More praise for *Behind the Veil*

"Suzetta Perkins spins a riveting tale of love, betrayal, and loyalty that will leave you breathless. Delicious reading!"

—PHYLLIS WILLIAMS

BEHIND THE VEIL

Published by

SBI

Strebor Books
P.O. Box 6505
Largo, MD 20792
http://www.streborbooks.com

This book is a work of fiction. Names, characters, places and incidents
are products of the author's imagination or are used fictitiously. Any
resemblance to actual events or locales or persons, living or dead, is
entirely coincidental.

ISBN 13: 978-1-59309-169-9
ISBN 10:   1-59309-169-9
LCCN 2006923553

First Strebor Books mass market paperback edition August 2006

10 9 8 7 6 5 4 3 2

Manufactured in the United States of America

For information regarding special discounts for bulk purchases,
please contact Simon & Schuster Special Sales at 1-800-456-6798
or business@simonandschuster.com

BEHIND THE VEIL

SUZETTA PERKINS

SBI

STREBOR BOOKS

NEW YORK LONDON TORONTO SYDNEY

To Teliza and Gerald (JR) —
the wind beneath my wings.

ACKNOWLEDGMENTS

My day has finally arrived, and I thank God from whom all blessings flow for empowering me with courage and the tools to pursue my desire to write. This has been a long road mixed with ups and downs, however, a smile sits upon my face because the labor was not in vain.

What a wonderful road to be on. It is because of the many wonderful people in my life and those that God allowed to cross my path, encouraging me, rooting for me, and believing that I would one day become a published writer that I do celebrate.

To my children, I love you from the depths of my heart. To my daughter, Teliza, thank you for just being there and saying the right things to keep me encouraged. JR, my creative other-half, thank you for always thinking of me, purchasing books every now and then to help me with my writing. You, along with your well of ideas that kept bubbling over, inspired me.

Patty Rice, you're awesome—not only as a writer but as a person. You didn't hesitate to look at my work when I asked. I will forever treasure your two-page, typed critique. You wrote, *What you will need: Writer's Market, Dictionary, Style Manual, Thesaurus, To read the work of authors that you intend to model to gain knowledge on sentence structure.* Priceless.

Thanks to LaWanda Miller, my co-worker, for reading my novel in its infancy, which consisted of eight lonely pages and loving my character Margo from the jump. That gave me the umph I needed to keep plodding on.

A special thank you goes to Evelyn Council who has believed in me from the beginning. You are my ray of sunshine. You read my first draft and thought it good enough to send to your sister in New York. It was your idea that I read a chapter of my book each time our book club met. You've been my rock. Thanks, and I love you.

A big sister hug goes to Carolyn Smith, my mentor. You are the epitome of everything good in life. During your busiest hour, you looked over my manuscript and gave me the value of your expertise. I trust you implicitly, and I love you with all my heart.

To my sistahs of the Sistahs Book Club—Wanda, Valerie, LaTonya, Melva, Brigette, Tina, Bianca, Latricia, Tara, Melody, Angela x 2, Bianco, and Jean, thanks for all your support. Fayetteville, North Carolina won't be the same. We'll have a great big book club meeting and invite all the local clubs. I'm already counting the book sales.

I'd like to thank my friends and supporters at Fayetteville State University—Dr. T. J. Bryan, Alfreda Cromartie, Mary Evans, and Dr. Booker T. Anthony.

A heartfelt, sister hug goes to my friend Phyllis Williams. I was so proud of you for being one of the finalists in the Romance Slam Jam short story contest in Durham. But it was your unselfish acts of kindness that make me forever grateful for your friendship. You took it upon yourself to occasionally send material to help me become a better writer, and without being asked, you took my synopsis and gave me advice on how to say it better. Thank you for being there for me.

When I think of unselfishness, Trevy McDonald heads the top of the list. While you were writing your own stories, you took time from your busy schedule to send me words of encouragement, advice, and material to help me be all that I could be. I can't thank you enough, Trevy, for all you've done.

To my road dawg and number one supporter, Mary Farmer, I thank you for being the kind of friend every writer needs. Your weekly calls to check on my progress, our monthly lunches to review your critiques of my manuscript (I added a chapter just for you), our fabulous trips to literary conferences, and your constant praise for a job well done has meant so much to me. I can't thank you enough for your faith in me…for believing that I have what it takes to be a good writer. Thank you from the bottom of my heart. I love you.

I would be nothing without the two people who took my written word and polished it like it was brass. To my editors, Robert Fleming and Annette Dammer, I will be forever in your debt. Robert, you gave me a chance and took my work and gave me the very best of you. That's why you're world renowned, and I thank you. Annette, you unselfishly took my work and made it your priority and refined my final drafts like new money. You constantly provided resources and advice to assist me with this venture. It meant the world, and I love you from the bottom of my heart for all you've done.

To Maxine Thompson, my agent, you're the greatest! From the first moment you expressed interest in my work and throughout the process of publishing my novel, you believed in me. You were just excited as I was about my work, and that made me a very grateful person. Thank you for believing in me.

This, my first manuscript, would not have materialized without the support of my two best friends, Glen Jubilee and June Ervin. You were a ray of sunshine on a cloudy day and your love, support, and encouragement will sustain our friendship for a lifetime.

And, to my ex-husband, Jerry, thank you for all your support and believing that I would accomplish what I set out to do although you didn't understand the best part of me.

PROLOGUE

Jefferson Myles put his foot on the brake and slowly turned onto Fuller Street. He brought the silver Mercedes to an abrupt stop and turned off the lights. He exhaled and looked out the window toward a brown, weather-beaten, single-story, wood-frame house, two doors down where others had gathered.

"Be quiet and stay put until I return," Jefferson admonished his companion, brushing her hand with his. "I won't be long."

Jefferson glanced at her again and quickly turned away. He patted his left breast feeling for the envelope that sat in an inside pocket of his brown leather coat. Satisfied, Jefferson opened the car door and got out, heading in the direction of the house two doors down. His stride was ardent and sure as he made his way down the street. He never looked back, and his companion, feeling alone and afraid, slid down in her seat. She did not like being on this side of town, especially late at night.

A moment passed, maybe two. She slowly eased up in

her seat, not wanting to be discovered. The Mercedes offered little cover, even under the cloak of darkness. There was a flurry of activity outside—men dressed in long, black, leather coats, walking nervously back and forth in great anticipation. Jefferson appeared to be embroiled in a heated discussion with one of the men who was adamantly trying to get his point across—his arms moving in strict staccato like a maestro slinging his baton, leading the orchestra in a resounding rendition of "William Tell's Overture."

Two figures standing at strategic locations caught her rapt attention. The one closest to her had something protruding from underneath his coat. It couldn't be, but there was no mistaking what she saw. It was a… gun, maybe a rifle! She put her hands to her mouth to stifle a scream. *Why did Jefferson bring me here?*

The sound of a car's motor met her ears. She quickly slid back down in her seat. Then there was the distinctive sound of car doors opening and shutting—must have been a van with so many doors sounding at the same time. She dare not look. She could hear people talking, but the voices were muffled. Then a second car cruised by—not in any hurry.

Suddenly, Jefferson appeared huffing, puffing and out of breath. He looked at her slouched down in her seat, a ghastly frown on her face. He slid his hand over her arm for reassurance. She flinched and pulled back slightly. Jefferson put the keys in the ignition and sped away.

What had she gotten herself into? She loved this man, and now he presented a side of himself she had not seen before. She was forsaking her marriage to be with her lover, who appeared to be mixed up in some illegal activity that might harm her. They were supposed to be enjoying each other's company, expressing and defining their love for each other, basking in the afterglow from their lovemaking. Instead, she found herself tightly clutching the armrest as if her life depended on it. The Mercedes swerved to the right causing the brakes to squeal.

Jefferson offered no explanation for the meeting that nearly soured only moments earlier, arousing a cloud of curiosity. He drove recklessly from the scene, oblivious to all else around him.

It was an obvious mistake taking her with him. However, circumstances and time were not on his side. His lips were dry, his hands moist from nerves, but he remained silent until she spoke.

"I don't know what was going on back there, but it made me nervous," said the hushed, soft voice.

"Nothing to worry about," Jefferson said very matter-of-factly. "Just try and relax."

"Who were those men you were talking to?"

Without answering, Jefferson forged ahead, noting

that his destination lay a few feet beyond the next set of traffic lights. "Business acquaintances," he finally said.

"Did you know that one of them had a gun? I'm not sure…"

"Everything is alright, baby. Chill, there's nothing for you to worry about. Trust me. Your job is to concentrate on how wonderful the rest of this evening is going to be."

Jefferson picked up her hand and drew it to his lips, placing a quick kiss on her dangling fingers.

She sat back in her seat without another word.

Jefferson breathed a sigh of relief, thankful that he and his companion were safely behind the door that hid them from inquiring eyes. The moment he envisioned some months ago had arrived, though with some difficulty. The pink neon sign blinked incessantly outside, announcing available residency.

Jefferson looked around the dimly lit room, noting that it was adequate for the purpose intended. There was a double bed planted in the middle of the floor, draped with a bedspread bedecked with a field of spring flowers. Matching curtains hung proudly and generously, covering the small window that looked out onto the spacious courtyard. A cheap-looking RCA color television set, with a loosened knob that threatened to fall, sat in one corner of the room on an old chest of drawers badly in need of a fresh coat of varnish. Or better yet, the nearest dump yard. It wasn't important though, for they wouldn't be staying long.

She smiled seductively, batting her long, curled eye-lashes at him. Her dress was plain and simple, much like the woman she was. She wore a pair of lined, white linen slacks with a teal and white, flowered, short-sleeve blouse that buttoned down the front. Pearl stud earrings dotted her ear lobes, and a pair of teal flats adorned her feet.

Jefferson went to her, holding her about the shoulders. *She's beautiful*, he thought, *a breath of fresh air*. Her long, silky, brown hair fell about her pale face, landing just below her shoulders in a casual flip. A hint of cherry-flavored lip-gloss glistened on her thin, perky lips.

Jefferson saw the worried look in her eyes. "There is nothing for you to worry about, love. It's just you and me, now. And I want all of you."

She smiled and swallowed nervously, as she watched Jefferson scan the length of her body. He seemed so uncomplicated, so in control of the moment. The egg-shell-colored, turtleneck sweater, made of imported wool that sat high on his neck brought out the richness in his flawless, medium-brown complexion. His brown eyes turned the color of amber with the reflection from the ceiling light. His closely cropped head held a field of neatly brushed waves that went into a slow fade at the temple and nape of his neck. And her heart skipped a beat.

He wanted to make love to her—passionate love—ever since she signaled that she wanted the same. At first it was just small talk, an occasional smile. Then it was the look that passed between them, the look that said, *I'm willing, are you?* And finally the smile that now registered six, if measured on the Richter scale, that said, *I'm ready!*

The smiles had not waned. This night had been chosen to commence an affair that had smoldered for some-time. It was a dangerous liaison for which they sought no repentance. There was no grief or regret. They were both in unhappy marriages, and their occasional smiles and small talk had gone beyond their expectations. Now it was time to put all their thoughts and dreams into action, although they were crossing a forbidden line that promised no real reward in the end.

It was unfortunate that she was a witness to the event earlier in the evening—an evening that was sup-posed to be totally and unequivocally theirs. However, it was preempted by a last-minute emergency for which Jefferson had no recourse but to respond. His business dealings had gone beyond legitimate, and the powerful alliances that he had found himself in bed with would never forgive his disobedience.

Jefferson put his thoughts aside and embraced her. They reached for each other without another word passing between them. Their lips met and the cherry-flavored lip-gloss caused him to linger longer than he had planned. She undressed slowly with Jefferson's eyes never leaving her for a moment. He removed his sweater, then his pants, trying not to seem too anxious. He took in all of her, noting that his imagination had served him well.

Spring flowers surrounded them as they fell upon the bed ready to unleash what seemed a lifetime of pent-up passion—passion that consumed them in each intimate caress. Jefferson traced her torso with his tongue in a relentless pursuit to have all of her. He was overcome with anticipation and desire—desire that burned uncontrollably in his groin.

Jefferson slowed his pace praying the night would last forever. His tongue sought refuge in the hollow of her waiting mouth. Their tongues mated, feverishly exploring every nook and cranny. His mouth became a vacuum as he sucked her bottom lip into the folds of his lips.

Their lips parted for a brief moment in order to catch their breaths. Jefferson continued to explore her body which trembled at his slightest touch. She was delirious with desire and a sense of urgency, as lust and greed consumed her being.

Jefferson took a deep breath and blew into her face—a few strands of her hair parting as he did so. Their bodies now entwined, Jefferson smothered her with kisses. He held her breasts and kneaded them like dough, sending tingling sensations down her spine. He massaged the length of her body, planting kisses along the way. He found the very essence of her waiting and ready, piercing the veil that gave him access. And she accepted what he had to offer.

Heat seared through their bodies as they moved instinctively to their own rhythm. They rode the tidal wave of passion until Jefferson could no longer contain himself and cried out for her to follow. She acquiesced, and it was a done deal.

CHAPTER 1

It was the twenty-third of December, a day Margo would always remember. It was the day that death came with great stealth in the still of the night. It was not death as is customarily associated with the dearly departed, but that of a dying soul whose heart would slowly be picked to the bone.

Margo had settled in for the night, waiting for her husband of nearly twenty-five years to come home after working late at the office. Jefferson and Margo Myles were like mortar to brick—they had a solid foundation and many people were envious of their varied accomplishments. She and Jefferson were both successful professionals, secure in their lifestyles. They owned a two-story Tudor brick home in the upscale neighborhood of Jordan Estates. Jefferson and Margo possessed the right combination of business savvy, having smartly invested in several diverse mutual funds, as well as optimum shares of blue-chip stock on the NASDAQ.

Besides the silver Mercedes Kompressor sports coupe that Jefferson drove and the Lexus sedan that was Margo's pride and joy, Jefferson was a collector of vintage automobiles that included a 1958 Edsel, a Rolls-Royce, and a Ferrari. He occasionally would be seen parading his menagerie of fine automobiles.

They had four wonderful children, and Margo was happy that her family would surround her this Christmas. Margo looked forward to the New Year—the new millennium as it had been hailed, a new century and a new decade full of bright promises.

Margo was grateful that her eighteen-year-old twins, Winston and Winter, who were in college, had made it home for the Christmas break. The drive from Virginia's Hampton University to Fayetteville, North Carolina, had been hectic with all the Christmas travelers trying to get home to family and friends for the holidays.

It was two days before Christmas—one of the most joyous times of the year. It was a time of celebration—celebrating the birth of the Christ child; however, the imminent feeling of love and family would not permeate Margo's home this Christmas season. Even the sound of the Wurlitzer grandfather clock that Margo and Jefferson bought in Europe ten years earlier gave no clue to the impending turn of events that would be forever etched in Margo's memory.

The volume on the radio was turned low. Margo perked up as the disc jockey on 99.1 The Fox announced the next set of soulful sounds. Luther Vandross' alluring voice began to croon "A House Is Not a Home," which resounded through the new set of Bose Acoustimas 10 surround-sound speaker system Jefferson had bought last month. Luther was Margo's favorite singer, and the rhythm and slow beat sent goose bumps riveting through her body. It was midnight, and Jefferson had not yet made it in.

The smells of the night's succulent, smoked, hickory-baked ham and candied, glazed yams still permeated the air. Ivy, the eldest of their four children, was famished after an evening of celebrating at A Touch of Class, a jazz nightclub for the young at heart. Ivy and three of her closest friends made going there an annual ritual, reminiscing about the past year's events. The spoils of the night that had been left on the stove were plenty reward after a full, callisthenic workout on the dance floor.

Margo had fallen asleep, unable to will her body to stay awake until Jefferson arrived home. It was unlike him to be out late, although he had called her earlier to say he needed to complete several portfolios and clean up some unfinished business before he closed the office for the holiday.

Margo was in the middle of a wonderful dream, and she sought a comfortable position as her body fought to continue into the abyss that her subconscious created. She absently reached over to Jefferson's side of the bed, hoping to feel the warmth of his strong, manly body to provide a nurturing cushion as she fell deeper still into her slumber. Through her sleepy haze, she realized he was not at her side, and she struggled to awaken.

Peaceful sleep overcame Margo's resistance only to have it broken by the telephone near her head, piercing the night with its sudden ring. Startled, Margo sat up and adjusted her eyes to the sea of blackness that engulfed the room. She grabbed the telephone certain it was Jefferson.

"Hello," Margo said. "Jefferson?" Silence at the other end.

"Jefferson?" Margo asked yet again. "Jefferson, is that you? Hello, hello, hello!"

Margo could hear faint breathing on the other end. She could almost count the number of pulses per second as time ticked away. And still not a word was uttered.

"Who is this?" Margo screamed into the phone, now frantically pacing the floor. "Answer me. Do you hear me? Jefferson, is that you?"

The phone made an abrupt click, and the line was dead.

"What's going on?" Margo shouted. She started toward Ivy's room before thinking better of it. It was probably a prank. But where was Jefferson? This was not like him. He certainly wasn't working at this late hour. Margo picked up the phone again and dialed Jefferson's office.

It seemed an eternity before the connection was made. Margo waited... one, two, three, six, eight, ten, twelve rings. No one was there. Maybe she had dialed the wrong number. She dialed again.

Margo laid the receiver back in its cradle and began to pace again. Their bedroom suddenly unsettled her, making the thought of a good night's sleep unlikely. The question lingered like a cloud. Who made the call?

As she continued to pace, she saw her Bible on the corner of her chest of drawers. Margo picked it up and proceeded to open it. It fell open to the Twenty-third Psalms. Margo picked her glasses up from the nightstand, placed them on her face, and began to read slowly.

The Lord is my Shepherd; I shall not want. He maketh me to lie down in green pastures: he leadeth me beside the still waters...Yea, though I walk through the valley of the shadow of death; I will fear no evil: for thou art with me...

Now why did that particular passage of Scripture jump out, she wondered...*walk through the valley of the shadow of death*. Margo closed the book and began to pray.

CHAPTER 2

Margo sat up abruptly at the first flicker of light. She was worn out from the all-night vigil that she had hoped would come to an expeditious resolve with Jefferson's arrival. Jefferson was a no-show, and Margo had cried softly until she fell asleep.

Now dawn brought a new anxiety. What should she do? Contact the police? It had not been twenty-four hours since she had last heard from Jefferson. Why had he not called? Was he all right? Maybe she should wait a few hours before doing anything. She definitely would not alarm the children until she had more answers.

"Mom, you up?" came the sound of Winter's voice getting louder as she approached her mother's bedroom. "What are you doing up so early?"

Margo masked her feelings and disguised the pain that was surely etched in her face. As Winter passed through the doorway wrapped in a pink terry cloth robe tied loosely at the waist, Margo's eyes examined her for clues that might reveal Winter had knowledge of her secret; but she could find none.

"I should ask you the same," Margo answered finally. "I was a little restless. I've got so much to do to prepare for Christmas dinner. I've invited all these folks, and I need to get a move-on."

"Where's Daddy?" Winter asked, looking around as she comfortably stretched her body across Margo's bed.

Winter was Margo's baby, an identical twin. She reminded Margo of herself as a young girl—so full of life and adventure. Today, Winter looked a lot like Margo, although she bore the resemblance of both parents. She was more reserved like Jefferson, while her sister Ivy was a warrior like her mother. And while Margo boasted a nice, medium frame, Winter was a little on the anorexic side. Winter had long, thick, jet-black hair that cascaded to the center of her back. She and her identical twin, Winston, had no distinguishable features, other than their anatomy, that would enable someone to tell them apart.

"Your daddy is business as usual. He wants to spend a lot of quality time with you all during the holiday, but he had to complete a project he's working on."

Winter leaned over and hugged her mother. "Mom, I love you."

"What's gotten into you?"

"I'm so happy to be home, Mom," Winter replied,

hugging her even tighter. "Being away from home gave me a greater appreciation for all the things I've taken for granted…like a good meal, clean clothes, a roof over my head, and a mother's warm embrace." Winter looked at Margo and smiled. "And knowing that your mom and dad always got your back."

Margo was overcome by Winter's sentiments.

"I'm glad you're home, too, baby." She touched the side of Winter's face, thankful for the tender moment, silently hoping that her early morning vigil was but a dream. As desperately as Margo would have liked for that to be true, her intuition gave way to the obvious.

Winter jumped up from Margo's bed and kissed her mother's cheek. Passing a window in the bedroom on her way to the master bathroom, Winter paused to look out when the sound of a running motor caught her attention.

"Umm, Mrs. Montgomery is out early. It's six in the morning. I'll have to get over to see the Montgomerys while I'm here."

Linda Montgomery was the last person on Margo's mind. She had yet to hear from Jefferson. Margo would not be able to hide the truth of Jefferson's where-abouts for long.

"OK," Margo said—more to herself than to Winter. She hadn't even realized that Winter had already left the room.

"I've got to call Angelica," Margo said aloud. "She would know what to do. I can always count on her."

Angelica was Margo's best friend. They had a unique friendship, one of endearment that many could not claim. They had known each other for three years, and it was an unusual set of circumstances that had brought them together.

One day Angelica walked into Margo's office looking for a real estate agent to help sell her home. Angelica and her husband, Hamilton, had recently ended a turbulent marriage that, on several occasions, brought the Fayetteville press to the doorstep of the Barnes' Bentley estate. Their front-page stories had probably sold more newspapers than the *National Enquirer*.

On that particular afternoon, Margo's schedule was sparse. Angelica, the diva she was, arrived at the door of the Century 21 Real Estate office dressed in a form-fitting, button-down, red jumpsuit made of calf leather with a wide, white, patent-leather belt slung off her hips. She had an exotic look that went well beyond her hazel eyes set in an oval-shaped face with a French-vanilla, cappuccino complexion, and her tossed, brownish-red mane that fell just over her shoulders. Margo extended her hand and welcomed Angelica, eager to make that next sale. She was already calculating her estimated commission. However, Margo was also drawn to Angelica. It might have been her grace and style, or her designer clothes, or it might have been her youthful look that spoke of an age of innocence. Nevertheless, there was an immediate bond that was secure as metal to a magnet—so secure that the bond was bound to last a lifetime.

The very first time Margo laid eyes on Hamilton, she had to suppress the awakened hormones (with God's help) that triggered every erotic sensor in her body as she sized up this six-foot hunk of German-chocolate cake. She felt awkward, especially in light of the fact that Hamilton had mentally abused his ex-wife, Angelica, and driven her to the very gates of hell on earth. Even in that brief moment, Margo fantasized about having a sexual interlude with this man. Hamilton, though, made her uncomfortable. She willed herself to let go of the silly fantasy that should not have been entertained in the first place.

But Hamilton, the fine specimen that he was, could not be characterized as the gift that every woman desired. He was vile and abusive, using his badge to hold women captive. It was rumored that Hamilton had raped many of the women who found themselves in his clutches. It could never be proven, as it was no secret that women threw themselves at him, begging to be his concubine. The man was rumored to be the last of the real black stallions with a sexual appetite to match. Hamilton had even physically assaulted some of the women who had not played his game the way he dictated, or when they'd threaten to tell his wife about their escapades because he couldn't keep up with their demand for his time.

It was Angelica who paid the ultimate price, taking the punishment for some of the unknowing souls fortunate enough to escape Hamilton's brutality when he turned from Dr. Jekyl to Mr. Hyde. But it was *The Code*, the secret brotherhood of law enforcement, which gave Hamilton the protection he didn't deserve.

Angelica not only gained a friend that day in Margo, but also found a real estate agent who was able to sell her big house of horrors and then stumble upon the perfect little home tucked away from the lights of Fayetteville, Fort Bragg, and prying eyes. It was situated in the midst of a small, gated community where Angelica felt more than safe.

Margo rose from her bed, stumbling over her slippers. It was only last evening that these slippers graced her feet as she walked back and forth in her bedroom with butterflies in her stomach, worrying and wondering about Jefferson. She located the phone sitting on the nightstand, anxious to solicit Angelica's help.

Margo hastily dialed Angelica's number, but was disheartened when there was no answer and Angelica's sexy voice broke the moment. "You've reached the one and only Angelica Barnes. If you feel you deserve the pleasure of my return call, you know the deal and keep it real."

Where was Angelica? It seemed that no one was in place this morning.

Margo could hear her children stirring and hoped she would have enough energy to get through the day. She had hoped to hear something from Jefferson by now. It was seven thirty-five a.m.

The telephone's ring startled her, and Margo lunged for it, praying that Jefferson's on the other end.

"Hello," Margo said.

"Hey girl, you rang?" boomed Angelica's cheery voice. "And how in the hell are you, stranger?"

"Hey, Angelica, I'm fine. Good to hear your voice. Where have you been?"

"I'm fine, doing great as a matter of fact. Where have I been? What do you mean where have I been?"

"When I called and your answering machine came—"

"Girl, I was in the bathroom taking care of Angelica business, if you know what I mean. I've got a lot of things to do today. I've got to run to town and finish Christmas shopping. I've got to pick up a few last-minute gifts that I hadn't anticipated purchasing. My brothers are coming for Christmas and both are bringing their girlfriends—not that I need to get them anything, but you know how it is. Do you mind if I bring them to dinner? I know it's last minute, but I didn't find out until last night they were coming."

"Sure, Angelica, that'll be fine."

"How's Jefferson?"

"Actually, that's why I called."

"Why are you whispering, Margo?"

"Look girlfriend, I have a problem."

"What's up, Margo?" Angelica asked, realizing her friend had something on her mind. "Spit it out."

"Jefferson didn't come home last night."

"Shut your mouth!"

"Then something strange happened. The telephone rang around three this morning. It startled me, but I certainly hoped to hear Jefferson's voice. I could hear someone breathing on the line, and after I repeatedly asked who was there, the line suddenly went dead. I'm worried, Angelica, and I can't file a missing persons report because it hasn't been twenty-four hours since I last spoke to Jefferson."

"Oh Margo, what are you going to do? You can file a missing persons report, although the police won't do anything until twenty-four hours has expired. But do you want to do that?"

"I was hoping you would have the answer."

"Margo, I don't know. I can't even think straight. You know, I saw Jefferson around eight yesterday evening. I was coming into Fayetteville on Bragg Boulevard when I saw his Mercedes roll into Richmond Heights."

"Richmond Heights? What would Jefferson be doing over there?" Margo knew that the Richmond Heights neighborhood was infamous for drugs and gang violence. Many citizens in the neighborhood had called attention to the rising violence there, but little effort was made to effectively rid that section of town of its notorious image. Gang-banging, drug solicitation, and street violence had not been deterred much by a strong police presence, and the likelihood that it would, with Lieutenant Barnes, Angelica's ex, at the helm was suspect at best.

"Well, you know Hamilton works down there," stated Angelica. "They put up a police substation in the heart of Richmond Heights to stop some of the crime plaguing that neighborhood."

"Hamilton? Of all people! What does Hamilton have to do with Jefferson?"

"I'm just guessing, Margo. I have no idea either. However, we both know that Jefferson does business with Hamilton."

"It doesn't make sense. Why would Jefferson go to the precinct to do business, especially late at night? I don't know, Angelica. Jefferson never mentioned anything about meeting Hamilton. He always lets me know where he is so I don't have to worry about him."

"I remember the first time I met Jefferson. Actually, it was a couple of years before the divorce. He came by the house to see Ham and show him some investment papers. Who would have guessed that investment would end up being a large part of my divorce settlement?" Angelica laughed. "Anyway, Jefferson was every bit the businessman, and it was quite apparent that he was the financial advisor, and Hamilton was the client. Any relationship beyond that seemed remote."

"What does that have to do with now?"

"Before, everything was business—after all, serious business was being conducted, but somewhere along the line Hamilton and Jefferson began to form an informal relationship. I believe they came to love each other like brothers."

"Funny, he never talked about Hamilton in that light." Margo digested what Angelica said. Maybe she didn't know Jefferson as well as she thought, even though they shared twenty-five years, four children, and a lifetime of dreams. "It still doesn't explain what he was doing in Richmond Heights last night, when he told me he had work he needed to complete before the holiday. What am I going to do about my pressing situation, Angie? You live with a person for a quarter-century, think you know them inside out, only to find that their life is hidden under a veil. I've got to do something. Maybe I'll call my pastor."

"Sit still a while, it may be nothing at all. What have you told the kids?"

"I told Winter that Jefferson had to take care of some work at the office."

"Good, that buys you some time. What's his secretary's name?"

"Ebony Wilson. What are you going to do?"

"Do you have her phone number? Maybe Ebony can shed some light on Jefferson's whereabouts. What about Malik? Did you call him? Now that's a p-h-i-n-e brotha, all six feet and two inches of him. Big, juicy nubian lips…girl, I'd never come up for air if I got a chance to get a taste of that. And those pretty white teeth against his ebony flesh. Have you noticed his muscles? Ripples through anything he wears. Makes me want to holler! Ooooh! I've got to get Jefferson to give me the real 4-1-1 on him with an option to buy, if the real estate is right. I don't understand why Malik has always eluded me. Sorry, sweetie."

"You are so crazy, girl." Margo laughed. "You're supposed to be helping me with my problem." It was the first time in almost eight hours, since the ordeal began, that she was able to release any emotional tension. "Well, we'll have to find Jefferson first. I haven't seen or spoken to Malik, but I'll get both of those phone numbers for you. They're on the Rolodex on Jefferson's desk."

As Margo put the phone down to retrieve the numbers, Angelica tried to refocus on the events of yesterday. Yes, she had seen Jefferson, but why was he driving into Richmond Heights at eight p.m.? Jefferson appeared to be alone in the car, but Angelica knew she would have to put on her best detective coat and hat for this snoop. After all, she was the queen of snoop. She'd gathered a rather fine portfolio on Hamilton that she presented to her divorce attorney, who helped to render a fine settlement on her behalf. Yes, the little mansion she was now living in, behind the iron gate that read Hawthorne Estates with the man-made moat running along the outer per-imeter, was testament to that fact.

"Hey Angie, here they are." Margo read the numbers to Angelica and bade farewell, promising that they would be in touch throughout the day.

As she hung up the phone, her door flung open. The twins came in bearing a tray of breakfast—homemade waffles, bacon, grits, scrambled eggs, and a glass of grapefruit juice. If this was any consolation, she knew she had the most wonderful children that any parent could ever ask for. After all, why wouldn't they be? She nurtured and guided them on the paths they were now pursuing, paths that gave credibility to all her hard work. They would make fine, upstanding citizens in whatever community they chose.

"I brought you the paper for your reading pleasure, Mrs. Myles," Winston said.

"Thanks, son. You know how to treat a lady, and always remember that."

"Yeah, Mom. Oh, Mr. Montgomery said hello. I was getting the paper when he pulled into the yard. He looked a little sad. By the way, where is Dad? Can't wait to shoot some hoops with him."

"I told you he went to work," Winter interjected.

"Well, maybe we should get dressed and surprise him—maybe offer to help him out a little, so he can chill with us."

"What are you going to do?" Winter asked. "One semester of college under your belt, and you still don't know anything. Dad doesn't need us around, getting in the way."

"He most certainly does not!" Margo interjected. She needed time. Margo had no earthly idea where Jefferson was, and she certainly did not intend to be caught in her own lie. Margo had to think fast.

CHAPTER 3

Margo shot a parting glance at the clock on the kitchen wall. It was now eight-thirty a.m. and still no word from Jefferson. She half expected Jefferson to show up in the early part of the morning, offering some tired, lame excuse for being absent from home. Now Margo's worry lines took on new wrinkles, because fresh fears were starting to surface and envelop her mind. Without answers, those fears were running rampant through her brain.

Margo dragged herself wearily through her spacious kitchen with its shocking-white, wood cabinets mounted on rustic-colored walls. The kitchen had an octagonal shape with three-tier planter shelves that ran along the upper perimeter of the wall, just slightly above the top of the cabinets' edge. There was a six-foot-long overhang that showcased Margo's gourmet pots and pans with their copper bottoms. Cooking was Margo's thing. She could turn any mundane meal into Chez Margo. The center of the kitchen sported a cook's island that boasted an electric grill and rotisserie. An exquisite, rustic-colored, Spanish ceramic-tiled floor, with an inset border of white marble and a hint of fool's gold sprinkled throughout, set off the whole kitchen and made it come alive. Margo designed the kitchen herself and was very proud of the look she created.

The quiet was deafening, and just as Margo allowed herself to exhale, the doorbell rang, startling and paralyzing her at the same time. She willed herself to move, but couldn't.

The bell rang a few more times, and Winter leapt from the top of the stairs and into the kitchen to see who was at the back door. She was a little perturbed when she approached the kitchen and saw that her mother was not making a move to silence the menacing attack on the doorbell.

"What is it, Mom?" Winter shouted. "Why didn't you get the door? You have been acting very strange this morning."

As soon as Winter began to speak, Margo seemed to be released from the trance that had left her momentarily paralyzed. "I was on my way to open the door when something just seemed to snap. I don't know what it was, but I'm all right now."

"Are you sure? Maybe I should call Dad."

"No, no don't do that. I wouldn't want to worry him needlessly. I must be stressing—thinking about all that I have to do to get ready for Christmas."

Winter went to the kitchen door, the gateway for

the frequent travelers who'd request a cup of sugar or flour from time to time. "Mom, it's Mrs. Montgomery."

"Hey, Linda, come in. What's up?"

"Nothing much. I wasn't sure anyone was at home. I thought I saw movement in the house, but after ringing the bell for the fifth time, I was beginning to wonder. Well, are you all ready for Christmas?" Linda asked, blowing into her hands, trying to warm them up.

"I'm getting there. We're expecting a house full, and I'm really behind. With the girls here, I'll get it all done. What brings you here?"

"I just returned home from taking Blake's mother an apple pie I made for her and stopped to see if Jefferson was home. We were supposed to finish those reindeer we were making for the yard. Christmas will be here and gone. Jefferson had only one left to cut out, and I still need to paint them. I'd get Blake out there to do it, but since he hurt his arm in that accident last week, he's had limited range of motion and can't do a blessed thing it seems."

"I hope he's getting better, Linda, and no, Jefferson is not home. He had to run into work this morning."

Blake and Linda Montgomery were the core of their cozy section of the neighborhood. Margo and Jefferson called them the first white settlers. They had welcomed many new residents into the neighborhood and had said goodbye to quite a few, as well.

Margo remembered how warmly she, Jefferson, and

the children were received when they first moved—
not only to Jordan Estates but also to North Carolina
ten years prior. Jordan Estates was predominately
Anglo, and the Myles family preferred a mixed neighborhood having lived in military settings during the
ten years Jefferson was in the Air Force.

The military was an outright supporter of racial
relations in the 1980s as families of all races, colors, and
creeds lived together, the only differences being that
living quarters were determined by rank and marital
status. The Myles' children experienced life that co-
existed with others of diverse cultures, with racial
differences often being second nature.

Linda went out of her way to acquaint Margo with
Fayetteville and helped her adjust to the Southern way
of living. Linda helped Margo enroll all four children
in school; two were high schoolers and the twins were
middle- graders at the time. There couldn't be a finer
display of Southern hospitality anywhere, and Margo
knew that while Fayetteville was not their first choice
of places to live, everything was going to be all right
with friends like Linda and Blake.

Some of the other neighbors who were part of the
elite group of first-comers to Jordan Estates sprouted
twigs of jealousy at the newly formed partnership
between the Montgomery and Myles clans. It soon
became common knowledge that each month the

Montgomerys or the Myles family would play cards together, alternating between houses, preparing scrumptious meals that were devoured before the high-stakes game of Spades took place—the women against the men.

Angelica once remarked that Blake and Linda must have thought they were Sally and Dave on *The Hughleys*, because they came and went as if they lived in the same house as Jefferson and Margo. And when Winter wasn't hanging out with her twin, Margo could almost always find her somewhere with Felicia, Linda's daughter, whether it was on the phone, going to the movies, or football games. That was before they both set out for college. They were inseparable and the Montgomery and the Myles families would always be friends.

Jefferson once spoke of moving to another subdivision, away from all of the encroaching development that was sure to signal possible annexation to the city. But Margo wanted to remain in her cozy setting, with her cozy neighbors, in their cozy community, with no thought of leaving the Mont-gomerys behind.

"Are you all right, Margo?" Linda asked, noticing the band of sweat that formed about Margo's forehead. Margo's nerves were starting to unravel, but she had to keep everything in check.

"Yeah, it's just that I've got a lot of things to do in so little time. Have a seat while I get a glass of water. Would you like something?"

"No, Margo. Thanks. I'm going to go so you can get back to what you were doing."

"I wish I had it going on like you!"

"How do you mean?" Linda inquired.

"Oh, you just seem to float along. I bet all your Christmas packages are bought, wrapped and mailed, if you had any to send. Up early this morning to catch the early morning specials, heh?"

"Huh?"

"Winter saw you pulling in early this morning. Figured you were trying to catch those early bird specials at the mall."

"Oh, that. No, I'm done. Had to go to the store to pick something up for Blake's pain. Let me get out of—"

Their conversation ended abruptly with the sudden ring of the telephone. Margo tried to make a beeline for the phone that sat on the secretary desk that completed the eighth wall of the octagonal kitchen. In Margo's awkward haste, the glass of water slipped from her hand, causing a loud crash that sent splinters of glass in all directions.

Linda couldn't help but notice Margo's discomfort.

"Are you sure you're all right, Margo? Let me help you pick up the glass."

"I've got to get the phone," Margo said, although it had stopped ringing a minute ago.

"Mom, telephone. It's Angelica," Winter said. "What happened in here?"

"Your mother dropped her glass while she was trying to get to the phone," Linda said, continuing to pick up the glass while keeping an eye on Margo.

"Well, she has been acting a little strange this morning," Winter put in. "I've just attributed it to her working so hard on closing those two real estate deals. And, of course, she invited all those people to dinner tomorrow and has probably worked herself into a frenzy. I'll be glad when my dad gets home. I'll finish, Mrs. Montgomery. Oh, how's Felicia?"

Linda was barely paying attention to Winter. So, Margo's been acting strange. Linda wasn't quite sure what to make of it. "Oh-h-h, Felicia's doing great," Linda said, coming out of her reverie. "She's home from school, also."

"Well, tell her that I'm coming over to see her in a day or two."

"OK," Linda said as she let herself out. "We'll probably come by for dessert tomorrow. I'll tell Felicia you asked about her."

"Angelica, what did you find out?" Margo asked, panting hard and trying to catch her breath.

"What took you so long to come to the phone? I thought you wanted information pronto!"

"My next-door neighbor was here, and when I heard the phone ring, I panicked. Thinking it might be Jefferson, I dropped the glass I had in my hand. I made a mess everywhere. I left Winter and Linda to clean up the mess, so I could find a place to talk privately."

"Well, get hold of yourself. If anyone didn't suspect anything, I'm sure their antennae are up now. And to top it all off, I didn't find out anything, but I wanted to let you know that I was still on the case."

"Nothing?" Margo screamed.

"Calm down, girl. There's an answer somewhere. Even Ebony came up empty. She said that Jefferson let her go early, about four o'clock on yesterday afternoon. Said he had to run an errand—and something about some white paint."

"Oh, that's probably for those freaking reindeer he and Linda are working on."

"I'm still trying to contact Malik, but keep it on the down low, my sistah. I've got your back. Love ya. Will talk to you later."

"I love you, too, Angie. Get back to me as soon as you can."

Margo took her time hanging up the phone. She sat on the bed in her bedroom with the door closed tight, contemplating her next move. Her head snapped at the sound of the doorknob turning. Before Margo could turn her head, Ivy stood in the doorway, looming tall over Margo with a quizzical look on her face.

"Mother, what are you doing in here and who were you talking to?" Ivy asked, walking into the room. "I could hear you yelling down the hall."

"Ivy, you worry too much. I just needed a peaceful and quiet place to be."

"Could have fooled me."

Very slowly, Margo said, "Ivy, I need some time to think. Angelica is going through some things, and I'm trying to help her through them."

"Oh no, not again. She's been through so much, and I thought she was on top of her world. Well, let me know if there's anything I can do, Mom."

"Thanks, honey." Margo got up and gave Ivy a big hug and tapped her on her butt.

"Out late showing off your new moves last night, eh?"

"Hey, you know me. My girls can't even keep up with Ms. Ivy B. Myles 'cause she's the baddest soul sistah in this here town."

Margo and Ivy laughed.

"Mom, are you all right?" Winter asked, her voice almost a whisper as she entered the cozy room, looking at Ivy for some 411.

"I'm fine. You girls worry too much."

"Just concerned, Mom. Look, we'll help you with

dinner, and when Dad comes home, we'll get the Christmas spirit flowing," Winter said.

"Where is Dad?" Ivy asked. "I didn't see his car when I came in this morning."

"You were probably drunk." Winter laughed, placing a pointed finger in Ivy's rib cage.

"I don't play that," Ivy said harshly, causing Winter to drop her eyes. "I know what I saw, and Dad's car was not here when I got home. And Mom, who rang at three o'clock this morning? It couldn't have been anyone in his or her right mind. You must have picked it up before I could get to it."

"So many questions. Slow down. But since you asked, it was a wrong number, sweetheart. Some crazy idiot lost his mind calling someone's house that early in the morning. Enough to give someone a stroke."

Ivy and Winter looked from one to the other.

"You sure you're all right?" Ivy asked one last time as she ushered Winter out of the room.

"I'm fine," Margo lied. "I just need to exhale for a moment."

"We'll be down to help you in a few."

Ivy and Winter walked briskly down the hall to Ivy's room, bumping into Jeff Jr. along the way.

"What's up with ya'll?" asked JR, as he was affectionately called in the Myles' household.

"None of your business," Winter retorted. "It's about time you got your lazy ass up from the bed."

"Watch your mouth, or I'll tell Ma," JR shouted back.

"Boy, you better recognize. We aren't running a hotel up in here. You know we have guests coming on Sunday, and if you think you're going to lay around without lifting a finger, you're wrong," Ivy said.

JR rolled his eyes at Ivy. "You're not my mama."

"Boy, get out of my way. Just remember what I said. I'll be watching you."

"You better charge it to the mind, you crazy wench." JR walked into the bathroom and slammed the door.

"He's a punk," Ivy continued. "Let's go to my room."

"What's up with you and JR, Ivy? I know that you all have had a few issues between you, especially since the time he took your car and crashed it."

"The fool was drunk…could've killed somebody. He never apologized…"

"Mom and Dad forgave him, and he's still your brother…"

"Look Winter, I didn't bring you in here to talk about JR. I think something's going on with Mom, and I think it has something to do with Dad. I don't think he came home last night."

"Umm," Winter moaned thoughtfully.

"Then I find her sitting in the closet talking on the phone. She claims Angelica has a crisis, but I don't buy it. Seems a little weird to me and so unlike her."

"Well, she has been acting a little strange. Maybe we should call Dad anyway, although she adamantly protested earlier when I mentioned it."

"See, that's what I mean. Give me the phone; it's laying by your foot."

The sisters lay sprawled across Ivy's bed. Ivy was a replica of Margo with her same cocoa brown complexion and curves that were all in the right place. Her hair was locked in short braids that she wore well. She had been many a guy's heartthrob. However, Ivy was sometimes cold and callous when it came to men. She had listened to many of the stories Margo and Angelica told about their heyday, and of course, Angelica's wild and crazy marriage to Hamilton. Ivy had seen Hamilton on the few occasions she and her mother had been out shopping together; and she liked what she saw. Hamilton had even winked at her once, but even then Ivy remembered the stories that Angelica told about how ruthless and vile he was toward women.

Winter picked up the black, cordless, Sony telephone and punched in *10, the hotline to Myles and Associates. After what seemed like the longest minute, the phone rang and then a voice at the other end answered.

"Hello," said the cautious voice while Winter's eyes

darted quickly toward Ivy who sat up abruptly, ready to take charge.

"Daddy, is that you?" Winter asked.

"Yeah, baby..." Jefferson was saying when Ivy reached over and snatched the phone from Winter, who gave Ivy a look of disdain.

"Daddy, when are you coming home?" Ivy asked, with some urgency in her voice.

"Why, what's wrong? Is someone hurt?" Jefferson asked.

"No, I'm...I'm just concerned about Mom. She's been acting very strange—talking in closets, dropping and breaking things."

"Talking in closets? What are you talking about?"

"Just what I said, she's been acting weird like something is really bothering her. She dropped a glass of water this morning, and then I found her whispering on the phone in the closet. It may not seem strange to you, but if you were here, you'd understand where I was coming from."

"Acting strange?"

"Yes, acting strange," Ivy said, with discontent in her voice at her father's obvious disbelief.

"There doesn't seem to be anything to be alarmed about, but I'll be home shortly. I was getting ready to call it a day anyway."

"All right, Dad. It's not an emergency, but maybe

you can talk to her and see what's up. We would feel a lot better," Ivy said, as she felt Winter's piercing eyes heavy on her.

"OK, babe. I'll be home in a minute."

Before Ivy could completely lay the phone in its cradle, Winter moved closer to Ivy. "Well, what did he say?"

"He said he'd be home in a few."

"Is that all?"

"Yep, that's all," Ivy said, in deep contemplation. "It was almost as if there was some relief in his voice."

"Hmm. We'll just have to keep an eye on Mom, I guess."

"Yep, I guess that's about all we can do right now."

"That call was from my daughters, man. They said Margo's been acting weird and tripping out, which I half expected. Anyway, they want me to come home now."

"You need to put your priorities in order, man. I'm not going to always have your back, and I'm certainly not with you, Jefferson, in this mess you're making."

"Listen, Malik. This is my ticket back into the house. I know you don't understand, and I really don't expect you to. I've got to come up with a good excuse right now. The girls are expecting me to come home any minute. You got any ideas?"

Malik looked at Jefferson and then turned quickly

away. "Did you hear anything I said, bro? You are screwing up your life, and someone's going to pay a price. And, bro, it might be you. Listen to what I'm saying, man."

"Malik, I hear you. I know what you're thinking. I have this wonderful wife who has suddenly worn thin on me, and I'm disrespecting her. And on top of that, I've got myself involved in some mess that could either make or break me. I can't deal with that right now; I need to deal with the moment, and I hope you have my back, bro. I've got to get through the holidays, then I'll think about prioritizing."

Malik let out a sigh. Jefferson was his best friend, but their relationship had become strained. Jefferson had gotten caught up in some dirty business and couldn't find his way out. And then last night—sneaking around on Margo right under her nose. Malik would love to have someone special in his life like Margo. As much as Jefferson sought after the finer things in life, he was neglecting the real treasure, and someone else would someday scoop it up right from under him.

"Jeff, you need to sever the ties with Barnes. Cop or no cop. Now you better get on home to your family. I don't know how you're going to explain it, but I'm sure your ass will come up with something. Have a Merry Christmas, and I'll see you tomorrow. I know Margo is going to throw down."

"Yeah, Merry Christmas, chump."

Jefferson was in deep, too deep to turn away from what he had already started. Money for guns, what in the hell was he thinking? Now there was a mistress to complicate the issue, but he couldn't help how he felt.

Jefferson raised his foot and kicked the nearest object to him. He recoiled in pain as his foot caught the broadside of his mahogany desk—missing the trashcan that was the intended target. Malik turned around, shook his head and walked out the door.

"Fool."

Jefferson sat pondering what he would say to Margo. Damn, it was eleven in the morning, and he hadn't talked with her since yesterday afternoon, although he tried unsuccessfully to speak with her. Her worried voice at the end of the line still rang in his ear as she frantically called out his name in the early dawn. Jefferson raised his foot again but thought better of it.

"Hey man, your watch over?"

"In a few minutes. I've got to finish this last report and fax it to the Captain. Then I'll be ready to ride on up out of here."

"OK. I'm going to make a quick run, and I'll be back in ten," Ray said.

"Do that, big fellow," Hamilton said, looking up from the paperwork he was completing. "Man, what do you make of Jefferson?"

"He's a hot potato getting ready to burst at the seams. He's got all the right fixin's, but the jacket is too tight. We're going to have to keep a close watch on him, especially since he's also playing with extracurricular toys. You just never know about folks, but the investment…we've got to protect the investment at all costs."

"I hear you, brotherman. At all costs." Ray Adams walked out of the police station.

Hamilton had been a highly respected law officer on the Fayetteville City Police Force. Hamilton was a handsome man who stood exactly six feet tall. He was in his early fifties. His skin belied his age, and his smooth, cocoa-colored complexion and head of thick, black, wavy hair only accentuated his other attributes. His robust, muscular build could stop traffic on any given day.

Hamilton laid down his pencil and scratched his brow. Even though he was a cop on the take and involved in some unscrupulous activities, it had not been his intent to drag Jefferson into the middle of it. Jefferson just happened to be a golden egg at the right time—a lucky pawn in the game. If Jefferson was not smart enough to realize that his involvement could possibly have some serious social and financial repercussions, so be it. I wonder what his p-h-i-n-e wife would do if she knew of his infidelity?

"Hmm, I wouldn't mind hitting on Miss Margo myself," Hamilton said half out loud. "Yeah, Miss Margo with the tight lips and voluptuous hips—hmm, hmm, hmm."

Malik was gone ten minutes before Jefferson made any attempt to go home and hopefully salvage the rest of the Christmas holidays. He knew he could not prolong the inevitable any longer. The girls would surely call again wanting to know what was taking so long. He was not ready to deal with Margo about his whereabouts last night, but he had no other choice but to go home and offer some type of explanation Margo would reasonably accept. He hated that people were depending on him to make their holiday bright, when his mind and thoughts were elsewhere.

It was high noon, and the beautiful, bright sun that shone above at a ninety-degree angle made a hopeful forecast of a white Christmas, null and void. Jefferson drove around the block five or six times, hoping to alleviate the tension that had his body all tangled in knots. He knew the longer it took to make his presence known, the tighter the noose felt around his neck. He still hadn't a clue as to what he would say to Margo, but he knew that precious time was wasting.

Margo stepped back as Jefferson's large frame loomed forward. Damn, she didn't expect to be the first person he'd encounter seconds after coming through the door. It was probably better this way—not prolonging the agony—get it over with hopes of salvaging the rest of the holiday.

Jefferson had promised to put some oil on that door hinge for weeks. The coils of the spring on the screen door sang his entry song, and Jefferson saw the welcomed relief on Margo's face as she stood over a twenty-pound turkey she was preparing for Christmas dinner.

Even in her relief, Jefferson could tell Margo was mad as hell. She examined him with her eyes from head to toe, looking for tell-tale signs of his whereabouts.

"Hey, Margo," Jefferson said, his eyes flitting over Margo's face, searching for a hint as to how she really felt.

"Jefferson," came the response. "I'm glad you were able to make it home in time for Christmas. We've been worried about you," Margo said sarcastically.

Yep, she's mad, really ticked off.

"Margo," Jefferson said, as he reached out to touch her, not expecting her to recoil so demonstratively, "I know you're upset, but I can explain why I didn't come home last night. You see," he stuttered, "I got drunk and lost track of time."

"Jefferson, don't even try it. Don't think you can come in here and try to offer some cockamamie story to me. I wasn't born yesterday. Furthermore, you must not realize it, but it's one in the afternoon. Maybe your concept of time is different from mine. You didn't even have the decency to call and let me know that you were yet in the land of the living. Give me a break."

"Hold on, Margo. I got really drunk last night."

"I'm having a hard time believing that, Jefferson. You told me you would be working late so that you could free up time to be with your family."

"True, true, but Malik and a couple of other buddies happened to stop by while I was still at the office. We ended up having our own company Christmas party and as the clock sped by, the drunker I got."

Margo's right hand took less than a minute to react to Jefferson's words. She slapped the left side of his cheek viciously. "Save your lies for someone who doesn't know any better," Margo said, as the tears began to form in the corner of her eyes.

Jefferson reached for Margo's arms, holding them tight. "Woman, I advise you never to do that again. Now save the drama for someone else." And he let her arms drop to her side.

"Listen, Jefferson, I'm tired of your foolishness. Don't think I haven't noticed your inattentiveness and sudden change in behavior. You haven't even kissed me these last few weeks, and you seem distant. What is it, Jefferson? You tired of this marriage? You got somebody else? What is it? Tell me!"

"You figure it out. Right now—"

"Hey Dad, you're home!" Winter interrupted, as she sped by her mother and embraced her dad. "We missed you. Winston and I came all the way from Hampton to be with you, and you're out working hard to get our tuition money for next semester."

"Hey, what's all the commotion about?" Ivy interjected, as she gave a searching glance toward her mother, eyeing her suspiciously. "Hey Dad, what's up? Working hard?" Ivy looked Jefferson straight in the eye.

"How are my baby girls? Look at my new college coed. She looks good, doesn't she, Margo?"

"Yes, she does," Margo said in a half-whisper.

"Dad, I'm not your baby girl anymore—well, you know what I mean. I'm all growed up now." Winter chuckled, looking in Ivy's direction. "You know the Scripture—*When I was a child, I spake as a child, I understood as a child, I thought as a child: but when I became a man* (a woman in my case), *I put away childish things.*"

"Girl, please. You're still wet behind the ears and wouldn't know a full-grown man from one who's still going through puberty if he got up in your face." Ivy smirked. Everyone in the room chuckled.

"I know more than you think I know," Winter stammered. "I'll certainly be the first Myles' daughter to wear a stunning white Vera Wang wedding dress when the time comes. At least, I'm going somewhere with my life."

Ivy put up her hand to Winter's face as if she was halting traffic. "Sister, you don't have a clue."

"Child, you need to stay young while you can and get a little more experience before you jump out there talking about wedding dresses," Margo chided.

"Oh Mom, that was cold," Winter said, a twinge of hurt clouding her face.

"And *you* better recognize," Margo continued, waving her hand in the air at Ivy for effect. They all laughed, even Jefferson, though he made it his business to avoid direct eye contact with Margo.

CHAPTER 4

Margo wasn't finished with Jefferson. The nerve of him waltzing back in the house with some flimsy excuse, acting as if time stood still for him. Yes, the brotha was going to produce some answers, or he might as well take his sorry behind right back from whence he came.

And why was Ivy watching her so closely? *The girl got her nose all in my business. Thinks she knows something. Well, she's barking up the wrong tree, or is she?*

"Ivy, I want you to wash the greens. Winter, pick up that bag of sweet potatoes on the counter and get to peeling. I want to get the pies out of the way." There was no immediate response, as Margo had anticipated. She stopped and surveyed the room to make sure the girls were able to comprehend her marching orders.

"What are those lazy good-for-nothing boys going to be doing?" Ivy asked, as she proceeded to scrutinize each collard green leaf. "Those boys need to get in here, Mom, and help peel these potatoes and chop the celery and onions."

"You're right. All those boys do is eat. I should have given them responsibilities like this before. Lord knows JR will be cooking his own food if he's going to eat because no woman is going to want a lazy husband. I don't know what I'm going to do with that boy."

Ivy rolled her eyes. "They're just pigs, and nothing's going to change that."

"JR, Winston!" Winter shouted, turning only to find two pairs of eyes staring at her as if she didn't have any sense. "Mom wants you," she said more slowly, two octaves lower. The boys bounced into the kitchen as if on command.

"What's up?" they said in unison.

"Mom wants you to peel sweet potatoes and chop some celery and onions," Ivy said.

"Mom, are you for real? We're in the game room with Dad. He's showing us some of his poolroom magic," Jeff Jr. said.

"Am I for real? Are you planning on eating tomorrow? You figure it out, and you better not take a long time. I will say this, you better pounce on those potatoes before I put you in the pot."

"Cut them some slack, Margo," Jefferson said, as he forced his way in the already crowded kitchen. "It's a father-and-son thing."

Margo looked at Jefferson with contempt. "They can bond with you later, that is if you'll be around long enough for that to be a reality."

"Come off of it, Margo. Don't use your anger to—"

Just then the phone rang. "Saved by the bell," Ivy crooned.

Margo grabbed the phone, as if she was Girl Friday, first day on the job, and eager to please her boss.

"Hello, Myles' resi—"

"Girl, this is Angelica. Have you heard anything from Jefferson?"

"Yes."

"Yes, what?"

"I know."

"Oh-h-h, you can't talk. Is Jefferson there?"

"Girl, yes. I started cooking an hour ago." Margo only hoped that Angelica understood her attempt at being cryptic.

"Say what? Just got home? What did he say?"

"I'll see you tomorrow."

"Look, call me when you can. I've got to get the scoop. What are you doing anyway?"

"Girl, I've got the whole clan in the kitchen cooking. Having children pays off at a time like this. Oh, by the way, did you get anything for me?"

"No, the trail is cold for now, I mean freezing cold. Clues aren't lying around like stray pennies on a sidewalk. You'd fare better at an Easter egg hunt."

"Better luck next time."

"Don't worry, girl, this baffling mystery will unravel soon enough. Chin up, my sister. I'm looking forward to tasting that succulent turkey and your almond dressing tomorrow. Talk to you later."

"Later, love." Margo hung up the phone and turned to a sea of inquiring eyes. "And what are you all looking at?" The gaze went around the room like a whirling steel ball in a pinball machine, trying to find its way out of the maze without getting hit by another paddle.

"Look, I've got to finish cutting that reindeer for Linda. I promised I'd have that done last week," Jefferson said, as he headed toward the garage—breaking what seemed like an eternity of silence.

Margo gave Jefferson a disgusted look. "You've just gotten home good, Jefferson. Surely one reindeer won't make that much difference. I'm sure no one will care since Christmas is tomorrow."

"I promised Linda, and it won't take me long to finish it. Look guys," Jefferson redirected his attention, "I'll be back in a few."

"Okay, Dad," JR said. "Don't be too long. I feel like putting a hurting on somebody tonight!"

Jefferson flipped JR a thumbs-up and walked out the door.

Margo was seething. If she could have turned a dark shade of red, it would have been crimson. Jefferson had been gone nearly a day and a half, and all he could think about was finishing those stupid reindeer. She didn't care who the reindeer were for, neighbors or no neighbors. "He's got some nerve," she said, under her breath. "You'd think he didn't have a family, and to think he tried to pass off some piss-poor excuse as to why he didn't come home. Yes, the brotha's got some explaining to do." She looked up at her children who were busy. No one dared return her stare.

There was definitely something going on between her mother and father, Ivy thought, and she planned to find out what it was. Dad was most definitely in the doghouse, but Ivy was still uncertain as to how short or long the chain was that was wrapped around Jefferson's neck.

"Helped her paint them, too—hmmm." Margo draped the purple, plush towel around her abdomen as she stepped from the shower. Jefferson slowly made his way into their bedroom, his eyes fixed on Margo. "I've even been to the mall and back."

Jefferson stood there without opening his mouth and abruptly turned away from Margo's stare. He looked around the room as if seeing it for the first time. The walls were still antique white. The purple and cream satin spread that draped their king-size bed, as well as the matching wallpaper border, was the same as it was the day before. Jefferson nearly tripped on the Chinese throw rug that had lain in the same place at the foot of the bed for the last two years. His mind was flooded with memories of another place and time, another set of circumstances that he had allowed to get out of control.

"What is it, Jefferson?"

"It's nothing, Margo. Look, I didn't mean to take so long with the reindeer. Blake has an injured arm, so I went ahead and painted the things. I'm sorry, Margo. Sorry for everything. I don't know what else to say."

Jefferson watched Margo as she digested his words. He had no idea what she was thinking, but he prayed that the night would pass by quickly.

"Are you seeing someone, Jefferson? Where were you last night?"

"Margo, I told you where I was and what I was doing. No, I'm not seeing anyone," he lied. "I don't know where you'd get an idea like that."

"Your mind certainly isn't on me. I love you, Jefferson, but you need to get it together. I don't know what's up with you, but you have a responsibility to me and this family. I didn't invest twenty-five years of my life for things to start falling apart now."

Margo marched around the room. The towel that

had covered her body had all but fallen down. Margo saw Jefferson's eyes scanning her nakedness, and she pulled the towel tight around her.

"You need to get rid of the itch or the bitch, because I'm not having any of it, Jefferson." She stood in front of Jefferson, proud of her closing statement.

Jefferson stared at Margo and dismissed her with a wave of his hand. "Margo, you need to get a life. I can't do any better than what I've told you." Jefferson walked into the bathroom and slammed the door behind him.

Jefferson slowly opened his eyes and turned toward the nightstand, barely making out the illuminated numbers on the Sony alarm clock. It was eight-thirty a.m. Arguing with Margo had left him drained, and sleep was the only safe haven from her grueling accusations. He lifted the blanket slightly so that he wouldn't disturb her sleep. He was not ready for a fresh onslaught of the wrath that he probably deserved.

The sun poked through the mini-blinds, casting shadows that looked like stripes on the American flag. Jefferson went to the window to peer out and saw Blake driving up in the driveway. He studied Blake like he was the answer to a problem.

Jefferson's movements, though quiet, roused Margo,

and she lay in bed staring at Jefferson as he backed away from the window. "What's going on?" she asked, startling him.

"Nothing," Jefferson responded. "Blake was just pulling in the driveway. Must have had to make an early store run."

"He's seemingly making a lot of those early runs." *Wasn't it just yesterday that Winston saw him pulling in at six in the morning?* "What time is it?"

"Eight-thirty-eight," Jefferson said, after popping the remaining contact in his eyes.

"Jefferson…"

"Not this morning, Margo. I'm not up to it."

"I'm not up to it either, Jefferson, but we need to talk."

"It's Christmas; let's just get through the day."

Margo continued to look at Jefferson as she sat propped up on her side of the bed. God, she loved this man, and she hoped he wasn't being foolish at this time in their lives.

"My God, I've got to get a move-on. Are you and the kids going to church? We've got all of this company coming. I can't possibly make it this morning. When are we going to open gifts?" Margo had a thousand things going through her head, and even with all that had gone on, she wanted this day to be perfect.

"Calm down, Margo. The kids and I are going to church."

She wouldn't be going in circles and wound up as she was if it hadn't been for him. Margo continued to watch Jefferson as he prepared for church like nothing had happened, no angry words spoken and no accusations hurled. If only she could read his mind.

With everyone out of the house, Margo took a breath and exhaled. Yesterday had been exhausting due to Jefferson's mysterious absence and sudden resurfacing without any comprehensible reason. Margo was trying to make the best of her *Nightmare Before Christmas*, still unsure of her next move. It would have to wait until after the holiday. Her energy was going to be directed toward watching happy faces as they consumed their meal and opened their Christmas gifts.

Each Christmas, it was customary at the Myles' home to share Christmas dinner with special friends and family. As much as Margo looked forward to it, so did all who came each year. Yes, Margo had to let her little trials with Jefferson sit on the back burner, but she'd keep her eyes on him, nevertheless.

Margo strolled into the family room to gaze upon the beautiful Christmas tree that she and Ivy had decorated. Festive holly and ivy were draped throughout the room, and over the fireplace hung six red and white stockings with each owner's name inscribed on it in green glitter. The tree stood seven feet tall and was decorated with red and white iridescent bulbs. Satin red and gold streamers also adorned the tree, accompanied by white twinkling lights. Margo collected wooden ornaments during her travels throughout the world, and they took their rightful place on the tree, as they had each year. Margo was also a collector of African-American ornaments. They hung proudly in their designated spaces as well.

The tree had stood the test of time. Purchased for eighty dollars at the military Post Exchange, it had been with the Myles family for fifteen years. It had served them well and probably would be utilized one more year. No one had the heart to throw it away since it had been with the them almost as long as the twins. The tree was a beautiful backdrop to the spacious room with its vaulted ceiling and creamy, textured palettes of eggshell and hues of brown.

It was going to be a good day. Jefferson's parents would be there, driving up from Atlanta that morning and probably staying until Tuesday. Margo's parents lived in Seattle and didn't feel like making the long trip to North Carolina. Margo would miss them and promised herself that she would fly out to see them next summer. She'd call them later tonight.

Angelica was going to be there, along with her two brothers and their girlfriends. Malik would probably be sporting a new girlfriend on his arm. Each preceding Christmas had established a pattern of his frolicking.

Everyone would stand and watch, speculating which sisterfriend's name would be recorded in Malik's record book this year.

Jefferson always invited Ebony, his secretary, to this annual event. She'd always have her sister, Katrina, in tow—probably to make her feel more comfortable. Lauren Miller and Latoya Jones, who worked in the real estate office with Margo and were dear friends, would also be a part of the cast of Christmas dinner guests. And, of course, Ivy's best friends, Erin and Kimberly, would hopefully be there. They were single and had ended up in Fayette-ville by way of the military.

Margo set about warming the food and setting the dining room table. The dining room was just off the family room, separated by two French doors. There was a certain elegance in this room that one could not elude. It was easy to be drawn into it. The beautiful floor-to-ceiling, beveled windows that stretched the full length of the southward end of the dining room gave way to a view of the saltwater cove that lay beyond. The pot garden that sat upon the deck was breathtakingly splendid. Most who ate in the room sat in awe for more minutes than could be accounted for, barely touching their food, as if the tranquil nature and beauty of the view hypnotized them.

The dining room was graced with an oval dining room table that sat twenty, surrounded by French Empire chairs upholstered in silk taffeta. Margo set the table with her fine Noritake china, a gift from Jefferson on their second wedding anniversary. Lenox starfire crystal champagne glasses, stuffed with Margo's best lacy-white linen napkins in a handsome fleur-de-lis fold, accompanied each setting. A beautiful Waterford crystal vase with a bouquet of yellow roses stood in the center of the table. Margo stepped back to admire her handiwork, and nodded her head in approval. Yes, the pale, calm walls and comfortable chairs would soothe the spirit, while the uncurtained windows revealed views to daydream by. Margo was happy.

But Jefferson and the kids would soon be home from church. Evil thoughts tried to resurface like bile in a blocked passage. Margo fought to suppress them. It was complicated, but as Angelica had said, the truth would come to light.

The aroma from the delectable, mouth-watering food to be served this afternoon filled the house. Margo was pleased. Now, all that was left to do was run upstairs and change clothes.

She reserved a beautiful red silk, swing jacket that swiveled slightly at the bottom just for this occasion. She wore a long, black velvet skirt that complemented the shiny, black buttons that graced the front of her jacket—a gift from Jefferson when she received the Realtor of the Year Award at the annual ball a year and a half ago. She had also won two free, round-trip tickets to fly anywhere in the continental United States. They spent two fabulous weeks in Hawaii this past summer, frolicking and rediscovering themselves as if they were newlyweds.

As she glanced once more into the floor-length mirror in her room, the doorbell rang. It was about one p.m. *It must be Jefferson's parents arriving from Atlanta*, she thought.

Allen and Fedora Myles were wonderful in-laws. They treated Margo as if she were one of their own daughters. Even though Jefferson had another brother, Allen Jr., and two sisters, Deborah and Faye, it was Jefferson and Margo who were always there for Allen and Fedora. Besides being present at all of the family reunions and weddings, any time Allen or Fedora needed help with repairs to their home, had car problems, or other financial needs, it was Jefferson and Margo who were there to the rescue. Never mind that the other siblings lived right in Atlanta within a ten-mile radius of their parents. Somehow they thought that Jefferson and Margo had greater financial means, especially when Jefferson was an officer in the Air Force. It seemed to be a common belief that all military personnel had money.

The doorbell rang again. Margo hastily made her way to the front door. A silver-haired, stately woman with eyes as bright as a UFO and magenta-colored lips stood on the porch next to a tall, lean gentleman whose silver sideburns made him very distinguished. The woman was a latte color with lots and lots of cream, while the gentleman sported a dark, rich permanent tan that made his graying temples sparkle. Her in-laws had arrived safe and sound with a bundle of Christmas presents, luggage, and good cheer.

"Hello, Mother and Dad," Margo said, as she affectionately embraced them and ushered them into the house. Jefferson was definitely his mother's child, although he got most of his dad's complexion.

"Hi, baby," Fedora said, catching her breath. "You look so beautiful, and girl, the smells coming from that kitchen are wonderful—whew."

"We're just in time," added Allen Sr. "How have you been, baby? You're certainly looking well, just like Fedora said. Where is everybody?"

"Come in and let me get you settled. Jefferson and the kids should be home from church any minute, and the others should start showing up around three o'clock. It's so good to see the both of you." *I am certainly blessed in the in-law department*, Margo thought to herself. *Certainly blessed.*

Margo led the way as she lugged their bags to the room they would occupy. This was Fedora and Allen's room. The Southerners called it the mother-in-law room. It was on the first level near the rear of the house between the laundry room and the garage. It came with its own private bath.

"So what's Jefferson up to these days?" Allen Sr. asked. "That boy of mine is always busy. Must be doing good, though."

As hard as Margo tried to suppress thoughts of Jefferson, little beasts kept gnawing at her subconscious, begging to be let out. "Calm yourself down, Margo," she uttered under her breath. She had to take control of her feelings. How she wished she could confide in them about what had transpired. But Jefferson was their son and in their eyes, he could do no wrong.

"Jefferson's been working real hard lately, almost to the point that he loses track of time. His business is doing great. And December is one of his busiest times of year."

"I noticed the pretty reindeer outside in the Montgomerys' yard. They always come up with such novel ideas and ways of decorating. How are they doing?" Fedora inquired.

Another opportunity to loathe Jefferson. Nothing against Linda and Blake, but Jefferson just had to finish those stupid reindeer after spending more than twenty-four hours away from home.

"Linda is doing well. Blake hurt his arm in an accident last week. But he'll live. They'll probably stop by for dessert later on."

"Well, darling, Allen and I are going to freshen up and get dressed so that we will be presentable when your other guests arrive." She kissed Margo on the cheek. Margo thought about her own parents, wishing they weren't so far away and could join them for the Christmas celebration.

CHAPTER 5

Margo was finally feeling the Christmas spirit. Even the events surrounding Jefferson's absence seemed a vague memory. A CD with Christmas carols and other enchanting holiday songs featured The Temptations, Boyz II Men, and Yolanda Adams—whose voice was as beautiful as a sparrow. Yes, it was going to be a perfect day. Sunlight shone through the bay windows of the living room adding warmth to a room that seemed full of love and peace.

As Margo stood mesmerized, she was suddenly alerted to the arrival of her clan as a chorus of wannabe singers rendered their own version of "It Came Upon a Midnight Clear." Jefferson, adding his baritone voice, gave the ailing group some credibility but still not enough to turn the heads of any record producer. Ivy was the only one in the group who had the gift of song, and to this day, no one knew from whom she inherited it. They were kind of comical, thought Margo, allowing herself for a brief moment to feel the distance that had grown between she and Jefferson.

"Hey Mom, where's Grandma and Grandpa? We saw their car in the driveway," Winston said.

"They're freshening up," Margo said.

Jefferson took a step toward Margo. She looked up at him, unsure what he had on his mind. Before he was able to utter the first word, Margo spoke up. "So how was church?"

"Oh, good. Reverend Bryant cut up today. You'd have thought that Jesus was born, crucified, and resurrected all on the same day. The folks were shouting up some."

"Yeah, Mom. Sis Carter shouted so hard that she walked right out of her shoes," interjected Winter. "When she realized it, she put her shoes back on and went to shouting again. Couldn't tell if she was happy because Christ was born or shouting because she had on a new pair of shoes." Everyone laughed.

"Stop, Winter!" Margo was desperately trying to keep her giggle to a minimum. Winter had a funny bone in her that she did not inherit from either Jefferson or Margo.

"Well, Ma, if she doesn't finish college, she'd probably have a good chance as a stand-up comedienne," JR interjected.

Every head turned in JR's direction. "Oh, please," Winston said, with an attitude reserved for a twin whose instinct was to protect his womb partner. "Just because you don't have anything in that vacant space you call a brain doesn't mean—"

"Hold it," Jefferson and Margo piped in simultaneously, looking at each other in disbelief that the two of them were in sync for the first time in forty-eight hours. Jefferson relented with a wave of his hand, giving the floor to Margo.

"That's enough. Today is Christmas, not that it matters that today is Christmas or any other day. We must learn to respect each other—"

"Hey everybody," came the sound of Grandma's voice as she and Grandpa rushed into the room.

Fedora wore a stunning, two-piece, charcoal and black ensemble that was comprised of a jacket and long, full skirt. The jacket bodice was made of black velvet with five, sparkling, crystal buttons running down the front and sported a silk, charcoal-colored box collar that hung off the shoulders. The full-bodied charcoal skirt matched the silk collar on the jacket. Pearl accessories rounded out her outfit.

Allen Sr. was decked out in a three-piece, charcoal, double-breasted Armani suit that Jefferson had given him several years before, accentuated by a white, flip collar, long-sleeved Armani shirt. He was the perfect complement to Fedora.

Allen Sr. and Fedora were met with "wows." Everyone took turns hugging and planting sloppy kisses on Grandma and Grandpa. Their timing was impeccable and probably saved what might have become a real damper on a quite promising day.

Ding-dong, ding-dong, ding-dong.

"Doorbell, someone please get the doorbell," Margo shouted, as she fastened her black lace hostess apron around her medium waist.

"It's Angelica and her family," Winter announced and opened the door. "Merry Christmas, everyone. Let me take your coats." She stepped aside to let the group pass.

"Hi, sweetie, Merry Christmas." Angelica kissed Winter on the cheek.

"This scarf is phat, Angelica." Winter fingered the pure silk fabric that was soft to the touch. "Whenever you get tired of it, remember your favorite play niece!! I know I would look good with this wrapped around my neck."

"It'll be yours, Winter, just for the asking."

Angelica's hair was pulled back into a tight French roll that wore well on her oval face. Her almond-shaped, hazel eyes highlighted her smooth, satiny, caramel-colored skin and gave off its own luster. Her nose was sleek and slender and sat above medium-size lips that were polished in gold lip color.

Angelica wore a full-length mink coat concealing a sleek, gold-leather, two-piece suit and ample breasts, with a collarless, three-quarter length jacket that closed along the side. She wore a pair of gold-studded, mesh sling backs that completed the outfit.

Her handsome brothers, bedecked in Brooks Brothers suits, testified to the fact that life was treating them well. Edward, a Howard Law grad, was a practicing attorney with his own law firm, which boasted being one of the largest minority-owned law firms in the D.C. area. Michael graduated from Johns Hopkins School of Medicine where he was a practicing neurologist, working alongside the world-renowned Dr. Benjamin Carson. No doubt the lovely ladies who graced their sides were vying to be the next Mrs. Thompson.

Margo rushed to the foyer, anxious to greet Angelica before they joined the others. Even though there would only be a brief moment to exchange greetings, there had to be a moment of solidarity.

"Hey Margo, my love," Angelica said, as she reached out for Margo and they embraced. "Girl, you look smashing. Turn around so I can see you."

"Girlfriend, you are simply gorgeous yourself. And if I know Angie, she's got the only replica of this outfit in the state of North Carolina. Girl, strut your stuff. Merry Christmas."

"Do you remember my brothers Edward and Michael?"

"Sure I do! Good to see you again."

"And their friends, Mary Davis and Pam Prentiss."

"Nice to meet you all, and Merry Christmas. Come on in and make yourselves comfortable. Jefferson, Mom and Dad Myles, and the kids are in the family room." Margo looked at Angelica on the sly, and Angelica gave Margo a wink that said, *we'll talk later*.

The doorbell rang again, and in waltzed Ebony and

her sister, Katrina. Ebony was a good and loyal secretary—a real asset to Myles and Associates. Jefferson appreciated all of her hard work and fortitude. She juggled a full-time job and went to college in the evening. Katrina was unsure about what she wanted to do with her life, although she was a counselor at Fayetteville State University, her third job this year.

The mood was right. The fireplace crackled. The smell of the pine embers put everyone in a relaxed frame of mind with the help of The Temptations as they sang "Chestnuts Roasting on an Open Fire." Winter and Ivy filled small crystal cups with eggnog and passed them out among family and guests—all engrossed in friendly conversation. Ivy was thankful that her mother appeared much calmer than she had been yesterday. Any hint of tension that might have been between her mother and father had now subsided. Hopefully, this was not the calm before the storm, because Ivy relished the peace and tranquility, as well as the gaiety of the moment. She was a little disappointed, though, that Erin and Kimberly weren't going to be able to make it. Ivy handed Jefferson a cup of eggnog. He winked at her and headed in Angelica's direction.

"Angelica, you look lovely as always."

"Thank you, Jefferson. You look debonair yourself. I probably had to work a little harder at it."

Jefferson politely smirked. "I don't think so." Jefferson's

eyes searched Angelica's face, making her very uneasy.

Angelica was sure that Jefferson suspected that Margo had confided in her, but she wanted to distract him and whatever he might be thinking. She certainly did not want to put herself in a position to be cornered by Jefferson while he was on one of his fishing expeditions.

"The tree is decorated so beautifully, I mean the whole room just makes me want to celebrate Christmas every day."

"Yeah, well Margo always does a fine job when it comes to decorating."

"Speaking of Margo, where is she?"

"She's probably out in the kitchen."

"Well, I should check to see if she needs any help. If you'll excuse me, I'm going to see if Margo needs me."

"Sure thing," Jeff said, as he watched Angelica disappear through the French doors. She sure had a body on her, and she looked good for her age. That was one of the first things he noticed when he first met Angelica, while helping Hamilton with some financial matters.

"Mom, Dad...are you doing all right?" Jefferson asked, turning his attention toward them and allowing his mind to briefly recall Angelica's exit from the room. It turned him on.

"Fine, son. We just love Christmases with you, Margo, and our grandchildren. They have grown so."

"Yes they have, Mom. I recall when they were first

born. It seems like it was only yesterday. Would you like more eggnog?"

"We're fine," they said in unison.

"Are you all right, son?" Allen Sr. cut in. "You seem so distant and a little agitated. What ya got on your mind?"

"Nothing, Dad, just the stress and strain of maintaining a business. Business is going well, but we're always at the mercy of the economic indicators. The economic indicators have been sporadic with the onset of a new presidential regime, and Alan Greenspan just raised the interest rate to slow down inflation, which means there will be an ultimate slowdown in consumer spending, according to the economists."

"Well, son, if you ever need me to help you out with anything, don't hesitate to ask."

"I won't, Dad. I won't, and you're the greatest. I'm going to move around and greet the other guests."

The doorbell rang yet again. Everyone turned their heads toward the door when they heard Winter announce Malik and his guest. The female guests wagged their tongues as they gazed upon the man some of them had termed, Mr. Hot Buttered Soul.

Malik's muscular body was wrapped in a three-quarter-length, black kid-leather coat that covered an ivory cashmere turtleneck sweater, and black silk slacks belted at the waist. He wore a half-carat diamond earring in his left ear, and his closely cropped hair seemed to glisten tonight. His smile was enticing, and the slight dimple on his left cheek made women weep. He was so handsome. There was no shame in their game, and the female guests refused to pry their eyes away from him.

Malik was better than David Copperfield, performing magic so effortlessly in his yearly performance of *Now You See Her, Now You Don't*. A new female specimen stood in the place of the old model. Everyone waited with baited breath for the unveiling of Malik's new feminine masterpiece.

She was petite with curves that demanded attention. She wore an elegant, two-piece, white silk suit. The jacket sported a sweetheart neckline and sophisticated beadwork outlined the edges. All heads turned in her direction, and Malik guarded her—no, almost suffocated her. She was the one.

"Merry Christmas." Malik greeted everyone and deposited his gifts with Winter.

"Merry Christmas, Malik," came the reply.

"I'd like for you all to meet Antoinette West, Toni for short." Malik hesitated a moment and then continued. "She is my soul mate for life."

"You go boy," Jefferson said, being the first to congratulate Malik. There were immediate high-fives among the men folk in the room.

The women stood around with scowls on their faces.

Yes, the brotha was p-h-i-n-e, and if Ms. Antoinette West seemed affected by the obvious cold shoulders, there was not a hint of it in her facial or body expressions.

Taking Margo's lead, the other ladies joined in reluctantly and welcomed Toni. She *won't* be here next year were their silent thoughts.

The chatter and laughter continued, and the flow of eggnog and cider warmed the hearts.

"Dinner is now served. Mom and Dad Myles, I'd like for you to take your places first," Margo said.

Everyone proceeded through the French doors. The room was breathtaking, as well as the scene beyond the floor-length, wall-to-wall window. Margo had outdone herself.

The Lenox crystal sparkled. The bone china reflected the faces of people who appreciated good living. Everyone took their places, ready to partake of the wonderful meal that Margo had prepared, with the help of her able-bodied young warriors whom she affectionately called her children from time to time.

The buffet was spread with turkey and almond dressing, succulent honey-baked ham, Cornish hens with chutney glaze, and a standing rib roast. There was a bounty of tasty homemade dishes, including collard greens, broccoli casserole (Fedora Myles' favorite), macaroni and cheese, sweet potato cobbler, and tangerine mimosa.

"Let's have every eye closed and every head bowed," Allen Sr. said softly.

"Thank you, Lord, for this gathering on this special day, a day in which we celebrate the true meaning of Christmas, the birth of your son, Jesus. As we sit and reflect on this past year, Lord, help us not to forget that it was Your Son who brought us thus far, Your mercy that allowed us to get up every morning, be about our business, acquire some of the niceties of this world, and kept us from death's door. It was no one but You. We celebrate life today, for if the Christ child had not been born, we would not have the chance to be a part of Your kingdom.

"Bless each family that is represented here today. Give them a renewed spirit. We ask You to bless the food which we are about to receive for the nourishment of our bodies. Bless the provider and the preparer. Sister Margo has done a fine job today. She's a special daughter, and I ask a special blessing for her, my son, and their children. And we all say, amen."

Someone in the crowd said, "Rise, Peter, slay and eat. Let's get this party started." Knives and forks clinked against platters and plates. All seemed to be having a wonderful time, and Margo was pleased.

Passing by Angelica, Margo whispered, "Don't forget, we have to talk."

Angelica took a casual glance around the table, then

her eyes locked with Malik's. She fluttered her eyelashes slowly and seductively until Malik turned away. Toni noticed that Angelica had been eyeing her man from the time they entered the Myles' home, but girlfriend was out of luck because, as Malik had so eloquently announced, *she was the one*.

Allen and Fedora were enjoying themselves. They wished their other children could have joined them. Jefferson and Margo invited them every year, but the rivalry was deep in their blood. So Mom and Dad celebrated Christmas with the others on Christmas Eve.

Ebony and her sister, Katrina, were in deep conversation. Ebony glanced occasionally at her boss hoping to catch his eye. Ebony had a secret crush on Jefferson. However, Jefferson had not returned her unsolicited affection.

After everyone had finished their last helping and the conversation died down, each diner pushed their empty plates toward the center of the table, eased back their chairs, and retired to the family room to wind down and open Christmas packages.

Ding-dong. Jefferson rushed from the room to answer the door. At the door stood Linda Montgomery and her daughter, Felicia.

"Hello, Linda and Felicia, Merry Christmas," Jefferson said, moving aside so they could enter.

"Merry Christmas to you, too," Linda and Felicia said, returning the greeting.

"Is Blake coming?"

"No, he needed to check on his mother, and Blake Jr. is at his girlfriend's house."

Linda gave Jefferson a hug and allowed her eyes to linger as she passed, catching up to Felicia as they proceeded to join the others in the family room. "Everyone, this is Linda and Felicia Montgomery, our next-door neighbors."

"Hi, Linda," the now stuffed group said.

"Hey, Felicia," Winter said, getting up to embrace her high school friend.

The family room had been transformed into a sea of colorful Christmas paper, clothing and small appliances as gifts were exchanged and opened.

Jefferson admired the nugget bracelet Margo had given him. A smile registered on his face, and he gave her a look of appreciation and mouthed the words, "Thank you."

Angelica hastily pulled the beautifully tied ribbon that circled her present from Margo.

"Oh Margo, it's so beautiful!" Angelica exclaimed.

"That is a serious, phat scarf," Malik said, moving closer to Angelica to get a better look.

"Oh Angelica, I'd rather have this scarf. It is so soft and purple is one of my favorite colors," Winter said, brushing the delicate fibers with the tips of her fingers. "This is soooo phat. I can't believe Mom hasn't bought me one; she knows I love scarves."

"Thanks, Margo; I love you. You're a special friend, and I wish you nothing but happiness in the new millennium." Angelica held and hugged Margo tight as tiny teardrops fled Angelica's face.

Margo wasn't aware that Hamilton had given Angelica a scarf for her forty-fifth birthday that was very similar to the one she had just given her. Angelica had run home to pick up a file folder she needed for work when she stumbled upon Hamilton entertaining one of his low-life, hoochie-momma groupies in their bed. She had Angelica's scarf wrapped around her neck as she performed a freaky Las Vegas number for Hamilton utilizing Angelica's scarf as a prop. The young girl was no older than nineteen. She pulled Angelica's scarf across her naked body as she begged Hamilton to make love to her.

Angelica ran out in horror, vowing to leave Hamilton once and for all. She did that very night. Angelica never wanted to see that scarf again, even though she loved it very much. The pain of the moment was too much to endure. And now Margo brought it all back; but this was not the same scarf. It was a special gift from Margo, and she would cherish it always. No hoochie momma would wear this one.

Mom and Dad Myles were elated at their gift. Margo bought a silver photo album that she and Ivy filled with pictures of their family, beginning with Margo and Jefferson's wedding through the twins' graduation from

Pine Forest High School. Fedora and Allen held each other's hand, looked in each other's eyes, and counted their blessings, acknowledging all the love that they had for each other. As they sat on the loveseat, Allen pulled Fedora close and they held each other tight.

Malik was opening his gift when JR decided to turn on the television. It seemed to upset the mood a little, although no one complained as they nursed full stomachs and continued chattering about who was going to play in the Super Bowl or who was going to be the next Denzel Washington.

"Is there a ballgame on, JR?" Malik asked, continuing to unwrap his tightly wrapped package.

"I think the Panthers are playing the 49ers," JR said.

"Thanks my man, you know how to hook a brotha up. This is real nice, Jefferson," Malik said, showing off his baby Rolex. Malik and Jefferson had been friends for years. They were frat brothers and shared a bond in their wonder years that seemed tighter than Jefferson and Margo.

Everyone wanted a peek at Malik's sensational watch. Each person took turns examining it, brushing their fingers over the twelve diamonds. It was an awesome piece of jewelry, and there was no wondering what made it the most-talked-about watch brand in the world.

A newscaster appeared on the TV screen interrupting the football game.

"We interrupt this broadcast to bring you a breaking news story from Fayetteville."

"Quiet, everybody," JR admonished.

"A shootout in the Richmond Heights subdivision, approximately five miles from Fort Bragg Army Base, has left one person dead," the newscaster announced.

Jefferson, Margo, and Angelica froze. Just forty-eight hours ago, Angelica was telling Margo that she'd seen Jefferson go there.

"A dark blue Ford Explorer was riddled with bullets from what appears to be an AKA assault rifle. The occupant of the Ford Explorer is a white male, mid-to-late forties. Lieutenant Hamilton Barnes of the Richmond Heights police station was first on the scene."

"Lieutenant Barnes," continued the newscaster, "can you tell us what you found upon arrival?"

Hamilton Barnes loomed large on the screen.

He is handsome, thought Margo, as she tried to focus on what he had to say.

"Yes, Sergeant Broadnax and I answered a 9-1-1 dispatch call that came in at approximately six-fifteen p.m. We rushed to the scene only to find a dark blue Ford Explorer in the middle of Fuller Street, riddled with bullets that appear to be from an AKA assault rifle. There was no movement in the vehicle, and upon opening the driver's door, found the occupant slumped over the steering wheel, apparently hit by gunfire. The victim is a white male, approximately fifty years of age. The name is being withheld until notification of next-of-kin."

"Thank you, Lieutenant Barnes. We will continue this live coverage and bring you more details as they become available. This is Denver Grey, reporting to you live from Fayetteville, North Carolina, WYZZ-TV."

Linda Montgomery collapsed on the floor in the middle of the Myles' family room.

CHAPTER 6

More than six Fayetteville City police cars lined Fuller Street with the forensic technician taking up the rear. One white male in a Ford Explorer lay shot dead, waiting to be carried to the coroner's van for later transport to the hospital. It appeared that the deceased was the intended victim, since his SUV was badly riddled. The police wondered why the man was on this side of town, eighteen miles from where he lived, alone on Christmas night when his family was enjoying festivities elsewhere.

"Lieutenant Barnes, my man, you've got a nasty mess on your hands—and on Christmas Day at that."

"Yeah, Captain Petrowski, a nasty mess. We're interviewing residents now to see if anyone saw anything suspicious that might shed some light on the matter."

"We're going to have to work fast on this due to the nature of the case."

"You mean because he was white in an all-black neighborhood—a neighborhood notorious for crime?" Barnes asked sarcastically.

"You got my meaning. Say Barnes, weren't you the first one at the scene?"

"Yeah, Bob. Sergeant Broadnax and I rushed down as soon as we received the dispatch. It probably took us no more than a minute to reach the scene."

"And no one has come forward yet?"

"No, Captain, not a soul. As I said, we're working on it. People were arriving at the scene about the same time we were—probably responding more to the sound of the crash than the hail of bullets."

"And how do you surmise that?"

"Considering the rather large crowd that gathered when Broadnax and I arrived, it leads me to believe that it had to be as a result of the noise made by the impact of the SUV."

"We've got to lock this up quick, Barnes, I do mean quick. Interrupted my Christmas dinner, it did." Captain Petrowski paced back and forth in his long, black trench coat that was buttoned up to the neck. The air had become a little more brisk with the sun on its final approach to sunset. "Somebody better talk before the night is over. I'm going back to the station."

"All right, Captain," Lieutenant Barnes said, as he watched Petrowski get into a squad car and drive away.

Captain Petrowski had been head of the Homicide Division for the last ten years. Fayetteville had seen some high-profile homicide cases during that time—

Junior French, a Fort Bragg soldier who went on a rampage and killed several diners, as well as the owners of a popular Italian eatery; the Golphen brothers who killed a N.C. highway patrolman and a sheriff's deputy on I-95 after they pursued the brothers after a minor traffic stop; two skinhead soldiers, also from Fort Bragg, who were looking for black people to kill—killing two innocent people on a cold December night in order to add a spider tattoo on their arm claiming victory for a job accomplished. Then there was the gang killing of two girls and the near homicide of another. It had been a tumultuous six years, and Hamilton knew Petrowski didn't relish the impact that this homicide was sure to create.

All mouths hung open as the news of the murder and Linda's subsequent collapse took on a reality of its own. Suddenly, the idea of chestnuts roasting on an open fire lost its appeal, and the perfect day that Margo had so longed for and nearly achieved was overshadowed by a breaking news story that affected everyone in the room like a collective slap.

"Linda, Linda, are you all right?" Margo called out, kneeling down on the floor and shaking her. "Somebody help me. Get a cold towel or something."

"Mom, are you okay?" interrupted Felicia, as she joined Margo. "Mom, answer me."

Jefferson knelt next to Margo, shaking Linda as well. "Ivy is bringing a towel," he said. Margo noticed that beads of sweat had formed across Jefferson's forehead.

Dr. Michael Thompson joined them, taking Linda's arm in his hand, checking for a pulse. "She's breathing and has a pulse. She'll be all right. She's fainted." Michael laid Linda's hand back onto the floor. "Pam, run to the car and get my medical bag. I have some smelling salts in it. Once I give Linda a whiff, she'll come to. Let's give her some air."

Margo noticed that the sweat was now running down the length of Jefferson's face. Linda had only fainted, according to Dr. Thompson, but why?

"A patrol car is pulling up in Linda's driveway," announced Angelica, as she peered out of the living room window, watching as Pam went to retrieve Michael's medical bag. Dusk had now fallen and the temperature along with it. Angelica noticed a few leaves were scurrying along in no real hurry, aided by a small brisk wind that was beginning to increase in speed.

"Felicia, you may need to go to your house. The officers are ringing your doorbell," Angelica motioned, as she continued to peer out of the window.

"What do you think caused Linda to pass out like that?" Margo asked Jefferson. "Do you think she knows the person who was killed?" Jefferson remained silent.

"Ford Explorer, white male...no...Jefferson, you don't think it's...no why would she assume? Jefferson, say something. It can't be Blake. What would he be doing in that area?"

"I don't know why Linda passed out, Margo," Jefferson said before Margo could finish. "I don't know."

Linda began to stir after receiving a whiff of the smelling salt that Dr. Thompson waved under her nose. Margo applied the cold compress to her head.

"Linda, are you all right?" She cradled Linda's head on her lap as Linda attempted to open her eyes. Linda started to say something when Felicia burst through the door screaming.

"Mom, Dad is dead!" Felicia screamed, trying to catch her breath at the same time. "Dad is dead! He was...he was the one who was murdered, but you knew that, didn't you, Mother?" Felicia continued to scream as she stood over Linda.

Linda stared back at Felicia, not saying a word. The room fell silent except for the noise coming from the televison, the deliverer of bad news. No one was prepared for what was to become the Christmas nightmare on Andover Street.

Margo hugged Linda even tighter.

"Mom, the police need to talk with you to get some information," Felicia whispered.

"I'll be glad to go over and talk to the police with you," Edward said to Linda who still lay limp in Margo's arm. "I'm sure my brother, Michael, would be willing to accompany you to the coroner's if you like."

Michael acknowledged his acceptance with a nod of his head.

Jefferson was visibly unnerved. He paced the floor incessantly, causing folks to look in his direction. Malik was studying Jefferson as he paced the floor. This was not just an ordinary news story that had grasped one's attention for five minutes and was now a blur. Blake Montgomery's death was going to rock a community.

One by one, the guests retrieved their belongings, thanked Margo and Jefferson for a wonderful evening, then slipped off into the night. Malik pulled on his three-quarter-length kid-calf, black leather coat.

As Toni and Malik were about to bid their farewells, Malik seized the opportunity to pull Jefferson aside.

"Wait for me in the car, Toni. I've got to run something by Jefferson."

"Okay, honey. Don't be long." And Antoinette West bid everyone a good night.

"Jefferson, what is this all about?" Malik inquired. "I sure hope Blake's murder has nothing to do with you."

"Look Malik, I don't have a clue what any of this is about, but Linda's passing out certainly aroused everyone's curiosity. I do not know why Blake was in that area, but I've got to find some answers. And Margo is watching me, man. I'm sure she is."

"That is your guilty conscience. You need to find some answers so you can make some decisions about the direction your life is headed. You need to compose yourself and be ready to move sensibly on whatever you find. I've got your back, dawg. I'm outta here. Stay in touch."

"Thanks, man."

Allen and Fedora were tired from the ride up to Fayetteville and bid a good night to all. "If you need to talk, son, I'm here," Allen Sr. said. No one had missed a beat, especially not the senior Myles.

"Margo, what do you make of all this?" Angelica asked. Angelica began pacing, trying to make heads or tails of what had just transpired, hiding the nagging feeling that this death was about to explode like the atomic bomb—a gut feeling that somehow Hamilton might be involved. She didn't have a chance to tell Margo that Ham and Ray Adams, Hamilton's sidekick, had come by the house last night. When she asked Ham if he knew anything about Jefferson's disappearance, both he and Ray visibly reacted to it without delivering any information.

"No Angie, I can't fathom what this is all about. Did you notice how quickly Linda reacted to the announcement without any verification of the deceased? Why don't you call Hamilton and see if you can get some information?"

"Yeah, I guess that's the only thing we can do at the moment. Let's wait until Edward and Michael come back, maybe they'll have some additional information."

"Margo," Angelica continued, "I have a strange feeling that the clues to your mystery will start showing up on the sidewalk."

"What are you talking about, Angie?"

"Gut feeling and bad vibes, girl. Haven't you noticed how Jefferson seems to be concealing his nervousness?"

"But what does Jefferson have to do with Linda and Blake?"

There was a staccato noise. "We interrupt this program to give you an update on the murder of a white male in the Richmond Heights area in Fayetteville. The victim has been identified as fifty-three-year-old Blake Montgomery of 2406 Andover Street in Fayetteville. A suspect has not been apprehended at this time. The investigation continues. This is Denver Grey reporting to you live from Fayetteville, North Carolina for WYYZ."

Margo and Angelica looked at each other. Linda had known right away that it was Blake. Margo looked over to where Jefferson was standing with his hand cupped to his chin. He avoided her stare, and the monsters that had lain dormant inside Margo's body began to resurface. She had to control them for now. She needed answers first.

It was going to be a long night.

Mary and Pam made themselves comfortable as they waited for Edward and Michael to return from helping Linda. Edward decided to accompany Michael, Linda, and Felicia to the morgue.

"Mom, is there anything Winter and I can do?" Ivy whispered.

"No, baby. Well, see if Pam, Mary, and Angelica would like something warm to drink."

"Alright."

"Jefferson," Margo said as she made her way over to him. Odd, he hadn't said anything else to her since the incident.

"Yes, Margo."

"You're awfully quiet. Do you have any idea what this is all about?" Margo looked at him quizzically.

"No more than I did the last time you asked. I'm just as puzzled as you are, Margo. I can't believe that Blake is gone. We've shared a great friendship these past years, and I feel for Linda and the kids."

"I do, too," Margo added. "Why do you suppose he

was in Richmond Heights? That seems to be the area of choice for a lot of people lately."

Jefferson turned around to look squarely at Margo. She did look good tonight. Jefferson remembered how proud he was when Margo received the Realtor of the Year Award. She was radiant that night, after the tribute for her successes in community and professional circles. Red and black looked good on Margo. Jefferson loved surprising his bride of twenty-five years with tokens of his affection. He truly loved Margo once, but lately, he wasn't quite sure what had gone wrong. What was happening to Jefferson took him from a path of security, acceptance, and love to what could be his eventual destruction.

"What do you mean that that's the area of choice?"

"Weren't you…?" Margo cut it short realizing she was saying too much.

"Were you what?" Jefferson asked, raising his voice, causing the remaining guests to look up.

"Don't raise your voice at me, Jefferson," Margo said, with fire in her eyes. "You know something, you're afraid. I see it in your eyes."

"You don't know what you're talking about, Margo. I'm just as upset about this whole thing as you!"

"Some of us are a little more upset than others. Remember, Jefferson, the truth will come to the light."

The children gathered in the family room, keeping

Pam and Mary company. Winston and JR were still feeding their faces with slices of sweet potato pie. Ivy and Winter passed looks between them, waiting to come to their mother's aid if necessary.

"Why don't you come and sit down?" Angelica asked, putting her arm around Margo's waist. She ushered her to the couch where Jefferson had been admiring his nugget bracelet only hours earlier. "Let me get you some coffee, Margo. Sit and relax."

"Thanks, Angelica."

Jefferson continued to stand and pace as if that was going to bring Blake back to life.

Linda, Felicia, Edward, and Michael rode to the coroner's office in silence. Edward drove, allowing himself a chance to go over the last twenty minutes of police questioning in his head. They didn't say much, just that they were there to notify the next-of-kin and elicit some vital statistics about Blake. Yet an abundance of unasked questions told Edward he'd like to be on this case or at least help uncover some of the vital details. The case reeked of high drama and high stakes, and Johnnie Cochran wasn't the only attorney capable of handling a challenge like this.

There was a sudden stillness in the air, reminding

one of death. This was a Sunday evening, Christmas Day, but something evil and ominous had killed the festive mood. The day that started off like so many others had now left tear stains on some faces and the question, *Why*, on others.

"Mrs. Montgomery, do you want to go through with this tonight, it being Christmas and all?" asked Dr. Gillespie, the forensic examiner, a short, round fellow in his mid-fifties.

It frightened Linda to be at the morgue, but Dr. Gillespie was so casual in his approach that he made it seem like another day at the office. He was eating a peanut butter and jelly sandwich with his ungloved hand.

"Haven't had a chance to eat Christmas dinner," Dr. Gillespie said, noting the stares of the foursome. "Do you want to do this now?" he again addressed Linda.

"I might as well get it over with," Linda said, wringing her hands together in an attempt to calm her nerves. "I've got friends here who will accompany me into the room. This is Dr. Michael Thompson and his brother, Attorney Edward Thompson."

"Pleased to meet you," the examiner said, shaking the brothers' hands.

As Dr. Gillespie turned back toward Linda, she noticed that he appeared exhausted. This had been a horrendous month for homicides. "Mrs. Montgomery, your husband's personal effects, pending your identification, have been turned over to our homicide division for analysis and possible clues. They'll notify you when they're through with the articles. At that time, you should be able to retrieve his belongings."

"Thank you, doctor," Linda said. "Felicia, I want you to stay outside. It's enough that I have to do this."

"Mom, I want to go in with you. That's my dad in there."

"Stay outside, Felicia. You need to call Blake Jr. and tell him about your dad."

"Are you ready, Mrs. Montgomery?" the coroner asked.

Linda nodded her head. "She's ready," Michael said.

The street was nearly cleared except for the few onlookers who hung around to discuss their theory of what happened. Sergeant Broadnax scratched his head in dismay after interviewing nearly thirty people and coming up empty. He headed back to his patrol car, and en route saw Lieutenant Barnes who motioned for him to come over.

"Anything yet, Carl?" Barnes asked.

"No, Lieutenant. No one seems to have seen anything. It baffles me too, almost as if it was perfectly planned."

"Well, we'll just have to wait until something surfaces. Look, continue your questioning even if you have to go house to house to get some answers. Captain Petrowski is hot on putting the wraps on this case, and hopefully we can give him something. I'm heading back to the station. You can radio me there."

"All right, Lieutenant Barnes. I'll see what I can come up with."

Sergeant Broadnax stepped off the curb making his way across the street where a few people were still milling around. The wreckage had already been cleared, but there were visible signs that an accident had occurred. The yellow police tape that cordoned off the area was now blowing. Sergeant Broadnax stepped on a piece of the SUV's reflector. It made a crunching sound. As Broadnax reached the other side, the few people who remained, turned their backs on him, sending out the unspoken signal that they had nothing to say. He was accustomed to this treatment. It was part of the territory, and it didn't move him at all.

"Hey, did anyone see anything at all?" The group ignored Sergeant Broadnax and continued mingling among themselves.

"I said…did anyone see anything? I know you aren't deaf," Broadnax said to the group.

"Look, if we saw something, do you think we'd tell you? White boy had no business being up in here no way," said a dark-complexioned, young boy who stood at about six feet two inches. He wore a gold tooth, and had a three-inch scar on the left side of his face running from his ear to the side of his mouth—obviously from a knife.

Sergeant Broadnax looked over the lanky kid with the big mouth who presented himself spokesman for the group. "You have anything to do with this, kid?"

"Man, do you listen? Must've got that badge from the local liquor store." A few giggles could be heard from the crowd.

Broadnax moved through the crowd, planting himself in front of the big-mouthed kid. He grabbed his collar and jerked him forward until they were nose to nose, and Broadnax could smell the odor of stale malt liquor on his breath.

"Look *man*, let me tell you something. If I find that your punk ass had anything to do with this, I'm going to personally give you the lethal injection. And don't let me see you with a beer can in your hand." He pushed the kid away and turned from the group in time to see a curtain move in an upstairs window of the house on the corner.

Marsha Wilson watched while Sergeant Broadnax questioned the group that stood in front of her house. She clutched her curtains, hoping those kids would go quickly to wherever they belonged. Now the sergeant continued to look toward the house, leisurely picking his teeth with a toothpick extracted from his shirt pocket. She watched him move in a slow gait, contemplating his next move. He determined that to be Marsha's front porch, and then she heard the doorbell ring.

Marsha did not move. She had nothing to say to any police officer. She didn't care that he was black. Sometimes they were just as bad as their white counterparts, asserting their authority like that fine Lieutenant Barnes. She was older by a few years than Hamilton Barnes, but it didn't stop her from tasting his luscious lips and seducing him to be a baaaad boy. Often, Marsha would scream out when they were in the midst of their love-making. *Bad boy, bad boy, whatcha gonna do, whatcha gonna do, my body's been waiting on you. Bad boy, bad boy.*

CHAPTER 7

Jefferson awoke early Monday morning. He had planned to spend the day with his kids, but after Blake's untimely death, he needed to attend to a more important matter immediately. Jefferson tiptoed around the bedroom, hoping not to awaken Margo. His effort seemed not in vain, as Margo's snoring was most distinct.

Jefferson moved swiftly in the dark. When he was finally dressed and looked at the clock on his nightstand, it was six-thirty a.m.

Jefferson deactivated the house alarm and quietly entered the garage through the kitchen door. Hopefully, no one would hear the garage door open or the motor of his Mercedes. All was quiet and still. At last, he was out onto the dark street, avoiding any questions or hassles from Margo.

Ivy stood, staring out of the upstairs window of the loft that was built over the garage and doubled as a rec room. She watched as the silver Mercedes backed out of the driveway and eased onto quiet Andover Street. She could see lights glowing from some of the other houses, probably folks preparing to go to work, hoping the week would go by fast in anticipation of the largest New Year's celebration to be witnessed—Y2K, the turn of the new century.

Ivy turned away from the window while her mind traveled in a maze covered with fog. Something was amiss. Ivy had heard her mother and father arguing on Saturday night, and there was no mistake that there was trouble on the front, and Ivy was going to get some answers.

"Morning, Sarge, back at it again, huh? Brought some coffee to wake you up," Lieutenant Hamilton Barnes said, as he walked toward his desk with the remaining cup of coffee in his hand.

"Yeah, Lieutenant, I could've used at least another hour of sleep. The coffee will help. Thanks."

"You come up with anything on yesterday's shooting?"

"No, Lieutenant, not a thing. Ran into a bunch of bad-mouthed kids who gave me a hard time, but I don't think they saw anything. Strange thing happened, though. I noticed someone peering out of an upstairs window at a house on the corner of Shaw and Fuller, but no one would answer the door. I rang the doorbell several times. I know what I saw. I was left studying an old architectural design on the door made by what looked to be a switchblade and shells from a .22-caliber pistol. Umm, this coffee is good." Sergeant Broadnax took another sip, allowing the heat to warm his face.

Hamilton watched Sergeant Broadnax's lips as he went on and on about his investigation. Hamilton tried not to look disinterested, but upon hearing about the corner house, some life sparked into him. "House on the corner, did you say?"

"Yeah, Lieutenant. A brown and beige two-story."

"You say you saw someone, but no one answered after you rang the doorbell?"

"Right again, Lieutenant. It appeared to be a female, but I could be wrong."

"I think I'd like to pay a visit to this house. Did you get a number?" Hamilton didn't need a number. He probably could walk blindfolded to 2334 Fuller Street. An old friend lived there and was probably due a courtesy call. Hamilton put it on his "TO DO" list for the afternoon.

"I've got it," Sergeant Broadnax chimed. "It's 2334 Fuller Street."

"Thanks, Sarge," Lieutenant Barnes said, without making an effort to write it down.

Jefferson bounded out of the car. It was eight a.m.

Earlier, needing to waste time, he stopped by a local Burger King and bought a ham and cheese croissant to keep his stomach from growling. He knew Hamilton was usually at the office by seven o'clock, and he didn't want to be a nuisance the minute Lieutenant Barnes arrived. Well, it was now or never. He walked up the couple of steps to the entrance. The street wasn't too busy since this was Christmas Monday and many people stayed home from work. Jefferson pushed open the door and entered.

The Richmond Heights police station was a small remote unit that housed three people and three different shifts. Lieutenant Barnes supervised the station with Sergeant Broadnax next in command. Sergeant Holly Walters served as dispatcher and secretary. A roving detective would rotate in and out of the station at least three times a week.

Jefferson walked up to the reception area where Holly sat, slightly distracted as she desperately cruised her brain for the answers to today's crossword puzzle. Holly was pretty adept at this word game, which had increased her vocabulary two-fold.

Twenty-year-old Holly always dreamed of becoming a police officer. She came from a family of them. Her grandfather, father, and older brother were or had been on the police force in Durham, North Carolina for the last forty-five years. Her grandfather had recently retired, and Holly was proud—and only encouraged her even more to push toward her goal.

Fayetteville was not Holly's city of choice, but an opening existed there. Since her passion to become a police officer was such a dominating force in her life, she accepted the post, finally realizing her dream. However, after being assigned to the Richmond Heights area for the past year and watching an overwhelming increase in crime in Fayetteville, she had begun to rethink her aspirations. A friend of hers directed her to Fayetteville State University, and she signed up for courses the next semester to possibly work toward a degree in elementary education.

"Seven across," Holly repeated as if saying it out loud would make the word materialize. "Friday or Dirty Harry, three letters. Now what could it be?"

"Ump," Jefferson said, clearing his voice for effect.

"Oh, hi, Mr. Myles, you caught me," Holly purred, quickly folding the paper and hiding it under a stack of papers she was supposed to be processing.

"Yeah, but it's alright. Knowledge is power. Maybe I can help you with that word when I come back through."

"Thanks, Mr. Myles. You here to see Lieutenant Barnes?"

"Yes, Sergeant Walters."

Holly pressed the button on the intercom.

"Yes, Sergeant Walters," came Hamilton's voice.

"Mr. Jefferson Myles is here to see you. Do you want him to come back?"

"No," Hamilton said, in a tone that was a little too anxious. "I'll be up in a sec. Thanks, Holly."

Hamilton gathered his holster and jacket, then turned to Sergeant Broadnax. "Sarge, hold down the fort for a while. If Petrowski calls, tell him a team is working on forensics and that I will be combing the area again this afternoon for clues. I've got to take care of a little business right now. You can get me through dispatch. By the way, do you know who took the personal effects of the deceased, if any?"

"City police did yesterday. Any other personal items were probably obtained from the coroner after he was done with the body."

"Okay, Carl, I'm out."

"Alright, Lieutenant; got you covered."

Hamilton proceeded to the reception area. Jefferson Myles was the last person he wanted to see this morning, but he needed to see what he wanted so that he could send him on his way. Hamilton came upon the water cooler that stood on the wall adjacent to the reception area. He needed a drink to wash down the coffee residue that he could still taste in his mouth. He wiped his mouth with the back of his hand. When he looked up, there was Jefferson pacing the tiny area with tension and fear written across his forehead. Jefferson rushed toward Hamilton upon finally seeing him.

"Cop," Holly said out loud. "Seven across is c-o-p."

"Hamil…" Jefferson tried to say as Hamilton ushered him out of the station away from prying eyes and ears. "What's up, man?" Jefferson said, attempting to finish his sentence this time. "Who killed Blake?"

"What do you mean who killed Blake? It's just another homicide that we are presently investigating."

"Don't give me that, Barnes. You knew who was inside that vehicle. What was he doing on this side of town anyway and on Fuller Street?"

"Maybe you can tell me. I've been wondering the same thing myself. Myles, you've got some nerve coming over here pointing your finger at somebody. I'm trying to find out the very thing you're asking. What you ought to be considering is how you might be linked to this."

"Linked, to what? Now what are you talking about, man? I was at home yesterday and haven't seen Blake since Saturday."

"Well brother, you're awfully tense for my taste. You better get a grip and stop acting as if you stole a fifty-pound canary. We will get to the bottom of this, Jefferson. Right now, why don't you go back to your wife and kids and let the big boys handle the action."

"Barnes, I know you had something to do with Blake's murder, and I'm going to find out just what."

"Is that a threat, Myles? Remember, I wear the badge."

Jefferson looked at Barnes and shrugged his shoulders. Barnes was ruthless. He would have to be extra careful from now on.

Barnes watched as Jefferson stepped into his silver Mercedes and drove off toward the All American Freeway. "Threaten me, did he? Hmmm, we'll see about that," Hamilton said aloud. He pulled his cell phone from its leather holder that was attached to his belt. Hamilton flipped the lid and proceeded to dial.

"Ray, this is Barnes. We've got problems. Meet me at eleven o'clock at the BP gas station on the Boulevard. We'll talk then." Hamilton closed the cover on the phone and got into his patrol car. He had to make one more important stop before meeting Ray.

Ivy didn't believe how easy it was to be a detective. She always thought she'd need some type of sophisticated gadgets and a keen mind to deal with the criminal element, but this was a piece of cake.

Go to the scene of the crime and *voila!!!* She had not quite made it to Shaw and Fuller Streets, but there in broad daylight was her father's silver Mercedes parked right outside the Richmond Heights police station. And then…a hole-in-one—her father and Lieutenant Barnes emerged from the station in what seemed to be a deep conversation—and not too friendly from Ivy's observation just one block away.

And the phone call Lieutenant Barnes made to someone after her daddy drove away. Ivy was sure that her father had no knowledge of that.

Ivy didn't want to be detected, so she sat until Lieutenant Barnes finally pulled away. She followed him, giving herself enough space so that she still had him in sight. She followed for four blocks until he suddenly turned and appeared to park on a corner. Ivy could also see crime scene tape and what appeared to be faint chalk marks on the ground. Ivy continued straight.

Hamilton seemed to have a laundry list of unpopular tasks today. That usually came with the territory, but these were indirect, out-of-the-way, unwanted, could-have-been-avoided tasks that took extra effort and energy Hamilton didn't want to expend. But they had to be dealt with anyway.

He peered up at the house across the street from the driver's side window wondering if Marsha Wilson was at home. Marsha was in his past, and a reunion wasn't what Hamilton envisioned. He had to find out, though, if Ms. Wilson had been a witness to any of the activities that occurred yesterday. He thought he saw a curtain move in an upstairs window, perhaps the same window that Sergeant Broadnax had mentioned.

Lieutenant Barnes crossed the street and climbed onto the porch that Broadnax had descended only yesterday. He remembered the gaudy structural design of the front door, remnant of the war on drugs.

Hamilton looked both ways, having rung the bell a number of times, watching for possible signs of escape or nosy neighbors who needed to mind their own business. One more ring, Ham thought, and he was going to break the ugly door down.

"Well hello, if it isn't Lieutenant Hamilton Barnes from the Richmond Heights Police Department knocking at my door. And how are you today?" Marsha cooed, opening the door slightly.

"Cut the crap, Marsha. Are you going to invite me inside?"

"All depends on what you selling."

"I ain't selling nothing, but you better let me in for your own good."

"Now, now, you don't have to be mean. I've always been very cooperative," Marsha said, smiling. She looked as if she might have expected Hamilton to show up today.

"Not according to my sergeant. Says you wouldn't answer the door yesterday."

"That fool! I didn't have nothing to say to him."

Marsha wore a skin-tight, red, Lycra dress that was at least four inches above her knees. It nursed every curve and bump with precision on her well-framed body.

She wore a pair of too-tight, red, high-heeled pumps that she could barely walk in. Her hair was neatly pulled back in a ponytail, even though there was evidence that a perm was badly needed. Her ruby red lips gave Barnes a most gracious smile against her velvety, chocolate skin that showed signs of aging before its time.

Hamilton didn't want to get comfortable. He focused only on the point of his visit. Marsha looked good, but his business was more important.

"Where were you yesterday at approximately six p.m.?"

"Honey, I was right here watching those Lifetime movies. I can't remember the name of the movie, but that woman who used to play in *Hotel*—what's her name? Uhh, uhh…Connie Selleca; she was the lead. And my girls, Ebony and Katrina, came by earlier before they went over to Ebony's boss' house for Christmas dinner. I think Ebony has a crush on him."

"Okay, Marsha. Did you happen to see anything out of the ordinary?"

"Out of the ordinary? You mean other than that man getting killed?"

"Well, yes and no. I'm talking about before the accident happened."

"No, I didn't see anything. Like I told you, I was watching movies all afternoon."

"I hope you aren't lying to me, Marsha."

"Why would I lie to you, Lieutenant Barnes," Marsha

said, seductively, encircling her arms around his neck and drawing her lips close to his, while looking him straight in the eyes. "If I saw something, you would be the first person I'd tell."

Hamilton made a small gesture to push Marsha away, but the tight-fitting red dress and Marsha's warm, sweet breath was making the bad boy weak. Marsha pressed her body tightly against Ham's, allowing no air to seep through the seam where their bodies joined. Marsha felt Hamilton's aroused hardness and knew that she had succeeded in taking his mind off his investigation.

Hamilton kissed Marsha forcefully, as if he had been deprived of a woman's lips for months, maybe years. Marsha responded just as passionately and felt Hamilton's big hands begin their search and seizure. He allowed his hands to roam the length of her back and then climb the hill, no the mountain—twin mountains that begged to be held. Then he pushed her against his hardness. It felt good and Marsha began to rub his head and bite his earlobe. She pushed herself further into him even though there was no place to go.

Hamilton kissed Marsha again and let his tongue travel from her mouth to her neck, making circular motions as he did so. Marsha's moans of pleasure hit decibels that could make one hard of hearing if they had a steady, daily dose. And Hamilton found her breasts, waiting like a large, neon, vacancy sign—begging him to stop, come in, and stay a while.

Hamilton cupped her breasts with his hands, feeling her erect nipples through the thin dress. His tongue sought her nipples that pulsated in his hands only seconds before, knowing that once he had them in his mouth, she'd be as pliable as a Raggedy Ann doll. And he laid her on the couch that had seen and felt more than its share of lust-filled bodies.

Hamilton was on his way to the main course when he abruptly loosened himself from Marsha's grip. He was jarred to reality by some sudden, unexplained force. He had already gone too far, and it was not in his nature to leave business unfinished, especially when business was this good. But he had to get control of his senses immediately and not allow himself to become trapped for a moment's indiscretion, leaving him without a clear head. It would be a mistake. A wrong turn or bad slip would be to his detriment.

He stood up and looked back at Marsha who stared back in disbelief. What was happening could not be happening! She was ready to ride to the peak, and now Hamilton left her in the middle of the mountain without a lifeline. The brotha was gonna pay.

"You better not be lying to me, Marsha," Hamilton said again, pointing his finger in her face and trying to straighten his clothes at the same time. "If I have to come back—"

"If you have to come back, what do you think you're going to do?" Marsha retorted, rising from the couch with fire in her eyes that said she was not afraid of Lieutenant Hamilton Barnes. "Just get your ass out of here right now. I told you I didn't see anything or hear anything except that loud crash, and everyone for miles heard that. Now get out!!!" she shouted at the top of her lungs.

"If I have to—" Marsha slammed the door behind Hamilton before he had a chance to finish his sentence.

"The nerve of him to come up in here and play with my affections. You're gonna pay for this, Lieutenant Hamilton Barnes," Marsha shouted from behind the ugly wooden door as she watched Hamilton cross the street and get into his patrol car.

CHAPTER 8

Blake Montgomery's funeral was set for Wednesday, December 28th. Neither Blake nor Linda had many relatives. Of the few they had, the one who lived the farthest was only five hours away. Today was Tuesday, and all who were planning on attending had arrived.

"Such a shame to die—and on Christmas Day," Margo said to no one in particular, although Jefferson sat only a few feet away. "How could something like this happen? So meaningless. And that poor family. Did Blake, Jr. ever come home?"

Jefferson sat stoically, as if Margo's mumbling was too much for his comprehension. Margo noticed that Jefferson had been standoffish, almost lethargic. He had risen very early on Monday and left the house without a word. Something was bothering him. This only added to the discord that threatened to upset the balance of things in the Myles' household.

Allen and Fedora Myles got up early and headed back to Atlanta. They expressed their condolences to

Linda and said they were sorry they wouldn't be able to stay for Blake's funeral. Urgent business compelled them to be home by Wednesday morning.

Margo spoke with Angelica briefly on Monday before Angelica left to go out of town on business. Angelica was not able to obtain any additional information about Blake's murder from her brothers. The autopsy report wouldn't be back for a week. And that would only determine the cause of death, but not who killed him.

Margo looked out of the window only to find overcast skies. Winter, Winston, Ivy, and JR were at the movies. Margo picked herself up from her parked position at the window with the view of Andover Street, deciding that she would go and see how Linda was doing.

Before Margo could get out of the door, the telephone began to ring. "Jefferson, would you please get that?" she called out.

"I don't feel like talking to anyone, Margo. I'm going to the office."

Jefferson grabbed his coat from the hall closet, leaving Margo with her mouth hanging open. She finally picked up the phone on the fifth ring.

"Hello, Myles' residence."

"May I please speak with Mrs. Margo Myles?"

"This is she."

"Hello, Mrs. Myles. I'm Captain Robert Petrowski of the Fayetteville City Police. I'm investigating the homicide of your neighbor, Blake Montgomery."

"Yes, sir. How may I be of assistance?"

"How long have you known the Montgomerys?"

"Almost ten years."

"Did they have many friends or acquaintances that frequented their home?"

"No more than anyone else, Captain Pet-ra-s..."

"That's Pe-trow-ski."

"They were very involved in their church," Margo continued, "and had many friends from Fort Bragg, but nothing unusual. It wasn't a party every weekend, if that's what you mean."

"Okay then. Were you aware of any problems that either Blake or Linda were experiencing—financial, business or otherwise?"

"No, Captain Petrowski. We were close, but not so close that they would confide in or share any problems with us. There were no visible signs, at least as far as I could tell. Is that at the crux of Blake's murder?" Margo asked thoughtfully.

"We're not sure of anything at this moment, Mrs. Myles, just preliminary stuff. I'm sorry to have disturbed you. May I call you Margo?"

"Mrs. Myles will be fine."

"Well, Mrs. Myles, if I need to speak with you further, I'll let you know."

Margo managed to mumble something and then looked at the phone as if it was responsible for the sudden change in her attitude. Why had she been singled out? Captain Petrowski had not asked to speak to Jefferson, and he was closer to Blake than she. There was another side to this story that she wasn't able to put her finger on. Margo hit the talk button and dialed Angelica's number, but got her answering machine.

Margo walked the few feet to Linda's house. There was something about mourning the dead that left her numb. Linda was taking Blake's death pretty hard. It was just last spring that Linda's mother and father were killed in a terrible auto accident, while on vacation.

Linda answered the door, casually dressed in a floral print dress. The dark circles around her eyes betrayed the depth of her grief. She appeared old, much older than her thirty-nine years. Her hair, usually so full of body, now hung limp at her shoulders.

Linda looked up as Margo crossed the threshold of the open door and moved into the foyer. She murmured a brief hello. Blake's death was a shock to everyone's system.

"Can I get you anything?" Margo asked Linda.

She missed Blake, too. After all, they had become very close neighbors and friends over the years.

"No, Margo. Thanks for everything."

Margo observed several others milling about the living room and decided to go in and see if she recognized anyone. Margo knew Linda was grieving. However, Linda seemed slightly agitated by her presence. She was probably making more of it than she should. Margo was probably agitated herself, not able to understand Jefferson's unexplainable mood. Yes, she was making too much out of a situation that was laced with grief.

Margo proceeded into the living room and immediately recognized Blake's mother whose silver mane sparkled under the iridescent glow cast by the black light from the family room. Mrs. Montgomery was a graceful lady who, in her slightly bent form, stood at least five feet eight inches tall. Upon seeing Margo, a smile illuminated her face, and she held her arms out wide as Margo moved toward her.

"You look wonderful, Margo," Mrs. Montgomery said, taking Margo's hand in hers. Her touch was soft and gentle, offering appreciation that Margo was concerned for their loss.

"Thank you, Mrs. Montgomery. However, you're the one who's beautiful. I'm sorry about your loss, but please know that our prayers are with you. How are Felicia and Blake, Jr. holding up?"

"Everyone is doing as well as can be expected. Linda is the one who needs our attention and love. She's taking this awfully hard and has put up a wall that even I'm having a hard time penetrating. Blake was my son, but right now I have to be strong for all of us. We'll get through this. Thank you for your concern."

"Blake's death touched the whole neighborhood. I want you to know that I'm right next door if you need anything."

"Thank you, Margo. Our family appreciates your kindness."

Mrs. Montgomery walked Margo to the door. Margo glanced back at Linda, who was noncommittal.

"Good-bye, Mrs. Montgomery. I'll bring some food by later."

"Thanks again, Margo, for coming by. I'll call if I need to." With that, Margo turned and pointed her feet toward home.

Ray Adams reclined the seat in his Lexus SUV, hiding behind dark tinted shades that gave him a sinister look. He bopped his head to the newly released Christmas CD by Yolanda Adams while awaiting Hamilton's arrival. They called off a planned meeting on Monday as an annoyed Captain Petrowski summoned Hamilton to his office for a briefing on the ongoing investigation. The Captain thought it was moving too slowly. Ray was a large, burly man who, in his day, could have easily competed in a Charles Atlas or Mr. World body-building competition. His muscular arms, stained with tattoos, spelled a threat to anyone who dared to cross him.

Ray was also ex-military, having completed twenty-five years of service with the Army, ending his career at Ft. Bragg. Barely a kid out of high school, he served time in Vietnam. The experience had hardened his exterior and his heart. He could never stay with a woman for more than a year, but it never broke his resolve to be with someone someday.

While an active duty soldier, Ray worked in armament and had also served a short stint as a Green Beret. Later, he kept many ties with the military. It was his life. Now he utilized those ties, having entered into a dangerous venture with political ramifications. He felt Jefferson Myles was on the verge of sabotaging the mission, because his indiscretions had caused a major catastrophe—Blake's death. Too much time, preparation, and money were invested in this mission to abort it. If it meant there had to be a sacrificial lamb, so be it.

The song was ending when Ray saw Hamilton's patrol car pull into the Krispy Kreme parking lot. Donuts were the mainstay of the officer with a badge, and what more appropriate place to shoot the breeze for a couple of minutes with the staff and few loyal customers there.

Ray got out of his car and walked to the entrance. Lieutenant Barnes sauntered in behind him, giving each other high-fives like old buddies who hadn't seen each other in a while. They purchased donuts and coffee, and waved to Brenda, the faithful donut attendant. They headed out the door, engaged in a hurried conversation, with Hamilton doing most of the talking.

"Look, Ray, we've got a problem. We have to watch Jefferson. He's on edge because of what happened to his neighbor. White boy had no business snooping around in our business."

"Okay, Ham. What do you want me to do?"

"I need for you to schedule a meeting with Jefferson and impress upon him the significance and importance of this mission. If you have to flex your muscle, don't hurt him. After all, he's our financial backer and we depend on him. Santiago called, said we should be ready for movement any day—probably New Year's Eve. We can't, I repeat, can't have Jefferson screw up this operation. Hear me, Ray?"

"Gotcha. I'll take care of it." Ray threw his untouched cup of coffee in a nearby trashcan and walked to his car, nibbling on the now sticky donut. Hamilton did the same. They shot each other a parting glance, and left in opposite directions.

Jefferson arrived at his office. His mind was cluttered. Too many things were going on, and he felt like his life was spinning out of control and headed for disaster. There was Margo who he had betrayed and who was now on the attack because of his carelessness. Then, there was Blake's death. It puzzled him. Why was Blake in that area? Had Blake obtained information about what he was doing? Did Hamilton have any responsibility for his death? Too many questions to answer all at once.

"Good afternoon, Jefferson," Ebony said, penetrating Jefferson's thoughts.

"Hey, Ebony. How are things this morning?" Jefferson responded as he headed toward his office.

"Things are well. Thanks again for inviting my sister and me to Christmas dinner. We always enjoy going to your house, and your wife is always the perfect hostess."

"You're welcome. Margo has a natural instinct and talent when it comes to entertaining. We look forward to you coming each year."

"Oh, before I forget, Lieutenant Hamilton called. Said he will call you later, because he'll be away from the office a while."

"Is that all he said?" Jefferson asked, looking for some small clue as to the reason for his call.

"That was it, although he didn't appear to be in a cheerful mood."

"Hmph, that bad?" And not waiting for Ebony to respond, he said, "Well, if he calls, find me if I'm away from my desk."

"Alright, Jefferson."

Ebony watched Jefferson walk into his office, disrobing him with her eyes. She'd like to make love to him one day, she thought. She might have to blackmail him in order to entertain that fantasy. Why not?

She'd watched her mother many nights and days sell her soul for a dollar here and a dollar there. Her father had been killed in a drive-by shooting, and her mother did the best she could to raise her and her sister, Katrina. Sometimes it was her mother's means to an end, and sometimes it was for a good time. The men came; they had sex. She'd even fix one a meal every now and then, but Marsha Wilson knew how to get what she wanted. Yes, Ebony wanted Jefferson. She knew that Jefferson embezzled money from his clients, but his secret was safe for now.

The sudden ring of the phone made Ebony sit upright, interrupting her lustful thoughts.

"Myles and Associates, Ebony Wilson speaking. How may I help you?"

"Is Jefferson Myles in?"

"Yes, sir, he is. May I ask who's calling?"

"Ray Adams. Tell him it's urgent."

"One moment, please."

Ebony pressed the intercom. "Jefferson, Mr. Ray Adams is on the line for you. He says it's urgent."

"Ray Adams," Jefferson said thoughtfully. "Patch him through."

"Ray, my man, what's up?"

"You got a minute this afternoon?" Ray said, skipping the formalities. "I've got something I need to run by you."

"Is it something we can do over the phone?"

"'Fraid not. How about you meet me at Smith Lake in an hour?"

"Look, Ray, I've got a lot of paperwork I need to catch up on. This doesn't have anything to do with Barnes' call to me, does it?"

"Look, Myles, I don't know why Hamilton called you, but I do know that you better be at Smith Lake in an hour. That's an order."

"I'll be there," Jefferson said with a slight quiver in his voice, angry from being told by some bully who thought he could scare him by telling him it was an order. He was no longer in the military. He hung up the phone, and Ebony laid her receiver down upon hearing the click at the other end.

Jefferson looked around the small office that seemed to get smaller each time he looked. What had he allowed himself to get involved in? They weren't going to let him back out, and now Ray Adams wanted to talk with him. He wasn't afraid of Ray. If he lifted a finger to touch him, he would be sorry. But, he'd go and see what Ray wanted.

It was a gorgeous day for a funeral. The sun shone brightly; and while the birds had already flown south for winter, there was a certain feeling, almost melancholy, that seemed to float away when the choir raised its voice in song.

Blake's funeral was short and sweet with very little fanfare. Many from the neighborhood came to pay their respects. They shook their heads solemnly as they passed by the coffin, still unable to comprehend how it happened.

It was quite obvious to those who were not deep in grief that members of the Fayetteville Police Department were present. Although in plain clothes, they watched the mourners as they passed the flower-draped casket and their movements throughout the service, hoping to elicit a clue that might help unravel this baffling mystery.

Jefferson and Margo sat behind the family that consisted of Linda, Felicia, and Blake, Jr.; Gladys Montgomery, Blake's mother; Blake's sister, Wanda; several cousins; Aunt Matilda and Uncle Walter; and Uncle George. It didn't go unnoticed that Jefferson was very much agitated throughout the service. He fidgeted in his seat and glanced occasionally in Linda's direction. He and Margo sat next to each other like strangers who would go their separate ways.

It was a nice service. However the reality of Blake's death was starting to set in, and Linda's new-found freedom left her frightened.

CHAPTER 9

Jefferson, Margo, Ivy, and Winter rode home in silence. The funeral and gravesite service left chills in Margo's spine. No one could shake the eeriness of Linda's constant sobs and those steely eyes that looked around at no one in particular. She was going to need therapy and someone to hold and nurse her through her grief.

The Myles clan single-filed into the house, dropping obituaries and coats at the front door. Margo moved slowly into the kitchen, still unable to loosen the services she'd just attended from her head. She felt the onset of a headache. Tylenol would probably help.

As Margo reached up to get a glass from the cupboard, she noticed the red light flashing on the answering machine. "Must be Angelica," she half-whispered to herself.

Margo pushed the play button, and immediately recognized Captain Petrowski's voice.

"This is Captain Petrowski with the Fayetteville Police Department. This message is for Jefferson Myles. Please call me at your earliest convenience."

Margo stared at the phone. *Why hadn't he asked for Jefferson the other day? Why hadn't he asked to speak to the both of them?*

"Who was that on the phone?" Jefferson's voice boomed, making Margo jump in surprise. She had not heard him come into the room.

"It was Captain Petrowski of the Fayetteville Police Department wanting you to contact him."

"For what? If it's about Blake's death, what could I possibly tell them? We were all here when it happened."

"Don't be so uptight. I'm sure he'll ask you the same questions he asked me about Blake's character and how well you knew him since you were his neighbor."

"You've talked to the police?" Jefferson asked, with surprise in his voice.

"On Monday. Remember, the phone was ringing and I asked you to get it, but you left the house, saying you didn't feel like talking with anyone? Well, it was this Captain Petrowski. Those were the kinds of questions he asked me. Why are you so irritable? I noticed you couldn't sit still during the funeral."

Margo moved closer to Jefferson. He turned his head as she tried to look him in the eyes. Then she noticed it—small, but yet, fresh. "How did you get that cut under your eye?" Margo asked, examining it with her finger until Jefferson pulled away. "It's a little bruised."

Jefferson made a motion, feeling for the cut he knew

was there. "Oh, that. I was pushing a filing cabinet so that I could get behind it, and the top drawer flew out, grazing my face."

"Did you put anything on it…some peroxide?"

"Just water. It was nothing—just a small scratch."

Margo looked at Jefferson. Something was not quite right, and she could not put her finger on it. Blake's death had made her temporarily forget that she and Jefferson had some unfinished business to discuss. Right now, she was tired and not in the mood. Today had been a long day—one she'd like to forget. A short nap would probably make her feel better. She needed some rest if she was going to go into the office tomorrow.

"Look, I'm going to stop by and see Malik a minute. I'll be home shortly," Jefferson announced.

Margo didn't care, especially since sleep was calling her name and the Tylenol 3 with codeine made it all the better.

Jefferson drove toward Fort Bragg military installation, eager to distance himself from his neighborhood. With Blake having lived next door, his death was a constant reminder of the last four days. He needed to call Petrowski—something he didn't relish, but maybe Margo was right. Maybe he only wanted to know bits and pieces of Blake's life. He needed to call Malik first. He would help put things into perspective.

Jefferson dialed Malik's number and quickly hit the *End* key. He had a sudden urge to dial another number, which he did apprehensively. His heart stopped when he heard the phone ring, and then there was her voice before he could hang up.

"How are you doing? I'm sorry that I've not been able to call you."

There was a long pause at the other end and finally the voice said, "I've missed you. I really can't talk right now. Send me an email."

"Alright, I'll do that. I've missed you, too. I…" There was a long pause, "love you."

The voice at the other end did not respond, and a clicking sound was all Jefferson heard. He didn't expect much else. It had been five or six days since they had been together, and a lot had happened during that time, making it impossible to get together again. Jefferson drove on and dialed Malik.

"Hey, man. What are you doing? I need to come by. I've got something I need to run by you."

"Come on. Wow, you seem to be in an awfully jovial mood. Didn't you go to the funeral today?"

"Yeah, buddy. I just talked to *her*. I just got off the phone—"

"You did what? Are you crazy?"

"Look, I needed to hear her voice, man. I'm going crazy not being able to see or touch her. I care about that woman, Malik. She's sweet, tender…I just missed her, alright?"

"Get your tail over here now. We do have some things to discuss!"

"That's not what I need to talk about. Captain Petrowski from the Fayetteville Police Department wants to talk with me about Blake's murder. I don't know why I'm nervous about this. Maybe you can help me sort it out."

"I'll be here when you get here."

Malik shook his head. He had warned Jefferson about the catastrophe he could see down the road. He was Jefferson's best friend, but that was not enough. He was not able to convince Jefferson to see the error of his ways. He had failed him miserably.

"Toni, Jefferson is coming by. He needs to talk about some very private business. Why don't you run on home, *love*, and I'll pick you up later for dinner."

"Okay, baby. I'll see you later."

"Hey, Ma!" Is there anybody home?" yelled the voice.

"Yeah, yeah," came the faint sound, after a prolonged silence.

"Hi, Ma," Ebony said, after climbing the last of nine

steps to find her mother sitting in her bedroom. Her hair was in curlers. She was watching *Living Single*, now in its fifth year of syndication.

"Hey, baby," Marsha said, finally breaking eye contact with the television that had her rapt attention and kept her company most days.

"Ma, it's six-fifteen in the evening, and look at you. Have you gotten out of this bed today?"

"What for—I don't go anywhere, and the men don't come by like they used to."

"Excuses, excuses. You need to get up and put some clothes on, get some fresh air, and maybe get a job. It won't hurt you."

"Girl, I know you didn't come up in here to get on my nerves today. I was doing fine before you brought your behind up in here."

"…And, you ought to lock the door!"

"You walked in here, didn't you?"

"That's besides the point, Ma. I'm your daughter, but I would have waited until you came to the door and opened it if it was locked."

"Yeah, yeah."

Ebony examined her mother's room. Nothing had changed much from when she and her younger sister lived at home. Marsha was always a sloppy housekeeper who didn't and couldn't cook a lick.

Marsha loved to look good, especially for the men

who strolled through the front door like it revolved. She held a job here and there—almost held one for two years. Her inability to get to those jobs on time always produced the dreaded pink slip, but in Marsha's case, it probably was a relief. She'd rather receive public assistance than use her head to rise above what she had become. It was too late now. She was content to live as she was and nothing else much mattered.

Ebony turned and saw the red dress thrown on the back of a chair that sat off in a corner.

"Where have you been wearing that little number?" Ebony asked, pointing to the dress. "This was my dress once," she continued, picking up the dress and examining it—reminiscing for a moment.

"Why do you want to know?" Marsha retorted.

"It's not so much that I want to know. It's just that on Sunday when Katrina and I came by, you were more or less in the same position you are now, except that the dress wasn't there. You hadn't been anywhere besides the grocery store in months."

"Well, if you must know," Marsha began, with a sly grin on her face, "that fine lieutenant down at the police station came by to talk to me the other day."

"What lieutenant? You don't mean Lieutenant Barnes?"

"Yes, that's the one." Marsha's eyes were full of glee as she recalled Hamilton's lips on hers, his warm embrace—and then his sudden rejection. And just as fast as the smile appeared on Marsha's face, it vanished. She still had not forgiven Hamilton for treating her like a whore.

"Yeah, he came by here searching for information about that murder on Sunday. Thought I might have seen something."

"What does that have to do with the red dress, Ma?"

"You figure it out."

"How's that boss of yours doing, Ebony? You know I've seen him around here quite a bit lately...and talking to Lieutenant Barnes."

"He's doing alright," Ebony said a little distracted. "You know it was his neighbor that got killed the other night. The news came as we had just finished dinner at Jefferson's house and began to relax in the family room. Jefferson's son turned on the television and boom— the news announcement about the shooting. And you know what else? The neighbor's wife was there, and she passed out cold in the middle of the floor before she even knew it was her husband. It was almost as if she had a premonition. Isn't that something?"

"I'd say it is. His neighbor is white, right?"

"Yes. Why?"

"No reason."

"C'mon, Ma. I know you know something that you're not telling me."

"No, not really. Just something I observed."

Ebony let it rest for a moment. She began having thoughts of her own. She remembered the telephone call from Angelica on Saturday asking about Jefferson's whereabouts on Friday. He was acting rather strange, constantly looking at his watch as if his life depended upon it. Something wasn't right. Just today, he had received a strange phone call from a Ray Adams who must have known Lieutenant Barnes. Maybe they learned that Jefferson was committing securities fraud. That couldn't be it... Ray Adams' tone was rather sinister, and the way he told Jefferson that meeting him was an order unnerved Jefferson. Something definitely was not right.

"Earth to Ebony," Marsha's voice echoed throughout the room.

"Sorry, Ma."

"What were you thinking about?"

"Nothing. Let's talk about something else."

"You know, I saw your boss talking to Lieutenant Barnes on Friday. In fact, he's in the area quite a bit. What you think he's got to talk with Barnes about?"

"Ma, I don't know! Anyway, you already told me you've seen Jefferson in the area. Was there a point in telling me the second time?" Ebony was a little irritated at her mother's annoying line of questions.

"Then, Hamilton comes asking me if I'd seen anything prior to that murder. Awfully strange to me."

"Why does that seem strange and what does one have to do with the other? Further, when did you get your detective badge?" Ebony questioned, trying to tone down her irritability.

"Look, Ebony, I don't know what it means. All I know is what I've seen. Barnes had the nerve to get all up in my face and threaten me about not lying to him."

"In your face?"

"Yes, in my face. The nerve of that fool! You know his reputation isn't so spotless. Sounds like somebody with a little something to hide. Even I've got enough sense to figure that one out."

"Ma, it was good seeing you. I've got to run. I've got some business I need to take care of."

"Baby, you've been here less than an hour. You can't leave now," Marsha protested.

"Ma, I love you. I do have to go. Please take care of yourself."

"Okay, baby. Tell Katrina not to be a stranger!"

Ebony kissed Marsha on her cheek and looked longingly after her. She retreated and then took the stairs, two at a time. She had urgent business she needed to attend to at the office. She had to do some more checking.

Marsha crossed the length of the room toward the

big window so that she could look out onto the street below. She watched Ebony as she crossed the street and got into her red Honda Accord. Her baby was all grown up. Marsha had witnessed many things while perched at this same window.

It was last Friday night when she saw the big silver Mercedes pull onto Fuller Street and stop at the brown house, number 2337 Fuller Street. She recognized the male occupant as her daughter's boss, having gone to Ebony's place of business on a number of occasions. She had been introduced to Mr. Jefferson Myles of Myles and Associates.

On this night, Mr. Myles wasn't alone. A female companion, who appeared to be Caucasian, sat in the front seat on the passenger side. Marsha couldn't tell much from her vantage point, but it did seem odd.

Then Marsha witnessed Hamilton Barnes and several other men coming toward the house at 2337. One of the men appeared to be armed. It was the way he held his arm under his trench coat. He and Hamilton kept glancing about, back and forth and over their shoulders as if they were sneaking around to make sure they were unobserved. Marsha saw the lady ease down in her seat.

Five minutes later, a blue Ford Explorer cruised very slowly past the Mercedes, then moved down the street. Marsha didn't get a look at the driver of the Explorer.

It was the way it seemed to have almost crept by the Mercedes, almost admiring it, that caught her attention. Then the same vehicle showed up again on Sunday, and that might not have been the only time. Marsha knew then she had too much time on her hands. Maybe she would become a detective. Silly idea.

CHAPTER 10

The light turned red and Jefferson brought his Mercedes to a halt. He allowed his mind to wander for a moment over all that had happened in the past few days. He couldn't keep his thoughts away from her—wished she were with him now. He wished there was a way they could usher in the New Year together—a celebration of new beginnings. As the thought faded temporarily, the DJ started a new set of music with Prince's *1999* heading the line-up.

The light turned green. Jefferson accelerated forward, popping his fingers to the beat of the music. He did not have much farther to go before he'd arrive at Malik's condo. Malik could be counted on for good advice.

Malik pulled two beers from the refrigerator awaiting Jefferson's arrival. His friend had pulled himself deeper into the quagmire, and no amount of talking was going to save Jefferson. And to complicate matters, he'd slept with "her," opening up the battlefield on all fronts.

Malik owned a two-bedroom condo that was warmly

decorated. A touch of masculinity was present throughout the room.

Malik was a collector of fine art. Several pieces from the Charles Bibbs collection hung proudly throughout his house, giving it a distinctive renaissance feeling. Charles Bibbs' paintings usually contained dark hues, all inventively rendered with a distinctive vertical flair that defined the artist. Everything else in Malik's condo made the accentuating painting stand out—from the cherrywood sofa table sitting comfortably behind the couch and loveseat placed in the middle of the room whose arms and legs were also carved from cherrywood, to the built-in bookshelves that housed hundreds of books. In one corner of the living room stood a beautiful cherrywood étagère that contained a small portrait of Malik and his fiancée, Antoinette; candles; and a few art objects.

There was also a fine display of sculpture from the Thomas Blackshear Collection, Ebony Visions. Malik was fortunate, and probably a selling point was that Antoinette was also a collector. A collaboration of their pieces would set off any museum. It had already defined them as a couple. If only Malik could get his buddy back on track. It would take some doing.

Malik opened the door upon hearing Jefferson's faint knock. Jefferson always did that.

"What it is, my brother?" Jefferson greeted Malik.

He stopped to give him a brotherly hug and handshake.

"You, my brother. It is you. I've got a couple of brewskies on the table, if you like."

"That sounds good."

Jefferson held the cold brew in his hand, paused, then took two quick swallows. He looked at Malik and sat down, watching his expression

"You seemed a little desperate when you called. What's going on?"

"I don't know, man. I really don't know. Things seem to be caving in on me."

"How?" Malik asked.

"You know I tried to cut my ties with Hamilton, but that's not going to happen. I have no choice but to do as they say—then Blake's death. Malik, I believe his death is tied in somehow."

"You sure about that, man? How can that be?"

"It's just a gut feeling I have."

"That's some pretty strong stuff you said there, man. Can you prove any of that?" Malik continued, as he gulped down two swallows of his beer.

"No, I can't prove anything right now. The Fayetteville police want to question me about the murder."

"Well, it's probably routine questioning, especially since you were his neighbor."

"That's what Margo said. Captain Petrowski has interviewed her already. Can't be anything else, but I've got this nagging feeling, a sixth sense if you will, that there's a lot more to this story."

"Your indiscretion and illegal schemes are haunting you. Yeah, that's your problem."

"What am I going to do, Malik?"

"You're going to go down there and march into that police station with confidence and answer their questions. And most of all, be cooperative."

"I'm probably all up in arms about nothing."

"True dat. You must do one thing, Jeff. Hear me out first. This information is important to your well-being."

"Well, spit it out!"

"You need to get rid of Linda. She will be a detriment and ultimately your downfall. Mark my words, brotha!"

"What are you talking about, Malik? I simply can't do that. I love her, man, and just as soon as I find a way to tell Margo, I'm going to file for a divorce."

Malik stared at Jefferson in unbelief. For sure, Jefferson was having a mid-life fling, but divorce? "Man, you're crazy and not making one bit of sense. Look at all that you stand to lose, over and above a beautiful woman who has devoted her whole life to you. I've finally found my soul mate in Toni, and hopefully, she's half the woman Margo has been to you—not that I'm comparing."

"Hand me another brew."

"Another brew is what you don't need. What's gotten into you? Can't you see that your life is in position for a roller-coaster ride to the bottom? I wouldn't want to be in your shoes."

"Well, Malik, you aren't in my shoes and you can't begin to know what my life has been."

"On outer appearances—I mean from where I sit and what I can see, things don't seem that good either. And I would bet my next paycheck on that."

"I came here for some brotherly advice, not a lecture," Jefferson said, rising to his feet and then sitting back down again.

"Calm down, it's going to be all right," Malik returned, tapping Jefferson's shoulder for reassurance. "I'm with you, but damn, man. You need to think about making some changes in your life, and I don't mean leaving Margo."

"Yeah, you're right. I'm going to see Barnes again and let him know that I will see this last deal through, but I want out. The risk is not worth it anymore. I don't know how I allowed myself to become involved in this."

"You've made some bad decisions, that's all. Now you'll have to find a way to correct them."

"It's not that easy, Malik. I've made a lot of money from this, and I couldn't resist the temptation. It all started…"

"No need to tell me," Malik said, abruptly interrupting Jefferson's train of thought.

"I need to tell somebody…so that someone will know in the event something happens to me."

"Nothing's going to happen to you. You're the man. You're the guy who went to Howard and got an MBA in Accounting and then went on to establish a lucrative securities business—"

"From which I've stolen thousands upon thousands of dollars to make millions of dollars that's safe somewhere in a Swiss bank because I'm afraid to use it. If I could do it again, I would—"

"Don't say it, because you don't know what you'd do if the opportunity presented itself again. Hopefully, you'll find a way out of this madness."

"This guy named Roberto Santiago is the big man in the United States and resides right here in North Carolina—Durham to be exact."

"You don't have to tell me anyth—"

"Yes, I have to. Santiago has people in Honduras, who are fighting a communist regime. We steal arms from Fort Bragg and then sell them to a buyer for this rebel group in Honduras. Santiago served in the U.S. military with Lieutenant Hamilton Barnes' henchman, Ray Adams. Adams is still connected to his boys in the military—even after doing a twenty-five-year stint. He has a lot of inside connections, buddies that are in the Army for the serious long haul. Adams' background is in armament, and he is well versed in where weapons and ammunition are stored throughout Fort Bragg."

"Stop, Jeff." Malik scratched his head and tried to comprehend what he heard. "You mean to tell me that this is going on right here in Fayetteville under the Post Commander's and General's noses? Damn! Sounds like the damn Ollie North Iran-Contra arms scandal all over again."

"Yeah, except we're not working for the U.S. government. We're stealing guns from them for this crazy Honduran whose motive for all of this is to avenge his murdered parents. I don't believe Santiago expected to get fat pockets from all of this, but since they became lined with all those greenbacks, he has yet to talk about suspending the operation.

"And not to say how risky it is. I just know that the more involved we become, the more likely we are to have a slip-up, and that's what worries me. Yeah, man, my eyes saw the dollar signs, but these boys are no joke. They're getting into some deep, serious stuff that has me a little scared. Truth is, someone was killed on the last mission. I'm not sure that Blake was another casualty of this war. I don't know how he fits in, but he was in counter-intelligence with the military before he retired. And I wouldn't put it past him to have somehow gotten his hands on something that may have placed him at the scene of his own demise."

"Jefferson, you are already in way too deep. No wonder Barnes is giving you a hard time."

"I thought that after the initial job, and even after the

second time he asked me to steal from my accounts, that would be it, because they made lots of money. After they paid everyone off, the profits were much more than what we paid for the guns, which was the sum of the money I stole at a given time. Thinking as an accountant, Hamilton could have taken his money and reinvested, and I would have been free to go my way. But I was so greedy, Malik, and I didn't even have the desire to resist. I can't believe I've been so stupid, stupid."

Jefferson rose from the couch and placed the empty beer bottle on the bar. He paced back and forth, until suddenly an idea came to him.

"Malik, let me use your computer. I need to check my messages."

"Alright, buddy. Go on back to the den. I'll be there in a moment."

Jefferson couldn't shake Linda from his mind. Since he couldn't be with her, he had to let her know that he was thinking about her, missed her, and loved her. He saw that she was online and told her all the things he wanted to, including how much he'd like to see her on Friday night.

She IM'd him, saying, *It's too soon, but I do want to see you, too. Just give me a little more time.*

CHAPTER 11

Police headquarters was alive with activity. The year was coming to a close. Only two more days remained both in the year and the twentieth century. There seemed an overabundance of small, petty crimes—the usual DWI's and thefts associated with this time of year. It made one think that the perpetrators purposely tried to hike the crime statistics before the calendar year ended to ensure its crime ranking in the state.

Petrowski sifted through the notes he had collected over the course of the last few days on the Blake Montgomery homicide. Nothing seemed to add up, and he was annoyed further still that Lieutenant Barnes hadn't produced any new leads in the case. Petrowski frowned as he continued to examine each note, trying to fit the pieces of a puzzle together.

"Umm, white male in late-model Ford Explorer in Richmond Heights," Petrowski moaned under his breath. "Why was he killed? Neighbor, Margo Myles, had not noticed anything out of the ordinary at the

Montgomery household. Umph—the victim had been in counter-intelligence while serving in the Army. Was he onto something?

"This was a strange one," Petrowski continued, rambling to himself. "Phone call from the Durham Police Department. They wanted to alert us to possible illegal activity—possibly arms sales, centering in the Richmond Heights area with possible police involvement. Is there a possible connection?

"Then, here's this letter addressed to Margo Montgomery, the victim's next-door neighbor, that we found on the deceased's body. There wasn't a return address listed on the envelope. This letter must hold some key to the mystery."

Petrowski picked up the envelope and fingered it, allowing his index finger to trace the words Mrs. Margo Myles, 2408 Andover Street, Fayetteville, NC. Petrowski tapped the letter on the edge of the desk, and decided to open it. It was now evidence. Every bit and piece of information, no matter how large or small, would certainly contain a clue even if it were part of a smaller picture.

Petrowski found his letter opener and sliced the envelope with one quick twist of his wrist. He pulled the contents from the envelope and found them to be a three-page, handwritten letter. The letter revealed that Blake suspected his wife, Linda, was having an affair with Jefferson.

As Petrowski continued to read, his eyes got wider with each new line and page. The letter revealed that Blake had followed the pair on a couple of occasions, but on Friday night, he had followed them on their rendezvous at a local hotel.

"Yes," Petrowski said to himself, taking a thirty-second stretch break and actually smiling. This certainly was a script for a romance novel. Petrowski leaned forward and picked up the letter again.

Blake went on about Linda and Jefferson sending emails to each other and how he had confiscated a few of the messages that Linda had downloaded onto the computer's hard drive. And then Petrowski's mouth flew open!

"Oh my God! Yes, there is a link!! God, I knew it. I've got to get Margo and Jefferson down here separately," Petrowski said aloud, rising from his desk and clasping his hands to his head. You'd have thought he was the million-dollar winner on *Who Wants to be a Millionaire*. It was a small victory, but small victories lead to larger ones.

Blake told Margo how he followed Linda to Jefferson's office at approximately seven p.m. on the Friday before Christmas, and when they came out of the building, they got in Jefferson's silver Mercedes. He followed them—going north, when Jefferson abruptly turned into the Richmond Heights area. He followed them to a house on Fuller Street. He cruised by the car slowly, not wanting to be detected, and saw Linda hiding down in it. He thought it odd, since she didn't know anyone in the area. Then he noticed what appeared to be an armed man with what appeared to be a police officer talking to Jefferson. There were several other men there, also.

Blake summarized that he believed some type of illegal activity was going on in the area, but he needed to go back and check it out.

Petrowski found his light jacket and bounded out of the police station. "I need to pay Lieutenant Barnes a little visit. I may know why he hasn't come up with any new leads in the case—because he might be the perpetrator."

CHAPTER 12

"**M**om, what are your plans for New Year's Eve? Can you believe it's almost the year 2000, Y2K or whatever they are calling it? That's going to be hard to say, two thousand."

"It's a little frightening, Ivy. I was in the post office the other day, and there was a digital display that announced the days, hours, minutes, and seconds until the New Year. It gave me an eerie feeling."

"Well, Kimberly, Erin, and I will probably go to Raleigh. A couple of our friends are throwing parties, so it looks like that's where we'll end up. I invited Winter to go along if she was interested."

"That was sweet of you, Ivy. What did she say?"

"She and Winston are meeting up with some of their classmates. Since they were the last class of 1999, the student body presidents of all the high schools in the area got together to organize this big 1999 New Year's Eve party at the Holiday Inn. I'd drop in myself if the guys weren't going to be younger than me."

"Sounds great. I wonder why Winter or Winston

hadn't mentioned it to me. At any rate, please be careful. There are going to be so many drivers who'll be driving while under the influence. And then there are the crazies who think something is going to happen to the world because it's the end of the century and they are Y2K'd in the head."

"Mom, you are so funny, but you don't have to worry about me. You still didn't say what you and Dad were going to do."

"We haven't discussed much of anything lately. He seems to have a lot on his mind, very preoccupied, especially since Mr. Montgomery's death."

"Do you think he'd do some investigating on his own?"

"Why? The police are handling it. I believe Angelica's ex-husband, Lieutenant Barnes, is working on the case."

"Well, I figured with Daddy and Mr. Montgomery being such good friends, maybe he wanted to be involved."

"Your dad doesn't want to talk with the police. They've even asked him to call them so that they could ask a few routine questions, but he hasn't done it yet. He's acting as if he were the suspect. Some of it goes back, though, to his childhood and the neighborhood he grew up in. The cops were always shaking down young black males, innocent and guilty. Your dad has never had a love for them."

"Didn't know that," Ivy said, thoughtfully. "Anyway,

I was wondering if you had plans. If you want, I can stay with you and we'll usher in the new millennium together."

"No, Ivy. You go and have fun with your girlfriends. I'll be fine."

Ivy bent down and kissed her mother. She couldn't shake the picture from her mind of her father talking with Lieutenant Barnes at the Richmond Heights police station on the Monday morning after the shooting. There was an explanation. Of course there was. There's an explanation for everything under the sun.

Captain Petrowski reached his patrol car and abruptly turned around. He needed to talk with the Myleses. Barnes could wait. He'd have plenty of time to talk with him.

Petrowski rummaged through his folder on the Montgomery case and retrieved a piece of paper with Jefferson and Margo's phone number written on it.

"I need to talk with them today," he muttered under his breath. "Better yet, I think I'll pay Mr. Jefferson Myles a visit at his office—a little surprise visit." Petrowski smirked. He leaned back in his chair, musing to himself, then picked up the phone and dialed the number to the Myles' residence.

Before Petrowski had finished dialing the last digit, the intercom light blinked. Petrowski was annoyed but quickly hit the intercom button, anxious to get back to his mission. He was further irritated when he heard the throaty voice of Amy, who manned the front desk reception station.

"Captain Petrowski?"

"What is it, Amy?" Petrowski responded in a rather unpleasant voice.

"I have a Mr. Jefferson Myles at the front desk asking to see you."

Petrowski tried to sit up straight and nearly tilted his chair over when he heard Jefferson Myles' name come across the intercom. *What do you know, Muhammad done come to the mountain!* "Yeah, send him in."

Petrowski had to commend himself on how well things were working out. Sure, he didn't have a murder suspect yet. However, he was beginning to feel better already about this new revelation that had eluded him the past few days. No thanks to Barnes, but he still planned to pay him a visit. It was a good day.

"Come in, Mr. Myles," Petrowski said, as he stood up and offered his hand. He could feel the tenseness in Jefferson's hand, mingled with an onset of perspiration.

"Jefferson Myles," came the reply as he withdrew his hand. "I believe you wanted to ask me some questions about my neighbor, Blake Montgomery."

"Indeed, I do. Have a seat." Jefferson sat in a metal

frame chair that was parked in front of Petrowski's desk so that the two faced each other. Jefferson twiddled his fingers. "I'm a little surprised to see you," Petrowski continued. "In fact, I was just dialing your number when I got the message you were here."

"Oh, I see. My wife said we received a phone call from you wanting to discuss the matter, and since I was in the neighborhood, I thought I'd stop by. This is just routine questioning, right?"

"Yeah, yeah," said Petrowski, trying to read Jefferson's thoughts. "Routine."

"Mr. Myles, may I call you Jefferson?"

"Sure, why not?"

"Well, Jefferson, let's get started."

"Alright," Jefferson said, intent on keeping his answers short and to the point.

"How long have you known Blake and Linda Montgomery?"

"Ten years."

"How did you come to know them?"

"Our families are next-door neighbors."

"Do you figure Blake to be a private person?"

"No, I don't believe so. He had many acquaintances, especially with his ties to the military at Fort Bragg. I don't think he would be inclined to share his intimate life stories with all of them, though. He certainly didn't share them with me."

"Would you consider your relationship close?"

"We were the best of neighbors, often sharing in projects. We would also get together once a month and play cards."

"What did Blake do for a living?"

"Well, he was retired from the Army, where I believe he worked in counter-intelligence. He worked for a computer company before he died."

"Did Blake indicate that he and his wife were having problems?"

Jefferson flinched, which didn't go unnoticed by Petrowski. He had touched a nerve and Jefferson's hesitation in answering only helped to validate the contents of Blake's letter. After a few moments, Jefferson spoke.

"As I said earlier, we were close; however, Blake never shared anything personal of that nature with me. If they were troubled, it's a mystery to me."

"What was their family life like…uhh, uhh…as a casual observer?"

"Blake and Linda had a very cohesive family. They seemed to enjoy life. They went on vacations each year and were involved in their church."

"Would you like something to drink, perhaps a Coke, Jefferson?"

"Uhh, yes, please," Jefferson said with a faraway look on his face. "A Coke would be fine."

"I'll be right back. Try and relax."

Jefferson felt a band of perspiration dot his forehead.

The interview had started off well but he was not ready for some of the questions that were being thrown at him. He did not want to give the appearance that he was nervous. He'd try to regroup. He saw Petrowski out of the corner of his eye and continued to stare straight ahead.

"Here you are," Petrowski bellowed moments later, handing Jefferson the Coke. "Let's finish this up. I'm almost done. Let's see, have you spoken to Linda Montgomery since Blake's death about her thoughts, or reasons why she thinks Blake might have been murdered?"

Again, Jefferson squirmed at the mention of Linda's name. It was as if Petrowski was digging tunnels from one place to another with all roads leading to one main event. This made Jefferson uneasy, but he'd get through this.

"Like everyone else, it's easy to assume he was murdered because his SUV was riddled with bullets. Linda has taken Blake's death rather hard, according to her mother-in-law, but neither I nor my wife have had more than a ten-minute conversation with her."

"Do you have any idea why Blake would have wandered into the Richmond Heights area on Christmas Day?"

"No, I was pondering that myself. We were watching television when the news flashed, and it was a shock to all of us."

"Is there anything else you can think of, Mr. Myles,

that might help us apprehend a suspect in this case?"

"Sir, I can't, since I have no knowledge of any activities Blake might have been involved in."

"One last question. Do you on occasion travel to Richmond Heights—let's say on business perhaps? You work in…" Petrowski thumbed through his folder, appearing to search for something. "Securities, correct?"

Jefferson sat staunchly in the metal frame chair that had suddenly grown too small and threatened to bottom out at any time. His lips were sealed, poignant eyes staring straight ahead into Petrowski's stare—a stare that demanded an answer for his "one last question." Petrowski knew he hit a nerve, but remained poised, waiting.

Jefferson lowered his eyes and leaned slightly forward. "Captain, I don't quite understand the reasoning for your question, but to answer it, yes. In fact, I have one or two clients who live in the area."

"If it's no trouble, may I have their names?"

"Look, I thought this was supposed to be routine questioning about Blake Montgomery's murder? My business clients are privileged information. Furthermore, what does that knowledge have to do with Blake's death?"

"Nothing, Mr. Myles. It was just a question, and I'm sorry I upset you. I want to thank you for coming here today. You've been a great help, and I hope I can count on your cooperation in the future."

Jefferson rose from his chair and turned to leave. "I'm glad that I was able to be of some assistance. Have a nice day." Jefferson left without another word.

A smile flew across Petrowski's face. *I done caught me a pigeon, and the best is yet to come.* He tapped his fingers on his desk, reflecting on the last half-hour. "Mr. Myles," Petrowski said to no one, "your ass is grass."

Petrowski twitched in his seat, contemplating his next move. He picked up the phone and dialed, then felt relief when he heard Margo's voice at the other end.

"Hello, Myles' residence."

"Mrs. Myles, this is Captain Robert Petrowski of the Fayetteville Police Department. How are you this afternoon?"

"I'm well, Captain," said a puzzled Margo. "What can I do for you today?"

"Mrs. Myles, if you have time today or tomorrow, I'd like for you to stop by the office. I have some additional questions I'd like to ask you that are of a more personal nature. Would today at four be okay?"

"What do you mean 'of a personal nature'? Our dear friend was murdered, and somehow I feel like I'm being prosecuted for it. What is this all about?"

"I'd rather not say now, but I do need your help. I'd also like for you to keep our meeting between us."

"You mean, not tell my husband?"

"You understand me well."

Margo stonewalled while she let what he said sink in. *Not tell Jefferson, why?* she thought to herself.

"Mrs. Myles?"

"Yes, Captain Petrowski. I'll come and see you. However, I'd like to wait until next week. I'm working from home today, and I have a couple of showings the next couple of days that need my attention. I'm sorry. I'm in real estate. How about Tuesday of next week?"

"Well, that will do. Tuesday it is. Happy New Year."

"Same to you."

CHAPTER 13

Margo was alone in the house. It felt cold and lonely. What did Petrowski want with her? Her spirit told her that Jefferson was connected in some way. There was Jefferson's not coming home, then Blake's murder. *What did all of this have to do with the other?*

Margo lay down on the couch in the family room, surrounded by pictures of loved ones taken when times were good and love was a constant. Margo remembered a time when the kids had gone to their grandparents' house for the summer, and she and Jefferson had the house to themselves. They were like two teenaged kids discovering each other for the first time. They were all hugs and kisses, a light dinner at Margo's favorite restaurant, and an occasional movie. They'd hold hands and share a box of popcorn, snickering at a funny scene or glancing at each other cockeyed during a hot and steamy romantic interlude.

Margo reached for the remote, surfing the channels for something, anything that would take her mind off of Petrowski's phone call. She lazily moved from channel to channel, stopping occasionally to view a favorite commercial or an announcement of an upcoming movie. Then she caught a glimpse of him—a fine brother dripping of caramel, encased in a taut, lean body. Shucks, he was married, but the brother had taste. The brother's wife, more than likely, graced the insides of an upscale health club to do a little kickboxing and treadmill workout. Oh, oh…a jealous diva in the mix. She wants girlfriend's husband—a fatal attraction. Kim Fields was playing the role, though.

It went to commercial after announcing that *Hidden Blessings* would return in a minute. Margo went to the kitchen and got a bowl of grapes to munch on, while she sank back into the movie that promised excitement on a dreary afternoon.

After an hour of TV drama, Margo dozed off into a light blissful sleep, encouraged by the voices that now echoed in her ears. The quiet was now comforting, her body relaxed, and she gave no thought to Jefferson, Petrowski, Blake, or any other person who had caused her undue stress in the past week. Sleep, restful sleep, called her name.

Margo had no sooner found tranquility when the opening and closing of the front door caused her to bolt upright. She sat in silence until she heard the distinct sound of rustling paper.

"Who is it?" she called out.

"It's me," Jefferson said half-heartedly.

"And what brings you home in the middle of the afternoon?" Margo continued, getting up from the couch, following the sound that had alerted her to Jefferson's arrival.

"I might ask you the same. I thought you had some homes to show?"

"Not until tomorrow. I decided to stay home and map out my routes. My client wasn't able to do anything until late this afternoon, so he postponed until tomorrow. You still didn't answer my question."

"If you must know, I took off early after seeing a couple of clients. Just didn't feel like going back to work. Ebony can handle things. I've got some work I can do from here."

"Have you spoken with Captain Petrowski yet?"

"Why do you ask?"

"Why are you answering a question with a question? The answer is either yes or no."

"Yeah, I've contacted him."

"And…"

"And what, Margo?"

"What did he say, Jefferson?" Margo tried desperately to control the tone in her voice. "What is it, huh? Did he say something you didn't like or did he ask too many questions? Better yet, did he accuse you of murdering Blake, because you sure are acting as if you did."

"Alright, Margo. You've made your point. I'm sorry. I guess this Blake thing has gotten the best of me. Petrowski asked me a bunch of questions about Blake and Linda's family life, who they saw, if they were having problems. For God's sake, the man was slain in the street while driving through a neighborhood. What does that have to do with his family life? I hate cops."

Catching his breath, Jefferson shifted his right leg in order to diffuse the stiffness in his joint—and to abruptly change the conversation that sent his temperature and blood pressure up. He looked around and turned toward Margo. "Where are the kids?"

"They're out. The twins are helping with the preparation of a New Year's Eve party the Class of 1999 is putting on. Ivy is over Kimberly's house and I'm not sure where JR is. By the way, do you think we can do something special on New Year's Eve...bring in the new millennium?"

Jefferson sighed. His eyes took in his wife of twenty-five years, unsure of how he really felt about her. She stood there in her slinky, yellow chemise that outlined the curves he fell in love with so long ago, batting baby brown eyes that ached for him. His head told him that the fire had died, but his body could not resist her totally.

Jefferson wasn't sure what had brought him to where he was now. He couldn't pinpoint the straw that broke the camel's back. Love for another woman had consumed him and taken control of his senses. She made him feel like new money, a million dollars, and the prince with the glass slipper. He had been reborn, and no one could tell him that dreams didn't come true. The exact moment it happened eluded him; however, there was no mistaking how he felt.

His eyes drifted away from Margo. "If you like," he said. But he knew there was only one person he wanted to be with on New Year's Eve. "I'm going up to my office. Call me when dinner is ready."

Margo was left staring after the man she loved as he retreated and went up the stairs. She searched within herself for an answer to this rift, their drifting apart, but could find none. She flopped down on the couch and wept.

Jefferson sat his eel-skin attaché case on the huge, mahogany desk. His office provided a place of privacy within his kingdom. Here he could be Jefferson Myles the financier, Jefferson the frat brother, Jefferson the aristocrat, and Jefferson the cyberspace lover. From the pictures that occupied the walls, to the leather-back chair and flokati rug that took ownership of its territory, Jefferson Myles' name was written all over this room. Margo was a decorator, but this room, his room, was truly all his—every piece of furniture chosen by him.

A glamour shot photo of Margo sat on one side of a double, four-by-six frame. Ivy, JR, Winston, and Winter occupied the other. Little artifacts from various places Jefferson had been throughout his military career in Europe and the Far East were scattered throughout the room. Jefferson glanced at Margo's smiling face, turned away, and hit the "On" switch of his personal computer.

Jefferson waited while it booted up. Something kept drawing him to Margo's picture—maybe guilt, but he couldn't keep his mind off Linda. Was she a novelty, like a new toy you couldn't wait to play with? Linda was fresh. She made him sing, made him feel alive, and made him feel good about who he was. She loved listening to his stories. She was sweet, succulent, revealing, passionate, gentle, and overflowing when they finally made love to each other.

Jefferson closed his eyes and transported himself to the illusion that he had allowed to consume his mornings and nights. It had been one week since he touched her, she touched him, he kissed her, she kissed him, he entered her, and she let him in. His moment was interrupted by the prompt on the computer that signaled all systems go.

He took the mouse in his hand and pointed to AOL. When prompted, he entered his screen name and password. This machine seemed magical the way it allowed him to be in touch with the whole world at the touch of a finger. He waited again while the PC's internal modem gave him access to the world outside.

When the large door opened, he was disappointed that she was not online. He checked his messages, "A bunch of garbage," he muttered, deleting most of them, some without opening them up, and then, *bling*. One of his buddies had come online.

It was her. It was Linda. A smile that looked like a mile-long crescent moon slung across his face, and he lit up like a Las Vegas marquee.

Jefferson immediately hit the IM symbol and typed, *Hi*. He waited a minute and received a *Hi* in return. *How are you?* he asked, typing as fast as his fingers would allow. "Much better," she typed. *I think about you every waking moment*, he spelled. *Me, too*, came her IM reply. He hesitated, but the voice in his head said, *Type it you fool, type it*.

Jefferson's fingers moved across the keys in double time. He sent the message. She read it. "Can I see you tomorrow night? We don't have to do anything but talk."

She couldn't touch the keys. She kept staring at the message and allowed her silent eyes to read and reread the message. Five minutes passed. He was still online according to her buddy list and she lifted her fingers and touched the keyboard and typed the word *Y-E-S* and sent the message he was waiting to hear.

Jefferson gasped out loud, then caught himself, not wanting to alert Margo. He had been waiting, it seemed, a lifetime for this answer. An answer he felt he'd not hear again, afraid it might have been buried in the cold grave along with Blake Montgomery.

He hurriedly typed, *Wonderful. Six o'clock at the Dairy Queen on Highway 210.* The answer was, *OK.*

CHAPTER 14

Ebony saw the patrol car slow, and then stop in front of the office. That was last night before closing. She had gone to the front to lock the door when the car suddenly appeared. She locked the door fast, stood back, and waited to see if anyone would approach. Her boss had left early that morning, and she hadn't seen him since. Now an unwanted stranger lurked nearby.

Ebony gathered her things and proceeded out the back door. She had her insurance package tucked safely under her arm, but needed a safe place to deposit it. Her boss was in deep, and she had enough goods to ensure a brand-new life for her mother, Katrina, and herself.

She had to be careful and work out the details of her plan. Jefferson had taken more than a million dollars from his clients without their knowledge. What he did with the money was anyone's guess, but something big was going on, especially with the amount of traffic that had been coming and going from Myles and Associates lately.

Now it was Friday morning. Ebony made a pot of coffee and opened up the door for business. The weatherman said it was going to be a nice day, a little sun once the clouds cleared. She hadn't heard from Jefferson since early yesterday and couldn't help but wonder if his disappearance could have something to do with the patrol car she had seen.

Ebony walked to her desk and retrieved the watering can she kept beneath it. She briskly walked to the small kitchenette, filled the can with water, and returned to the large ficus tree that stood in the front lobby. She gave it a healthy watering, stopping at short intervals to caress the leaves and sing a few bars of *Summer Breeze*. The tree was only a twig when Jefferson first gave it to Ebony, now it was a towering giant. It made her smile.

As Ebony prepared to make her first call of the morning, the door chimed, announcing the arrival of either a client or a prospective one. There was something different about this one. He walked with a purpose, almost defiant—looking for something but not wanting to buy.

The man approached Ebony's desk, scanning the premises as he did so. It was obvious that the owner of the business was quite successful. There was no expense barred on the lavish décor and furnishings. A beautiful Tiffany lamp sat on a small, mahogany table in the lobby along with the latest copies of *Ebony, Black Enterprise,* and an old edition of *Newsweek* that had a feature article about Jefferson's rise on the corporate ladder as one of America's new, top, black businessmen.

As the gentleman got nearer, it was apparent that his business there had nothing to do with purchasing stock. The man quickly examined Ebony's nameplate and nodded his head. "Good morning, Ms. Wilson, I am Captain Petrowski of the Fayetteville Police Department." He flipped his badge on cue, like a well-rehearsed scene from a Broadway script.

She scrutinized him from head to toe like a bloodhound sniffing for drugs. "And, how may I help you, Captain Petrowski?" Ebony finally asked, making mincemeat out of his name.

"Is Mr. Jefferson Myles in?"

"No," she said, locking eyes with the captain.

"He left a glove at my office yesterday. It must have fallen out of his pocket."

"I'll take it and make sure that he gets it."

"Do that," Petrowski said, making a slight, pivotal turn to gain a better view of the office layout.

"Is there anything else I can help you with, sir?" Ebony was anxious for the captain to leave.

"There just might be. How many accounts would you say you handle here?"

"I'm sorry, sir, but I'm not at liberty to give out that kind of information. It would be better if you spoke with Mr. Myles. He should be in later this morning, and I'm sure he'd be happy to answer any questions you might have regarding his accounts."

"Well, alright. I'll call back then. I bid you a good day."

Ebony watched Petrowski until the door shut behind him. "What was that all about?" she half whispered to herself. She hoped she didn't appear to be on the defensive. *Out of the blue, this cop comes marching up here. Well, I'm not going to tell him anything. The package will be safe with Momma until I figure out what to do with it.*

Jefferson rose early, finding Margo already up and dressed. *She must be in the kitchen getting a cup of coffee,* he mused to himself. *She's showing some houses today.*

Jefferson reset his alarm and lay back down for a few minutes. He slept well last night as his thoughts and dreams were of Linda—what he would say to her and how he was going to hold and kiss her. He could think of nothing else but her. He wanted time to rush by.

His thoughts drifted a moment. Then he remembered…the $250,000 wrongfully withdrawn from the accounts. By him. No one else. The money needed to be in place by noon today so that they could purchase the guns for delivery to Robert Santiago by Saturday morning.

"This will be the last time," Jefferson said to himself. "The last time."

Santiago put down his glass. He always had a drink in the morning. If he was to ensure that everything would go according to plan, he needed a clear head today. He was a little troubled that Jefferson might sabotage the project, but he'd come through before, and Hamilton had assured him that all was in order. Santiago picked up his glass, again.

He wrapped his silk smoking jacket about him, bringing the brandy snifter to his nose, relishing the smell, and took a sip of the smooth drink. It pacified him for the time being. Santiago looked around him. This lavish lifestyle was far from the squalor he left in Honduras as a poor farm boy. A sea of floral splendor surrounded his Mediterranean-styled villa, with each flower carefully selected and planted meticulously throughout the grounds. The gold trimmed columns and marble floors were quite inviting, and a spiral staircase, bedecked in gold specks, suggested the residence of royalty.

Santiago's favorite room was his studio. Its outer structure was shaped in the form of a dome and sparkling, beveled glass. It was furnished completely with Italian furniture, tapestries of Roman design, and Persian rugs strategically placed throughout.

Santiago enjoyed the spoils of the United States, but not without some cost. He came to America with an uncle who had lived in New York a number of years. Santiago later enlisted in the Army.

During the next few years, there was civil unrest in his country. He was unable to see his family. His training as a Green Beret prepared him for what he knew he must do, get back in the country to see his parents and possibly bring them to the U.S. In the process, his parents were arrested and slain by the Honduran government as traitors. Santiago vowed he'd avenge their deaths.

He solicited the help of some rebel guerillas who agreed to do his bidding if he could provide them with guns and ammunition in their continued effort to fight the fascist regime in that country. They were already funded by an unknown source. With another source of supply, the rebels had a better chance against the government forces.

Using old connections, Santiago solicited the help of his old Army buddy, Ray Adams, who was a veteran of clandestine military operations. Santiago promised that it would net Ray a great financial reward if they could carry this out. It didn't take much to convince Ray of the advantages of an effective partnership between them. The money and other perks outweighed the risks.

Money was the name of the game. But with tighter restraints placed on many of the critical areas in Fort

Bragg, no amount of expertise would allow the duo to extract the number of guns and ammunition needed without inside help. However, everyone had his or her price.

Adams hired the services of two trustworthy foot soldiers working in munitions and supply. Both were well versed on the types of weapons the military possessed, where they were stored, and the Army's inventory system. For a reasonable fee, they carried out the operation dubbed "Operation Stingray" right under the Army's nose. So efficient was the operation, the rebels wanted a continued supply of arms, which their financial backer was willing to support.

Ray Adams brought in Lieutenant Hamilton Barnes, his best friend, who was also a former military policeman. Barnes would sell his soul for the opportunity to make the kind of cash that was presented to him. He would provide police protection by keeping his eyes and ears open for possible detection and infiltration, running interference when needed. And then there was Jefferson Myles, the owner of his own securities firm.

Jefferson was at the pinnacle of his profession in the Fayetteville area. To honor his achievements, the Minority Business Professionals awarded him the Minority Entrepreneur of the Year for his outstanding career in financial securities and his contribution to the community. They said his talent to make money grow made him the most sought-after investor of capital.

Santiago looked at his diamond-encrusted Rolex. It was eleven-thirty a.m. He needed to dress, and then he'd wait for a call from Hamilton Barnes, who now headed up "Stingray" in eastern North Carolina.

CHAPTER 15

Petrowski's day wasn't starting out as he had planned. He had run up against a tough one in the name of Ms. Wilson. Well, it was still early, and since he was already out, Petrowski decided to pay a visit to Lieutenant Barnes. The neighborhood seemed unusually quiet today, unlike last Sunday when a crowd of people came to view the bullet-riddled Ford Explorer. This was nothing new here—violence was almost the norm—except the victim, the "man from downtown," was lurking in their neighborhood where he shouldn't have been.

Petrowski pulled up in front of the station and jumped out of his patrol car. He looked around noting that only one cruiser was parked outside. He proceeded through the double doors and found Sergeant Holly Walters reading today's news. She quickly threw the paper under her desk when she saw Petrowski coming.

"Good morning, Sergeant Walters," Petrowski's voice boomed.

"Good morning, Captain Petrowski." Holly smiled,

hoping Petrowski had not seen her reading the newspaper.

"A lot of bad news, ehh?"

Holly knew then she was busted. "Well, the crime report was at a minimal today, but the critics say they expect a busy weekend." Holly was proud of herself for coming up with that one at the last second.

She's smart, too, Petrowski thought to himself. "I'm sure it will be with all the planned celebrations." Abruptly changing the subject, "You here by yourself? I noticed only one cruiser parked outside."

"Sergeant Broadnax should be back in about thirty minutes. Said he wanted to talk to some kids who were mouthing off about seeing a car with out-of-state plates in the neighborhood on Sunday."

Petrowski's eyes arched at that little bit of news. "I see," he said thoughtfully. "He seems to be putting in a lot of footwork on this case."

"He follows a lead when he gets one, but not much has materialized."

"How about Lieutenant Barnes? Has he said anything about the case—such as where he might be with the investigation? I really need to speak with him some-time today."

"No, Lieutenant Barnes has not shared anything with me. I believe he confers with Sergeant Broadnax on his cases." Holly watched Petrowski. She sensed he was fishing for something. He'd come by and occa-sionally check on a case that might have been ongoing, but there was something about this one that seemed to peak his curiosity.

"Well, let Lieutenant Barnes know I need to speak to him—today!"

"Yes, sir," Holly replied.

"Oh, by the way, how's your father doing? I hear they're up to their ears in alligators."

"Yeah, Dad's been working hard. He's been working on a big case that involves stolen guns that they believe are being sold and shipped to South America from this area. I believe he said there might be a possible link with Fort Bragg. Didn't my father alert you to that?"

Petrowski's antenna was already working overtime. Yes, he had received subsequent phone calls and a subtle hint that said there might be police involvement and possible corruption in the Fayetteville area. He was very interested in what Holly knew. He wanted to remain casual on the issue since he had no evidence to support his theory, which wasn't much of a theory at the moment. After all, the Feds had a virtual stronghold on the case. Sergeant Walters was becoming invaluable by the minute.

"Uhhh, yes Holly, I remember your father's phone calls. I'll have to ring him and see where they are on the investigation."

"Look, Holly, I mean Sergeant Walters, keep your eyes and ears open. You might be instrumental in solving this case."

Holly's eyebrows arched toward the ceiling, apparently missing Petrowski's bait. Her eyes searched his for an answer that didn't seem forthcoming. But by the look on her face, Petrowski knew she'd eventually figure it out. She remained silent, wanting Petrowski to go on.

"How long have you been on the Force, Sergeant Walters?" Petrowski probed.

Holly maintained her puzzled look. "A little over a year."

"With the right connections, you could really go places with the Force. You're smart, and your grasp and attention to detail is a major plus on your report card. You've got potential."

Holly continued to watch Captain Petrowski, understanding his meaning. "Thank you for the vote of confidence, Captain Petrowski. I'm counting on you to mean what you say."

"I'm good as my word, Sergeant Walters," Petrowski said reassuringly. "I believe you and I will talk again real soon. In the meantime, remember that every action and reaction is a clue, a key that may unlock one door or a slew of them. Don't forget to give my message to Lieutenant Barnes."

Captain Petrowski tipped his hat and started out of the door. He turned around, catching Sergeant Walters' placid face looking after him. "We'll talk later, okay?"

Holly nodded, mouthing the word, "Okay."

CHAPTER 16

Sergeant Carl Broadnax received an anonymous phone call from one of the kids who had been hanging out with the bad-mouth kid on the day of Blake Montgomery's murder. He was nervous—said his mother made him call, because she had seen too many Perry Mason stories where an innocent bystander who had important information about a case suddenly became "the suspect" because they didn't come forward. He said some guys in the group were talking about this man who was in the neighborhood on Friday night driving a bad, black Lexus SUV with Florida license plates. He cruised slowly—seemed to look for something or even watch something or someone. But it wasn't until he got out of the car on Sunday—yes, he was in the area again on Sunday, and they saw the AKA-50 assault rifle with a scope affixed to its body.

This was the first bit of information of any value that had trickled his way, and Sergeant Broadnax was on it.

He found the kids huddled in a vacant lot at the other end of the 2300 block of Fuller Street. At first, his presence on their turf angered some of them. However, after a few high-fives and a Michael Jordan ski-high, over-the-rim slam-dunk on the backboard of a freestanding basketball goal that produced a round of Oh-h-hs and ahhs, he was one of them—except with a badge.

The boys said they were used to *phat* vehicles coming through their neighborhood, but this car was seriously phat. The driver of the car was not friendly like the others who stuck their heads out, signaling for some of them to come over to talk. It was the way he rode up and down the street—like he owned it. Then a couple of other cars showed up and the occupants went into the house at 2337 Fuller Street. Then the Lexus came out of nowhere—almost ran out like he was gunning for the finish line at the Indianapolis 500. Then there was a loud noise. That was about the time the Ford Explorer was hit.

"Where were you boys when this was going on?"

"We were at our boy Smitty's house. But we—"

"Which one of you is Smitty?"

Smitty raised his hand slowly after a little hesitation.

He must have been the one who called, Broadnax said to himself.

"What did you see, Smitty?"

"I didn't see anything. Max and Bobby saw it. I was too scared to look out of the window."

"Why were you scared?"

"They said they saw guns."

"One gun, Smitty," Bobby corrected.

"Okay, boys. Have you told this to anyone else?" Broadnax asked.

"No, man. That was a big gun."

"Okay. I don't want you all to say anything to anyone else about this. I need to check something first."

"What about that other cop? He must know something," Max interjected.

"What cop?" Broadnax asked with a frown on his face.

"You know, man," Bobby said. "The one you were with the other day. He's about your color."

"Lieutenant Barnes?"

"If that's his name," Bobby continued. "He's in the neighborhood all the time—that cocoa-colored police officer. My momma says she could go for him, but she likes a little cream in her coffee." The boys laughed.

"What do you know about cream in your coffee. You're still drinking milk."

"'Cuz my momma drinks coffee. She has a cup every morning to get her started." Bobby grinned. "Says she really doesn't like it, but if she puts lots of milk in it, it tastes okay."

"So you know a little something about coffee. Have any of you ever committed a crime and been locked up?"

The boys cringed at the thought of being in jail. "No, man. We haven't committed any crimes," Max said, speaking for the whole group. "We're just ten years old, and—"

"And what, Max? You're a fast-talking one. Do you know that many young boys your age have committed crimes and are in detention homes? Don't look at me like that. I'm telling you the truth. Now run on and don't let me ever see you at my jail unless you're inquiring about a career in law enforcement. Or maybe we can shoot some hoops sometime."

"Okay," the boys said in unison.

"Remember, no talking to anyone about this."

"Yes sir," was their reply.

"What's your name?" Smitty asked, finally getting up enough nerve to open his mouth.

"Sergeant Broadnax, son. Sergeant Carl Broadnax."

"Okay, Sergeant Broadnax," Smitty said, giving him a thumbs-up. "We don't trust no cops down here, but you're a cool brother."

CHAPTER 17

Carl Broadnax strolled down the street toward his patrol car, passing remnants of what were once very nice homes. Old, beaten-up cars stood hostage in yards with wilted lawns and homemade driveways. Every now and then he'd come upon a home whose owner maintained and preserved the look of the old neighborhood in its nineteen-hundred-square footage of occupied space. Carl remembered it well because he had been a product of this neighborhood, born in this neighborhood. Memories flooded his mind of the community when it was alive and vibrant, when you had twenty mommas instead of just one, and each had permission to dust your behind if you were out of line. Many people had come and gone since he lived here and only a handful remained that he had known during his childhood.

Something the boys said disturbed him—the reference to Lieutenant Barnes. He could not shake the nagging feeling that something was not right. In fact, nothing seemed to add up the way he thought it should. *How did Barnes factor in?* Such a strange set of circumstances—the name Barnes sticking out like a sore thumb.

Broadnax continued down the street until a good-looking woman, must have been in her late forties or early fifties, encroached upon his space, blocking his path.

"Hello, Sergeant. Mighty fine day we got here."

Carl tried to tactfully move out of her way, but she caught his arm and hung on. "It's a nice day, ma'am. Would you mind giving me back my arm?"

"What if I don't want to?" came the reply.

"Well, Ms…"

"Ms. Marsha Wilson…"

"Ms. Marsha Wilson. I have to get back to work. Just trying to keep the street safe for the citizens."

"You want to keep me safe? I didn't catch your name."

"Sergeant Broadnax."

"Umm, Sergeant Broadnax. See, I live in the house on the corner, and I could use some company."

Carl perked up. This was the house he'd gone to while investigating the Montgomery murder. This was the house where he'd seen someone look out of an upstairs window—someone who refused to answer the door when he rang. She was a good-looking babe, although a little rough around the edges, and this was definitely an opportunity he couldn't let slip by. He could charge it to the investigation.

"On second thought, you can leave your arm there. I could use some company myself. Do you have something cold to drink? I'm a little thirsty."

"Not so fast. Just a minute ago you had to get to work."

"I still do, but a little refreshment won't hurt, if you have a cold drink."

"I have that and a whole lot more," Marsha said, pulling Carl Broadnax to the other side of the street, clicking her high-heeled shoes against the cement pavement.

Carl glanced quickly to his east and then his west. He made an attempt to look south over his right shoulder when Marsha snatched his arm to pull him inside. Probably out of habit because of the job, he'd been looking over his shoulder a lot lately. And Ms. Marsha was a feisty one. Hopefully her feistiness would become foolishness and he'd be able to bag a few bits of information that might happen his way. This was proving to be some morning.

Carl walked up the flight of stairs that led to Marsha's apartment. Marsha led the way, auditioning for the part of temptress in her black, skin-tight, Lycra dress. Carl didn't mind a little shaking and a little teasing on his behalf. After all, it did wonders for his ego. Right now, though, he needed to be alert just in case a tidbit or two fell his way.

"This is my place," Marsha said with emphasis on *my place*, as she waved her hand to welcome Broadnax into her humble abode.

Not as neat as the dress laying on that sculptured figure, he thought to himself.

They passed what he figured to be her bedroom before entering her living room. Even with the door slightly ajar, he could see the turmoil that lay within. She hadn't dusted in a while. Broadnax wasn't sure that he wanted to sit on the sheet-draped couch, but he didn't want to make her feel bad. So he sat while she went out to the kitchen with a promise to return.

Carl scanned the scantily decorated room. It was painted a pukey green. An old, floor-model television set in one corner. With at least a half-inch of dust on the glass shelves, a brass étagère, whose legs and arms were well beyond tarnished, occupied the east wall. The étagère held family photos and a few whatnots. And then he noticed the window that looked out onto Fuller Street, with the lacy curtains that had provided cover for curious eyes a week earlier.

Carl got up from his perch on the couch and went to the window. He peered through it and found an extraordinary view of Fuller Street, a stakeout cop's dream. Had this woman seen anything?

"Taking in the view, honey?" Marsha said, startling Carl, who had been lost in his thoughts. Marsha handed him a beer as he walked clumsily away from the window.

"Yeah, nice view from here. I was thinking about a time long ago when I used to live in this neighborhood."

"Oh, you're from here?" Marsha gave Broadnax a look of surprise and took a sip of her beer.

"As I said, it was a long time ago. I was born here. As a matter of fact, I lived three blocks over. My parents are both dead. I was an only child. I came back to the area to help out a sick uncle and ended up staying."

"Well, Sergeant Broadnax…"

"You can call me Carl."

"Alright, Carl. Who do you think killed that man in the Ford Explorer last week?"

Carl was caught off guard. This woman amazed him. Here she was cool, calm, and collected, looking straight into his eyes which was somewhat unnerving—all the while sipping her beer. He was sure she couldn't read his mind, for surely she'd know that he was using her to get information. He looked back at her, not touching his beer and said, "We don't have a suspect yet, but we're still working on it."

"Is Lieutenant Barnes working on the case?" she plowed on, having finished off her bottle of beer.

"What is your interest in this case, Marsha?" Carl threw back, catching her a little off guard.

"Nothing, but it did happen in our neighborhood— almost in front of my home. Curious, I guess."

"Why did you ask if Lieutenant Barnes was working the case?"

"It was nothing, Carl. But…well, Hamilton—I mean Lieutenant Barnes." This was the second time today Barnes' name had come up in conversation. Then he remembered Barnes' apparent interest in 2334 Fuller Street after he told him he had gone there. That nagging something was bothering him again.

"Did he have any reason to think that you knew something?"

"No." Marsha watched Broadnax as he digested the food for thought she'd just shared. Should she impart another slice of pie? She owed Hamilton, and Sergeant Carl Broadnax might just be the vessel to use. "I'm going to get another beer. Drink up."

He sat longer than he had planned. Marsha told Broadnax her life story— the husband she lost to gang violence and the girls she raised alone. She loved her girls, and was sad about not giving them the better home that they deserved. But they were doing fine now. One was a big-time secretary at a securities firm and the other was a counselor at a local university.

There were quite a few men in her life, she told him. Many helped to sustain her through tough times, and others were there to soothe a broken and lonely heart. But she had fun, too. "Let the good times roll," Marsha had said, reminiscing. She popped her fingers and turned on some music to take her back to a moment (and there were plenty of them) that made her feel good.

Carl understood the attraction. In another time and

place, he might have been one of Marsha's "good time" men. She made him laugh. She made him sad. She could tell a story. And underneath all that veneer was a woman who was still beautiful but yet vulnerable. There was a woman who needed to be shown love—love that neither of her children could give her.

It was time to leave, and Carl hated to go. Carl was unable to fathom why, but it had felt good talking to Marsha. He was no closer to solving the murder, but he felt something in this room—this dusty, shabby room that was waiting on love.

Carl reached for Marsha's arm and rubbed the length of it.

"I've got to go now. Got to get back to the station before they miss me. I'm not sure what we accomplished here today, but…I think I'd like to come back sometime."

Marsha blushed. Carl was a true gentleman, unlike that psycho, Hamilton Barnes.

"I'd really like that, Carl." Marsha brushed Carl's cheek with the backside of her index finger and placed a small kiss on his lips.

Carl's eyes lit up, and he fell slightly backward, overcome by Marsha's display of affection.

"Okay. I'll call you."

"I'll be waiting. Let me walk you down the stairs." And she kissed him once more.

CHAPTER 18

Lieutenant Barnes checked his watch. It was eleven fifty-nine a.m. One minute to go before verifying that the money was in place. He was counting on Jefferson to hold up his end of the deal. Santiago was breathing down his neck and wouldn't stand for another upset. Santiago was counting on him.

It was noon. He calmed himself. He quietly accessed the account via his PC and breathed a sigh of relief upon seeing that the money was there.

"Thank you, Jefferson," Hamilton said to no one and picked up the phone to call Santiago.

Ray Adams spent a lot of time waiting these days. Waiting always had a way of paying off. He remembered his mother's favorite saying when he or his sister asked for something they wanted right away. She'd say, "Patience is a virtue." Ray didn't fully comprehend the meaning of that saying until he was older. And now he waited for Hamilton's phone call to proceed with Operation Stingray.

His long-awaited call finally arrived at twelve-thirty p.m. By the sound of Hamilton's voice, Ray knew all systems were go and to proceed with the next phase. Under the veil of night, the exchange would be made, one hundred M16 rifles and hand grenades were to be readied for shipment with final destination, Honduras. The exchange for transport to the Latin American country would take place at Fuller Street. With all the activity in the past week, Ray wondered if a change of venue might not be in order.

Hamilton was pleased that all was going well. All phone calls were made and the plan set in motion. It was time to make his appearance at the office. He'd drive by Fuller Street first to make sure everything was readied for tomorrow morning's exchange.

He drove past the station and noted that only one cruiser was parked outside. Broadnax or Walters must be at lunch. He'd be back in a minute.

Nearing Fuller Street, he slowed down so that he could make his eventual right turn. Barnes felt on top of the world, and the broad smile on his face said the same. He eased onto Fuller Street and stopped abruptly, the engine idling high.

He watched as Broadnax rambled down the stairs of 2334 Fuller Street. Walking with a slow gait—not going anywhere fast, head bent slightly downward. The sergeant turned around slightly, lazily waving his hand in what appeared to be a goodbye. Barnes quickly moved on, finally noticing Broadnax' cruiser, but Broadnax saw him as well and tipped his hat in recognition. Lieutenant Barnes decided not to stop at the house on Fuller Street and drove directly to the station.

Broadnax watched Lieutenant Barnes take off down the street. What was his interest on Fuller Street? Marsha had pointed out a house. Was Hamilton headed toward that house? He decided to go to the station and maybe get some answers.

When he arrived, Barnes' cruiser was already there. "Hey, Sarge," Holly called out, as Broadnax came through the front door, his face glowing. Using sign language, she informed Broadnax that the lieutenant was not in a good mood, especially after she told him Captain Petrowski was there earlier and wanted to talk with him. Carl nodded his head, and mouthed a big "Okay."

The air was thick in the room. Broadnax hummed a tune as he strolled to his desk, throwing his hat on the desktop. "Afternoon," he said to Barnes, who did not return the greeting. Ignoring the snub, Broadnax turned his back and took out a notebook to make some notes.

"What were you doing at Marsha's?" Barnes finally asked, smoke smoldering in his voice.

So he assumed right away that I was with Marsha, Broadnax made a mental note to himself. "I was following up on the investigation of that shooting on Sunday. I don't know what propelled me to stop, but it was as if I saw that curtain move again, and I needed an answer. So I went up to the house and rang the doorbell. This time, someone answered," Broadnax lied, watching Barnes' expression.

"So what did she say?"

"So, you know her?" Broadnax countered very methodically.

"Many people know Marsha, Sergeant Broadnax." Barnes twiddled his fingers while looking straight at Broadnax. "She doesn't have the most spotless reputation in town."

"She said she didn't know anything, hadn't seen anything, and that she had already given that information to Lieutenant Barnes who had failed to tell me. Otherwise, I probably wouldn't have stopped."

Barnes caught the accusatory message that Sergeant Broadnax tossed at him. He was doing his job. *He's a good man and a good cop*," Hamilton thought. *I don't want a rift between the two of us.*

"Sorry, Sarge. I didn't mean to sound ungrateful or untrusting. Captain Petrowski is on my case about solving this murder, and we haven't had any real leads. I did forget to mention that I had spoken with Marsha and that was probably due to the fact that I had come up empty-handed again."

"Look," Hamilton continued, "I have another case I need you to work on. It's a robbery at T & W Pawn Shop on Bragg Boulevard. One of the owners was shot. They may have the suspect on camera. Let me handle the Montgomery case. Petrowski is leaning on me pretty hard. It's not that you're not doing a fine job, Broadnax, but I need to be more personally involved in this one."

"Alright," Broadnax said, taking a toothpick out his shirt pocket and putting it in his mouth. "I'll get right on it."

"Good, and Carl, you're my right hand."

Broadnax gave Lieutenant Barnes a wink and a thumbs-up, but he was not giving up this case, even if it meant working his own undercover. He was convinced more than ever that the lieutenant's involvement in this case went beyond his sense of duty. Marsha had something, and what little it happened to be was enough for him to start his own investigation.

There was something about Marsha that tugged at Broadnax's heart. He found a woman who wanted to be loved and to love in return. Broadnax couldn't get her out of his mind, and something inside of him longed to get to know Marsha better.

Some would call him silly. After all, Marsha was noth-

ing but a stray piece of well-used tail from the street.
But he didn't care. Marsha was seeping into his system,
and he had a feeling that he'd like to learn more.

"Richmond Heights Police Department."

"Hi, baby, it's your dad."

"Hi, Dad," Holly chimed.

"How's my favorite girl, and how are things going
around there?" Detective Walters asked.

"I'm fine, Dad. Signed up for classes at Fayetteville
State University. I'll start in January."

"Good, baby!"

"As far as business goes, we've had a lot of activity
because of that murder on Sunday. In fact, Captain
Petrowski came in today, looking for Lieutenant Barnes.
He casually asked me about you, and I told him you
were working on some case that had to do with guns
and Fort Bragg. He said he remembered that you had
called him about it. Very interested in your investigation—said he was going to call you…"

"I'll call him," Detective Walters cut in. "We believe
something is going down this weekend. In fact, we
have a tail on one of the principal players—we believe
the liaison between the U.S. and Honduras. We're
watching to see where his trail leads, although the FBI,

for all intents and purposes, has taken over the case. I'll keep you informed."

"Thanks, Dad. Why don't you let me pass that on to Captain Petrowski? I'm looking to advance my career."

"I see. Last week you weren't sure that you wanted to remain with the Force."

"That was last week. This is now, and with your help, I may become a career officer."

"My, my, my what a different tune. Well, I've got to go. You can count on me. Love ya."

"Thanks, Dad. Love ya, too. Bye, bye." Sergeant Walters was on a high. She was staring into space when she suddenly noticed Sergeant Broadnax watching her.

"Sergeant Broadnax, what's wrong?"

"Holly, did I overhear you say guns and Fort Bragg?"

"Well, yeah," Holly said, reluctantly. She didn't need anyone else getting the glory for the case that could possibly make her career.

"What did Petrowski want to know?"

"Captain Petrowski came by this morning looking for Lieutenant Barnes to discuss the shooting, and it kind of came up."

"Look, you and I need to talk, but later. I've got to run out now." And he left Holly with a puzzled look on her face.

CHAPTER 19

Jefferson had completed his task for Operation Stingray. No phone call was an indication that Barnes had found everything in order. He'd hear from them again on payday.

His thoughts weren't focused on Barnes or Ray Adams. Everything seemed to be taking a turn for the better. He would see Linda at six tonight. He was restless and anxiously wished for the hours to fly by, so he could enjoy that first kiss. He couldn't get her off of his mind. He wanted to hold her and tell her that everything would be all right, that nothing could keep them apart.

Then a vision of Margo loomed larger than life—standing over him, reminding him that she had given him the best twenty-five years of her life, along with four beautiful children who adored him. They had a wonderful marriage and he was throwing it all away, because he felt he was getting old and needed something new in his life to make him feel young and vibrant. Jefferson shook his head to erase the vision. But it was still visible, however faint.

"Maybe if I go to the office, I can lose myself in some work," Jefferson thought out loud. *Yeah, that's what I'll do. Margo will be occupied for the day, and I won't run the risk of running into her. I'll leave for Dairy Queen straight from the office.*

Jefferson looked at his reflection in the rearview mirror and ran his fingers across his front teeth. "Myles, you're a handsome devil." And he dashed from his car for the office.

"Ms. Ebony, how are you doing this afternoon, my love?" Jefferson said, in his most cheerful voice.

My love, Ebony thought. *Right!* "Good afternoon, Jefferson. You have several messages, and a Captain Petrowski came by looking for you. He was asking about your accounts, and he left this glove. Said you left it at the police station yesterday."

Jefferson stopped in his tracks. "Petrowski here? What did he want to know about the accounts?" Jefferson asked, turning around to face Ebony.

Ebony watched Jefferson with great interest. The "accounts" struck a nerve. His neck did a version of that old dance, the snake—moving in the shape of the letter "S." And he was very familiar with Captain Petrowski's name. He had left a glove at the police station on yesterday. What was that all about? Her little package was becoming more valuable by the minute, even though she had not determined how valuable.

"He wanted to know how many accounts we had. I thought it was an odd question. In fact, I didn't get it at all. I told him that he'd have to talk to you since I was not allowed to divulge that kind of information."

Jefferson stood staring at Ebony, who stared at him. Little thoughts began to run through his mind. *How did she get to be so smart? I would expect her to be nothing but loyal. I must give her a nice bonus when the time comes. Did she wonder why Petrowski was curious about the accounts? I'm wondering why he's interested in my accounts. Before he died, did Blake have information that the police was now in possession of? Why was Blake in Richmond Heights?* He shook his head. When it cleared, Ebony was still staring at him.

"What is it?" he asked.

"Nothing, boss. I like your eyes. They seem mysterious—almost as if they hold the key to some hidden secret."

"Now, you're getting deep on me."

"You are deep," Ebony said, in a low seductive voice that was not wasted on Jefferson. "Deep in your own umph," she said under her breath as Jefferson walked away. He halted mid-step to glance back at Ebony, who was yet staring at him in an odd way. It gave him an unnerving chill. It made him a little tense, not knowing what to make of it.

Ebony let her eyes drift back to her desk. She picked

up the phone and dialed her mother. The phone was on its fourth ring. Marsha tried to get to it but Hamilton Barnes had her trapped. He finally released her and Marsha ran to the phone.

"Hello."

"Hey, Ma. Are you all right?"

"Yeah, baby. I had to run to get the phone, and I'm out of breath."

"Well, catch your breath. Exhale. I'm just checking on my package."

"Your package?"

"Yeah, Ma, my package. Is it all right? Did you put it up out of the way?"

"Yes, baby. I remember now. It's in a safe place."

"Ma, are you sure you're okay? You seem out of sorts."

"Girl, I'm just trying to straighten up this house. You saw it the other day, and you're right. I need to get up and fix this place up, make some changes in—"

"Ma. Ma…*click*…Umm, the line went dead." Ebony quickly redialed the number but got a busy signal. "What is she up to?"

"What were you talking to Sergeant Broadnax about?"

"He came here looking for answers just like you did. Wanted to know if I saw anything. I told him no."

"You lying wench. I saw him come out of this house. Why didn't you tell him that at the front door?"

"Because he said he wanted to ask some questions, and I offered him a cool drink which he said would be nice. Maybe that was his way of checking me out."

"You've got a line for everything, don't you? I'm going to be watching you. If I so much as hear or see you talking with one of my subordinates, you're dead. I'm gonna squash your guts all over Fuller Street if I hear that you've been holding out on me."

Hamilton pulled Marsha to him and slapped her full force on the face. She stumbled, fell backward, her high-heeled shoes coming out from under her, while the force of her body knocked over a chair that stood in her way. Blood oozed from her nostrils, which seemed to make Barnes madder. He reached down and slapped Marsha again, making her head spin as if on a broken axis. Her swollen left eye now closed, Barnes issued his threat again. "If I see you talking to any of my people or holding out on me, you'll be eating dirt."

He left her lying on the floor and went to the kitchen to wash the blood from his hand. Then Barnes spotted it, a manila envelope—the package that she must have been referring to when she was talking on the phone. He quickly grabbed it from the shelf where it rested, unclasped the fasteners that held it shut, and took out the contents.

He'd barely finished reading "Myles and Associates" when he heard a click that made his heart stop as he turned around. There was Marsha standing nearby, her bloodied, swollen face before him, her shaky hand holding a .22 revolver aimed at his heart.

"Put it down," she said coolly. "Now get the hell out of my house. Don't you ever set foot in here again. Don't let me hear that you've come near my place, up on my porch, because I'll come looking for you and it won't be pretty."

Lieutenant Barnes was outdone. He looked from Marsha to the gun and back to her angry face. Struggling, he dropped the envelope and its contents on the table and turned to leave. He pursed his lips to utter something to Marsha, but she raised the gun higher. He got her meaning.

He turned to walk out. Marsha let her guard down, as he anticipated, leaving her vulnerable. He dropped low, grabbing and twisting her arm, hoping to wrench the gun from her grasp. But Marsha held on.

They fell to the floor knocking over some of the whatnots on the étagère— gifts from her daughters and world-traveled suitors who occasionally stopped at Marsha's. Marsha's high-heeled shoes lay somewhere between here and there, and the dress that had hugged her every curve now rode high above her hips. Hamilton tried relentlessly to pry the gun away, but as Marsha pulled, he clung to her like glue—like two awestruck dancers doing the last tango in Paris.

Hamilton underestimated Marsha's strength. She was a survivor, but this game had only one victor, and he intended to be it. She clawed and bit him trying to break free of his hold. They fell to the floor, once more. With Marsha on her back and raging like a bull, Hamilton lunged at her. Marsha tried to pull the trigger, but the collective force of Hamilton's body and the backhand slap to her already bruised face forced her head backward. She landed on the side of the console, and her head fell forward.

Hamilton caught his breath and jerked the gun from her hand. He pointed the gun at her, and then, her eyes—those eyes, those penetrating, soulless eyes stared back at him. Then he saw the blood that ran from behind her head, from the point of impact. Hamilton stood looking at her, afraid to touch, not sure if she was dead or alive.

"God, why?" he cried.

He had to get out of there fast. Whoever phoned might come and check on her. "Take the gun," Hamilton whispered to himself. "I'll get rid of it." It wasn't fired, but he had to take it. He was almost out of the door when he remembered the envelope. He didn't even know what it contained except that it was something to do with Myles and Associates. Someone on the line was inquiring about it. He picked up the envelope and the pieces of paper that had dropped on the table.

He crept to the door and looked out. He brushed his clothes with his hands, likewise his hair. He walked briskly to his patrol car that he had parked around the corner. He eased in the car and sat a moment overcome by what had just happened. He felt a teardrop, then two and said, "I've got to protect the investment."

CHAPTER 20

Fridays were always busy—the last day of the workweek. Out-of-town employees rushed to get home early before the rush-hour traffic made it impossible. Shoppers made last-minute purchases for their out-of-town fun—maybe a trip to the beach or to the mountains. But this was the end of an era, a decade, a millennium—a bridge to a new one, and shoppers were out taking advantage of the New Year's sales spectaculars. It was a chance to celebrate the new year with friends and family, take in a college football bowl, or whatever suited the fancy.

Margo had just finished showing her client the last of four houses and was ready to call it a day. Everything was still festive downtown. Garlands hung from street lamps with large snowflakes extending from them.

Maybe Jefferson would like to meet me for dinner. That would be nice, she thought. They hadn't done that in a while, and it certainly beat going home and cooking. The kids could certainly fend for themselves.

Margo pulled out her cell phone and dialed Jefferson's number.

"Myles and Associates, Ms. Wilson speaking."

"Hi, Ebony," Margo said. "It was good to see you last Sunday."

"It was good seeing you, too, Mrs. Myles. I was telling Mr. Myles how my sister and I always look forward to Christmas dinner at your house."

"Well, you're welcome anytime. Is Jefferson in?"

"No, he left about ten minutes ago."

"Alright then. Happy New Year to you."

"Happy New Year to you, too."

Margo looked at the clock on her console. It was four p.m. Maybe Jefferson was heading home. He couldn't be far. She dialed the number to his cell phone.

She let it ring, but there was no answer. Jefferson's voice mail prompted her to leave a message. "Jefferson, this is Margo. I've finished my last showing for the day, and I'm famished. Want to meet me for dinner? I'm going to make a stop and then go to Trio's. I should be there by five o'clock."

Jefferson saw Margo's number flash in his caller ID box. He let it ring while his mind concentrated on other things. He needed to stop by the florist to purchase a bouquet of roses. He had plenty of time before his planned rendezvous, and he wanted it to be perfect.

Margo drove on, hoping she'd hear from Jefferson soon. As she rode down Hay Street, she noticed some of the changes that had taken place in the city's attempt to revitalize the street. A small theater called the Cameo Theatre had cropped up along with a small quaint eatery called Rude Awakenings that invited you to sit outside if you liked. The newly renovated R. C. Williams Business Center, named after a prominent citizen in the city, that housed the electric company, Public Works Commission (PWC), sat tall and beautiful on one corner nearly taking up an entire city block.

Margo proceeded past the Fayetteville Police Department, which had replaced some of the hottest strip joints in the city. Passing the police department caused Margo to think about Petrowski and his wanting her to come to the police station. *But why? Why did he not want Jefferson to know?* She drove past and looked at her cell phone that refused to ring.

It was five p.m. Margo sat at a round table that could have held one to two people. She looked at her watch, then the phone. She had called her house before entering Trio's, but no one answered.

The waiter brought the menu, and she decided on duck that was prepared in an orange sauce. The clock ticked, the minutes flew by. When the clock rounded the half-hour, Margo surmised that this would be a meal for one with no one else picking up the tab.

Margo ate in silence, her heart beating frantically like the wings of a startled bird. She was unable to calm the turmoil that was building inside of her. Her anxiety caused her blood pressure to rise, and memories of Jefferson's behavior over the past few days began to resurface.

With her head slightly bent, Margo applied pressure to her left temple with her finger, hoping the ensuing headache would subside. She fidgeted in her seat, twisting the napkin that lay in her lap. She could sit no longer and rose to leave.

The pain in her head intensified as she walked to the car. A burden that seemed to weigh a thousand tons lay heavy on her heart. She tried to dismiss it, but the burden remained.

Margo rummaged in her purse until she located the card with Captain Petrowski's phone number. She retrieved the cell phone from her purse, paused, then dialed Petrowski's number.

"Fayetteville Police Department."

"Yes, may I speak with Captain Robert Petrowski?"

"Speaking."

"This is Margo Myles, Captain Petrowski. I was to meet with you next Tuesday."

"Yes, Mrs. Myles, I remember," Petrowski said, stumbling all over himself. He must have been living right to have both Myleses come to him.

"I'd like to come and talk with you today if you have some time."

"Now is fine. Just go to the desk and ask for me. How long will it be before you arrive?"

"Maybe fifteen or twenty minutes."

"That will be fine. I have nowhere to go tonight," Petrowski lied. He'd promised his wife that he was coming home early to spend some quality time with her, but that had to be put on the back burner. One of the moments he had envisioned had just arrived. He also knew that what he was about to do might have a Kamikaze effect.

"I'll see you in a few minutes."

"I'll be waiting."

The pain in her head slowly subsided. Margo peered at her console once more. It was six p.m. and still no call from Jefferson. She dialed home and Winter answered. Jefferson wasn't there, and Ivy and her girlfriends decided to go to Raleigh a day early. Winter and Winston were heading out to a meeting with some of the committee members to iron out last-minute details for their New Year's Eve party. Margo drove on.

The street she had passed through only hours earlier seemed different somehow. Before, there was a gaiety type of presence that offered smiles, indifference, a laxness associated with the climate of a welcomed social change. However, a cloud of darkness dampened the spirit that was once alive. Margo passed the new Airborne and Special Operations Museum, crossed Winslow Street, passed the new Subway sandwich shop now housed in the old train station, and then saw the Radisson Hotel loom into her field of vision—a landmark that said she was nearing her destination.

She pulled into an available parking space at Dawkins Plaza, which was named for the late mayor, and took a deep breath. Margo wasn't sure why she chose to come, but something inside her head said she would find the answers with Petrowski. She looked at her face in the rearview mirror. Her lipstick was perfect and her teeth devoid of traces of her last meal. She got out of her car, brushed her suit into place, and walked the ten feet that took her into the police station.

There was no loitering or loud talking that one associates with police stations, as defined by those TV police dramas that invade millions of households each week. The entrance was a rather dull yellow and absent of people. The dispatcher's station lay straight ahead, shielded by a long window and a sign which announced the Fayetteville Police Department and its motto: *Faith in Service, Pride in Commitment, Dedication to Excellence*.

Margo walked to the reception desk and asked for Captain Petrowski. It was apparent that she was expected, because no other questions were asked of her, and the receptionist announced that she had arrived.

Captain Petrowski appeared at the front desk in less than thirty seconds.

Petrowski escorted Margo to his workstation and then showed her to an available office where they could talk more privately. Margo's head began to thump again—almost anticipating some unforeseen event that lay ahead. She was all up in arms about nothing, after all this was about Blake's death, even though she was baffled by the secrecy surrounding her visit.

"I thank you for coming, Mrs. Myles. I realize that I may have caused you some concern, however, we are very anxious to find the perpetrator of the crime against Blake Montgomery and bring that person to justice. Unfortunately, we have the unpopular task of having to ask a lot of questions that we hope will point us in the direction we need to pursue, as well as follow up on any leads that lend themselves to expediting this investigation."

"I understand that, Captain Petrowski. I would like to see justice brought to Blake's killer, also. I'm just a little confused as to how else I can be of further assistance after having told you all that I knew when we spoke the other day."

"It's a little more complicated than that, I'm afraid."

"Complicated how?" Margo demanded, new lines of concern forming on her forehead. She began to tap her foot, her nervousness and anxiety returning.

"We believe that Blake may have stumbled onto something, the knowledge of which might have caused his death. We know that he stumbled onto this information accidentally while following your husband."

"Following Jefferson? Why would he follow Jefferson? Jefferson was at home when Blake was killed. In fact, we had a house full of people at the time of Blake's death."

"Mrs. Myles, we found among Blake's personal effects a letter addressed to you. I've already reviewed the contents of the letter. It is now considered evidence in this case. However, I'd like for you to also read the contents before it becomes public knowledge. I'm sorry that I have to share this with you in this manner. However, you'll understand once you read it."

Margo sat quietly fingering the envelope that Petrowski passed to her. *What was she going to discover that he knew would upset her? What did it have to do with Jefferson?*

Petrowski watched her closely while she continued to toy with the envelope. He could see the apprehension on her face and lowered his gaze, avoiding hers, knowing full well that Pandora's box was about to be opened.

Margo pulled the letter out of the envelope and unfolded it. She counted the pages, trying to avoid looking at the contents. After another minute had passed, she dropped her eyes and viewed the first line.

December 24, 1999
Dear Margo,
  It is with much regret that I write this letter to you. I find it difficult to formulate the words that are and will be devastating to the both of us but yet have to be said.
  I had reason to believe, and have now more than confirmed, that Jefferson and Linda are having an affair.

Margo gasped. Her hands began to tremble and she dropped the letter to the floor. Petrowski leaned forward to offer assistance. She looked at Petrowski, and then picked up the letter. She closed her eyes, then reopened them and began to scan the letter again, bracing herself for the worst. She read on.

  I have followed them several times. I'm not sure how long they've been seeing each other, but for sure it may have been six months or more. I've confiscated e-mail messages from Jefferson that were sent to Linda, including an "I love you" on-line greeting card.
  They met once at a drive-in restaurant, another time at Wal-Mart. They talked most of the time with a kiss here and a kiss there, but last night was different.
  Linda told me she was going to meet her friend, Jolene, who had invited her to their company Christmas party. Linda was still in the driveway when Jolene called to see what Linda was doing and if she was up for a quick run to the mall. She had no plans to meet Linda.

I ran and jumped into my car and followed Linda from a safe distance. She drove to Jefferson's office, went in, came out with Jefferson and they got into his Mercedes. I followed them to the Richmond Heights area.

"Richmond Heights?" shouted Margo out loud. She didn't want to believe that this revelation was somehow tied to Blake's death. She read on.

I parked a block or so from them after I saw that Jefferson had pulled over. Jefferson got out of the car. After a few minutes had passed, I started my car and drove slowly by the Mercedes. I saw Linda hiding down in the seat. I didn't linger to avoid being detected.

Up ahead, I saw Jefferson talking to some men—one appeared to be a policeman. Then I noticed a guy standing at a distance. I believe he saw me looking, and that's when I noticed that he might have had a gun, because there appeared to be an object protruding from underneath his coat. He might have been a bodyguard.

I don't know what was going on, but my counter-intelligence experience told me that I needed to check this out further. I put in a call to a friend of mine who works for the FBI and asked him to watch the house where they were all gathered.

I drove around the block and parked. Maybe fifteen minutes later, Jefferson got back in the car and took off. They turned around and passed me. I ducked, and I don't believe

*they saw me. I was able to catch up with them and followed
the car until they pulled into the parking lot of a small motel.
I went on but circled back. They were together until four
this morning.*

*You may think I'm crazy, but I needed to know. Linda
doesn't know that I suspect her of anything, even though I
questioned her about how long she stayed out at a company
party.*

*I'm sorry you had to find out like this, but I couldn't find
another way to tell you. My only thought was that you should
know. We'll talk after you receive this letter.*

Blake

Margo sat paralyzed in the chair, not looking at anything in particular. She willed her tears to stop, however, the dam broke, and she cried uncontrollably.

Petrowski put a tissue in her hand. She took it and
wiped her face, the crying now turned to sniffles. After
a long silence, Petrowski spoke. "I'm sorry, Mrs. Myles."

Margo said nothing. She clutched the tissue, and as
seconds turned to minutes, the tissue became a ball and
the fingers that gripped it were ready for war. Margo
looked into Petrowski's eyes. "Is this the reason you
needed to see me so urgently?"

"Again, Mrs. Myles, I'm sorry. I realize that this has
come as a complete surprise to you. However, we can't
overlook the implications this letter has raised. Blake

Montgomery was killed near the place where he followed your husband and his wife. Mr. Myles' subsequent interaction with people in this area has raised eyebrows."

"This letter doesn't indict Jefferson for killing Blake. As I've already said, Jefferson was at home when it happened."

"What is Jefferson's relationship with Hamilton Barnes?" Petrowski asked, ignoring Margo's determined eagerness to place Jefferson far away from the crime scene.

Margo sat up straight locking her eyes onto Petrowski's. "What do you mean, what is his relation-ship…?"

"Are they business partners, good friends, for example?"

"Jefferson is Hamilton's financial broker. Ahh…the letter mentioned a policeman. Is it Lieutenant Barnes?"

"Don't know yet."

"What is this all about?"

"We're still checking things out. Federal agents are already involved in the murder investigation. I wanted you to be aware of this since the letter is considered evidence. I didn't want you to hear about it later. Secondly, I'm not sure what direction this case may go."

"Captain Petrowski, this has been a day of revelation. I can't say that I'm at all happy about it, but my life has just been altered because of it. I don't know who killed Blake and what Jefferson's involvement, if any, happens to be, but you have certainly been successful in making my life miserable. If that is all, I'd like to leave now."

"There is one other thing."

"And what might that be?" Petrowski could see the fury in Margo's eyes. She looked straight at him, straight into his soul without flinching, ready to deflect any more pain that might be hurled her way.

"Have you noticed any excessive spending by your husband, Mrs. Myles, in recent months?"

Margo sighed. "No."

"I know this has been tough for you today, and if there's anything I can do for you, please give me a call."

"You've done enough already. You've done enough."

Margo hurried from the building, anxious to put some distance between herself and the police station. She fought back the tears that insisted on coming anyway.

As Margo stood at the curb, she brought both hands to the side of her face and hollered out loud. "Whyy-yyyyyyyyyyyyyyy, Jefferson? After all we've been through, you choose now to become a sorry, low-life, cheating jackass." Margo stomped her feet and flung her hands in the air, then from side to side. She hollered out again, stomping her right foot in rapid succession like a tribal warrior in the midst of a tribal ritual. "Somebody is going to pay for this! SOMEBODY IS GOING TO PAY!!!!"

She reached her car and sat behind the wheel, drained from the ordeal. Margo's head found the headrest and allowed her eyes to stare at the roof of the car. Her head fell forward onto the steering wheel and she began to cry out to God.

"Lord, I need your help. I need it desperately right now. God, what have I done to deserve this? I've tried to be a good wife and mother. I've tried to be a good Christian. Lord, if I've ever needed you, I truly need you now. Help me. Help me," Margo whimpered.

She lifted her head, flipping the radio dial to the oldies but goodies. The day was not going to be kind. At every corner, there seemed to be someone who wanted to let her in on the secret they had kept from her. And if the last half-hour was not enough, the recording artist began to moan, *You've abandoned me, love don't live here anymore*. And Margo lowered her head back and let the tears fall.

CHAPTER 21

He dismissed the thought that something might be wrong with Margo. Relief shone on his face after listening to Margo's message asking him to join her for dinner. Jefferson pitied his wife who no longer set him on fire, and his pending rendezvous with Linda made his foot lay on the accelerator, increasing his speed by five miles per hour.

Linda drove toward Spring Lake and hung a right at Highway 210. She wanted to be with Jefferson. She anticipated their meeting, ready to be in his arms again, hopefully to rekindle the fire that had burned between them before life took a sudden spiral turn downward. She had not expected Blake's death, and things were not any easier because he was gone.

While Linda's marriage had suffered, Jefferson had offered an alternative to her misery. He made her feel brand-new, alive, and resilient. She felt she could do just about anything against all odds. This relationship had posed one big difficulty. They were both married and still lived with their spouses. Now Blake was dead, and Margo remained the only obstacle.

They had talked about commitment, leaving their spouses. They believed they could have a wonderful relationship together. Linda stared at the open road while she played and replayed of upcoming episodes with Jefferson.

Something was not right. A nagging feeling invaded her body; she couldn't seem to purge it. There was a feeling that shouted within her saying Blake's death was because of her and was somehow linked to Jefferson. This feeling was strong, and radiated strongly through her, causing her to suffer guilt and anxiety. She didn't know the how or the why. Maybe when she saw Jefferson, the guilt and pain would flee. She did love Jefferson, and her agreeing to see him would let him know just that.

Dusk had come and the sun was setting fast. Linda looked at her watch. She would get there in time. "Gotta shake this thing," she said out loud. "I'll be alright; I will."

Jefferson arrived ten minutes ahead of Linda. The lot at the Dairy Queen was sparse with cars, and he parked to the side so that he'd be able to spot her easily upon her arrival. Jefferson watched as the white Honda Accord turned off the main highway and headed in the direction where he sat, waiting to be in her arms once again. A smile crossed his face, and he sat anxiously until she peered through her car window, not taking her eyes from his.

The next move was his. Jefferson slowly opened the

door to his car and got out. Linda did likewise, both unwilling to let the other out of their sight. He stood in front of her, she in front of him. He touched her face; she gazed in his eyes. He kissed her lips; she kissed him back. His arms held her tight; she collapsed in his. He wanted to speak but found his tongue paralyzed. She wanted to say something, but her eyes uttered a million words.

After seconds passed into minutes, Jefferson pushed Linda back from him, and with a seductive smile, he formulated the words, "I love you." Her sensual eyes blocked everything else from view, and her lips mouthed the words, "I love you, too."

They kissed again and fought the urge to throw caution to the wind and let passion take its course. It had been a long week. A lot of things had happened, terrible things for which they could not let down their guard for fear of being exposed. Jefferson held her face again, riding the wild waves of lust. He coaxed her inside the building for a banana split treat. He remembered that he had a little surprise and ran back to the car to retrieve the roses he had picked especially for her. She beamed when he brought them in and gave them to her. The few customers there gave quick glances at the two, and elicited a couple of smiles.

They sat in a booth, teasing their banana splits and acting like two teenage lovers on their first date. Then he spooned a scoop of his ice cream and brought it to her mouth as she opened wide, receiving willingly what he had to offer, letting her tongue slowly drag across the surface of the spoon. She stroked his fingers—slowly building up speed on her third lap across, building speed whose friction ignited sparks, sparks that aroused passion, passion that whispered sweet nothings, making the heart race, making it hard to continue sitting in their chairs. They watched the ice cream melt over a bed of nuts and bananas that reminded them of themselves when they made love and the covers slipped to the floor.

"Let's get out of here," Jefferson said, uttering the longest sentence to come out of his mouth since they had whispered, "I love you."

"I'm willing," she said, all hint of her fear and misgivings having disappeared like the sun on its journey to the next hemisphere.

"Where would you like to go?" Jefferson prodded.

"It doesn't matter to me as long as I'm with you. There must be a small inn in the next town. I want to be with you, Jefferson," Linda said, surprised at her own admission. "I want you to hold me and tell me that everything is going to be alright."

"It will, love. Let's find a place, and I'll hold you all night if you want me to."

"I'd like that." Linda turned and grabbed Jefferson around the neck. He held her waist and they kissed passionately, throwing caution to the wind.

CHAPTER 22

"Girls, this New Year's is going to be the bomb," Kim said, moving her lips a mile a minute. "Johnny and Tripp said they were coming to Freda's party and bringing some more brothers with them. We're gonna have fun, ladies. Look out, ya'll, 'cause here we come—oohhh, oohhh…"

"Girl, you're a trip," Erin interjected. "I'm ready. I've got on my Nine West black stiletto heels and my long, slinky, black, fitted, knock-off, Vera Wang dress…"

"You mean the one with the cleavage that meets your navel and the one hundred-somethin' rhinestones running from North to South?" Ivy hollered, trying unsuccessfully to suppress her laughter.

"How about that? I won't even be able to wear my new Victoria's Secret push-up bra." The girls broke out into another fit of laughter.

"With that dress hugging your hips like paint on a fence," Ivy continued, "you wouldn't think you already had a man."

Ivy and Kim laughed again until tears had almost washed away their mascara. "And keep your hands on the steering wheel," Kim managed to say to Erin between the continued bouts of laughter.

"Quiet, quiet!! Ya'll are just mad because the back of my dress slings down to the round of my fine hips," Erin said, popping her fingers, "where Tripp's hands will be all night long while we're jammin' to Tyrese. Can't stand it, can you? Ha, can't stand it." Erin smiled to herself, because she knew the girls were jealous.

They rode on until the laughter had somewhat subsided. They were glad that they had decided to go up a day earlier. Now, they would be able to help Freda with her party and be able to enjoy the festivities without all of the rush. And they could avoid the crazy folks who'd be out on the street trying to get to their destination so they could be with loved ones to celebrate the end of a century.

They eased on down Highway 210. Kim frowned as she looked out of the window. In the corner of her eye, she saw what looked like a familiar car and a familiar face. "Ivy, isn't that your...dad...?"

"My dad, where?" Ivy asked from the back seat, now straining to look in the direction Kim just pointed out. "Where, at the Dairy Queen?"

"Uhh, uhh..."

"Uhh, what," Ivy began, not quite sure what Kim was trying to say. "Turn around Erin and go back to the Dairy Queen we just passed."

"Why don't we keep going?" Kim cut in. "It wasn't your dad."

"Well, I'll just see for myself. What is it, Kim; why are you acting so strange?"

"I see the Dairy Queen," Erin shouted. "Let me get in the turn lane and I will drive... Oh my God, it is your dad, Ivy. Who's the woman with him?"

Kim popped Erin upside her head. It was too late. Ivy had already seen what the others saw. There was her dad and Mrs. Montgomery.

"Oh my God!" Ivy wailed, balling up her fists and throwing her hands in the air. "No, this can't be. I don't believe this."

"Calm down, Ivy," Kim said, consoling Ivy the best she could.

"What do you want me to do?" Erin said.

"Drive over there. I want to confront him. I want to get up in his face so he can see the whites in my eyes, while he tries to explain to me why he's laying all over that slutty bitch. I just can't believe he would do this to my mother. I knew something was wrong between my parents, but this? Damn, this makes me angry!"

"Ivy, you may be taking what you saw out of context. He probably ran into her and was consoling her. After all, she did just lose her husband and violently at that. Can you imagine the toll it has probably taken on—?"

"Girl, don't go there. Tell that to somebody else. You

saw them just like I did, and you can't sit there and deny that they were all into each other. And if my daddy was consoling his grieving neighbor, as you seem to think, he's certainly having a good time while doing it.

"I'm sorry about her husband, but that doesn't give that bitch the right to have her arms wrapped around my daddy's neck and her lips all over his face. If that's what you call consoling, Ms. Know-It-All, then you still have a lot to learn about life. I hate my dad for this... he makes me sick."

"Chill, Ivy. I wasn't kissing your dad," Kim retorted.

Ivy jerked around and looked dead into Kim's eyes. "And if I ever see you with my daddy, I'll kill you right on the spot. And you better know that I will."

"Hold up, hold up, Miss Thing," Erin interjected. "That's enough. Kim didn't mean it like that, Ivy, and you know it. You're hurting and rightfully so, but we are your friends and are here for you. After all, we are supposed to be going to a party to celebrate."

"Celebrate? How can I celebrate at a time like this? I need to confront my dad, *NOW*."

"No, Ivy. I'm not going to stop. You've got to handle this some other way. He's still your dad, and he's still due some amount of respect because he's our elder. We would look foolish driving over there to confront him. Your dad will get his. But you need to apologize to Kim. That was a very nasty thing you said."

Ivy dropped her head and sighed. She drew her mouth up in a tight line, exhaled, and turned to Kim. "I'm sorry, baby," Ivy said, stroking Kim's arm that were crisscrossed over her chest.

Kim was sulking and did not want to look at Ivy. "I'm sorry, I didn't mean to take it out on you."

Kim scrunched her face. Water had formed in the corner of her eyes. Ivy's words had hurt her to the bone. And when she looked up, Ivy was still staring at her waiting for her to respond.

Kim unfolded her arm and reached out for Ivy. Ivy grabbed her friend and held her in an embrace for dear life, wishing she could take back every word she had spoken. "It's all right," was about all that Kim could muster.

"I'm sorry," Ivy repeated. "I don't know what got into me. You and Erin are my best friends. What would I do without you guys in my life?"

"We'll be here," Kim spoke up. "You won't make it without us." The girls laughed until their sides hurt.

"You know, guys, I'm not really in the mood to go to the party. Where's my cell phone? I need to call my mom."

Ivy felt her stomach churn. Now she understood what was at the root of the tension brooding between her mother and father. Worst yet, their next-door neighbor was at that root. At one time, Ivy believed the tension was credited to something else, remembering her father's early-morning encounter with Lieutenant Barnes the day after Christmas, but tonight explained everything, and she was an eyewitness.

She dialed her mother's number, and after several rings, heard her voice. The last thing she wanted to do was arouse her mother's suspicious nature.

"Hi, Mother, what are you doing?"

"Oh, it's 'hi, Mother' today," Margo said, mocking Ivy's upbeat voice. "I'm relaxing," she lied. "It feels good to have the house to myself."

"Where's Dad?" Ivy pressed.

"He's out right now, baby."

"Are you alright, Mom?"

"Ivy, what's wrong with you? I said I was fine." Margo tried to regain her composure. Ivy was a snoop and always wanted to know why this or why that. Today, she certainly didn't feel like answering a whole lot of questions. "Aren't you and your girlfriends going to Raleigh?"

"We're on our way now, but if you need me to come home, I'll have them bring me back."

"Absolutely not! For the love of God, Ivy, I'm fine. I promise you. I don't understand why you're asking me all these questions."

"I guess I was feeling a little guilty about leaving you with the new year coming and all."

"I'm curled up on the sofa with a good book, enjoying

the peace and solitude. Anyway, your father and I are going out tomorrow night."

"You are? I don't recall you having told me that you were going out."

"Ivy, sweetheart, I don't need your permission to go out on a date with my husband. You know—your father. Anyway, we talked about it last night, even though we aren't sure where we are going."

Margo wasn't sure about anything. She was in a fog now, not sure of her next step. She wanted to hate Jefferson at this moment, but she needed to wait for his explanation. *Petrowski could have written the letter, but why would he do that. Think, Margo, think.*

"Ahh, Mom," Ivy said, shaking her head, "are you still there?"

"Look, honey, you ladies have a good time, and… Happy New Year."

"Happy New Year to you, too, Mom." Ivy hit the *End* button on her cell, sat back in her seat, and let the tears roll silently down her cheek. "Yeah, Happy New Year, Mom."

"Happy New Year," Margo uttered to herself. "It's going to be one big bang."

CHAPTER 23

Lieutenant Hamilton Barnes could not go back to the police station. He was in a state of disarray, no matter how many times and ways he tried to make his uniform look neat. Combing through his thick crop of hair didn't alter a thing. His altercation with Marsha made him perspire badly. He could not hide the obvious, and now, he needed to run home and change clothes. He hated that Petrowski had been hanging around the station, but hopefully, it wouldn't take long for him to change and be back at the station before Petrowski showed up again.

That bitch had it coming, he thought. He had warned her, but she was a stupid broad with marbles for brains. How could he have allowed himself the pleasure of seducing her? It was easy. She was an easy lay with no cares in the world and going nowhere. Not one ambitious bone could probably be found in her body. There might have been marbles in her head, but she could make a man lose his mind.

Marsha knew how to love a man, knew how to make

him sing "Stormy Weather" in the key of "C," knew how to turn his midnight into day, and knew how to make a man scream her name. Poor Marsha. She just had to go snooping around and mess up everything.

There were too many things to juggle in his head today. The arms shipment had to be protected and this was to be a big payday. Jefferson came through. Monies were deposited. It was nearing four in the afternoon, and Hamilton awaited word from Ray that their cargo was in his hands and all that was left to do was make transfer with Santiago in the morning.

"Damn that Petrowski and Marsha," Hamilton rambled on, pounding his fist on the dash of his car. They were complications he did not need, trouble-shooter or no troubleshooter. Santiago's men were ruthless, and Blake Montgomery's death was a testament to that fact. Death was one of the perils of war.

Hamilton pulled up in front of his Spanish-style condo. After he and Angelica had gone their separate ways, he decided a large estate like the two had shared was much too large for him. What he lacked in space, which was minimal at best, he replaced with a lavish décor and artifacts that spoke of someone with taste and money. Even though Hamilton was the benefactor of his mother's estate a couple of years earlier, it would take more than a lieutenant's salary to supplement the lifestyle he had become accustomed to.

One would have thought that he'd like to bring less

attention to himself, considering his recent outside activities that reeked of criminal stench, but Hamilton Barnes didn't have a subtle bone in his body.

Hamilton's condo was decorated with imported Italian furniture done in hues of beige and brown. The spacious living room was adorned with an open-hearth, half-moon fireplace surrounded by African art and artifacts. The tribal masks and fetish pieces were made in Ghana and had become popular in many African-American households.

The kitchen was designed with a Mediterranean flair. It also flaunted a half-moon kitchen window that boasted a terrarium where many varieties of herbs lay basking in the noonday sun. The window was encircled in layers of terracotta brick. The ceramic tiled floor added to the rustic, carefree atmosphere that made the kitchen a lounging area, as well as a place for eating.

Hamilton ran through the shower and threw on a fresh uniform. A bottle of Giorgio Armani aftershave sat on the marble-like counter that Hamilton quickly picked up, pouring a small amount into the palm of his hand. He put his hands together, allowed the liquid fragrance to saturate both hands, and slapped both sides of his face, letting the liquid seep into the pores of his skin.

Next, he patted his hair and sucked his teeth, while examining his profile in the bathroom mirror that covered a full wall over the countertop.

"No one will be able to tell what kind of day you experienced this morning, Lieutenant Barnes," Hamilton uttered out loud, admiring himself in the mirror. "You look like fresh lilies in your favorite lady's crystal vase. Boy, you know you look good."

Hamilton rushed from his condo and hopped into his vehicle. As he moved forward, he caught a glimpse of a Ford Crown Victoria he thought he'd seen earlier. It didn't mean much at first, but the driver's sudden move and his obvious attempt to stay at a certain distance certainly marked the driver as a tail.

Hamilton watched him for a good ten minutes and decided to make an abrupt turn into a coffee shop. He saw the driver slow down, but then drive on. Hamilton believed the driver knew he was outsmarted. There still remained the who, what, and why. Hamilton hoped this weekend would pass quickly.

He plopped his right hand on the seat of the cruiser. He felt it. He had completely forgotten about the package.

"Damn, wish I had left it at the house," Hamilton said aloud, "but I can't worry about it now."

CHAPTER 24

The Richmond Heights Police Department was busy all afternoon. There was still no break in the Montgomery murder case, but Sergeant Broadnax had an uneasy feeling about the investigation. He went over and over the conversation he had with the boys and Marsha. Broadnax noted, also, how often Marsha had put Lieutenant Barnes' name on the lunch menu, even though he was not sure what she was trying to convey to him—if she was letting him in on a secret or a clue that might help him solve the Montgomery case.

Broadnax tried desperately to erase the thought that Barnes could somehow be involved. Can't be, but what did it all mean? Maybe he would give Marsha a call and get together for New Year's. What would it hurt?

He picked up the phone and dialed the number Marsha gave him. The line was busy; he'd call again.

"Sergeant Broadnax," came the voice over the intercom.

"Yes, Sergeant Walters. What's up?"

"I believe someone was trying to call you, but her voice became very inaudible. I'm not sure if she hung up on me or not."

"Did you catch the name?"

"No, she didn't say."

"Maybe it was Marsha," Sergeant Broadnax mumbled.

"What…?" Sergeant Walters asked.

"Holly, I'm going to make a few phone calls. I want you to keep this conversation just between the two of us, okay?"

"Well…okay," Holly said, not sure what he was referring to.

"Look, I need your word on this. I'll explain later."

"You've got it."

"Thanks, Holly."

Sergeant Broadnax leaned back in his chair and dialed Marsha's number again. Who could she be talking to? The phone still rang busy. She didn't appear to have that many friends.

Holly grabbed the phone on the first ring. She was getting good at this. Fewer distractions.

"Sergeant Holly Walters, Richmond Heights Police Department."

"Hey honey, it's Dad. Got me on speaker, eh?"

"Hi, Dad. Nobody's here except for Sergeant Broadnax. What are you up to?"

"Catching criminals is the name of the game, and

that's my final answer." They both broke out in laughter.

"Dad, you could become a comedian if you wanted to."

"That's what the guys here say. I just may take them up on it if I ever retire this uniform."

"Well, what's the word from the DPD?"

"The feds are closing in on the arms ring. They have had surveillance on the supposed ringleader for months. His name is Robert Santiago. He's a Honduran native and seems to be helping a rebel group in Honduras by providing them with arms. Remember me telling you that we believe he's getting his arsenal from Fort Bragg?"

"Yeah, I remember. Can you imagine—right at Fort Bragg and under our nose. You would have thought security would be much tighter considering it's a military base."

"They also believe that several soldiers, green-beret types, may be on the take. No one is making a move at this moment. The feds are watching the operation, hoping to catch the whole gang. And remember me telling you that the feds believe that a local cop may be involved?"

Holly nodded.

"Although they haven't confirmed it yet, I believe they have a good idea who it is."

"A Fayetteville cop? Ooh hi, Lieutenant Barnes." Hamilton nodded and remained planted just inside the main door.

"Huh?"

"Hey, Daddy. I was just saying hello to Lieutenant Barnes."

"Oh. Well, I better let you get back to work."

"Okay. I love you."

"Love you too, honey. I'll call you tomorrow."

"Okay, Daddy. I have the day off. Will talk to you then."

Lieutenant Barnes moved from his position and walked toward the reception desk, not taking his eyes off Holly. His eyebrows arched—almost menacing in appearance. "Interesting conversation you were having there, Sergeant Walters. Care to share it with me?"

Barnes' question took Holly off-guard. The strange manner in which he asked the question made her a little uneasy. It was not uncommon for Holly to talk with her father about police business. However, the stealthy way in which Lieutenant Barnes approached was what unnerved her.

"I was talking to my father about how hard the Durham Police Department had been working, especially with all of the New Year's celebrations going on this weekend."

"Well, that's nice, but I was especially interested in what you were saying about a local Fayetteville cop. Is there something I should know?"

"I'm not sure what you mean, Lieutenant Barnes," Holly stuttered. "My father said a local cop might be involved in a case that originated in their jurisdiction that the feds are now handling…"

"The feds?"

A frown crossed Holly's face. "Did I say the wrong thing? Do you know something?" Holly asked excitedly.

"No," Barnes said, his tone noncommittal. "This is the second time I've heard about cop involvement but haven't seen an APB or case history surrounding any alleged involvement. Do you know what the cop was involved in?"

Something started to register with Holly. Local cop, Lieutenant Barnes' sudden interest, and Sergeant Broadnax's swearing her to secrecy. Could there possibly be a link? Something was going on. Lieutenant Barnes was much too inquisitive about the cop thing, and Holly was going to make sure he didn't get anything out of her. Local cop, Hamilton Barnes—that's a thought.

"Daddy didn't say, Lieutenant Barnes. He said that they had a hot case the feds were trying to crack, and that was the highlight of their week."

"If you should hear anything else, Sergeant Walters, please let me know. Maybe we can assist somehow."

"Alright, Lieutenant Barnes."

Holly followed Barnes with her eyes as he walked away from the lobby. Her puzzled look became one of realization—some very strange goings-on were happening right under her very nose.

CHAPTER 25

There was certainly no doubt in Hamilton's mind that this day was the worst he had experienced in a long time. "D" Day, Black Sunday— Hamilton was experiencing his own dark Friday. His world was spiraling downward, but he had to gain control. There were too many glitches that shouldn't have been. First, there was Petrowski, then Marsha, and now the partial conversation he overheard. Oh, and yes, Broadnax. Did Marsha tell him anything? If so, what?

"Get a hold of yourself," Hamilton's voice whispered softly. "You'll need your strength for what's about to come. You've got to call Santiago and warn him."

Hamilton walked toward his office coming up behind Sergeant Broadnax. Broadnax put the phone down when Hamilton passed his desk. "Any leads on that robbery, Carl?"

Broadnax jumped, startled by Lieutenant Hamilton's voice. "I do have a lead on a possible suspect, sir."

"Good. Keep on it."

The robbery was the last thing on Broadnax's mind.

He had been dialing Marsha's number for over an hour, and her line was still busy. She didn't seem the type to hang out on the phone.

"Lieutenant Barnes…"

"What is it, Broadnax?"

"Nothing. It was nothing, sir."

"Spit it out. I've had a bad day. What did you want, Carl?" Hamilton's blood pressure was pushing the limit.

"I'd like the day off tomorrow. I want to celebrate the New Year with a cousin in Virginia."

Hamilton gave a sigh of relief. Maybe it wasn't a totally bad day.

"Look, take the rest of the day off and have a happy New Year. The night watch should be here any minute."

"Thanks, Lieutenant. You have a happy New Year, too."

Broadnax grabbed his things and headed for the door. He gave Holly a nod that she understood to mean they would talk later. They wished each other a happy New Year, and Broadnax walked out the door.

He sat in his car and contemplated what he should do. Lieutenant Barnes had warned him to stay away from Marsha, but something kept nagging at him, a sixth sense that would not allow him to get her off of his mind.

Broadnax started his car and put it in gear. He drove away from the station heading toward Bragg Boulevard Before he reached the boulevard, he made a left turn and then a series of lefts and rights until he reached Fuller Street. Sergeant Broadnax had Lieutenant Barnes' number, and he knew how to outsmart a fox, if he had to.

He parked one street over and walked the short distance to Marsha's. He rang the doorbell, but no one came. Then he noticed that the door was not completely closed. Broadnax leaned into it, and it flew open.

He called out Marsha's name, but silence met his ears. His instinct told him to stay on course, and he climbed the stairs.

There was an eeriness that crept over Carl. Compounded with the deafening silence, it made him shudder. He couldn't shake the feeling, but thought he might be overreacting. He reached the top of the stairs and called out Marsha's name again. He stopped upon hearing voices, which moments later he determined to be the television.

He softly called out Marsha's name yet again, but still there was no response. He passed the bedroom he recalled from his first trip. He moved on until he came upon the entrance to the living room. He stopped abruptly, fell slightly backward, clasped his hands to his face, and let out a shrill cry.

The room was in utter chaos. Marsha lay in a pool of blood in the midst of it. Papers were strewn throughout; slivers of glass, broken figurines, and discarded shoes lent themselves to the mayhem. It spelled foul play and an apparent struggle, with a winner and a definite loser.

Broadnax reached for Marsha's arm to check her pulse. Finding none, he looked for the phone in order to call an ambulance. He almost stumbled over it as he tried to tiptoe through the debris, careful not to touch the evidence as he'd been trained to do.

Carl picked up the phone with his jacket and heard the busy signal when he put the phone to his ear. If he had only come earlier, he might have saved her. He decided to use his cell, and dialed 911. Broadnax looked at Marsha again, and then turned away. Tears welled in the corners of his eyes, and he brushed them away with the back of his hand.

Broadnax couldn't stand it any longer and decided to wait downstairs for the ambulance. Before he reached the bottom, the door flew open, and there was Marsha reincarnated standing before him. Broadnax's eyes grew large like he'd seen a ghost, and he stared at the uncanny likeness of a woman he had just met.

"Excuse me," the young woman said. "Is my mother up there? And who are you? Do I know you?"

"Mother?"

"Yes, my mother. I'm Ebony, Marsha's oldest daughter. Didn't you just come from up there?"

"Momma must have a thing for police officers," Ebony muttered to herself.

"Jesus," was all Carl Broadnax could say.

"What's going on?" Ebony shouted, now upset. "Where's my mother?"

She tried pushing Broadnax aside in an attempt to mount the stairs, but his strong arm held her at bay. "You can't go up there."

"Take your hands off of me, and get out of my way. Who in the hell are you, anyway?"

Before Sergeant Broadnax could answer her, the siren's deafening scream made them stand at attention. Sergeant Broadnax looked at Ebony. Ebony stared back at Sergeant Broadnax. The arch in his eyebrows and the glaze in his eyes told a story fear had elicited only moments earlier. Now that fear had become truth.

She looked at Broadnax again, searching for an explanation or some kind of reassurance that all of this fanfare had nothing to do with her mother. As the ambulance pulled into the yard, its siren now only a vibration caught in the ear, Broadnax lowered his head and pointed upstairs.

The paramedics obeyed Broadnax's direction, followed closely by several police units from downtown. And then there was Lieutenant Barnes. His eyes searched Sergeant Broadnax, and then shifted toward Ebony. Not saying a word, he followed the others to the top.

"My mother is dead, isn't she?" Ebony asked in a low, still voice.

"Yes," Sergeant Broadnax said, staring off in space and avoiding Ebony's piercing eyes.

"I want to see her."

"I don't think it's a good idea."

"I'm going up now, and if you don't move out of my way, I'll…I'll…"

Sergeant Broadnax let Ebony pass and watched as she ascended the stairs. The forensic technicians had finished their task, passing Ebony on the stairs as they headed back to their cars. Broadnax leaned up against the wall, standing guard at the door, when he heard Ebony's blood-curdling cry, as she lamented over her mother's fate. And then it was quiet except for the movement of the paramedics' trolley.

They brought Marsha's body down—invisible inside the black body bag. The police followed, now ready to question Sergeant Broadnax who had made the 911 call following his discovery. Lieutenant Barnes held up the rear, consoling a sobbing Ebony. Ebony glanced up when she passed Sergeant Broadnax and immediately let her head drop without asking another question. Hamilton passed without even a nod, moving hurriedly to catch up with Ebony to offer his condolences. And Carl Broadnax's internal notebook was filling up fast.

Outside on the street, the police questioned Broadnax at length, wanting to know why he was there, his relationship to the victim and how long he knew her, what time he arrived on the scene, what time he called 911, why he didn't radio his own unit, why did he park around the corner, why, why, why.

Lieutenant Hamilton Barnes watched and listened from a short distance, hoping to obtain the answers he also wanted to know.

Outside, Denver Grey of WYZZ News set up camp and was gathering information. He interviewed the police, the paramedics, and Ebony, who pointed her finger in Sergeant Broadnax's direction—the man she'd seen coming down the stairs from her mother's house. It was time for him to share with the world what he knew—what little it was—but he knew that this was not just a simple murder.

All of a sudden, Ebony ran back into the house, first scanning Sergeant Broadnax thoroughly before entering. Lieutenant Barnes tried to run after her, but Sergeant Broadnax blocked his way, telling Barnes to let her be.

Lieutenant Barnes scowled at Sergeant Broadnax but backed away. A confrontation was the last thing he could afford with Petrowski leaning on his back. He did not follow Ebony, although he had a strong feeling why she might have gone back into the house. No, he couldn't take any chances.

Denver Grey approached Carl. Lieutenant Barnes stood quietly by.

"Sir, Sergeant Broadnax…?"

"Correct, B-R-O-A-D-N-A-X," Carl responded, as if the newscaster had forgotten his name.

"Sergeant Broadnax, I understand you were found on the stairs of the victim's house when her daughter arrived."

"Yes, sir. I was."

"Can you tell me what you were doing here?"

"I spoke to Marsha Wilson earlier in the day regarding our investigation into last Sunday's Montgomery murder. While she didn't give me any information that would aid us in the case, I sensed that she possessed some vital information but was afraid to say.

"While at my desk this afternoon, I decided to call her because of a nagging feeling I had. I tried calling her, but the line was busy. I tried several times over a period of an hour and a half, and the phone remained busy. Concerned, I decided to stop by Ms. Wilson's house and check on her before going home.

"When I arrived, I rang the doorbell, but there was no answer. It was then that I discovered that the door was not completely shut. I proceeded up the stairs, and it was then that I made the gruesome discovery."

"I have one last question for you, Sergeant Broadnax," Denver said. "At what time did you discover the deceased?"

"It was approximately five-fifteen p.m."

"Thank you, Sergeant Broadnax." Denver continued

talking into the microphone for another minute or two before he hollered, "It's a wrap."

Almost on cue, Ebony appeared, looking straight at Sergeant Broadnax.

"It's not there," she said through clenched teeth.

"What's not there?" Sergeant Broadnax asked, a quizzical look on his face.

"You know what I'm talking about."

"Ms. Wilson, why don't we talk?"

"Why don't I speak with Ms. Wilson," Lieutenant Barnes interrupted, moving closer to Ebony and Broadnax. "She apparently doesn't trust you."

"I don't want to talk to either of you," Ebony countered, storming off to her car, sobbing as she went. "I've got to call Katrina and tell her about Momma. Oh, God, what am I gonna tell her?" Ebony got in her car, not daring to look back at the house where Marsha, who had raised two beautiful daughters, once lived.

And Captain Petrowski sat in the cruiser observing, while his rookie gathered evidence that would be shared with him later.

CHAPTER 26

Dusk turned to night. Margo walked silently throughout the house, moved methodically between rooms watching, waiting, and looking while the grandfather clock announced that another hour had come and gone. This time Margo stopped, upon hearing the chime, to record the time. It was ten-thirty p.m. She sat down on the couch.

The afternoon's revelation came running back to her. "Dear Margo: I could find no other…Linda and Jefferson are having an affair…" Margo bolted upright from the couch, hurriedly rushing to the window that faced Linda Montgomery's driveway. The driveway was still empty, just as it was a half-hour ago and a half-hour before that.

The anger that had lain temporarily dormant began to well up again, ready to boil over and spill its guts. Margo wanted some answers and someone would provide them soon.

Margo knew that Linda was with Jefferson. She could feel it. It didn't take an educated guess to figure it out. Jefferson didn't even have the decency to return her phone call. She contemplated even now whether to call his cell—just to interrupt what she believed was going on. She walked to the window again and viewed the driveway that was still unoccupied.

Margo picked up the phone and dialed Jefferson's number; he did not answer. There was no need to leave a message. He knew that she was looking for him. Margo gazed at the phone hoping it would ring. And the silence continued, except for the wind that suddenly picked up, echoing in the night.

CHAPTER 27

The sudden sound of the familiar melody interrupted Jefferson's groove. He reached over Linda's begging body to ID the caller. He immediately recognized the number, turning off the power without acknowledging the caller's name.

He rushed back to recapture the moment, not wanting to miss a beat. Their bodies were entwined and the rhythm of their lovemaking was so in tune. He kissed her lips and then her breasts, feeling her body arch as his mouth went from place to place.

His hot breath rose like steam. Her panting was that of a secret code that only Jefferson would be able to decipher. He entered her, and she allowed him safe passage.

They were at the height of passion when, for a fleeting moment, Blake's image flashed before Linda. He seemed to mouth something, words she tried desperately to understand. Blake's lips moved slower, mouthing what Linda made no mistake in deciphering… "You and Jefferson will pay for my death." As abruptly as the image had appeared, it was gone.

Linda tried to pull away just as Jefferson was going for the home run.

"Stop, Jefferson, I can't do this."

"What is it, Linda?" Jefferson asked, stroking her hair while taking in the sight of her and wanting very much to get back to the business at hand.

"Stop, please stop. I thought I saw Blake's face trying to warn me."

Jefferson pulled back and looked at Linda. "Linda, Blake is dead. Only you and I are in this room, and we were so close to being on top of the mountain."

"I can't go with you right now." Linda pushed Jefferson away and covered her nakedness with the sheet. "I'm having reservations. Things don't feel quite right."

"Don't you love me, Linda? We were both unhappy until we found each other, and I want to be there for you, always." Jefferson lifted her chin and brought her face to his. "I love you. I won't let anything happen to you."

"I wish it was that easy, Jefferson. I've struggled with myself over something ever since Blake's death. I don't know how to ask...to say this, but I guess I'll come right out with it."

"What is it, Linda?"

"Did you have Blake killed?"

The look in Jefferson's eyes told Linda that she had asked the wrong question. While there was a look of surprise, a certain hostility seemed to rise that scared Linda a little.

"You disappoint me, Linda. How could you even think such a thing? I could never kill a soul, and you know that I was at home when Blake was killed."

"You could have set it up," Linda said, becoming a little more defiant. "I watched you and those guys last Friday in Richmond Heights, and I'm sure you're involved in something that may not be on the up and up. I saw the gun, Jefferson, the gun that one of those guys tried to conceal. Tell me please, tell me I'm wrong."

The groove, the high, the passion had vanished in an instant. Jefferson examined Linda with renewed interest, trying to figure out where she was coming from. Only minutes ago, they were in the midst of hot and torrid lovemaking, now she had the nerve to try and implicate him in the murder of her husband. He needed to get away from this place. The thought of life with Linda was beginning to sour.

"I told you before, those guys were business associates. We had to conduct some emergency business. My question is, what was Blake doing over there? Can you answer that?"

Linda paused. She had not asked herself that question. Why was Blake there? "I can't answer that question, Jefferson, but I do know that I felt uncomfortable being there…in Richmond Heights…and those guys looked like gangsters."

"I'm not going to stand here and defend my honor with you. I thought you knew me better than that.

You're a fool if you believe otherwise. And stop trying to rationalize about what I was or was not doing in Richmond Heights. Now, get dressed, it's time for you to go home. If you can't trust me, then there is no point in your being here."

"Jefferson, I do love you, but something keeps eating away at me. I have a hard time eating and sleeping, and this knowing feeling that keeps wearing at me. You may not directly have anything to do with Blake's murder, but my spirit says you're involved somehow."

Jefferson grabbed Linda by the shoulders. "I don't know what you're talking about, but know that I had nothing to do with Blake's murder. Blake was my friend, despite the fact that I fell in love with his wife. Now get ready. I've had enough for one night."

Linda went into the bathroom without another word and shut the door. As soon as Jefferson heard the shower door close and the sound of water running, he turned on his cell phone to see if he had any messages. Two messages. One from Malik and the other from Hamilton. They couldn't be important. Jefferson was surprised that Margo hadn't tried calling back.

It was eleven p.m. Jefferson was seething. He hadn't expected Linda's outburst—questioning his character, accusing him of a horrendous crime against her husband. He was many things and some not so good, but a murderer? Never. The only crime he was guilty of was being in love with the dead man's wife and stepping out on Margo.

Now he was left with no alternative but to go home to Margo, who probably had her accusing finger ready to condemn him to the pit of hell. She was probably asleep—mad but asleep—angry because he had not returned her phone calls. He looked at the phone in his hand. Just as he was about to lay the phone down, it began to ring.

"Jeff, that you?"

"Yeah, Hamilton, it's me. It's late. What do you want?"

"Where are you?"

"What do you mean, where am I?"

"Look, I don't have time for your sarcasm. We've got a problem," Hamilton went on. "Ray Adams was arrested tonight on F Street."

"Say what?" Jefferson's voice sounded the alarm.

"It was as if they lay in wait for him. They also seized the arsenal of weapons."

"Damn, damn, damn!" Jefferson shouted, walking briskly back and forth in the room. "How could this happen?"

"I don't know, but they knew. It was the feds."

"Feds? Jesus, that means they have been watching us. What about Santiago?"

"Haven't called him yet. Oh by the way, your girl at the office…what's her name…?"

"Ebony?"

"Yeah, that's her. Her mother was found dead tonight."

Jefferson raised his left hand in the air and slammed it on the dresser out of frustration. "How did it happen?"

"They're investigating it now. You'll probably have to wait for the autopsy report for the cause of death."

"I'll call Ebony and see what I can find out. I don't believe this."

"I'd also keep an eye out on Ms. Ebony."

"What do you mean?"

"Just keep an eye out."

"Look, keep me posted. I'm out of town at the moment, but I should be back in a couple of hours."

"A little booty call, eh?"

"I'll talk to you later." And Jefferson pushed the *End* button.

Linda stood on the other side of the door, taking in what she could.

CHAPTER 28

Hamilton was a nervous wreck, not quite the all-knowing cop who seemed to be affected by nothing. He had to be on top of things so his indiscretion did not catch him in the loop. He could count on Ray to keep quiet.

But Santiago was another story. He would not be pleased with this turn of events. Even though it was not his money backing the buy, Santiago stood to receive a bundle hidden under a cloak to oust the dictatorship government in his country while also getting revenge. While he might not suffer the fate of Jefferson's next-door neighbor, Hamilton knew that something close to that would remind him that he messed up.

He picked up the phone and after a couple of seconds, put it back down. He continued this game for the next ten minutes before deciding it was now or never. And it had to be *now* because he wouldn't live to see *never* if he didn't.

Sweat poured from his face. Hamilton had not experienced fear like this. The phone rocked in his hand, and he put it down again.

Other things were beginning to possess his psyche. Montgomery and Marsha. Even Sergeant Broadnax somehow fit into the equation. He'd deal with him later. Broadnax was too slow in solving a simple petty larceny when the evidence was out in plain view. Everything would be taken care of before Sergeant Carl Broadnax could figure anything out.

It was evident that Broadnax had no knowledge of the package. The package—it somehow fit in. Hamilton had to get it and study its contents tonight. Can't leave any stone unturned. ·

What will Santiago do if we can't deliver? Have us eliminated because we know too much? Damn. At least Jefferson is getting a booty call while his poor wife sits at home unattended. Like to have some of that.

Hamilton picked up the phone again to call Santiago. This time he wouldn't chicken out.

CHAPTER 29

Margo dozed off. She was exhausted and her body gave in, although she wanted to be Jefferson's welcoming committee when he came through the door. She also wanted to be a witness to Linda's arrival home, if indeed the two of them planned to show up on Andover Street tonight.

WYZZ News was on the air. Margo's internal instinctive clock aroused her from slumber in time to catch the top news story of the hour. Wiping her eyes, Margo made out the face of Denver Grey, dubbed the voice of doom. Margo yawned and tried to focus her eyes when all of a sudden she stiffened at the announcement of another homicide in Fayetteville's Richmond Heights area.

Margo stared at the screen in disbelief. Denver Grey said that a woman in her fifties was found dead in her home on Fuller Street. *Wasn't Fuller Street the same street where Blake met his death?* And as if Denver Grey had heard her question, he confirmed that Blake Montgomery was also murdered on that very street, nearly in front of the latest victim's house, last Sunday.

"Foul play, yet to be determined by autopsy, seems to be the culprit of this latest fatality," Denver continued.

But that wasn't what made Margo gasp, clutch her chest, and hope that what she heard was not true. The victim's name was given as Marsha Wilson whose daughter, Ebony, worked for Myles and Associates owned by Jefferson Myles. Coincidently, Blake Montgomery was Jefferson Myles' next-door neighbor. No connection had been made between the two murders.

Margo couldn't believe her ears and wasn't sure she trusted the information that had just come forth. She exhaled and all of today's activities came to the forefront of her thoughts. Petrowski knew something—something more than the letter he had given her to read. It was in the way he probed her mind with X-ray vision, hoping she'd shed some light on a few facts he might have held. Poor Ebony; she'd call her tomorrow.

A tire screeched. Margo rushed to the window, the window she had peered out of at least ten other times tonight. It was eleven-thirty p.m. Margo saw Linda emerge from her white Honda, quickly look toward Margo's house, then turn back, apparently looking for the house keys that were probably at the bottom of her purse. Then Margo noticed the flowers—could have been roses. It was hard to tell from her position, but she wouldn't get the chance to find out since Linda was now in the house. Margo had no plans to enter that house again.

Margo moved from the window and paced the floor. *I wonder how long it will be before Jefferson comes home?* He was probably giving Linda time to get home and get settled, putting as much time and distance as necessary between their arrivals. It was the 30th of December, and many things were about to change.

It was twelve-thirty a.m. when Jefferson finally arrived home. Margo lay on the couch in the family room, waiting to watch the late-night viewing of *Oprah*. They were going to announce the "Book of the Month." Margo was a faithful book club member.

Jefferson heard the sound coming from the television, but he walked toward the staircase rather than follow the noise. Margo had been waiting on him for more than seven and a half hours, and tonight someone was going to tell her the truth, part of the truth, or something. There was going to be no more waiting until the morning to discuss what was ailing them. The time was now.

"Is that you, Jefferson?" Margo called out.

"Yeah Margo. I'm going up to bed."

"I've been waiting for you to come home. Did you get my messages? I've been trying to contact you all evening."

Jefferson came in the room where Margo now sat at attention, with something most definitely on her mind.

"Look, Margo, I've had a long day and just want to

get some rest. By the time I got your message, it was eight-thirty p.m. I was on the way to a client's house."

"Well, I have had a very long day also, Jefferson…a long and quite interesting day, in fact."

"Where are the kids?"

"Ivy went to Raleigh tonight with her girlfriends." Margo didn't miss the twitch of his eye. "Winter and Winston are still out with their friends, finalizing plans for tomorrow's celebration."

"I see. Sorry about dinner. You should have called Angelica. She would have loved to dine with you."

Margo looked Jefferson straight in the eyes. "What kind of statement was that? Are you implying that you don't enjoy dining with me? I haven't spoken with Angelica in a few days. She went out of town."

"I don't want to argue tonight, Margo. Why don't we just go to bed?"

"You've already been to bed."

Jefferson watched Margo intently, tried to feel his way through the bits and pieces she kept feeding him. With hands on her hips, Margo continued on her soapbox, not giving Jefferson an opportunity to respond.

"I guess I don't deserve any flowers, although I've put up with your behind for the last twenty-five years. No, let me correct that. I've loved you with all my heart and soul for the last twenty-five years. But I guess it wasn't good enough for you, huh? The thrill is gone, right, Jefferson? I don't move you like I used to?"

Margo went to Jefferson and brushed up against him, her firm breasts and extended nipples protruding through the thin, pale, blue chiffon camisole. Jefferson pushed her away, but Margo grabbed his face in her hands and tried to plant a hard kiss on his lips. Jefferson pulled away.

He looked at Margo for the longest time, unable to conceal his engorged member that responded to the sight of his beautiful wife. Her skimpy underwear defined every heavenly curve on her well-manicured body—a confectioner's delight. He just stood there.

"I guess Linda Montgomery has the right combination that unlocks your passion and love."

Jefferson continued to stand in the middle of the room. For sure, this was the downfall of man—a woman, a beautiful woman clad in next to nothing, revealing her total self in humble submission. However, the woman before him was not to be played. She would readily give him all that she possessed and become his slave—slave to the generous master who would have been eager to give all.

But he held a secret, and she must have gotten a whiff of it. He was dumb-founded, not quite sure what Margo knew. Was she playing his bluff, trying to get him to admit to what she may have only speculated, or did she have knowledge of his affair with Linda?

"Nothing to say in your defense, Mr. Myles?" Margo was not ready to share her knowledge of Blake's letter.

It would manifest itself soon enough. She wanted to hear from Jefferson's own mouth that he and Linda were a twosome.

"What do you want to know, Margo?" Jefferson asked, sure that he knew but needing confirmation anyway.

"Did you hear anything I said?"

Margo was doing her best to retain her composure, but her tolerance level was at an all-time low. She had had a little more than seven hours to calm down, but she found it difficult to remain civil when something within her kept crying out, *Punish him, punish him.*

"I know that you and Linda are having an affair," Margo continued, "and that it has been going on for some time. I want to understand why, Jefferson, and why Linda? What in the hell were you thinking, and what can she give you that I haven't already given you seven times over?

"You see, Mr. Myles, I know I'm the real deal, and there will never be anyone else that'll be able to satisfy you like *your* sweet, chocolate sistah. I know what I'm talking about, because when the newness wears off, you'll wish you had this vintage behind of mine…vintage, just like those cars you've got outside—made to last a lifetime. Mark my words; she's going to bring you down."

"Yes, Margo, I love Linda—I think."

"You think?" Margo shouted to the rafters. "I don't get you. You're out there making a mockery out of our marriage and all you can say is *I THINK?*"

"Shut up, Margo. I love Linda, and that's that. I want to be with her. We've just been thrown a curve with Blake's death."

Margo slapped Jefferson squarely in the face. "You're sorry…You've been thrown a curve? What in the hell do you think I've been thrown you self-centered, ego-tistical, cheating SOB? A million dollars from Publisher's Clearinghouse or the dream vacation of a lifetime? No you fool, I've been given the vacation from hell, and I do mean vacation because I don't plan to stay long. You can treat me anyway you like, but you and that wench are going to pay, and hell will probably look pretty good to you then."

"Margo…"

"I'm not finished. Did you know that Ebony's mother was found dead tonight?"

Jefferson looked up at the woman who had been his soul mate for the past twenty-something years and nodded his head in the affirmative.

"The news media mentioned that Ebony worked for Myles and Associates whose owner is Jefferson Myles. Said that it was coincidental that you had a connection with both of the victims who were killed on Fuller Street. Do you know how that sounds?" Margo watched Jefferson flinch—trying to hold onto what little respectability he possessed.

"If I can speak now, what else did the media say?"

"They said that there was no connection, at this time,

between the two murders except that one was your neighbor and the other was the mother of one of your employees."

Jefferson sat in the nearest chair. How did he get in this mess? He should have listened to Malik, but it was a little too late for that now. And here's Margo standing in front of him hurling her accusations and exhibiting violent behavior. If she weren't right, he'd probably haul off and knock her out of her misery. He was probably getting what he deserved.

"God, what am I going to do?" Jefferson said out loud.

"What are *we* going to do, Jefferson? If you think I'm going to sit by and do nothing, you're wrong. There will be no you and Linda."

"And what does that mean? I'm sorry, Margo. What else do you want me to say? I've been unhappy for some time, and I'm not going to compromise my happiness any longer. I'll stay as long as I have to…to make sure that things are in order for you."

"Jefferson, I'm not going to give you a divorce. You better tell that wench that it's over, or else."

"Linda and I can have a good life together. We love the same things and have a lot in common. She makes me hap—"

Margo lunged for Jefferson. She couldn't stand it another moment. Jefferson deflected her attempted blow and threw her on the couch.

"I'm not giving up!" Margo shouted between tears. "But know this, you better watch your back because whatever else you're up to, the police have got their eyes on you."

Jefferson stopped cold, turned, and looked at Margo again. He didn't know where she had gotten her information, but he knew that she meant what she said. And Ray was arrested tonight. Jesus, everything was falling all around him. Got to call Malik. He'll know what to do. ...And what did Hamilton mean by "I'd also keep a watch on Ms. Ebony?"

Jefferson stormed from the room, picking up his coat. "I'm going out." He slammed the door.

"Oh, Mr. Myles, it's just beginning," Margo said to the door. She picked up the phone and dialed Linda's number, then thought better of it and put the receiver down.

CHAPTER 30

"**H**amilton, I've been waiting for your phone call," Santiago said, taking a sip of brandy. "Yes, I've seen the news, and now I want to know what you're going to do about it. It was your job to be the eyes and ears of the operation, thwarting off any unwanted threats and enemies, intercepting any messages that would keep us a step ahead of the feds. You've failed miserably, and I don't take kindly to failure.

"What am I going to tell the people who I was supposed to make delivery to tomorrow?" Santiago questioned. "We had a slight delay, our contact called in sick, or that I have idiots working for me? They don't want to hear excuses. They want the merchandise!! You have twelve hours to get it to me." Santiago slammed down the phone. "Idiot."

"Pour me another brandy, sweetheart," Santiago said to his voluptuous, caramel-flavored lover. "Barnes doesn't know who he's messing with."

"Maybe I can be of some assistance."

"How can you help?"

"I've thought of a plan that might just work. I don't foresee getting additional money as a problem, only how we execute it. Jefferson may need a little reinforcing."

"My, my, my. Didn't know I had one of my biggest assets right under my nose."

"I want to make sure these diamonds continue to sparkle on my arms and fingers."

"Give me a kiss, sweetness. We're going to have a long future, and I'll see to it that you have everything you ever want and need."

Their tongues tasted each other and their bodies lay exposed upon the Persian rug in the light of Santiago's favorite room—the light shining through the dome of beveled glass that sparkled like crystal.

The tires on the Mercedes Kompressor burned rubber and left a three-foot-long tire track in the driveway. Jefferson couldn't believe the turn of events. All hell was breaking loose.

First Linda, then Margo, and if that wasn't enough, Ray was arrested along with the stolen weapons that cost him two hundred-fifty thousand dollars—money he had funneled—no stolen—from the accounts of clients who depended upon him and held him in the highest esteem. Now he wouldn't get paid—the money gone.

He had to talk to someone. Just like his life, his wife, and possibly his lover, he might lose everything.

Jefferson tried calling Malik again, not succeeding on his first ring. He let the phone ring until Malik's answering service picked up. He tried Malik's cell phone, but no answer there, either. Must be a night out on the town with Toni.

Jefferson continued driving toward Ft. Bragg. Maybe he could make it to the NCO Club before they made the last call for alcohol. He needed a drink. It would probably take two or three of the watered-down variety they served at the NCO Club to make him feel good. Who cared? It would give him time to think things out. It was going to take a lot of thinking.

As he neared his turn onto Reilly Road, Jefferson's cell phone rang. "Malik is on time, didn't want to sit in the bar by myself, anyway," Jefferson murmured to himself.

But upon viewing the digits on his caller ID, he clicked the "Off" button and turned into the driveway of the NCO Club. He didn't have anything to say to Hamilton. Operation Stingray was Barnes' baby, and he needed to handle it because Jefferson T. Myles was finished.

He ordered three rum-and-Cokes that seemed to be more watered down than he remembered. Better yet, the bartender sensed him, and was making sure Jefferson wasn't going to drown his sorrows from the counter of his bar. Jefferson needed to be alone, although he spotted a couple of sexy sisters who might have some intelligent conversation and maybe a dance or two so he could knock the rust from his dancing shoes.

He really wasn't good company and the longer he sat, the more depressed he became. What was he going to do without the money? He surely couldn't dip into the accounts. He knew that Santiago probably wanted that shipment, come hell or high water.

Last Friday was a prime example. They were late with the shipment and Santiago's contact couldn't stay put. They were penalized for their tardiness and had to come up with the extra cash to move the weapons to a new drop-off point. Then Santiago demanded a new shipment for the following week. Certainly after last week's fiasco, Santiago was not going to be nice.

I can't do this anymore, he thought. But Jefferson knew the noose around his neck would not be cut unless they were removing his body from it.

"Damn," he said aloud, causing some to look in his direction.

Jefferson turned around when he heard a familiar voice call out his name. Oh, she was a welcome sight. She put her index finger to her lips, admonishing him not to speak, only gaze.

"How are you?" Angelica whispered. He looked as if he needed a friend, if only for one night.

"Fine…no, lousy," came Jefferson's reply. He wished his intake of alcohol had mellowed him out. It did nothing for him and his blues still hung on him like the aroma of a breakfast meal eaten five hours earlier from a mom-and-pop establishment.

"Wanna dance?" she asked, not believing her good fortune.

"Yeah, I need to try out my dancing shoes. Maybe I can dance off some of this funk."

And he had them, she observed. "Okay, let's do this."

They made their way to the dance floor, losing themselves in the lure of the beat. Then Erykah Badu's "Bag Lady" resounded throughout the club, slowing things down. Jefferson knew that this was his song. He was definitely carrying a lot of garbage and needed to get rid of it. Jefferson looked at his dance partner and begged off, but she had a better offer.

"Why don't you come home with me?"

"You can't be serious…"

For the second time in one night, the silent finger went to her lips, and Jefferson relaxed, took a deep breath and said, "Let's go."

CHAPTER 31

I t was the 31st of December, the last day in 1999, and the last day of the twentieth century. There were to be celebrations all over the world, unprecedented by any other event like it. There were reports that terrorists might seize the opportunity to attack America, especially in the wake of the World Trade Center bombing. Authorities had already cancelled planned festivities in Seattle.

The last day in the year of 1999 was going to be a gorgeous one, although Margo doubted she'd enjoy it much, especially after a rather sleepless night. She was awake most of the night and early morning wondering if Jefferson would come home. It was almost becoming a routine weekend thing, with Jefferson a no-show on Friday night. This weekend had a slight curve in the story. Margo exposed Jefferson's unfaithfulness, and he chose the door.

As Margo prepared to get up and start her day, yesterday's event flashed before her like unwanted paparazzi, blinding their subject with a one-hundred watt bulb—photographing a memory that seemed destined to be with her for the rest of her life. She had some unfinished business. And she was going to make certain that all items on her priority to-do list, which amounted to two things, were completed.

Linda saw Margo move nervously toward her as she stepped outside to retrieve the daily paper. Maybe it was in the way she moved, the sway of her hips that sounded the alarm. Margo's body language was serious, and a smile had yet to part her lips.

"Hey, Margo, nice day for a New Year's Eve celebration," Linda charged, wanting to be the first to speak, guilt on her like white on rice.

"For some it might be."

"You all right?" Linda asked, sensing Margo's mood.

"I'm fine, Linda."

Not looking at Margo, she forced the next sentence from her mouth. "You and Jefferson have plans for New Year's?"

"You beat me. That was my next question to you."

Linda looked at Margo quizzically. *What in the hell is she talking about?* Margo noticed her look of confusion.

"Maybe I need to clarify or, better yet, restate my question." Linda struggled to look Margo in the eyes.

"Do you and Jefferson have plans for New Year's? And don't look at me as if you don't know what I'm talking about, you stupid bitch. You smile in my face, eat from my table, and act like you don't have a clue to what I'm talking about. I just want you to know, you no-good cheatin' heifer," Margo continued, snapping her fingers and making imaginary geometrical designs in the air, "I have found you out. Oh yeah, I've got your number."

"Look, Margo, I'm going in the house now. I don't know what you're talking about, and until you calm down, you and I can't have a conversation."

"Oh-h-h, no, no, no, no. You're not getting off that easy. You act as if you're the epitome of this neighborhood with your self-righteous, pious-acting self. But I'm here to serve you notice that if I catch you with my husband, within two feet of him, I'll beat you down like a carpenter with a hammer."

"I've had enough, Margo. You come over here with your unfounded accusations—"

"Unfounded, you say unfounded? Then tell me you were not with my husband last night and the Friday before that. It probably killed poor Blake."

"Shut up, Margo. You leave Blake out of this. My husband is dead!" Linda shouted, moisture forming in the corner of her eyes.

"It's a little too late for that, Miss Linda. You see, Blake wrote me a letter telling me how he followed you and Jefferson to a motel last weekend before he died."

Margo watched Linda's face turn ashen white. She knew she had her now, and she was ready to reel the fish in. Linda stood there in an apparent state of shock.

"Yes, I know about your emails, your rendezvous—especially last Friday. But I have another piece of news for you. Blake never was able to mail the letter to me. The police found it on him when he was killed last Sunday. Some strange coincidence, huh?"

"Margo, you're a liar. You're trying to make everyone as miserable as you."

"Miserable? Who said I was miserable? Did Jefferson tell you that? You still have not answered my question."

Linda shook her head at Margo. She'd never seen her like this, but she understood why. Just surprised how she found out, if what she was saying was true.

As if confession was good for the soul, Linda blurted out, "Yes, I was with Jefferson, Margo. We love each other, and I believe we can have a wonderful life together."

Margo's eyes glazed over, and she slapped Linda across the face. "How is it that you think you're going to have a life with Jefferson when I'm the one who's married to him? You crazy bitch! The only kind of life you're going to have is a miserable one from having to look over your shoulder every minute of your days, wondering when I'm going to strike next. I'm going to be your worst nightmare. You see, I'm not only a woman scorned, I'm a black woman scorned."

The tears came rushing down. Margo stumbled back to her house, all the while pointing back at Linda, admonishing her to watch her back. Linda stood dumbfounded, occasionally rubbing her cheek, with the newspaper still laying at her feet.

CHAPTER 32

Margo plopped into the nearest chair, trying to turn her faucet of tears off. It hurt her more to know that her dear friend and her husband were having an affair under her nose. It hurt badly, and to think she had to find out from the grave.

She must call Angelica. She needed a shoulder to lean on, someone to keep her sane, to be her sounding board. Yes, Angelica should be back in town; said she would be gone a few days.

Margo dialed Angelica's number and let it ring. Finally, she heard a familiar voice on the fourth ring.

"Hey, girl. How have you been?" Angelica asked.

"Fine, no awful. Got a minute?"

"You know that I always have time for my girl, but right now is not such a good time."

"Oh-h-h," Margo said, with a hint of recognition of the situation in her voice. "You got a b-o-o-t-y call?"

"Well a, yeah…something like that."

"You don't have to be coy with me. I'm your sister girlfriend, and I know the deal."

"Right," Angelica whispered, not wanting to disturb her groove. "Talk to you later."

"Okay."

"So my girl is already celebrating," Margo murmured to herself. "Good for her."

Margo rose from the chair and decided to make herself a cup of tea. Tea seemed to have that soothing power, a power that allowed her to believe everything would be all right. After putting the cup of water into the microwave, a vision of Jefferson radiated in front of her—him reaching out to stroke her swollen face, swollen from the tears shed because of his betrayal, infidelity and love lost. He even seemed to say everything would be all right again.

Margo closed the door and set the microwave on one minute. She didn't want Jefferson to touch or pity her. She wanted him to denounce his love for Linda and tell her that this nightmare was a big mistake. She wanted to hear that Linda had come on to him, and after much resistance, he had succumbed. She wanted to believe that so badly.

Margo's thoughts were abruptly interrupted by the microwave and telephone simultaneously. She reached for the phone, wondering if it was Jefferson.

"Hello, Mrs. Myles?"

"Yes," Margo said. "Is this Ebony?"

"Yes, it is. May I speak with Mr. Myles?"

"He's not here right now, Ebony. Is there anything I can do for you? I'm so sorry about your mother."

"Thanks, Mrs. Myles." Ebony sighed. "She's probably in a better place," Ebony said half to herself. "Would you please ask Mr. Myles to give me a call at home? I would appreciate it very much."

"I will, Ebony. Let me know if there's anything I can do for you."

"I will."

They hung up the phone. *So much tragedy*, Margo thought. *First it was Blake, then Ebony's mother. Can't believe their deaths happened at almost the same place. Just coincidence.*

Before Margo could exhale, the phone rang again, making her want to take it off the hook. *Winter, Winston, and JR must be taking luxury naps this morning*, she thought, since no one other than herself moved to get the phone.

"Hello, Myles' residence," Margo said, irritated at the intrusion.

"Margo, this is Hamilton. Sorry to bother you so early in the day."

"Well, well, I haven't heard your voice in a while except on TV...when our neighbor, Blake, died."

"Yeah, it's been a while. Look, is Jefferson there? I need to talk to him right away."

"Well, you are out of luck because I haven't seen

Jefferson since late last night, and then it was only for a minute." Now she had said it. Put Jefferson's business, whatever it was, in the street.

"Do you happen to know where he is?"

"Have you tried his cell phone? You might have better luck with that, although I haven't had any. Sorry, I couldn't be of any more help."

"Thanks anyway."

CHAPTER 33

Jefferson looked at his watch. It was nine a.m. He could not believe the night he'd had. He wasn't sure how an evening gone bad materialized into one he wouldn't forget. Now he had to get out of the place that had provided comfort and cover for the last seven hours. He needed to check his messages.

There were several calls from Hamilton, including one that had been received only minutes earlier. There was a message from Ebony who needed to speak with him urgently. His boy, Malik, had called. He'd call Malik first, once he was outside the confines of Angelica's place.

"Breakfast?" questioned the magical voice of his midnight enchantress. She was clad in a short green and lavender silk robe that hung loosely around her shoulders, exposing her ample breasts, even though a thin belt made of the same material was very casually tied around her waist. Strong, honey-glazed legs extended beyond the hemline of the robe for Jefferson's further viewing pleasure. A pair of green satin slippers cushioned the soles of her feet.

The beauty of her shapely, hourglass legs transfixed

Jefferson, and it took everything in him to resist any further temptation. First Margo, now his mistress of the night. Who would have thought Angelica would come to his rescue? He had held out the white flag one time too many, and he was not going to surrender this time.

"No, I've really got to go. I've got a busy day ahead."

"You'll need nourishment for all of that. Go take a shower. You'll feel better and breakfast will be ready when you're finished."

"I guess you're right. Anyway, who in their right mind would turn down an offer like that? In fact, who would turn you down?"

"Alright, go and get cleaned up," she said, patting him playfully and shooing him into the shower.

Alone, it took Angelica only several minutes to scan through Jefferson's cell messages. Hamilton was definitely afraid, she surmised, noting the number of calls he'd made to Jefferson. *I need to veer Jefferson in the right direction.* Who would have thought she would strike gold as she did? Her luck was certainly running high.

The plate of eggs, ham, grits, and toast was inviting, and Jefferson wasted no time consuming all that was set before him. He followed it with a few gulps of orange juice that must have been freshly squeezed. Jefferson noticed that his host hadn't eaten a bite.

"Not eating?" he quipped.

"I'll eat a slice of toast in a minute. I'm enjoying watching you eat."

"I guess I was famished, and now I feel a little sleepy. I really need to be going, but I might have to hang out a few more minutes."

"Relax. I wasn't going anywhere at the moment."

"Not going to celebrate the new year?" Jefferson asked, his speech beginning to slur.

Before Angelica could say another word, heavy breathing replaced unwanted, unsolicited small talk as Jefferson fell into a deep sleep. She seized the moment to browse through all of Jefferson's belongings. Nothing of any real significance. A receipt for a dozen red roses from Dale's Florists, another for a couple of banana splits from Dairy Queen, and oops, a hotel receipt dated yesterday, December 30th.

Must not have stayed long, because she found him at the NCO Club at one a.m. Who was she? How could he so easily accept an invitation to her house after what seems to obviously have been a lover's rendezvous? He was a married man, although she had lured him home. But it was all business—her mission possible. And if she took slight advantage of the situation, oh well. She'd put it on her expense report under entertainment.

She continued digging, and then she spotted it—what appeared to be access codes. She copied the information and placed the other back in Jefferson's wallet. Santiago would know what to do.

Jefferson's cell began to ring.

She raced over to retrieve it from its resting place

and moved to another room, not wanting to arouse Jefferson from his slumber. She pressed a button and the caller's frantic voice was the next voice she heard.

"Jefferson?" the caller shouted.

The phone lay at her ear, but she did not respond.

"Jefferson, what's up with you? You think this is just my problem? It's our problem. Santiago gave us only twelve hours to complete this operation, and seven of those hours are gone. Are you reading me? Well, say something."

She hit the disconnect button. The phone rang again, but she ignored it, turning it completely off.

So Hamilton desperately needs Jefferson to accomplish the mission. She'd help him make that happen.

CHAPTER 34

Saturday morning, December 31st. Ebony and Katrina sat in the comfort of Ebony's condo. The sisters sat holding hands, most of their tears shed for the moment. Their mother had been taken from them so savagely. Marsha may not have been able to boast Mother-of-the-Year, but she was their mother and she loved her girls. She tried to do right by them, and they both turned out all right. Ebony was a secretary at a well-established financial planning/brokerage firm while Katrina worked as a counselor at Fayetteville State University. While Ebony was the oldest, Katrina could hold her own.

They had to make preparations to bury their mother. It would be a small funeral, more than likely held in the mortuary's chapel. Their mother had one brother who lived in New York. There was not much else in the way of relatives. Ebony would ask Ivy Myles to sing. She had a beautiful voice.

Something else bothered Ebony. It was the envelope. It was clear to Ebony that Broadnax knew nothing about the envelope that detailed the unusual client account activity she believed was made by Jefferson. Broadnax wanted to talk and she would give him a chance. Right now, she wanted to talk with Jefferson. Too many unexplained coincidences. She believed Jefferson was caught in the thick of it.

The girls removed their hands from each other upon hearing the doorbell. Neither was interested in any company, but went to the door since their visitor seemed awfully persistent.

Ebony peered through the peephole, recognizing immediately the visitor who sought to gain entrance. She looked at him thoughtfully, thought she saw him wink. "He must be here because of Momma." She opened the door.

"Good morning, Ms. Wilson," Captain Petrowski said. Taking off his cap, he gave Ebony a faint nod.

"Good morning, Captain," Ebony said very curtly.

"May I come in? I'm investigating your mother's death."

Ebony moved aside and allowed him to enter. Katrina sat, not bothering to move or acknowledge Petrowski's presence.

"This is my sister, Katrina."

Captain Petrowski nodded again. He sat on the imported, Italian leather love seat while Ebony joined Katrina on the matching couch. Petrowski crossed his legs and made himself comfortable, as he looked around.

The living room was warm, decorated with modern

furnishings. Candles of various sizes stood on wooden pedestals throughout the room. There were two rather large art deco paintings on the wall. The paintings reminded Petrowski of several frescos he purchased for his wife a few years earlier.

"I wish to express my condolences to the both of you," Captain Petrowski began.

The girls gave a faint nod.

"I have only a few questions and won't take much of your time. Can you give me a list of your mother's friends or associates with whom she would be in frequent contact? Any enemies?"

"My mother had frequent male visitors," Katrina began. "We couldn't begin to know who they all were—"

"While my mother," Ebony interrupted, giving Katrina the evil eye—no need of putting their mother's business in the street, "may have had a few visitors, she had two close friends— Virginia Ross who lives a few doors down, and June Perry. I will say also that one of your own, Lieutenant Hamilton Barnes, used to frequent my mother's house a lot. In fact, he was over there a couple of days ago on the pretense of getting information about the other murder."

Petrowski sat upright at that news. He recalled how Barnes seemed to hover over Ebony after Marsha's body was found.

"By other murder, do you mean Blake Montgomery?"

"Yes."

"When you said Lieutenant Barnes came on pretense, just what did you mean?"

"I went to visit my mother the day after Lieutenant Barnes had been to see her, and when I arrived, I saw this skimpy little sexy number that used to be mine on the back of a chair. Since my mother had been in a slump—not getting out much or taking care of herself like she should, I was amazed to see the little snappy number laying out."

"What does that have to do with Lieutenant Barnes?" Captain Petrowski queried.

"I'm getting to it," Ebony continued. "I asked my mother what she had been up to and she told me that Lieutenant Barnes had come by to question her, and then one thing led to another."

"Just what do you mean by 'one thing led to another'?"

"Do I have to spell it out? SEX. S-E-X. Lieutenant Barnes used to be a frequent visitor to my mother's home."

Katrina twisted her head in Ebony's direction and gave her a sharp look with her piercing eyes. She couldn't believe Ebony, after she had slapped her earlier with a nasty stare for divulging too much information. Captain Petrowski stared at the sisters, trying to digest what he had just heard. He made a notation in a small leather book he took from his pocket. When he finished, he laid his pen down and looked up at Ebony.

"What about Sergeant Carl Broadnax of the same police station who found your mother?"

"I don't know him. Yesterday was the first time I had met him. He seemed genuinely concerned about my mother's well-being."

"Is there anything else the two of you can think of that might help us in our investigation?"

"Well, there is one other thing," Ebony continued. "When I was visiting my mother that day, she gave an indication that she might have seen something in conjunction with the first murder. She didn't come right out and say—she sort of hinted at it."

Captain Petrowski looked toward Katrina who did not part her lips.

"Well, good day, ladies. I thank you for your help. If you should think of anything else, here's my card. Please call." And he was gone.

"And who do you think you are, silencing me? And then had the nerve to turn around and make Momma look like a whore in front of that white man?" Katrina lit into Ebony. "You don't know everything. Momma's killer is out there, Ebony. Everyone is a suspect until they find the perpetrator."

"Are you finished, Katrina? I know what I'm doing, and Captain Petrowski has the information he needs." Ebony had a gut feeling about things. She caught the action between Sergeant Broadnax and Lieutenant Barnes. *Something was not right. Lieutenant Barnes was too clingy; I've got to talk to Sergeant Broadnax.*

I'm going to save my boss for last. Ebony knew she was

on to something—didn't have all the pieces to the puzzle, but she believed it started the day Blake Montgomery died or even before. But she had to find that package, and she believed she knew who had it.

"Katrina, I'm going to get to the bottom of this. I owe it to Momma."

"I'm sure you will." Katrina sighed.

CHAPTER 35

Hamilton hadn't had an ounce of sleep. Where could Jefferson be? He had tried relentlessly to get in touch with him. He needed two hundred-fifty thousand dollars to secure the guns. He visited Ray, using his badge as cover, to obtain the names of the contacts, so he could secure the additional arsenal. But he needed Jefferson, because these guys were not going to release anything until they were paid in full. They had further stipulated that there would be no additional supply for at least another six months because of possible troop deployment. The contacts were risking their necks obtaining the additional merchandise.

Jefferson, please call.

Hamilton hadn't had this kind of anxiety since he dated his first girlfriend. The two really couldn't be compared, because his life now could hang in the balance. He knew he was expendable, but before that happened, someone else would pay.

Why did he give both Sergeant Walters and Broadnax the day off? Although Sergeant Craig had sat in many times for Broadnax, he didn't feel good leaving him in charge, but he needed to go out.

"Sergeant Craig, I need to make a few rounds. Should be back in an hour."

"Okay, Lieutenant. I've got it covered."

"Okay. Any emergencies, radio me."

"Okay, Lieutenant."

Hamilton walked out into the brisk air. Something was a little unsettling. Tonight there would be celebrations all over; some of the celebrating had already gotten underway. He hoped he'd be here to enjoy the year 2000.

A slight vibration caused Hamilton to reach down and pull his cell from its holder. "Damn, it's Santiago."

"Hello, Hamilton," came Santiago's voice before Hamilton could say a word.

"Yes, Robert."

"How are we doing down there?"

"It'll be ready. Just a few minor glitches."

Santiago passed on the location of the new drop-off point. "Three hours."

"I hear you, Robert." *Click. I've got to get the money. Please call, Jefferson*, Hamilton prayed.

Santiago laughed to himself. His sweetness would soon give him what he needed.

"God, what time is it?" Jefferson asked. "I feel like I've been asleep for hours."

"It's ten a.m., and time for you to get up. You were sleeping so well, I couldn't bear to wake you."

"Margo. Oh, God. What am I going to tell her?"

"Shh. Don't work yourself into a frenzy. Relax a minute, and then if you gotta go…"

"I really enjoyed this, Angelica. Maybe we can get together again. It's been a while, but I haven't completely forgotten."

"Well, maybe we can do it again sometime. Right now, maybe you better get going."

"Yeah, you're right. I might be right back."

"I'm going to be out for a good while, so if you should return, I'll leave a key under the mat. I'll tell security at the front gate to let you pass. Help yourself."

"Thanks." And she covered his lips once again with her finger.

CHAPTER 36

The morning slipped by fast. Margo already entertained a serious headache after her altercation with Linda. "I should have beat her down," Margo said out loud.

"Beat whom down, Mom?" Winter asked, yawning with a puzzled look on her face.

"Someone who deserves it," Margo replied, not offering any more information.

"Without a doubt, Mother."

"Don't worry your pretty little head over it. Are you all ready for the big celebration tonight?"

"Yes, and it's going to be slamming, too. What are you and Dad doing?"

"Probably nothing. We'll watch all the excitement on TV."

"Where's Dad? Missing again?"

"What do you mean by that, Winter?" Margo responded rather harshly.

"Lighten up, Mom. Ivy seems to think Dad might be running around. I think she's crazy myself, but she says she's got the goods."

"Where would she get a crazy notion like that?"

"Dad didn't come home last night, did he?"

"Answer my question, Winter. Where did Ivy get an idea like that?"

"She called me last night with some crazy story about seeing Dad when she was on her way to Raleigh."

"Was he with someone, Winter?"

"She didn't just come out and say it, but I gathered he must have been."

"Did she say it was Linda Montgomery?"

"Mrs. Montgomery next door?"

"One and the same."

"Mom, you can't be serious."

"Since you seem to know so much, yes, I'm serious. I spoke with her this morning. Seems they love each other, or as your father put it, 'he thinks.'"

"Shudda beat her down, Mom. Want me to go and do it?" Winter shouted. "She's not going to get away with this."

"Shh, let's not make an announcement, okay," Margo cautioned.

"This is war. Her husband may have just died, but she just signed her death warrant."

"That's enough, Winter. There's more. I found out from the police that Blake Montgomery left me a letter. He suspected your dad and Linda of having an affair. He followed them on several occasions and was able to verify his suspicions."

"My God, and right under our noses!"

"Yeah, and your dad might be involved in something else. I have this strange feeling."

"Like what? It can't be worse than sleeping with… Oh-h-h, this makes me sick. And worse yet, she comes parading over here like she's Miss Innocent. I'm ready to go off on somebody."

"Your father is to blame, too. He's going to fall…"

"Look, Mom, I don't have to go tonight. You don't need to deal with this by yourself."

"Like I told Ivy, go and have a good time. There will be tomorrow, and I'll need you then."

"No, I'm not going…"

"What did I say? Go and have fun with your friends. You'll be going back to school soon; so enjoy this time."

"Mom, are you sure? I don't want to leave you, especially in the state you're in. I'll tell you this. Dad's going to have to answer to all of us."

"He's only got to answer to me and God. Now, don't go sticking your nose where it doesn't belong. I can handle your daddy."

"Alright, Mom." Winter backed off, but she turned around at the last minute and looked longingly at Margo. "I love you."

"I love you, too."

Winter hugged Margo for what seemed an eternity. "I've got your back, Mom."

"I know." And Margo smiled.

Margo sat in the kitchen, sipped on her second cup of tea and thought about her conversation with Winter. She looked at the kitchen clock; it was eleven a.m. Where did the time go?

Jefferson hadn't called, but she barely cared. His wrongdoing would be exposed soon enough. And he'd probably have nerve enough to ask for forgiveness. She might welcome him back, but he'd have a long road to hoe, and forgiveness wouldn't come easy.

Lost in her thoughts, Margo was suddenly brought back to earth with the ring of the phone. That seemed to happen a lot lately.

Margo reached for the phone but was not ready to hear Linda's voice so soon.

"Please don't hang up, Margo," Linda pleaded.

"Why shouldn't I? You are now the enemy," Margo responded.

"I understand, and you have every right to hate me."

"So why are you calling? To offer me some friendly advice on how to get over Jefferson or to tell me he came on to you and you tried to resist time after time after time? What is it, Linda? Tell me."

"Margo, I believe Jefferson may be indirectly involved in Blake's murder."

Margo's ears perked up. "I overheard him this evening

talking to someone about a guy named Santiago and something going wrong. Yes, I was with Jefferson last Friday night, and we went to Richmond Heights. There were these suspicious characters, even a guy toting what appeared to be a machine-gun. Some kind of transaction took place, and Jefferson was in the middle of it. I was scared as hell."

"Why tell me now? That's what you get for being where you shouldn't have."

"I think Jefferson may be in serious trouble," Linda said, ignoring Margo. "It was the way he was acting. I called it off tonight, or otherwise—"

"You'd be with him?"

"Maybe."

"Doesn't excuse anything. Why haven't you gone to the police with this information?"

"I do care for Jefferson."

"Bitch!" Winter screamed, listening on the phone.

"Get off the phone, Winter. Now!"

The phone clicked, but Margo offered no apologies for Winter's outburst.

"I just wanted you to know what I knew," Linda began, "…in case the police do question me again."

"And what are you going to tell them?"

"The truth as I know it."

"You would betray Jefferson like that?"

"Blake was my husband!"

"But you temporarily forgot that fact when it was convenient. Jefferson told me he was contemplating divorcing me, but it will never happen."

"You've spoken to Jefferson about us?"

"Yes, he was home briefly…all of five minutes, if that. But I haven't seen him since."

"Maybe he's at Malik's."

"Oh, Malik's, eh? So Jefferson has taken you around his circle of friends. Well, I don't know where he is since I've not spoken with either Jefferson or Malik."

"Margo, I've got to go. I just wanted to share that with you in the event—"

"Don't go now. We're on a roll. Are you going to call the police?"

"No."

"Well, good day." And Margo slammed the phone in its cradle, causing it to fall to the floor. Plastic and metal pieces flew across the floor like an unexpected meteor shower. *The nerve of that woman, who only hours earlier had confessed her love for my husband. Now she's about to rat him out. Serves Jefferson right. Angelica made the break, so can I, if need be. Let me call my girl and see what she's into.*

"Hey girl, you free now?" asked a tickled Margo. Angelica was keeping secrets. "Can't keep girlfriend out in the cold."

"No girl. It really wasn't like that."

"So what was it like, huh?"

"Get out of here, Margo."

"What are you doing tonight in the way of celebrating?"

"More than likely, I'll be going to Durham to a party. Would ask you to go, but I'm sure you and Jefferson have a big night planned."

"Right. I haven't seen Jefferson since twelve-thirty a.m. this morning. Am I worried?"

"What?"

"You heard me, and guess what, Angie? He's having an affair with my next-door neighbor, Linda Montgomery."

"Girl, stop. Not the same Linda Montgomery who fainted in the middle of your living room last Sunday?"

"One and the same."

"Get out of here. What are you going to do? Cuss her out, beat the hell out of her? Girl, I don't believe what I'm hearing."

"Well, believe it. She said she loved him. He told me he thinks he loves her. Don't choke, girl, this is for real. She and I have already had words. Then she had the nerve to call me back later to tell me she believes Jefferson is involved in something that could mean big trouble."

"Big trouble like what?"

"She didn't tell me much. She overheard him talking to someone last night about some kind of trouble. Then she went on to tell me that she and Jefferson were together last Friday. They went to Richmond Heights. That must have been when you saw him. And she said they met up with a sinister-looking bunch. One of them carried a machine-gun."

"My goodness, Margo. Do you think Jefferson could really be involved in something illegal?"

"That's what Linda seems to think."

"What else did she say?"

"She mentioned a name—Sundee, Santee, no it was Santiago. Yeah, that was it."

"Who is that?"

"She didn't say. I don't think she knows, either. I believe she heard Jefferson say his name to whomever he was talking to."

"And guess what else?"

"What, Margo?"

"Linda said she would tell the police the truth as she knows it."

"But what does she know?"

"Nothing. Just a hunch that Jefferson may somehow be indirectly responsible for Blake's murder."

"Get out of here! But we were all at the house when Blake was murdered. How did she come up with that equation?"

"You asking me? I say it serves Jefferson right. You know Angelica, even though you've been married to someone for over twenty-five years, you never really know what lies beneath the veil. I thought I knew my husband. We had a wonderful marriage, four beautiful children, good jobs, traveled all over the world, and now look at us. It boggles my mind.

"Then take Linda Montgomery, this so-called perfect specimen of a friend who I put all of my faith and trust in, the epitome of the loyal neighbor. She was all that I considered to be good in a person. Just goes to show, you can't trust anybody. If you can't trust your best friend, then whom else are you going to trust?

"It saddens me, Angelica, because these were people I trusted so much. I trusted them with my life. I'm so grateful I have you as a friend. I don't know what I'd do without you. This has been hard for me because I've been so trusting. And the one person above all others who I would have laid down life and limb for, has made a mockery out of everything we were as husband and wife. I hope to never lose you as a friend. I guess this is life and I'm learning some of life's hard lessons.

"And all these things people are saying about Jefferson. I can't believe they're true. If he really is dealing with unscrupulous people, why haven't I been able to see the signs? I live right up under him, and there has been nothing, to my knowledge, that would indicate that anything other than our daily lives was happening."

"You didn't know about Linda," Angelica said. "And that was happening right under your very nose. You'll get through this, Margo. And I want you to know, I love you. I hate to leave you hanging, girl, but I've got to go. I'll call you when I get back. We've got some serious talking to do."

CHAPTER 37

Ebony lay sprawled across the bed. She couldn't sleep. Her dreams were so vivid—and she tried to block out Marsha's face.

She reached over and picked up the card that Sergeant Broadnax had given her from the nightstand by her bed. She stared at it and twirled it between her fingers, allowing her subconscious to revisit the scene on Fuller Street after her mother's body had been brought down. There seemed to be something honest about Sergeant Broadnax. She felt it in her heart. He seemed to genuinely care for her mother. She twirled the card again and decided to make the call.

Sergeant Broadnax answered on the first ring—almost as if he anticipated her call. He had a pleasant voice, Ebony thought—deep, with a calmness that was quite soothing.

"Sergeant Broadnax?" Ebony asked.

"Yes, it is."

"Hi, I'm Ebony Wilson, Marsha's daughter." She could hear the surprise in his silence.

"Uh, Ms. Wilson, I'm so glad you called. How are you feeling today?"

"As well as can be expected," she said. "I'll let you know when the arrangements for my mother have been made."

"Thank you. I'd like to pay my respects. You know," Carl continued, more hesitantly than before, "I thought your mother was someone special, even though I only knew her a short period of time—I do mean short. She had a way about her, and I believe she needed someone besides her children who could really love her."

"You realized all of that in just a short period of time?"

"I did. That's why I went back there yesterday afternoon. Was gonna ask her if she wanted to celebrate the New Year…with me." Carl sighed. Again he saw Marsha's blood-soaked body.

Ebony listened thoughtfully and then spoke up. "She was special. She didn't have the opportunity or the chances to make her life right." Ebony paused again, reflecting. "I think you would have made my mother happy."

Sergeant Broadnax was glad Ebony couldn't see him through the phone. He had the broadest smile on his face. If only he'd had the chance to possibly make Marsha happy.

Snapping out of his daydream, Sergeant Broadnax realized Ebony didn't call to see if he had feelings for her mother. "Is there something I can do for you?" he inquired.

"Hopefully, you can," Ebony replied. "If you have a minute today, I'd like to meet with you. I have some suspicions that I'd like to share. I feel that I can speak candidly to you about them."

"I'm off today. Any time would be good for me. Where would you like to meet and what time?"

"Would noon be okay at Mi Casita's on Ramsey Street? I have this sudden taste for Mexican food."

"That would be fine."

"I'd like to bring my sister along, if that's alright with you."

"Sure. That will be fine. Will see you at noon."

"See you then."

Jefferson looked at his watch. It was ten-fifteen a.m. What a morning! He couldn't believe his luck.

He weaved in and out of traffic, not sure where he was going, but he knew he needed to get home. He didn't feel like fighting with Margo, but after the kind of morning he'd had, he felt he could conquer the world.

"Got to make some phone calls," Jefferson mumbled aloud. "Can't avoid them forever."

He decided to call Malik first. After several rings, Malik finally answered. Malik was concerned after he had returned Jefferson's initial phone call and didn't get a response. He tried subsequent times into the wee hours of the morning and still no response.

Jefferson gave Malik the 4-1-1 on all that had transpired. Malik was astonished at Jefferson's revelation and shook his head as Jefferson gave him a blow-by-blow account. Malik felt sorry for Jefferson. There was little else he could say or do to cause Jefferson to see the light of day. Malik had warned, pleaded, and talked until there was nothing left to negotiate. Now Jefferson must face the consequences of his actions. He loved Jefferson like a brother, but Malik wanted no part of his friend's self-destruction.

Realizing that he would not find any solace with Malik, Jefferson ended the conversation. *Some friend,* he thought. But Jefferson knew he couldn't blame his troubles on Malik.

He dialed another number, partly because he was running out of options and needed to know if he had a lifeline left, and because any voice other than Margo's was comforting regardless of the danger he was in.

"Hey, Hamilton…"

"Where in the hell have you been, Jefferson? I've only just called you ten dozen times in the last eight or nine hours."

"Hold it, man," Jefferson said matter-of-factly, trying to bring calm to a very irritated Hamilton Barnes.

"Hold it? What do you think I've been doing for the last ten hours? Even a full bladder has to have release sometime."

"I'm sorry, man. I was detained, and my cell battery was dead," Jefferson lied.

"Where have you been? I spoke to your old lady, and she said she hadn't seen you in a while."

"You spoke to Margo?"

"You do still speak English, right?"

"What did she say, man?"

"She said you weren't there! What's up with you? Oh, you were with your white mistress from the neighborhood. I get it now—and poor Margo still doesn't know."

"She knows. I don't know how she found out. Maybe she suspected and put it all together. After last weekend, she seemed to be ready for me."

"You're completely screwed up, Jefferson. If I had a hot number like that, my radar wouldn't be looking for any more lost ships."

"And certainly you have room to talk…the emperor of whoredom…player of the week," Jefferson roared back. "And for your information, Margo is not a hot number. She's every bit a lady."

"Testy for someone who has the taste of someone else on their mouth."

"Look, I didn't call you to discuss my life situation.

I'm returning your phone call. What did you want?"

"You have an hour and half to obtain two hundred fifty-thousand dollars. The bank closes at noon, which means you only have one hour to have the transaction complete. Santiago is accepting no excuses. By the way, I'll handle the process from this point."

"Absolutely not!!" Jefferson shouted.

"What part of what I said did you not understand, Jefferson? One hour or no excuses?"

"I can't tap into those accounts again. I do not have any guarantee that this will be a successful drop."

"If you don't take care of it, you'll never know. My cell is on, and I better hear from you in fifty-five minutes or less. Got that? …And oh, one more thing. I've got a package you'd be interested in—account transactions."

Silence lay between the two of them. Hamilton didn't wait for Jefferson to respond. "Fifty-three minutes. Can I give that beautiful wife of yours a call since you don't seem to be interested?" And the line was dead.

CHAPTER 38

It was eleven fifty-seven a.m. Ebony was going to be late. If the traffic light would only be kind and allow her car to slide through, she'd be all right. Ahh, she made it. She'd only be a minute late.

She pulled into the parking lot and scanned the area, hoping to get a glimpse of him. Sergeant Broadnax spotted her first, peering through the smoky glass door from inside the restaurant. He didn't want to appear anxious, standing outside and become the topic of an unwanted gossip of lunchtime customers as they strolled into the restaurant. Ebony looked so much like her mother—Ebony the diamond, Marsha the diamond in the rough.

"Hi, Ms. Wilson," Sergeant Broadnax said, opening the door when Ebony approached.

"Hi, Sergeant Broadnax," Ebony replied.

"You can call me Carl."

"Okay, Carl. Sorry I'm late. I tried to be on time."

"Late? Late by a minute?" He chuckled.

"It could mean the difference between life and death," Ebony said in a strained voice.

Carl became somber. If only he had gone to check on Marsha earlier, he might have saved her.

This was the first time Ebony got a real look at Carl Broadnax. Civilian clothing replaced his uniform, but he was a handsome man. He appeared to be in his mid to late forties—a little salt and pepper sprinkled throughout his crew-cut head with more pepper sprinkled along the temples. He stood at least five feet eleven inches in a medium frame with a nice round behind. It must have been the result of all that walking—beating the streets. Most remarkable was the small gap between his slightly protruding two front teeth when he smiled. It was priceless.

Rich, dark chocolate would appropriately describe the color of his skin. Ebony melted when she gazed into his round, medium-brown eyes. Slightly thick lips that were definitely made for kissing sat just above Carl's chin, and a long, slender nose met at the top of his lips, flaring a little at the nostrils.

"This treat is on me," Carl said, retreating from his thoughts. "Where's your sister?"

"She wasn't able to come, so I guess it's you and me."

Carl was glad Ebony had chosen to come to Mi Casita. They ordered the chicken taco salad with plenty of guacamole and sour cream. They picked at their food, prolonging the purpose for their luncheon, neither of them displaying any signs of real hunger. They continued to play with their meals until Ebony suddenly and without warning broke the silence—her eyes looking deep into Carl's.

"How well did you know my mother?"

Carl looked up and put down his fork. She sure was pretty. Her cocoa color and the long, curly lashes that begged him to come near were so much like her mother's. Marsha. And those thin sweet lips that Carl longed to taste made him quiver. He glanced away, unable to keep his thoughts in check.

"As I've said before, I didn't know Marsha but for a little while, a few hours to be exact. I saw a light sparkling in her eyes, a heart big as a watermelon, and a smile to die for. She spoke kindly of her girls that she loved with all of her heart. She'd longed to be the kind of mother they would be proud of. But Marsha was dark inside. She harbored a lot of secrets—secrets that may have cost her life and are possibly connected with the murder of the man in the Explorer."

"She shared that with you even though you just met?"

"I believe your mother sensed that I cared. She sought me out. We laughed and talked so easy-like. I believe she wanted to tell me something...something she wanted someone else to know...Someone who might take the information and do something with it."

"What did she tell you?" Ebony asked. She needed to be sure that Sergeant Broadnax could be trusted, even though her instinct and gut feeling told her that he was all right.

"She hinted that she might have seen someone that I know near the scene of last Sunday's accident-murder. She spoke mostly in riddles."

"Did she mention Lieutenant Barnes?"

Ebony watched Sergeant Broadnax's reaction to her question, although Carl tried to camouflage it.

"She hinted that Lieutenant Barnes may be tied to the murder. I'd rather we not speak about that in public. Marsha was not the only person who suspected that Lieutenant Barnes might be involved in some un-scrupulous activity. I even have my suspicions."

"I believe he killed my mother," Ebony blurted.

Carl looked at her wearily. He wished he had an answer for her. Inasmuch as it could be true, he hoped that Hamilton Barnes wasn't stupid enough to commit such an act. He knew of Barnes' reputation with women and of his sometimes abusive behavior—but to kill Marsha?

"Why do you believe that?" Carl asked.

Ebony moved her lips slowly, formulating her words so Carl would not misunderstand. "Lieutenant Barnes visited with my mother earlier in the week. Asked her all kinds of questions about what she might have seen. After Momma told him she hadn't seen anything, he threatened her. Said he'd take care of her if she'd lied."

"My mother loved Lieutenant Barnes once," Ebony continued. "He would have sex with her and used her to satisfy his lust, and with Momma being so enamored, she allowed it to happen. He even tried to put the make on her the other day." Ebony noticed the disappointment etched in Sergeant Broadnax's face, but she wanted to continue.

"There's more. I believe my boss is also involved somehow. My mother told me she saw the two of them across the street from the house, along with some sinister individuals, the Friday night before that guy was killed. The crazy phone calls and Captain Petrowski's visit to my office aroused my suspicion. My boss may be involved in some type of misconduct."

"Catch your breath, Ebony. So...Captain Petrowski from the Fayetteville Police Department came asking questions?"

"Yes, and I'm not finished. I started checking some of the client accounts— I'm not sure why—but guess what I discovered? I noticed that large sums of money had been taken from several key accounts. I keep ledgers on all transactions, and there were at least ten profile accounts that showed transactions that did not make the ledger. They were all done on the same day."

"Some detective you are! So what did you do?"

"I made copies of these accounts for insurance purposes. Initially, I thought about blackmail, but changed my mind. I needed a safe place to hide them, so I took them to Momma's house and told her to put them up for me. She didn't ask me about the contents of the package.

"I called to check on Momma yesterday, and it was apparent she had someone with her."

"What time was that?"

"About three in the afternoon. I asked her about the package—if she had put it up in a safe place."

"I remember you mentioning something about a package when you came out of the house last evening."

"Yes, that's what I was referring to. When I went back into the house, I searched and searched, but my package was gone."

"…And Lieutenant Barnes was so attentive, wanting to talk with you—to get you by yourself," Sergeant Broadnax interjected.

"That's why I believe it was Lieutenant Barnes who killed my mother. I believe he has the package, too. But there's more to it. I feel it, and the evidence I had points to it."

"Wow. You've been a wealth of information."

"I want it to be more than just a wealth of information, Sergeant Broadnax, excuse me, Carl. I want my mother's death avenged. I'm sure that this information, if given to the right person, will unlock a few doors to find the answers."

"I'm sure you're right. I didn't mean to seem non-chalant about it. I'm a policeman first, and I weighed everything you said carefully. I feel, too, that those responsible should be apprehended—and soon. I'm going to personally see to the handling of this."

Carl stopped, looked down at his plate, and picked up a forkful of chicken and lettuce. Then his eyes met hers, her hands resting on the cleft of her chin. He batted an eyelash, she batted both of hers. He moistened his lips, she licked her teeth.

"You're beautiful, Ebony, but I'm sure you hear that all of the time."

"Not from you." She understood why her Momma liked Carl. He was a little old, but she wouldn't mind going out on a date with him if he should ask. Jefferson Myles was history anyway.

She's a little sarcastic, but I don't mind, Carl thought. "Would you like to go out on a real date? Maybe cele-brate the New Year?"

"Carl, I'm not Marsha. I won't be replacing my mother."

"I know, and I'm looking forward to getting to know Ebony."

"I'm flattered, Carl. I don't know about this evening. Katrina and I will probably spend time together—getting things ready for Momma's funeral. We will have it sometime next week, maybe Wednesday. I'll be free after that time, and I think I'd like to see you again."

"I'd like that also, and forgive me for being inconsiderate. If you girls need anything, let me know. We will catch Marsha's killer."

"Carl," Ebony said thoughtfully, "if you'd like to come by tonight, Katrina and I would be grateful. It doesn't hurt to have a friend or two around." Then she smiled, and he smiled.

"I'll be there at eight o'clock. I'll bring along some refreshments."

"That will be fine."

CHAPTER 39

It was eleven thirty-five a.m. and not a word from Jefferson. Margo knew he was not with Linda. Maybe he spent the night at Malik's. Seems he would have called by now. Why should she care? He was a lousy, good-for-nothing adulterer. Leaving him seemed like a good idea.

Margo decided to get some air, do a little shopping, and maybe get something to eat. She wished Angelica were available. This was their kind of day, but today Margo would have to go it alone.

Got to find out who her new man is. She's trying to keep a well-guarded secret, Margo mused to herself.

"A motor running?" Margo said out loud. She ran in the direction of the sound. She pulled back her kitchen curtains in time to see Linda pull out of the driveway.

"I wonder where she's going. Could she be going to meet Jefferson?"

Just at that moment, the phone rang. "Hello, Myles' residence," she said gruffly.

"Margo, this is Jefferson. I'll be home—"

"What lie is it this time, Jefferson? Probably going to meet your girlfriend who just plowed out of the driveway."

"What girlfriend? I just can't talk—"

"What's wrong with your brain? You know what I'm talking about, your girlfriend just left here."

"Margo, I give up. I'll be at the office, and I don't know when I'm coming home."

"Why bother at all? Every time I turn my back, you push the knife deeper."

"Believe what you want. I've got to go."

"Well go!" Margo hollered into the phone. "Mark my words, Jefferson Myles, you're going to pay for your sins. I can't believe you're disrespecting me like this!"

"Gotta go." And the line was dead.

Margo sat down in the comfort of her kitchen, shaking her head as she began to pray. "Lord, if you're listening, I want you to know that I love Jefferson. I don't know what makes me react this way whenever I hear his voice. Lord, I want my husband back; I can forgive him. It just hurts right now.

"When I think of him and Linda together, it makes me crazy. I know that underneath that exterior, the man I fell in love with, the man who fell in love with me resides. God, give me the strength to endure and have patience with me, because I get a little weak— like I did a few moments ago.

"But I love him so, even though he's confessed his love for someone else. I'm asking You to intercede, God. I know You can work miracles. We haven't come this far down the road to allow this sudden detour to get the best of us. Thank you, God, for listening. I love you."

Jefferson unlocked the door to the office. He relished the quiet and solitude. Today was Saturday, and he expected no one. So much had transpired in the past week, in the last twenty-four hours, and now he had to save his own life. He couldn't take any more money, but what other recourse did he have?

He glanced at his watch. He had twenty minutes to make the transaction. If he didn't do it, it was his death. If he did do it, he was still dead. He was sure to be found out eventually.

What did Hamilton mean, he had a package I'd be interested in? Jefferson found this puzzling. *Nineteen minutes and counting.*

Access was finally given, and once Jefferson entered the code, he'd be able to transfer the money from the accounts. Maybe he should take enough for himself, purchase a one-way ticket to nowhere, and drop completely out of sight. It did sound like a good idea—no more Margo, Hamilton, Santiago...or Linda.

He'd miss Malik and Ebony. He should give Ebony a big bonus. She was a gem, the best office assistant a boss could have.

"I'm finally in."

Jefferson pulled the profile on the first account. "Something's strange here. It appears that a transaction has already taken place—today—in the amount of twenty-five thousand dollars. How could that be?" Jefferson went to the next account and found the same thing, and so on and so on until he came to the tenth account.

"What in the hell is going on?" he shouted at no one. Who could have accessed these accounts? These transactions were made today. *Gotta get Hamilton on the phone. I need to know about that package.* He looked again at his watch. Ten minutes to go.

Jefferson dialed Hamilton's number post haste. Hamilton picked up on the first ring.

"Everything cool, man?" Hamilton asked, excitement in his voice.

"No, it's not cool."

"What are you talking about, fool? Don't you realize our lives are at stake, and we're only nine minutes from 'D' day?"

"What's in the package, Hamilton?"

"The package—what does that have to do with the money we need? Time is ticking."

"Tell me what's in the package!" Jefferson shouted into Hamilton's ear.

"Copies of records from some of your accounts. I found them in Marsha's apartment."

"Marsha's apartment? What were you doing at Marsha's apartment? How do you know the records are from my accounts?"

"To answer your question, I had some business to take care of with the lady. But you have a bigger worry. Those records have your freakin' name, company logo, and address written across the top. Now how did they get in Marsha's apartment? Do I need to be more specific than that? Eight minutes."

"Someone already tapped into my accounts this morning, Hamilton, to the tune of two hundred-fifty thousand dollars."

"Say what?" Hamilton gasped. "I'm sorry about that, Jefferson. I told you to watch Ebony. But you're going to have to access those accounts again. Our lives depend on it!"

"You do what you have to do, Hamilton. I'm not touching those accounts. I need to find Ebony."

"Are you crazy, Jefferson? Do you realize you're signing our death warrant?"

"Is your behind all you care about?"

"Look, Jefferson, why don't you rethink this? Since you're already in too far, what would it hurt to do it one more time? You can replace the money with your cut."

"You slay me, Hamilton. All you can think about is you. I have more at stake. My business and my integrity are already shot to hell. My money will keep you in your lifestyle, and with my share, I'd be only able to hide a portion of my indiscretions. Well, I'm not going to subject myself further."

"Jefferson, you're going to—" Bits and pieces of plastic scattered throughout the room as the phone crashed into the side of the wall.

Jefferson got up and walked the length of the office to Ebony's desk. "No bonus for you," he muttered. "You could have had it all, but now you get nothing."

How did Hamilton get the package, Jefferson wondered. He searched Ebony's desk for any other signs of misconduct. Was Hamilton in Marsha's apartment before she was murdered? Why? The questions ran rampant in Jefferson's head.

He needed to call Ebony. He needed to get to the bottom of this. *Why, Ebony, why? I've been there for you, got you out of jams, hired you when no one else would.* Her phone continued to ring until the answering machine kicked on. Jefferson left a brief message asking Ebony to return his phone call as soon as possible. He tried her cell, but it was conveniently turned off.

He needed Margo. She always made him feel safe. Why had his life turned out the way it did? Although things had been going on for some time, this was the week of reckoning, and it didn't look to be a good new year. *Should've prepared my doomsday kit. A little too late for that now!*

CHAPTER 40

Sergeant Broadnax had enough information to help Petrowski get a search warrant and a possible arrest warrant on Lieutenant Barnes. He needed to call Holly first. There were some things Holly had said which could also possibly implicate Barnes. And there was the sketchy account that the boys on the playground had given him. If Barnes was indeed a corrupt cop, the police needed all the ammunition available. Then, if there were a conviction, he would stay locked behind bars for the rest of his life.

"Where is Holly's number?" Carl stammered. "Oh, here it is; I hope she's home."

Carl stopped to contemplate why he was actually calling Holly. He was getting ready to open a can of worms. If he was wrong, it could be detrimental to their office relationship. He would tread slowly with Holly, only eliciting information, if possible, and not divulging any.

"Okay, take a breath, Carl," he said to himself. "If you're right, you might be promoted to Lieutenant."

❖❖❖

Sergeant Broadnax wasn't the only one daydreaming about replacing sergeant stripes with lieutenant bars. Captain Petrowski had said as much, if Holly would be his eyes and ears. And thanks to Daddy, that just might be a probability.

Holly wasn't a cutesy, pin-up sergeant sitting behind the reception desk. She may have worked a few cross-word puzzles on long stretches from time to time, but she was an observer. Not much passed her by that she didn't make a mental photograph of, paying attention to small detail.

After all, she went to the academy and trained to be a cop—a cop like her grandfather and father before her. She'd do the desk thing for a while, but it wasn't going to be forever. She was going to Fayetteville State in the spring. If she didn't get a position as an instructor at the academy when she was through, there was no way she would remain in Richmond Heights. She'd have some kind of pivotal role as a homicide detective or forensics specialist, instructing a group of recruits on the science of it four times a week. "This female will be a viable force in the police department someday," Holly lamented.

Brring…brring. Holly jumped.

"Hello?"

"Sergeant Walters?" the voice inquired.

"Yes, and…Sergeant B-r-o-a-d-n-a-x, Sergeant

Broadnax, is that you?" recognizing the voice at last.

"It is. I'm glad I caught you at home."

"Well, what do I owe the pleasure of this surprise?" Holly asked.

Carl wasn't sure where he should start, but he knew that he needed to get as much information about yesterday's phone call as possible. It could have been Marsha, and the time of the call could become crucial in apprehending Marsha's killer.

"I need to ask you about the phone call that came in for me yesterday."

"Yes, I remember. It was a woman's voice. The voice was faint and then faded like someone who was in the twilight zone—if you get the picture."

"Yeah, yeah, I get the picture." Carl wasn't amused. "Do you remember what time that call came in?"

"It was shortly before three-thirty p.m.—around three twenty-five to be more exact."

"Are you sure?"

"Yes, because a dispatch call came in right before the call in question, and I logged the time in the log book at three twenty-five p.m. I'm sorry I wasn't able to get anything more."

"My suspicion tells me that that call came from Marsha Wilson…"

"You mean the woman you found dead when you left work yesterday?"

"Yes, I believe she was trying to contact me to let me know she was in trouble."

"Yeah, Lieutenant Barnes turned white as a ghost when he heard you found her. You'd have thought he got caught stealing a million dollars."

"He did, did he? Did he say anything?"

"He asked if I had spoken with you personally and whether or not Fayetteville Police had been dispatched."

"I see."

"Sergeant Broadnax, I don't know if I'm doing the right thing by asking you this question, but after this, I think I must."

"What is it, Holly?"

"Do you think that Lieutenant Barnes might be a corrupt cop?"

"Holly, what would make you say something like that?"

"I knew I shouldn't have said anything."

"No, it's alright. I didn't mean to come off like that. I was surprised by your question, and I'm certainly curious about what may have motivated that question."

"Do you have a minute? I think I need an ally in the office."

"I've got plenty of time."

Holly shared the details of the investigation of stolen weapons from Ft. Bragg, being conducted by the Durham Police Department and the Feds, as given to her by her father. She also divulged that a Fayetteville

Police officer was believed to be linked to the crime, and Hamilton Barnes might be that person.

They had arrested one person involved. The man was caught with the stolen arsenal and happens to be a good friend of Lieutenant Barnes, according to the Feds. Also, they picked up the guy near the site of the last two murders.

Holly went on to tell Sergeant Broadnax how Captain Petrowski had been snooping around, asking questions, admonishing her to keep her ears and eyes open.

"My dad had been in contact with Captain Petrowski. It now appears they have suspected Lieutenant Barnes for a short while.

"Yesterday, I was talking on the phone with my dad about the case when Lieutenant Barnes appeared out of nowhere. He had been out all day. He apparently overheard me talking to my dad about the case and remained planted in the same spot until I finished my conversation. Listen to this. He walked over to me and inquired about my conversation, specifically about Fayetteville cop involvement."

"Have you shared this information with anyone else?"

"Well, uhh, yes—Captain Petrowski. Is that a problem?"

"No, that's fine. I need to share some information with you. I'm even more convinced that Lieutenant Barnes may be more deeply involved than just the arms case."

"What are you trying to say, Sergeant Broadnax?"

"Try double homicide."

"What!" Holly exclaimed. "Are you sure?"

"I'm more than sure, and Holly, I don't want you to talk to anyone about this until we have Lieutenant Barnes in custody. I'm going to call Captain Petrowski as soon as I hang up. I guarantee you our lives are going to be different. If need be, go stay with friends or your parents as a precautionary measure."

"Precautionary measure? What are you saying?"

"I'm saying, if Lieutenant Barnes gets wind of this before he's apprehended, he may come after one or both of us. He has a reputation for violence. If I'm correct, I believe he killed Marsha and may have either killed or indirectly killed Blake Montgomery. I guess I've said that before, but I want to reiterate to you the kind of person we are dealing with. Most of our evidence is circumstantial, but he seems to be the top candidate. The Feds have enough surveillance information to link him to both crimes."

"Oh my God. I think I'll go to my parents' house. I'll feel safe in the company of a police officer."

"Good idea. I'm going to give you my cell number in the event you need to get in touch with me right away. Holly, we need to get scum off the streets even if they are family. But even more so, those who took an oath to uphold and defend the law, and then take it upon themselves to break it, must pay the penalty."

"I understand, and you have my word that I won't say anything."

"Thanks, Holly. Get going."

Sergeant Broadnax did not relish what he was about to do. It frightened him a little, but he had to do it.

CHAPTER 41

"Hey, Sweetie, I missed you."

"Missed you, too."

"Everything go well for you in Fayetteville?"

"Better than I could have ever expected."

"Let's sit so I can look at your beautiful face."

Her tan, cashmere, Donna Karan sweater accented her brown tweed trousers, made for lanky legs like hers, and blended well with the décor in Santiago's favorite room. She looked like one of the many valuable and beautiful treasures that lay throughout the room. Santiago in his crème, lamb's wool jacket and slack ensemble offered the optimum complement.

"You are truly a princess, my love," Santiago said. He took her face by the tips of his fingers and turned her toward him, planting a light kiss upon her lips.

"And you are my prince. I've brought you a priceless treasure. Well, I wouldn't exactly call it priceless, but a treasure nonetheless."

"What is it, my sweetness? Do tell."

She loved the way he spoke to her when they were in their playful mood. She loved the way he made her feel magical. She loved the way he made love to her with the same love and tenderness a mother gives her new-born baby. She was fortunate to have found him. It was divine intervention. One moment she was alone and needing someone and the next, she was picking diamonds from the soles of her shoes.

She hadn't told her best friend about him. Wanted to keep him to herself, because it didn't seem real. She'd been badly hurt by love, and by keeping this a guarded secret, if only for a moment, she could protect herself from scrutiny, especially if things went wrong.

But things were so right. She had everything she needed and then some. Not that life was bad before, except for an abusive husband. She wasn't sure about love, but it was bound to be forthcoming. He adored her. She was crazy about him. She was beautiful, and he could fall in love.

"So what treasure have you brought me, my princess?"

"Oh-h-h, some magic numbers that produce other magical numbers. Let's say, these numbers produced the sum of two hundred-fifty thousand dollars, and I didn't even work up a sweat."

"Oh, you've made the prince very happy, and the prince shall make *you* even happier. Lay with me for a while. I have some very important business I need to attend to."

"You happy?"

"Very happy."

CHAPTER 42

Santiago drew the shades and placed a huge chiffon throw pillow under the head of his sleeping princess. Pleased with her accomplishment of the day, it was time to make the phone call. His time in Durham had been served, and a new venue would be welcomed. The Adams, Barnes, and Myles trio was now expendable, like the sixth digit on a hand.

There was something comforting, even sensual, about sitting in a semi-dark, quiet room preparing to carry out an executive order on demand. The stillness of the moment rendered Santiago intoxicated with his own power—holding the key to life and death. He withdrew his cell phone from the end table with the ornate legs that dripped of gold leaf and dialed the number that would put an end to "Operation Stingray."

"This is Santiago," Robert said, in a hushed whisper once he heard the familiar voice. "It's time. Both Barnes and Myles must be eliminated—quietly. We will deal with Ray Adams later. No fanfare and definitely not on Fuller Street. Other than that, handle it any way you see fit until the job is done. Use the code to notify me that the mission is completed. Once I hear from you, I will call from an undisclosed location and advise you where we will meet. If for any reason the order is not carried out, do not make connection—only if it's an extreme emergency. And, I don't know what that could be. Understood?"

"Understood," was all the voice on the other end said. And the line was dead.

She dozed off, but was slowly awakened when her body realized that it was alone nursing an oversized pillow. She did not stir. But in the stillness, she heard Santiago engage in a mysterious phone call. Although he spoke in a voice that was almost inaudible, the silence throughout the room allowed the alarming words to float to her ears.

There was no misunderstanding the words, "Both Barnes and Myles must be eliminated—quietly." It was imperative that she get out of there and warn them, princess or no princess; two hundred-fifty thousand dollars wasn't enough money to sell out two people who had meaning in her life. If she wanted diamonds, she could afford to buy them herself. She might be signing her own death warrant, but she had to do what she knew she had to do. A tangled web she had woven, and she'd have to use all that was in her to save Hamilton and Jefferson.

CHAPTER 43

Her shades covered half her face. The large scarf that covered her head and draped the back of her neck gave the appearance of a Muslim woman in her ethnic burka—embarking on an important mission.

Linda cautiously looked over her shoulder as if she half expected someone to pounce on her at any moment as she walked to the police station. To the casual observer, she was a funny sight—a foreigner in a strange place bound by the rules of her homeland.

But she was no foreigner in a strange country, only a frightened female on the verge of betraying her lover in order to soothe her guilty conscience. Blake had visited her again, admonishing over and over that she was going to pay for her sins. She didn't need another attack on her psyche to prompt her to call Captain Petrowski.

She told him all she knew, which was not a lot. However, she was able to corroborate previous information that Petrowski held. The Feds weren't much help, almost territorial in their handling of the case. Petrowski wanted any information in his possession to be well worth its weight so that he might obtain the proper credit for it.

The story unfolded into a bizarre scene of lust, greed, and death—two stories merged into one, and by mere happenstance. Petrowski's crime scene board, which once looked like odd pieces of a giant jigsaw puzzle, was assembling nicely. He needed to get the crucial pieces so that he could put it in a frame and call it a job well done. His board looked a little like this:

Middle-class, African-Americans in scheme to purchase guns for a Honduran-American who was helping to back a rebel fundamentalist group in his homeland.

Guns were stolen from a supply arsenal at Ft. Bragg, NC. Inside help. Fayetteville City policeman possibly involved.

Blake Montgomery is killed in Richmond Heights area on Fuller Street. Dark-blue Ford Explorer was riddled with bullets. Montgomery is white, married, and lives in the Jordan Estates subdivision.

House on Fuller Street under surveillance. Reportedly, drop-off point for arsenal of weapons, per reports submitted by Durham Police Department and FBI.

Letter found in Blake Montgomery's personal effects written to Margo Myles, next-door neighbor. Letter contained information about an extramarital affair his wife, Linda, and Margo's husband, Jefferson, were having. Blake followed them into the Richmond Heights area the Friday night before he was killed and observed suspicious activity Jefferson Myles might be a party to. Montgomery was ex-counter-intelligence.

Marsha Wilson is killed five days later in her home, on the same street where Blake Montgomery was killed. Montgomery was killed almost in front of the Wilson house.

Both murder victims were familiar with Jefferson Myles: Montgomery, next-door neighbor; Wilson, mother of Myles' employee, Ebony Wilson.

Ray Adams arrested with arsenal of weapons on Fuller Street, three houses down and across the street from Marsha Wilson's house. Handled by FBI.

Linda felt drained but relieved after purging her soul of details she felt she needed to share with the police. She wasn't totally sure why she was compelled to tell. After all, Blake was dead, and who believed in spirits?

She sat a moment longer, gazing around the room. She hoped she'd receive some sort of assurance that things were going to work out.

"Why did I sell Jefferson out?" she said aloud, but just a little too late. "He's going to hate me." But those voices kept ringing in her head and she had no other recourse but to do what she did.

Petrowski watched her with interest, not sure where she was coming from. Some cases were so cut and dry; and then there was the unpredictable. The players were characters out of a fairy tale movie. Petrowski bet that this case was an obvious candidate for movie-of-the week. He'd like Dennis Franz of *NYPD Blue* to play his character. Franz was so cool.

Petrowski was suddenly taken by surprise by her words.

"May I see the letter Blake wrote to Margo?"

"Letter?" Petrowski repeated, not quite sure she was talking about "the letter."

"Yes, the letter. Margo told me that Blake wrote her a letter that was found with his things. She says that's how she found out about Jefferson and me. Not that I don't believe her, because Jefferson and I did have an affair, but I'd like to see it for myself."

Petrowski weighed her request, then pulled the folder marked "Blake Montgomery." He retrieved the letter and passed it to Linda, who was a little hesitant at first in taking it. But upon opening it, she read the contents intently, focusing on each word.

She looked up at Petrowski when she finished. Meeting his gaze, she said, "Do you think I'm a bad person?"

Petrowski arched his eyebrows and returned her gaze. "Who am I to judge? I don't even know you."

"If I was your wife and cheated on you—and then with a black man, would you hate me?"

"Mrs. Montgomery, I've been happily married to my wife for the past thirty-five years. You aren't my wife, and I'm not planning on straying from mine. What you do is your business."

Linda sighed and sat back in her chair. Petrowski could tell that she was seeking absolution, but she was getting nothing from him. He could also sense her anxiety and thought maybe he should say something.

"Do you feel better that you came here today?"

"Somewhat."

"You want to see your husband's killer apprehended, don't you?"

"Sure I do. But I love Jefferson, and I don't want anything to happen to him. It was those visits from Blake, and these strange feelings I was having."

Petrowski appeared uninterested.

"Even though I don't believe that Jefferson was directly involved in Blake's murder," Linda continued, "he was somehow involved."

"Well, thank you for your time. You have been a great help in this investigation. Can I call if I need to ask any additional questions?"

"That will be fine."

"Have a Happy New Year."

Linda's heart raced as she hurried to her car. No one appeared to notice her, and her only thought now was to go home and lock herself in her room. She did what she had to do, and there was no taking it back.

Petrowski was glad Linda Montgomery was gone. She seemed to be a little touched in the head—talking to spirits and all, but he believed her conscience was kicking her behind. She didn't know how to deal with it. She was somewhat helpful, but Petrowski had another important visitor.

And his information would likely be essential in obtaining the document needed to bring down Lieutenant Hamilton Barnes.

Lieutenant Barnes' history was well known, but he had many allies who shielded his various vices and unscrupulous behavior from the eyes of Internal Affairs. He was about to run out of luck. There would be no court, high or low, that would save his behind if the information he had proved to be right. There was nothing worse than a dirty cop, and Petrowski relished the thought of putting Barnes away. *Ahh, there's the intercom now.*

"Sergeant Broadnax is here," Amy said.

"Thanks, Amy."

"Some New Year's Eve," Petrowski said to Sergeant Broadnax.

"Yeah, and the fireworks are still to come."

The collaborator and the investigator traded information and updated the crime board. A warrant was finally issued for Lieutenant Barnes' arrest. Sergeant Broadnax felt good, and now he needed to go home and get ready for his date.

CHAPTER 44

The afternoon slowly turned to dusk, with only hours left in the twentieth century. While the world proclaimed Y2K with thousands of parties and events taking place around the globe, Margo walked throughout the house, room to room, trying to quiet her anxiety.

She hadn't given Jefferson a reason to treat her the way he had. And what was all this talk about him possibly involved in some type of illegal activity? What had Jefferson gotten into?

Margo climbed the stairs. Maybe a nap would make her feel better. *Yeah, a nap would do me some good.*

Nearing her room, Margo was drawn to Jefferson's home office. She turned the knob. The door opened easily. She hadn't been in the room since the previous Saturday. It was a beautiful room which probably held more secrets than Margo was aware.

She paused at his desk, then sat in the oversized leather chair that made her feel like a queen. She twirled from left to right, remembering when she had occasion to sit in her daddy's big chair in his office back home.

Margo brought both hands down in the middle of the massive mahogany desk. She was not sure why she had come into the room or what she had hoped to find. Her eyes slowly scanned the length of the desk, noting that nothing seemed out of place. It was fairly organized with manila folders stacked in neat little rows on the left side. Margo's glamour shot photo from some five years earlier peered at her from its frame alongside the photo of the kids. The beautiful desk accessories, Margo's gift of three Christmases ago to Jefferson, held hostage several Mont Blanc pens, Post-It notes, loose paper, paper clips, and other paraphernalia.

Margo looked at the file folders again, hesitated and then picked them up. *Myles and Associates, Investment Portfolios Pending, Referrals, and MISC*, she read to herself. *Nothing out of the ordinary.*

She thumbed through the first folder, tagged "Myles and Associates." It appeared to be a company portfolio with a listing of old and newly updated stock options. There was a quarterly and year-to-date summary of earnings along with other financial statements. *Myles has been very profitable*, Margo mumbled. *With quarterly statements like this, we ought to be living off the interest.* Margo moved to the next folder. It contained client worksheets listing their market interests and the type of portfolio they desired. As Jefferson was well established, it was not unusual for him to be laden with many requests and prospects.

Margo was tired from her search but at the last moment decided to peer into the folder marked "Miscellaneous." Business cards, brokers' telephone numbers, and expense receipts were all tucked in the pocket of the folder. She took a hard look at the receipts, not sure what she'd find. There were several gas receipts; the Mercedes certainly used a lot of fuel. There was a receipt from Office Depot and another from Lowe's, but the one that captured her attention was dated December 23rd.

The word Budgetel was written across the top. Margo held it in her hand, staring at it as if it would share some secret with her. Although it was just a piece of paper, the secret was out with its mere presence.

Margo crumpled the receipt in her hand and tossed it across the room. Blake's letter had exposed the unknown while Margo was in denial. But a receipt with a signature didn't lie, and the calm had now become the storm. Margo tore through the rest of the folder, finding little else of interest. She slid her fingers along the base of the pocket and pulled up a small sheet of paper. There were ten sets of numbers that didn't make much sense to her, but she'd seen enough spy movies to know that this paper contained some kind of code—to what she did not know. She decided to pocket it, and closed the folder.

Steam still rising from her nostrils, Margo looked through drawers and credenzas not finding a thing. Still unsatisfied, she continued to search, knowing for sure that she had overlooked something. She got up from the chair and searched the bookcase, looked behind paintings and in the trashcan. The longer she looked, the more infuriated she became. *There must be something else in this room.*

The mounting tension drove Margo mad. A sharp pain hit her in the base of the neck, and she lightly rubbed it hoping to ease the throbbing that seemed to settle there. It was nerves. That she was sure of. Her nerves were being torn to shreds by Jefferson's unfaithfulness. Margo wasn't sure if she could take much more.

Margo plopped down into the chair and spun around a couple of times. She rested her elbows on top of the desk when her joyride came to an end. She let her head fall forward, coming almost face to face with the desk calendar that protected Jefferson's desk. Jefferson loved vintage cars. December featured a red and white, 1957 Buick Special. That was Margo's favorite picture, because it reminded her of her daddy's car when she was growing up.

As Margo sat gazing at the picture, something made her take the corners of the calendar and lift it up. She spotted several folded-up sheets of paper and pulled them out. She nervously unfolded one of the sheets and barely let the word "bingo" roll off her tongue.

It was an email from *Reindeer10 (Linda Montgomery)* to *MONEYMAKER (Jefferson Myles)*. There was a profession of love for Moneymaker and how Linda longed to be with him forever. She spoke of their many emails and phone calls, especially the Blue Mountain Christmas Card that Moneymaker had sent her. They were gearing up for the millennium where a new change, new lives, would begin. They couldn't wait for that moment. The hardest part would be telling their spouses and children. How would they handle the troubled aftermath of their decision?

Margo didn't stop the tears from falling. She hurt all over the words danced over and over in her head. Seeing it on paper made the pain much more unbearable. Margo couldn't read the others and decided to take them back to her room. She would read them when she felt she could.

The bedroom seemed smaller upon entering. Margo looked around, letting time take her back to happier moments, when she and Jefferson made love to each other with reckless abandon, their passion sparked by just the sight of one another. He was her king and she was his queen. No amount of money, come hell or high water, would ever separate the two of them. Margo lay down on her bed and cried into her pillow. She fell fast asleep, taking solace in the memory of what life had once been for her.

CHAPTER 45

Angelica looked for an excuse to leave the house. She needed to warn those she had betrayed, and there was no way that could be done from Santiago's fortress. At this moment, she hated herself—she hated herself for allowing greed to take her soul. It was no accident that she was there. She had been privy to some information that she used to get Robert Santiago's attention, and the rest was a piece of cake.

She knew of his wealth and lavish lifestyle, and set out to claim some for herself. At first, she didn't want a "real relationship." They were too cumbersome and most times caused more pain than a doctor could cure. A weekend guy was what she wanted—someone she could have sex with on a regular basis, who would buy her expensive gifts, didn't make big demands of her time, and basically wanted the same—a weekend girl with no strings attached.

But she was falling in love with him, and he had treated her well. He gave her anything she wanted and made her his princess, and he had become her prince.

They made love instead of having sex, and he knew well how to please her. She had been living this life for six months, and it would be hard to throw it away.

There *was* someone Angelica would have liked to fall in love with, but Malik belonged to someone else. He was in every sense of the word a "real man" and not that "men are from Mars" crap. He had good taste and looked so good in his clothes. His Versace, three-piece, smoke-gray suit made her want to call out the National Guard. She had often envisioned being wrapped in his muscular, sturdy arms, kissing those big, fine, wonderful lips, and massaging the length of his body while she made him scream out her name. What had she done wrong?

She could not afford to continue daydreaming. Getting out of the house was her main objective. She had to protect those she betrayed while betraying yet another. Santiago seemed to be waiting around for something, but she didn't have time to waste. Yes, she'd make an excuse to go home—*she left her stove on.* It did sound a little lame, but it was better than what she had a moment earlier, which was nothing. She got up, hoping her plan would work.

Santiago was in his built-in gymnasium when he saw her approach. *She is so beautiful and smart,* Santiago mused to himself. *How could I be so lucky? I not only have a concubine, but a concubine with a head on her shoulders. I*

*might have to give her an assignment if she continues to
show me this kind of aptitude.*

Angelica approached slowly, smiling seductively
while he looked back. Maybe she was pouring it on too
thick, because he was grinning that grin. She toned it
down a little and upon reaching Santiago, she put her
arms around him and kissed him on the lips. He was
quickly aroused and pulled her close to him. She
attempted to move backward, but he held her tight,
rubbing his hardness against her body.

"I need to run home, baby," Angelica said, trying
earnestly to pull away. "I believe I left my stove on, and
I've got to go and turn it off."

"I'll buy you two houses, Princess," Santiago said in
between breaths, as he continued to press her with kisses.

"I really need to go."

"Don't you have someone you can call?" Santiago
continued, not missing a beat. "Woman, I want you
here and now. Let me help you out of that beautiful
cashmere sweater. It may be soft like you, but I want to
feel nothing but you."

"But what about…"

"A few more minutes won't make that much difference. I want you now."

Angelica couldn't afford to aggravate him so she
allowed Santiago the pleasure he anticipated. She came
on too strong. Now he had her pinned to the floor in

all of her nakedness, arousing the passion within her that even she couldn't ignore. She needed to save Hamilton and Jefferson, but she had to save herself, too, from the burning desire that tingled throughout her body and between her legs. She fell deeper into Santiago's spell that only he could relieve.

Afterward, they were spent and lay catching their breath from their carnal journey. He kissed her lips as any prince would to claim his sleeping beauty. The moment was magical until the telephone disturbed them.

Santiago was unhappy with the intrusion. His instructions prohibited any phone calls unless things did not go well. He answered it on the third ring, unable to keep the anger from his voice.

"What is it?"

"Santiago?"

"Hamilton?"

"Yeah, Robert, it's me. Jefferson got the money, and we're ready to deal. We're only an hour behind schedule."

"Oh-h-h, I see. Well, I cancelled the order. Just wait until you hear from me again."

"What do you mean you cancelled the order? We put our necks out to make sure that this operation was completed."

"Operation Stingray is officially over as you know it."

"You can't do this, Santiago. You can't just cut us off like that. We have the money."

"Operation Stingray is dead." And the line was disconnected. "It's too late now," Santiago murmured to himself.

Angelica had to get out of the house now. Otherwise, it would be too late to save Hamilton and Jefferson.

CHAPTER 46

She ran through the shower knowing that each minute she remained inside Santiago's mansion meant precious moments wasted in her resolve to save Hamilton and Jefferson. Angelica quickly put on her clothes, glancing in the mirror for only a second to make sure her makeup had not completely marred her face. Opening the door to Santiago's grand bedroom was like walking from a Roman bath into a celestial garden, only it didn't seem so celestial as the prince was irritated and in a foul mood.

"Going somewhere, Princess?" Santiago asked, demanding an answer.

"I really need to get home and turn my stove off. I'm almost sure that I left it on, and I certainly don't want my house to catch on fire."

Sweat formed on Angelica's brow. Her nervousness threatened to betray her. Santiago was agitated, which forced a change in his mood, but that had nothing to do with her. What was she afraid of? This was a man who just made love to her, who bestowed praises upon her for a job well done. This was the man she was falling in love with, the man who made her laugh and smile. But now, this very instant, she was fearful of him, having been exposed to the realm of his capabilities.

"If you must go, leave now. I won't be available for a while, but you can always leave me a message."

"I'll call you as soon as I get home." And with that, she walked out the door.

"I know who you really are," Santiago said aloud to no one, "but you won't be able to save them."

"Holly, I wish you hadn't insisted on coming with me. If something should go down, I'd hate for you to be in the thick of things."

"Oh Dad, you're so overprotective. After all, I'm a cop, too, sworn to uphold the law. Since this case has gotten big attention, I thought it would be cool to see it from a different vantage point. Anyway, sitting on a stakeout like this probably won't get us much action. You keep saying that the Feds have got everything under control, but I do hope I get a chance to use these binoculars."

"I know. The only reason I'm out here today is that we're short-staffed because of the holiday. Let the Durham PD handle it today, the Feds say."

"Attention, all surveillance units!" the crackled voice

said over the radio transmitter. "A black Lexus with a female driver has just left the Santiago premises. The car is heading east on South Street. Do not apprehend. Monitor movement. Ten-four."

"Ten-four," Captain Walters repeated, turning to look at Holly. She seemed more than eager to see some excitement. "I guess it's show time."

The elder Walters and daughter sat perched on the side of the Exxon station that gave a clear view of South Street running east to west. If the car passed their way, they would follow it a distance until another unit picked it up and tracked it for an unspecified duration and so on.

The Feds really wanted the big fish, Santiago. In order to make any type of arrest, he would have to be caught in the act of committing a violation. Though the Feds seemed to have more than enough information to make an arrest, they seemed to want something a little more, something that would make a conviction stick. Hopefully, today would be the day.

"Look!" Holly shouted. "The black Lexus is coming this way. In fact, it's stopping here to get gas."

"Just remain calm," the elder Walters cautioned, moving his hand to illustrate his point. "We don't want the occupant to get wind of us, or the next thing you know, we're in a high-speed chase. Let's just see what happens."

The car rolled to a stop in front of the first open

pump. A very attractive female emerged from within the car, briefly looking about, but in an apparent hurry to get gas. Holly raised the binoculars to her face to get a better view.

"It couldn't be…"

"What?" Detective Walters asked.

"I believe that's Lieutenant Barnes' ex-wife, Angelica. What in the world would she be doing coming from Santiago's house?"

"Are you sure, Holly?"

"I could be mistaken, but I don't think so. Look Dad, I've got a plan. I'm going to get out of the car and walk over to where she is and pretend that I just happened to be in the station and recognized her."

"No, Holly. You are not on duty here, and you aren't to interfere with my orders."

"But…"

"No buts." Holly had already slipped out of the car, setting her plan in motion. Detective Walters did not want to cause a commotion, but he and Holly would have a long talk after this. He was upset with himself for even allowing her to come with him.

It was just her luck that her car was low on fuel at the moment she needed to travel toward a destination eighty miles south of here. *This will cost me another five minutes,*

Angelica said to herself, *but I can't help them without it.* She pulled up to the pump and fumbled around in her purse for her credit card. "Here it is; this shouldn't take long."

She squeezed the trigger hard as if this would cause the fuel to pour faster. *"God, I need to hurry. I've got to save Hamilton and Jefferson."*

"Mrs. Barnes, is that you?" came the voice that made Angelica jump and almost drop the nozzle.

"Holly?"

"Yes. I thought I recognized you."

"Holly, I need your help," Angelica said in desperation. "This is going to sound strange, but I can explain the whole story later."

"What do you need me to do?" The excitement rose in Holly's voice.

"Lieutenant Barnes and a friend of his, Jefferson Myles, are in big trouble. A contract has been put out on their lives, and I need you to radio the police in Fayetteville so they can help save them. I'm on my way, but I would be too late, if I could do anything at all."

"Who ordered the hit, Mrs. Barnes?"

"I can't say. Just trust me on this. I desperately need your help in getting this information to Hamilton and Jefferson, if it's not already too late."

"Well…Mrs. Barnes, I'm going to need some additional information from you."

"Holly, we don't have much time."

Holly knew that she was already in trouble with her father. However, since Hamilton Barnes was her boss, she felt that in some way she owed him this—no matter what was being said about him. She looked at the desperation in Angelica's eyes and knew she had to do what she had to do. "Alright, I'll see what I can do. I can't promise you anything. I will need to get some information from you now."

"Holly, I appreciate what you're going to do, but I really don't have time to linger. I'm on my way to Fayetteville now."

"...But, we do need to talk." And Holly stood and watched as Angelica drove off.

Holly called Sergeant Broadnax and updated him on what had just transpired with Angelica Barnes so that he could have first-hand knowledge and get the ball rolling. She and Sergeant Broadnax were in this together, and together they would see it to the end.

CHAPTER 47

Captain Robert Petrowski whistled a happy tune. The judge had signed the order to issue arrest warrants for Lieutenant Hamilton Barnes and Jefferson Myles. It would make him a very happy man to be able to bring both Barnes and Myles in before the New Year. Either way, things were looking up, and with it, hopefully the answer to many unanswered questions.

He sat absently at her desk, trying to understand why she had done what she'd done. Hadn't he done more for her, going well beyond anything expected of a boss with a loyal employee whose work had risen from mediocre to exemplary? Now she was seen as someone who put pizzazz into an otherwise dreary place and was respected by the clients because of her attention to detail and the excellent way she handled them. And more than that, she and her sister were permanent guests for Christmas dinner since she had started working at Myles and Associates.

Jefferson picked up the picture frame sitting on the corner of Ebony's desk. It contained a picture of Ebony with her sister, Katrina, and their mother, posed together and taken at Olin Mills Studio. Ebony was the likeness of her mother, a younger version, of course. So tragic was Marsha's death. Jefferson didn't know her well, having only met her on the few occasions that she happened to come by the office either to borrow money or catch a ride to a destination the bus didn't travel.

He was still studying the picture when a slight creaking of the office door caused him to take his eyes away and look up. He met Ebony's surprised gaze with a smile.

"Didn't expect to see you, Jefferson—it being New Year's Eve and all."

"Well, this is my office and I decided to drop in. I do that quite a bit. I must say, though, I'm surprised to see you. I'm sure you and Katrina have your hands full with having to make arrangements for your mother."

Ebony lowered her eyes. She didn't want to think about her mother lying in some cold funeral parlor. "Yes, it has been stressful."

"Do you need any assistance?" Jefferson offered, while masking the inner conflict that fought against his will to remain civil.

"Well…no. My Uncle Johnny is going to help us with the arrangements."

"So what brings you here? Did you leave something? Or—"

"What's wrong, Jefferson? You've been acting strange ever since I walked in the door. I can see that faraway look in your eyes that says you have something on your mind. And why are you holding my picture?"

"There is something on my mind, Ebony." Jefferson rose from the chair and came and stood directly in front of her. He could see the agitation in Ebony's body language. She longed to be in control of this situation.

"Okay, Jefferson, what is it? Enough of this cat and mouse stuff." Ebony put her hands on her hips—a defense mechanism she utilized to let Jefferson know she meant business, too.

She was really on edge now, Jefferson noted. He methodically folded his arms and paced in a semi-circle.

"I feel that I've been a very good boss to you. I've bent over backward to see that you excelled at Myles and Associates. You did better than expected, and I've rewarded you time and again for all of your hard work and dedication.

"It appalls me, Ms. Wilson," Jefferson continued, "that in light of all that I've done, you would go behind my back and betray my confidence in you."

Ebony knew where this was going. Somehow, he'd found out about the "package." She decided to let him ramble on.

"If you needed money," Jefferson continued, "why didn't you just ask me?"

"Whoa, back up a minute. Money, what money?"

"You know what money," Jefferson shouted. "The two hundred-fifty thousand dollars."

"Back up, sir. What two hundred-fifty thousand dollars? Do you mean the money you stole from the accounts which added up to a lot more than any two hundred-fifty thousand dollars per my calculations?"

"Oh, you want to play games, Ms. Wilson. Your job is to—"

"Hold it. No, I don't play games and especially not the dangerous game you're playing, whatever it might happen to be. What I'm trying to tell you is that I didn't take any money. Yes, I've copied records for my protection since I'm smart enough to realize that all these people who have been snooping around asking about your accounts and threatening you don't have your best interest at heart. It certainly has given me cause for concern. And yes, I did a little checking on my own. Yes, I discovered discrepancies in several of the accounts for which I have no ledger entries. And while you may think that I don't have a clue about some things, I'm smarter than you think. You're the one who needs to look in his back pocket before shaking an accusatory finger at someone else."

"Are you finished, Ms. Wilson? Remember, I'm the boss and I do the accusing."

Ebony smirked at this sad creature she thought she loved even if it was only in her dreams. "Accuse all you want, Mr. Myles," Ebony emphasized to Myles. "I didn't take, or should I say, steal any money."

Jefferson took in Ebony's profile noting that her clothes accentuated her medium brown skin. Her taste in clothes spelled expensive, and she made a good enough salary at Myles and Associates to afford the best. Although her hair was not all her own, the long, black strands flowed effortlessly down to the middle of her back and were pulled off of her face in a clean sweep. She wasn't bad to look at, Jefferson thought, but she'd always be his girl Friday. For some odd reason, he believed her when she said she didn't take the money. But if she didn't, who did? Ebony's eyes had not left his since the beginning and only the sound of a phone ringing forced them to look apart.

Jefferson grabbed his cellular phone from its holder. This had to be good news since he had transferred the money and Hamilton's telephone number was showing in his ID box. And if things went well, payday was just around the corner.

"Hamilton, my man, what's up?"

"I've got bad news. Santiago cancelled Operation Stingray."

"Say what? Hell no, no way!"

"Hell yes, and I don't have a good feeling about this, Jefferson. Something is up…It was in the way that he said 'Operation Stingray is over as you know it.'"

"What about the money? I've already transferred it to the account, and there's no way I can retrieve it."

Jefferson hesitated slightly. How quickly he'd forgotten that Ebony was standing in front of him and he undeniably had spewed out information that was very damaging to him. "Just a minute, Hamilton. Let me get to my office. It's Ebony," he whispered, moving out of earshot.

"She's in the office?"

"Said she didn't take the money but admitted that she made copies of the accounts for insurance… I guess in the case of my business demise. According to her, with all the inquiries about my business accounts, she became suspicious and did a little investigating on her own."

"You believe her? I wouldn't put anything past that bitch. Just like her old lady."

"That's enough, Hamilton. I don't think she stole the money, but it doesn't tell us who did. It still doesn't let her off the hook, because there's the matter of the copied records. I can't fire her just now with her mother dying and all, but I'm going to deal with her."

"Look, have it your way. I'm going back to the station. I don't know what it is, call it a premonition if you like, but Santiago has it in for us."

Jefferson hit the *END* button on the cell and sat staring at the walls in his office. He had made something of himself—becoming someone his family proudly admired. He could feel the walls collapse around him as he scanned the room taking in the many accolades, diplomas, and other citations that celebrated his success and achievements.

He was uncertain about his destiny, but somewhere deep within, life as he knew it was about to change drastically. Without a doubt, he had made a mess of his marriage because of his need to be free of the dull routines of his life. He wanted spice. Linda had given him that temporary release, but sitting in this chair at this moment, he suddenly realized that Margo had given him the best years of his life.

He picked up Margo's photo and looked at it longingly. She was a good woman, the mother of his children, and he needed to make it right with her before it was too late. There were a couple of things he needed to do first, but begging Margo's forgiveness was paramount.

Jefferson pushed the prefix for Atlanta and dialed the rest of the digits to his parents' home. He needed to talk to Dad, someone he could trust with his feelings, someone who wouldn't throw him by the side of the road because he had fallen from grace while on a misguided road to lust and greed.

He was glad his father answered the phone. He knew he could share the information with his mother as well, but right now it had to be a father-and-son conversation. While Alan Myles had sensed that something was amiss with his son, he didn't know the depth of it.

Dad offered Jefferson some sage advice. "Son, we sometimes get caught up in things we shouldn't, but it takes a bigger person to recognize and admit their mistakes. Take charge. Clean up your mess and make restitution. Do this whether the outcome is positive or negative and move forward. You have to accept responsibility for your actions. Then ask God's forgiveness and let Him show you the path to take in order to make things right."

Alan loved his son. But what was more important to Jefferson was that his father still believed in him and would always be there when Jefferson needed him.

Jefferson walked out of his private office toward the front where Ebony still stood. Another time and place, he would have wanted to confide in Ebony. It was amazing how a little knowledge could make you look at a person differently. Regardless of her role, he could not trust her.

"I'll deal with you later," Jefferson said to Ebony. "I've got to make an important run, then I need to find my wife."

Ebony's eyebrows arched at the mention of his wife. She was quite aware that he was unfaithful to Margo. He must have had a talk with God, Ebony surmised. Whatever it was, Jefferson seemed to be different somehow—like a burden was lifted.

"Alright, Jefferson. I'll leave in a moment."

CHAPTER 48

The sun was on the verge of bidding farewell for the day. Only a slight hint of its existence in the sky remained as it continued its trek due west. The house was quiet with everyone gone. At the slightest sound Margo flinched, her nerves and fears getting the best of her. Loneliness had crept in, but she wasn't about to start feeling sorry for herself now.

Every muscle in her body ached. She went to the bathroom to splash cold water on her face to wake her from her stupor. As she passed her window, she quickly glanced out, noting that Linda's car had now taken residence in the driveway.

She'd really done it this time. Jefferson had not bothered calling again. What had she expected? Margo knew that if she hadn't been so selfish, he would have been there now even if they were hardly speaking. She missed him.

Margo was a fighter and she was not going to let some fickle woman take from her what took twenty-five years to cultivate. Most of those years were great.

She would wait until whatever bug had infected Jefferson died. She got on her knees and prayed.

Here I am again, Lord, your begging child. I need strength that only You can give. You've been so good to me, and I can't thank You enough for what You've already done. I'm willing to wait on You, because I know You're a midnight-hour God. I know all power is in Your hands, and there is nothing too hard for You; when the time is right, I know You'll deliver.

But I need strength, God, to get through. I love Jefferson, and my children need their father. Whatever test this is, Lord, I'm learning that patience is a virtue and love conquers all. I thank you again, God, for everything.

Margo got up from her knees feeling rejuvenated. She and God would usher in the millennium, and she'd pray that Jefferson would join them.

"Was that the doorbell?" Margo muttered to herself. She was so filled with God's praises that she wasn't sure what she heard. "It is, and could that be? No, Jefferson would have used his key."

Margo peered through the peephole surprised to see Malik standing outside. He was handsome. She thought for sure that he and Angelica would hook up. He certainly would have been a good catch. Antoinette, though, was quite fortunate to have won his hand. She evidently possessed the qualities the others didn't. Margo would make a point to get to know Toni better.

"May I come in?" Malik asked, as Margo continued to gaze at him.

"Yes, Malik," Margo said, somewhat subdued. "I'm sorry, I have a lot on my mind."

He was Jefferson's friend, but so unlike Jefferson in his temperament and character. He was a gentleman and a man of conviction—the kind of man who could be the next up-and-coming person in the community. A leader of sorts. Jefferson was kind and gentle once. Margo couldn't remember when he was that way last, although it couldn't have been that long ago. Margo and Malik embraced, almost suffocating each other. She needed that.

"Hey, Margo." He pushed her slowly aside to get a better look at her. "How are you doing?"

"I'm okay," she said, flopping down in what had become her comfort couch.

"It's me, Margo. How are you?" Malik asked again, observing the faraway look that now covered her face. *How could you not love a woman like that*, Malik thought. Her hair smelled fresh, her perfume soft and feminine. She made him want to lay his head in her bosom. He was glad that he found Antoinette, and he truly loved her. He shook his head thinking how foolish Jefferson was for treating Margo as he did.

"I'm fine, I guess," Margo said, somewhat resigned. "Is Jefferson here?"

"No. He's…I have not seen him since last night, Malik."

"Margo, I want you to listen to me."

"What is it?" Margo jerked upward, now fully alert. "Has something happened to Jefferson?"

"Not that I know of… but I need to share something with you. I'm not sure just where to begin…"

"Try the beginning."

"I guess that would be logical if I knew where the beginning began." Malik paced back and forth clasping his hands together, opening and closing his eyes in meditation at the task he was about to embark upon.

"Margo…uhmm, Jefferson is in a lot of trouble." He waited for Margo to digest and respond. Surprised that there was no response, Malik continued. "Jefferson has embezzled large sums of money from his clients, money which he used to help fund an extremist group in Honduras that is trying to overthrow their government. Jefferson is involved in an operation backed by a powerful guy, Roberto Santiago. They have used the money to purchase weapons in a corrupt deal where Santiago received large cash payments in return from an unknown source in Honduras. Hamilton Barnes is also part of the group.

"Jefferson is so deeply involved that his attempts to get out of the group have failed. Sure, he had no business becoming mixed up in this mess from jump street, but he allowed the power of the almighty dollar to suck him up in the vacuum. Now he can't get out."

"Hold it, Malik. You mean to tell me that Jefferson is taking money from his clients and not putting it back? How long has this been going on?"

"Jefferson is being paid handsomely. At first, he put the money back, but as Jefferson became consumed with what he was doing, the power he was wielding, and the profits he was making, less and less of the money was replaced. Santiago is ruthless, and Jefferson believes he might have had something to do with Blake's murder."

Margo sat staring at Malik. *Jefferson may also be indirectly involved with Blake's murder*, but she was not going to share that tidbit with him.

"How long have you known?"

"Just found out last night. In fact, I didn't want to know, but Jefferson insisted on telling me in the event something happened to him."

"So, you've seen and talked to Jefferson?"

Malik saw the dejected look in Margo's eyes. "He was feeling pretty desperate at the time—kind of like sinking in quicksand with nothing to grab on to. I don't think I made him feel any better."

"What are we going to do?" Margo sighed. "I love him, Malik."

"I know you do, Margo. We've got to help him; I just don't know how yet. Margo, I feel that I've also failed him. You see, I told him how sorry he was for getting involved with uhh…"

"It's okay. I know all about Linda."

The look of disbelief was written all over Malik's face. Margo seemed so calm. When did she find out? How…when…? "Are you alright?" he finally asked.

"I'm okay. Finish telling me what you told Jefferson."

"Well, I told him in so many words that he was destroying himself and his family—that he was walking out on the best thing that has happened in his life, the woman who has been there walking by his side, sharing his life, raising four beautiful children, and who steadfastly loved him. I washed my hands of him and turned my back on him, at least temporarily. I was so upset with him because he never listens to me." Malik patted Margo's hand.

"You're a good man, Malik. I love you, my brother. I'm sorry about my husband, but unfortunately, he'll have to suffer the consequences for his mistakes."

Malik sat next to Margo and held her. "We're going to get through this and bring Jefferson back."

"I hope so."

CHAPTER 49

Jefferson drove blindly through the streets, unsure of his destination. He felt better now that he had spoken with Allen, Sr. In some ways, he felt like the little boy who needed to hold his daddy's hand for reassurance—an assurance that would certainly make things right.

"Jesus," Jefferson shrieked, almost hitting a pedestrian that had the right-of-way in a crossing zone. He finally noticed the screaming red traffic signal that loomed in front of him. "Got to get a hold of myself," he muttered, grabbing his head. He was glad to see that the pedestrian was still a whole person and was now at the opposite end of the street. The light turned green. Jefferson inched forward, afraid that he might make the same mistake again. With horns blaring behind him, he finally picked up speed and moved on. His head was clearing. It was time to make a decision.

Margo, Margo, Margo. What do I say to you? I messed up? I was out of my mind? I had amnesia and didn't know who I was or what I was doing? I have to tell her how sorry I am… and… and I love her. I do love her.

She'll say, why the sudden change of heart, Jefferson? Your girl kicked you to the curb? Was the grass not greener on the other side? Or was it that she didn't love your sorry ass no how—just using you like I told you she was. Didn't want to listen to what I had to say, but you just knew that you were through with me and I was old, tired, and used up and you needed a fresh face to look at.

I'd tell her my love was there all the time but lust, greed, and temporary insanity took away my senses—suffocating me in all its dirt, changing the person I was into the one that I had become. I became the devil's advocate—doing his dirty work. In fact, I kinda liked what I saw—made me forget what used to be. Foolish, that's what. Then my curiosity was pricked. It pricked the very fabric of the veil I had used to shield myself until I realized that I was on the wrong street, in the wrong house, and going nowhere. Trapped. "Damn."

Another red light lay ahead, daring Jefferson's vehicle to violate the boundary it had set. *When I say STOP, that's what you're supposed to do,* roared the stoplight in Jefferson's head.

Jefferson saw a drug store in the distance and headed for it. There seemed to be one on every corner, Eckerd vs. CVS. As he approached, he pulled over to regroup and purchased a bottle of aspirin. He'd end up killing someone if he didn't.

Jefferson couldn't face Margo just yet. After all he had done, he didn't want to appear that he was crawling back home because he had nowhere else to go. And knowing that Margo's instant rejection was sure to come, made it that much harder. *I'll go to Angelica's house for a while until I can muster up enough courage to face Margo.*

Nothing happened last night, he assured himself, *or did it?* It was a strange coincidence meeting her at the club and then ending up at her condo for the night when she knew he was a married man. Angelica was his wife's best friend. Jefferson rubbed his chin and drove on.

He shaved, bathed and now slapped his face with his favorite cologne. Carl Broadnax peered into the mirror that dared to look back at him, giving him the thumbs-up. "I'm going on a real date," he mused to himself. "Well, sort of one. I'm going to see Marsha…no, no Ebony."

Ebony was a beauty in her own right. The uncanny likeness of the two, mother and daughter, made him shake his head.

Carl's fingers tingled with excitement, although fear was getting the better of him. He had no need to worry. Katrina was going to be there, also—a small party among intimate friends, Broadnax hoped.

He would help them with arrangements for their mother, if needed. Otherwise, he'd console and try to lift their spirits.

Carl glanced at himself once more in the mirror, and now assured, grabbed the bag of goodies bought earlier to make the evening lighter. He did a full glance of his small, tiny apartment, turned off the lights, set the alarm, and walked out the door. It was going to be a good New Year.

CHAPTER 50

*N**ew Year's Eve! I should be out with a pretty woman—dinner for two at Angus Barn and a carafe of the best Chardonnay money could buy. Then we'd go dancing at one of the many parties in town—getting our Electric Slide on, waiting for the countdown, back to my place for a drink or two, soft music, a little cuddling and kissing, and getting our groove on. Oh-h-h, she'd be a sweet tendaroni, hourglass figure, sweet-ebony lips, and thighs that would squeeze me oh so tight.*

The station seemed quiet. No crazies milling about or loud-mouthed relatives attempting to get their know-they-broke-the-law loved ones out of jail. Hamilton pulled his cruiser into the first available space. Sergeant Craig's car was still parked outside. Hamilton needed to speak to him before he left. Sergeant Craig was a good kid.

Hamilton checked out the area, and then stepped out of his car. It was almost too quiet to be the last day in the year. As he headed up the steps, Hamilton turned slightly in time to catch a glimpse of a slow-moving vehicle. He wasn't sure of the make or model, but it came to an abrupt halt in front of him.

Then he saw it—almost too late. One of the vehicle's occupants aimed a semi-automatic in his direction. Hamilton dropped to the ground just as the hail of gunfire erupted. Wounded, he crawled on his belly until he reached the side of the building leaving a trail of blood. Then the driver of the vehicle sped off.

Sergeant Craig descended upon Hamilton who was bleeding profusely. "Lieutenant Barnes, are you alright?"

"No, I've been hit," Hamilton managed to say.

"I'll call an ambulance."

"It was a hit, Craig! S-a-n-t-i-a-g-o-o-o," came the faint sounds from Hamilton Barnes' mouth.

"What, Lieutenant Barnes? What did you say?"

"Sant-e…" And Hamilton passed out.

"Jesus," Sergeant Craig exclaimed. "Who'd want to put a hit out on the lieutenant?"

The ambulance and Captain Petrowski arrived on the scene within seconds of each other. Sergeant Broadnax was next to arrive, making his way swiftly toward Captain Petrowski and Sergeant Craig, who were both kneeling at Lieutenant Barnes' side. Surprised to see Sergeant Broadnax, Captain Petrowski walked over to meet him.

"Thought you had the night off?" Captain Petrowski inquired of Sergeant Broadnax, hoping this was going to be a solo act and that he wouldn't have to share any of the spotlight.

"I did. However, I received a phone call from Sergeant Walters who was on stakeout with her father in Durham. Said that Lieutenant Barnes' ex-wife, Angelica, drove into the gas station they were observing from. Holly, Sergeant Walters, recognized Ms. Barnes and approached her. Ms. Barnes told Sergeant Walters that Lieutenant Barnes and Jefferson Myles of Myles and Associates were marked men. She overheard the order for the hit, but would not say who ordered it; did say, though, that she was on her way to Fayetteville to try and help them. How, I don't know. The strange thing was that Ms. Barnes was coming from Robert Santiago's house."

"What?"

"Can you believe that? Well, I ran to the station as soon as I got that message. Apparently, I'm too late."

"Nothing surprises me anymore, Broadnax, in this line of work. The paramedics say that Lieutenant Barnes was hit in the shoulders and buttocks by several bullets, but he'll live. That guy must have twenty-nine lives. Let's read him his rights and we'll find out what happened from Sergeant Craig."

"Okay, Captain."

Captain Petrowski and Sergeant Broadnax returned to where the paramedics had now placed Lieutenant Barnes on the stretcher. Captain Petrowski tried to elicit a response from him, but Hamilton did not respond. Petrowski looked into his face, but saw that his efforts would be in vain. He turned to Sergeant Craig, looking for answers.

"What happened here tonight?"

"There were shots, sir—several rounds of continuous fire on the wall of the police station. I got dispatch to call the main police line immediately, because I didn't know what the situation was outside."

"How long was it before you went outside, Sergeant Craig?"

"I would say in the minute or two after the shots had ceased."

"And how long was that?"

"About five minutes total."

"What happened when you went outside?"

"I found Lieutenant Barnes lying on the ground, blood oozing from his body."

"Did he say anything to you?"

"He said he was hit or that it was a 'hit.' He also tried to say a name that sounded like san-tee."

"Santiago," both Captain Petrowski and Sergeant Broadnax said simultaneously.

"That could have been it," Sergeant Craig continued. "Then he passed out."

"I need you to write all of that down in a statement," Petrowski instructed.

"I'll take care of it right away, sir," Sergeant Craig responded.

Captain Petrowski turned toward the paramedics who were about to put Hamilton into the ambulance. "I'm Captain Robert Petrowski of the Fayetteville Police Department," he said, flipping his shield for verification. "I have a warrant for Lieutenant Barnes' arrest."

Sergeant Craig's eyes searched Captain Petrowski's and Sergeant Broadnax's faces for understanding. Finding none, Sergeant Craig walked back into the station to write his statement.

Captain Petrowski informed the paramedics that he would place armed guards around Lieutenant Barnes during his hospital stay. No one would be allowed to visit except those authorized. The paramedics nodded and proceeded to transport the patient to the hospital with a police escort.

CHAPTER 51

Jefferson turned into the entrance and headed for the guard gate. As he approached, the friendly face waved him through, having been given instructions to let the driver of the silver Mercedes with license plate NC MONEYMKR through. Jefferson felt some solace behind the gate that promised security—somewhat like God putting his arms of protection around him.

He wasn't sure why he had come here. It was against the rule, but he had broken so many rules lately; he wasn't sure what was right and what was wrong. There was solace with Angelica. She made him feel warm—not like Linda, but in a more lustful way. *I guess she used me and I used her.*

"Margo can never know about this," Jefferson said aloud, almost in a panic. "She would die. So many lies lay beneath the surface. So many phony faces and so much distrust. Margo hadn't asked for any of this!"

Jefferson pulled in front of Angelica's condo. Her car was not in sight and Jefferson smiled at the thought of having some time alone to sit and think.

The Lexus appeared out of nowhere, barreling down like it was in a hurry to show off its new luxury features. The car skidded to a stop beside Jefferson, wasting no time in emptying its precious passenger.

Jefferson saw the glazed look on her face as she headed toward his car. He sat unmoved, unsure if he should open the door. Angelica looked frantic, distressed as she beat upon his car window, begging him to listen to her. He relented and rolled down the window.

"What is it, Angelica?"

"What is it? Is that all you can say? Your life, that's what. Why aren't you getting out of the car?"

"What are you talking about, and what do you mean, my life?" Jefferson got out of the car, curious, wanting to understand.

"Your life is in danger. So is Hamilton's. I'm here to warn you."

"Slow down. Now, where did you get a crazy notion like that?"

"You've got to trust me on this, Jefferson. I came home hoping you would be here, and now we've got to find Hamilton."

"You need to tell me something, girl. I've got a lot on my mind. I want to make it right with Margo. I want to go to her and explain to her what I've done, why I did it, and how terribly sorry I am for what I've put her through. I don't want any more secrets between us. I miss her. I didn't know how much I missed her until a little while ago, and now you show up to tell me that my life is in danger."

"Your life is in danger. I'm happy that you want to make it right with Margo, but now is not the time. We need to get out of here!"

Jefferson reached for Angelica, pulling her close to him as he spoke. "What aren't you telling me? Who's after me? Tell me something before I go off on you."

Angelica tried to shrink from his grasp. "For a financial analyst, you're pretty slow. This is a word problem. Figure it out."

"I've had just about enough of you. Now, talk to me, woman. Apparently, you know something I should. Let's go in the house. I'm not interested in making a public display."

"Jefferson, we don't have much time," Angelica pleaded.

"Well, we're going inside and you're going to start explaining." Jefferson nudged her arm and ushered her inside.

Angelica had no plans of telling him anything. She had warned him. Now it was up to him whether or not he took her advice. *Men can be such fools sometimes*, she thought.

She went to the kitchen to get a glass of water and noticed the flashing light on her answering machine. *One message—it could be Santiago—can't risk Jefferson hearing this.* She thought better of it and pushed the "play" button.

"Alright, Angelica. Time's up," Jefferson said, entering the kitchen.

"Be quiet. My answering machine is running."

"You can't hear it if you don't turn it up."

"Shh…"

"Ms. Barnes, this is Sergeant Broadnax with the Fayetteville Police Department. I'm calling from Cape Fear Hospital. Lieutenant Barnes has been shot and is now in surgery. I'm not sure of his condition at the moment. If you should come by the hospital, please ask for me." *Beep*, and the machine clicked off.

Angelica grabbed her throat. Jefferson stood frozen in his tracks. Was this the work of Santiago? Hamilton had hinted that he felt something was amiss with Santiago. Was Angelica trying to tell him the same thing? What would she know about Santiago and their business with him? Angelica was right. They needed to get going.

Angelica was in a frenzy. She was worse for wear and felt her own world caving in. "Let me get my scarf. It's breezy outside," she said, struggling to get up on her feet.

"Hurry up, we've got to get out of here—NOW!"

"Now you're suddenly in a hurry," Angelica said, rushing back to the living room so they could depart.

"Who told you that Hamilton and I were in trouble?"

"Let's not start that again. Let's go."

Jefferson dropped the conversation at least for the moment. "I'm going to get to the bottom of this. Let's take my car. I'll take you to the hospital."

"No, let's not go there. It…it won't be safe."

Jefferson turned to her as he backed out of the driveway. "I want to know right this minute what you're withholding from me."

The look in Jefferson's eyes told Angelica her time was up. She wet her lips, sucked her teeth with her tongue, and turned her face toward the window. It never crossed her mind that she would be placed in a position that would require her to explain to her best friend's husband that she betrayed him. And…the money, yes the money; she couldn't tell him about that just yet.

"Drive."

Jefferson drove through the security gate and headed east. He wasn't sure where he was going, but he knew this road did not lead to where he should have been going.

They drove on in silence, neither wanting to be the first to start what would probably become mindless chatter. Angelica steadied her gaze on the vast countryside while Jefferson stewed over another bad decision and his desire to make some sense of it all.

The white Range Rover kept its distance. It had been following them for some fifteen minutes. It was difficult not to notice it on this rural road. Traffic was very sparse. The New Year's revelers, whether going to church or an organized New Year's event, took to the main roads while others stayed at home. It was not long before Jefferson spotted the Range Rover again. It was shadowing them.

"Seems like we've got company," Jefferson calmly announced to Angelica.

She squeezed her hands together, took a chance and turned around. She knew that an order had been issued by Santiago and that Hamilton may have already received his visit from the gangsters. Angelica was afraid, suddenly realizing that she might be a target as well, having left Santiago as she did. He wasn't a stupid man.

"Jefferson." Angelica paused, unable to force her mouth open any further. Jefferson made her uncomfortable as he drove on without acknowledging her attempt to tell the information she knew.

"Jefferson," she attempted again. "There is a hit out on you and Hamilton."

"A *hit*? What do you mean a hit, and just how do you know that, Angelica?" Jefferson shouted.

"Because…I was with…I was…I was with Santiago when he issued the order."

All that could be heard was Jefferson's breathing— labored and louder with each passing second. Then he put his foot on the accelerator while Angelica watched the speedometer climb from fifty-five miles per hour to sixty-five, seventy, eighty, then ninety miles per hour. The white Range Rover's speed also increased. There was no doubt in anyone's mind that the search and destroy mission was underway.

"What were you doing with Santiago?" the harsh voice asked.

"Would you slow down, please…please. See, I was… his princess."

Jefferson snatched Angelica from her seat, grabbing the collar of her beautiful cashmere sweater. As quickly as he had grabbed her, he released her in order to navigate an unexpected curve in the road.

"You were his damn what?" Jefferson shouted. "I guess you were playing me last night and our meeting was not so coincidental."

"It was in a way. I had planned to contact you, but I wasn't sure how I was going to go about it. Who would have guessed in a million years that I would hit pay dirt without lifting a finger?"

"You disgust me, and I thought you were trying to comfort me."

"I was in a way."

"By taking from me?"

"What are you talking about, Jefferson?"

"Angelica, you know what I'm talking about. You took advantage of me and stole the codes and embezzled the two hundred-fifty thousand dollars that's missing from my accounts. It is now very clear to me. Keeping me there a little while longer so that you could get what you needed. I blamed Ebony for taking the money, but I know now it was you. You pathetic piece of trash."

"You're pathetic, Jefferson, and you're the bigger thief. Margo will do well to get rid of your sorry behind. You have a wonderful family, beautiful home, great job, but your brains are scattered like a field of wildflowers—sold your soul to the devil for thirty pieces of silver. Now you're left with nothing, forfeiting everything, and for what? You may even lose your life before it's all over."

"How poetic. And you of all people got the nerve to tell me what my life is or has become. You only have to look at yourself. I bet you never told your best friend, Margo, that Hamilton picked you up from a strip joint and gave you everything including respectability. And now you betray me and Hamilton for one lousy piece of silver."

Angelica did not respond.

"Tell me," Jefferson continued, "was it as good as the first time? You will never be the woman Margo is, you know. She is a God-fearing woman, upstanding and upright. See, you not only betrayed me, but you betrayed the very person who showed you kindness and allowed you into her home and her soul. She didn't know that lying beneath that exterior frame of yours was a conniving, cheating woman who brought some of her trouble on herself. I know that you suffered abuse at the hands of Hamilton, but you went in with your eyes open. Then I allowed you to seduce me when I should have resisted. I guess I'm not much better. But using Margo the way you did—because I know that you didn't just happen upon her real estate office that day. I had talked so much about my wonderful wife that you had to find out for yourself what Margo Myles was really like. You never counted on becoming her best friend, even though I do think you came to love Margo as a sister, and—"

"Shut up, Jefferson!!" Angelica shouted. "You don't have any idea what my life has been like…and who are you to judge? Seems to me you're the one who's made Margo's life a living hell."

"Once a whore, always a whore. How else did you expect Hamilton to treat you?"

"Jefferson, you're so wrong. I've had to prove myself my whole life. My brothers were the good guys in my family. Both went to college and grad school; one became a successful lawyer and the other a successful doctor. I wasn't so fortunate because I had a daddy who liked his pretty young daughter that matured at an earlier age, and everywhere I turned he was making googly eyes at me when Mother wasn't looking. And then one day it happened— when Mother wasn't home and my brothers were playing football out of town. My daddy wanted

me to play with him...play with him...play with..."
Angelica broke down and cried.

For a fleeting moment, Jefferson digressed to the time he allowed Angelica to seduce him. It was as if it were yesterday, although Jefferson had given their encounter little or no thought in the couple of years since. Angelica and Hamilton were having their troubles and she had chosen Jefferson to unleash her burden.

It was common knowledge among the rank and file that Hamilton had an appetite for other women besides his wife. The stories on the street were none too pretty. One particular evening, Jefferson had gone by the Barnes' home hoping to catch Hamilton. He had revised an old portfolio of Hamilton's and was anxious to get his approval. The market was ripe, and although President Clinton's approval rating was faltering, the economy was faring rather well.

All sense of urgency and excitement left Jefferson when he saw the puffiness around Angelica's eyes. It seemed she had been waiting for him to rescue her from distress. She fell into his arms like a child whose mother had been gone all day and finally arrived home.

Jefferson pulled her face to him and held it in his hands. Oh how he wished he could make her pain go away. She was worn from the abuse she suffered at the hands of her husband, even though her natural beauty was still apparent. Jefferson tried to get her to tell him what happened, but to no avail. Angelica would never tell. She held onto Jefferson for dear life, as if that would make the difference.

There must have been a moment when Angelica let her wounded soul take a side seat. So much heat and warmth had radiated between them as he held her tight. And Angelica saw an opportunity to pay Hamilton back.

She told Jefferson that Hamilton would not return home until the next day. On the pretext that she needed him to help her lift a table that had been knocked over, she led Jefferson like a lamb to the slaughter into her large expansive bedroom that was larger than any of the bedrooms Jefferson had seen during his childhood.

The room was tastefully decorated in gold and cream brocade with silk swag curtains and a matching double-king comforter of the same color. The large four-poster bed sat on an oak platform that was befitting of royalty. Two Queen Anne chairs subtly upholstered in gold and cream brocade, with a hint of a light peach rope pattern running through it, were parked on either side of the bed. A six-foot-long chaise lounge, covered in the same fabric, held up the large picturesque window that overlooked a well-tended bed of roses in several varieties. Jefferson was overwhelmed by what he saw, and was puzzled, wondering how Hamilton was able to afford this place on his meager policeman's salary.

It wasn't the size of the room or how ornately it was decorated that left Jefferson dumbfounded. During the time Jefferson had spent gawking at the room and beautiful scenery, Angelica had completely disrobed, leaving him aroused and vulnerable—wishing he was anywhere else but in that room. His eyes traced her outline. If there ever was a stunningly attractive woman, Angelica definitely was she.

Angelica swayed and moved her hips in a slow, sultry pattern. This was Hamilton's wife, and Jefferson was a married man. Hamilton had a temper. Jefferson loved his wife. This was taboo. He had no intention of getting caught in such a precarious position, but the persuasive call of the flesh was causing Jefferson to forget his resolve to resist. Angelica had temporarily forgotten the reason for her tears that had stained her face only minutes earlier.

Jefferson relented, enjoying every moment of it, but he hated himself the moment the physical act of sex ended. And now there was last night—giving in once again to his male prowess. It was all coming back to him. Now he was riding to who knows where, a haunted man, sold out by his partner's wife who had deceived him while he was only too eager to be deceived because he was a love-sick idiot.

Angelica lifted her head turning toward Jefferson and saw the large semi-automatic pointed her way. She and Jefferson had gotten so carried away that they did not realize the Range Rover was upon them.

"Jefferson, watch…"

The Mercedes swerved to the right. Jefferson lurched forward, closely pursued by the big white car. A volley of shots struck his car with a series of metallic pops.

"My God!" Angelica screamed.

"Hold on, Ang-e-l-i-c-a. I've been hit."

Jefferson's voice faded and he fell forward—his hands relaxing, then falling from the steering wheel. The car moved in a free roll, rolling more rapidly after jumping an embankment, and finally coming to rest against a large magnolia tree.

Angelica remained crouched on the floor in the front using her hands to shield her from harm. Not a sound came from the driver's side. Jefferson looked like a mangled mess, and the car was a tangled wreck at the root of the tree.

Angelica waited in silence, biding her time, hoping that the would-be assassins were satisfied with Jefferson and her dilemma. Five minutes passed, then ten. She wanted Jefferson to say something, but his voice was still.

"Jefferson," Angelica called out softly. "Jefferson, do you hear me?"

Again, silence answered and Angelica remained in her curled-up position on the floor. Another ten minutes passed before it occurred to Angelica that no one was around to call for help—that they were wrapped around a tree waiting to die because no one had any idea where they were.

All sorts of thoughts flooded her head but she never once thought to pull her cell phone out of her purse and call for help. When the idea finally penetrated her brain, she fumbled around until she found her phone and dialed 911. "Jefferson could die because I was so stupid," she said out loud, waiting for the 911 dispatcher to answer. "Hurry, for God's sake, Jefferson can't die."

Then a bombshell fell on her thoughts. *How would she explain her being with Jefferson when the car crashed?* She had to get out of the car now. She could not afford to be found in the car with a man who might be either dead or alive. Jefferson was her best friend's husband, and there would be no explaining her way out of that.

She scrambled to release herself from the tangled piece of scrap metal that was once a silver Mercedes. She was blessed to be alive—it must have been the position she assumed on the floor. Angelica pushed upward until she was able to look out of the shattered passenger window. From where she knelt, she could see what appeared to be miles and miles of barren field. Turning her head to the right and much further back, there appeared to be an orchard of some kind. Maybe if she ran into the orchard, she could find refuge.

As she inched further up in her seat, Angelica noticed for the first time the spasm that shot through her shoulder blade that now radiated through to her right arm and neck when she moved. She sat a minute twisting her head from side to side, hoping to find relief. Then she looked Jefferson's way, reached over to check on him. He had a slight pulse but was barely breathing. She had to hurry, and she prayed that someone would be there to help Jefferson shortly.

Angelica pushed against the car door, finally forcing it outward. Another pain shot through her shoulder, but she had no time to waste. She crouched down outside the car, unsure which way she should travel. The orchard seemed like a safe haven, but it appeared to lead nowhere. "If I can just make it back to the main road," she mumbled, "I'll have a better chance of getting away."

The car rested approximately five-hundred yards from the road. There was a slight incline, but Angelica resolved to make it, although the extreme pain in her shoulder was making it difficult.

She made it to the road—which was devoid of any cars. Dusk had fallen and a distinctive need to find a safe haven overtook Angelica.

She walked to the other side of the road and headed

for a group of trees nearby. Then she heard it—the siren warning the countryside that it was in search of a victim. She strained to see from which direction the vehicle traveled. The wailing sound became more intense as it drew near, and for the first time fear enveloped Angelica as she thought about Jefferson's helpless body lying down the embankment on the other side of the road.

The fire truck, followed by an ambulance, must have spotted the car as they careened to an abrupt stop. There was a lot of activity. Angelica prayed they could save poor Jefferson's life. She stayed hidden in the clump of trees hoping the rescuers would depart soon so that she could find her way home.

CHAPTER 52

The hospital emergency staff was on full alert for the impending arrival of their patient. "Two this evening," said one of the nurses in triage.

"I had hoped for a quiet evening—even if it is New Year's Eve," said another. "I'm glad I'm not out there with all of those crazy folks." They both laughed.

Within minutes, the ambulance arrived at the emergency room. Dr. Graham barked orders to get things rolling. Their patient had suffered severe trauma to the head and some internal organs. He also sustained several deep lacerations to the upper body. Notably, there were two bullet entry wounds to his side. It was a miracle he was still alive.

Interns in their crisp, white cotton smocks transferred Jefferson to a gurney for quick transport to the operating room. It was feared that Jefferson was already in shock with his vitals reading very sporadic and failing. If there was such a thing as luck of the draw, Jefferson could count himself among the fortunate. Dr. Graham was one of the best cardiologists and surgeons in this region.

"He lives way on the other side of town, according to his driver's license," said one of the nurses at the nurse's station. "The police are taking care of notifying any relatives."

"Margo, I've got to go," Malik said, rising from his seat. "Toni and I have reservations at Angus Barn tonight and we'll eventually end up at a party at the Hilton given by the husband of one of Toni's girlfriends who happens to be a banker in Durham. You're welcome to come along if you like."

"No need to pity me; I'll be alright. I'm just worried about Jefferson and how I'm going to help my husband, if he lets me. I'd just be a third wheel, and besides, you and Toni need to be alone."

"We'll be with other people."

"Remember, dinner at Angus Barn. Sounds pretty romantic to me."

"I guess you're right about that. I love you, Margo, and I'm glad to see you're not giving up on my brother."

"I love you, too, Malik. Jefferson is fortunate to have you as a friend."

Malik and Margo embraced and Malik got that feeling again. He knew there would be nothing to it, but Margo made his body quiver all inside—and her hair, always so fresh to the nose, made him want to lay his head on hers. He couldn't afford to spend another minute this close to her. They released each other and Malik headed for the door.

The phone rang as they silently walked to the front of the house. "Hold on, Malik. I want to walk out with you. It might be one of my children on the phone."

A little of the old spark had been rekindled in Margo. The way she bounced as she hurried to answer the phone was evidence that she had received and accepted the encouragement of a good friend and was ready to meet life head-on. Malik watched as her once smiling face turned to a muted frown.

"Fayetteville Police Department…and…yes…," then a long pause. "My God! Where? Yes." And her sobs that were coming every half-second became uncontrollable.

"What is it, Margo?" Malik called out, the phone now lying on the floor. Malik walked over, picked it up, and spoke to the caller at the other end.

"Hello, this is Malik Mason, a friend of the Myles' family. Mrs. Myles is quite upset. May I ask what's going on?"

The caller replied in a voice that had performed this ritual many times before. "This is the Fayetteville Police Department. Mr. Mason, Mr. Myles was in a terrible accident and has just been taken to Cape Fear Valley

Hospital. He is very fortunate to be alive. Seems that his car veered off the main road and hit a tree head-on. His car was completely totaled. We're not sure why his car careened off the road, but we're checking it out now. May I speak with Mrs. Myles again?"

"She has passed out. I'll have her call you later. I'm going to take her to the hospital now."

"Alright, sir. Let Mrs. Myles know that we will be in contact with her."

"Yeah, I will."

A thousand thoughts ran through Malik's head. Was it an accident? Or was this the attempt on his life that Jefferson had casually alluded to?

His first course of action was to get Margo to the hospital. She was going to need him, and he would stay as long as she did.

Malik dashed cold water on Margo's face. She had a puzzled expression on her face when she opened her eyes. Malik helped her to the nearest chair and let her collect herself before repeating the contents of the phone call. He took a moment to call Antoinette and fill her in on what had transpired. Antoinette was disappointed, but she told Malik to do what he needed to do. She knew she couldn't compete with a friend's love and didn't want to. That's part of what Malik loved about her. Yes, he was blessed.

Margo looked at Malik for guidance—maybe some

kind of confirmation that it was but a dream. The vague look on Malik's face was not reassuring, and when he spoke, all hope diminished.

"Margo, we need to go to the hospital," Malik whispered. He was not sure of her mental state, because it had been a blow to his own composure. He didn't want to believe that anything had happened to his beloved friend. He fingered his Rolex.

"Jefferson," Margo stuttered. "Jefferson…accident… terrible accident. Oh Malik, we've got to get to Jefferson. We've got to help him!"

"Calm down, Margo. Get your purse and a light jacket. I'll take you."

"Thanks, Malik," Margo said, standing up and holding onto him. Just as abruptly, she pulled away. "Toni is waiting on you to take her to dinner. You go on, I can drive myself."

"Toni is already aware of what happened to Jefferson and knows I'm going to be with you as long as I'm needed. See Margo, my lady is not a selfish woman. I'm sure she's disappointed, but Antoinette and I will have many New Year's Eves together. Right now, we've got to see about Jefferson."

"Thanks, Malik. You're a special friend."

Malik and Margo rushed from the house and got into Malik's car. Linda stood by an upstairs window looking out into the dark vastness when they emerged hurriedly from Margo's house. She strained to see them. A sudden state of fear rose within her as she tried to analyze what she saw.

Margo wasn't dressed up, neither was Malik. They did not appear to move casually. There was something alarming about the way they seemed to rush to the car. Could it be Jefferson? She hadn't seen his car all day, or since they were together, for that matter.

She gave up her right to know when she waltzed into that police station and ran her mouth to the police.

CHAPTER 53

Malik must have flown to the hospital. Margo was certain the clock on the dash said eight-ten p.m. when they started out. Now it was eight twenty-five p.m. What normally would have been a twenty-five minute ride was accomplished in just under fifteen minutes. Maybe it was also Margo's apprehension at finding the worst. She must be strong. Besides, Malik was with her for support.

The emergency room was full of folks who looked as if they'd settled in for the night. A woman with a red and white head rag tied around her head full of rollers, with three young children in tow, took up a whole row of seats. She didn't seem to care that two of her children were scooting on the floor and pulling on the backs of the chairs of the occupants in the preceding row. There was an older gentleman and a woman who appeared to be his wife who coughed in three/four time. They must have been there a while, because none of the other twenty-five or so emergency room dwellers paid the man or the woman any mind.

Margo and Malik stood in line, waiting their turn for assistance. Margo tried to waltz her way to the front of the line, but the stares of those sick patients who had waited their turn prompted her to retreat to the end of the line.

They finally made it to the information window and were met with a bright, polite smile. "May I help you?" Ms. Wiggins said—her name according to the name-plate pinned above her left breast.

"Yes," Margo spoke up. "My husband, Jefferson Myles, was in an accident…"

"Yes, Mrs. Myles. He was taken to the operating room for emergency surgery. Have a seat, I'll get some-one to assist you."

"Thank you," Margo said, as they walked away from the window. "The way she cut me off," Margo continued as she turned toward Malik, "you would have thought she personally attended to, bandaged, and escorted Jefferson to the emergency room herself—almost as if he was her private property."

"Margo, you're exaggerating. Yeah, she was a little forceful, but that's probably her demeanor."

"Yeah, yeah. I guess I'm a little uptight. I just want Jefferson to be all right."

"He's going to be all right, Margo." Malik rubbed Margo's back, hoping to relieve some of her tension.

They found a couple of chairs far away from head

rag momma and her wide-awake children. Almost as soon as they sat down, Margo heard her name called. She and Malik hurried to the window for the next set of instructions to get them through the maze to find Jefferson.

The nurse gave them directions to the waiting room on the third floor, backing her words with a series of fancy hand gestures. They rushed through the double doors and down the corridor that led to the elevator.

They rode in silence. When the elevator opened, Margo paused, looked up at Malik, grabbed his hand, and disembarked.

The waiting area was virtually deserted—an elderly gentleman sat off in one corner, his head slightly tipped over. He must have been there for some time because his snoring was at a steady pace. He was unmoved when Margo and Malik entered the room.

The receptionist looked bored and distracted— probably not wanting to be there but duty called. Margo approached the desk to see if she could get an update on Jefferson's condition.

"Ma'am, they're still in surgery. He was messed up pretty bad. He had several bullet wounds. You'll have to wait for the doctor for any other information. I'm not sure how much longer it's going to be. I'd suggest that you make yourself as comfortable as possible."

"Thanks," Margo said dejectedly. She walked the few

feet to where Malik sat and slid into the seat next to him. Tears ran down her face for the second or third time today.

Another hour, half-hour passed. Margo decided to get up and stretch her legs while Malik went to get a hot cup of coffee for the both of them. Margo walked up the hall past the reception desk and noticed for the first time a police officer sat inconspicuously at the end of the hallway. Her mind raced, but she pushed the thoughts to the back of her head. He might have been extra security hired just for the holidays or maybe he was taking a break. After all, he was sipping a cup of coffee, which she desperately needed at this moment.

Margo was glad to see Malik, who held two cups of steaming coffee in small white Styrofoam containers. It was going to help calm her nerves.

The hot brew warmed her insides. But before her lips could take the next sip, a tall man draped in a long white coat and blue surgical wear approached.

"Mrs. Myles?"

"Yes," Margo said, standing to her feet and extending her hand.

"I'm Dr. Graham, your husband's physician."

"And this is a friend of the family, Malik Mason," Margo said, gesturing toward Malik. "How is he, Dr. Graham?"

"Mrs. Myles, your husband has suffered a lot of trauma...trauma to the head and neck and some internal organs. He has several cracked ribs, which we have set. We removed a bullet from his side while another passed through his body. It's a miracle no vital organ was pierced by the bullets, although they sustained trauma due to the impact of the car hitting the tree. Let's sit down.

"Your husband is paralyzed on his left side. However, we hope it's only temporary. We'll know more once he wakes up."

Margo gave a long sigh and lowered her face, then brought it up again.

"How long will he have to remain in the hospital, Dr. Graham?" Malik asked, when it became clear that Margo was unable to speak.

"He's going to be around for a while, Mr. Mason, considering the type of injuries he sustained and the inability to move his limbs on the left side."

Margo's eyes were wide and glassed over, but she managed to open her mouth. "Will…will he fully recover?"

"We are unable to say at the moment," Dr. Graham said, choosing his words very carefully. "Again, we hope his paralysis is temporary, but it all depends upon the damage to the neck area and skull. We have run a full CT scan on him and are awaiting the results. We operated immediately to stabilize and control the bleeding along with removing the bullet lodged in his side. We successfully removed the bullet, but the rest will be up to Jefferson and God."

"Do you believe in God, Dr. Graham?"

"Yes, Mrs. Myles, I believe in a higher order. I do believe in God. I know that He's given me the skills necessary to help save many lives. I know an angel was watching over Jefferson."

"Thank you, God," Margo said, looking up to the ceiling, thankful for a sign. "You said you would always be with us and thanks for showing up in Dr. Graham. I know nothing is too hard for you."

"I must go now, but I'll be back in a little while. Jefferson is in recovery, and we'll wheel him to ICU after that. Why don't you go and get something to eat?" Dr. Graham paused and looked at Margo reassuringly. "Again, Mrs. Myles, I do believe in God."

Margo managed a smile and watched Dr. Graham until he disappeared into the elevator. She wrapped her arms around her waist, absorbing the good feeling the doctor had left with her. Jefferson was going to make it. He would live!

The movement of the police officer caused Margo to temporarily lose touch with her good feeling, but she made no move as he walked from one end of the corridor to the other. Malik noticed her sudden agitation and suggested they go to the vending machine to get another cup of coffee.

Malik and Margo rode the elevator to the first floor, anxious to get another cup of coffee and return to Jefferson. When the door opened out onto the first-floor lobby, Angelica nearly bumped into them on her way in.

"Malik, look who's here? It's my long, lost friend, Angelica. What are you doing here?" Both Margo and Malik saw the look of surprise on Angelica's face. She hadn't expected to run into Margo, and prayed that her countenance would not give her away.

"Hey, Margo," Angelica said, half whispering. "Hamilton was shot tonight while going into the police station." Both Margo and Malik gasped. "I'm on my way to see him. He's in ICU. Evidently, you weren't here to visit Hamilton."

"No, Jefferson was in a terrible car accident. They had to perform emergency surgery. He's in recovery now."

"My God, Margo! I'm so sorry. Is he going to be alright?" Angelica asked, concern rippling through her voice. She prayed that Jefferson would be all right. Right now, she was happy that he was alive.

"The doctor is not sure if he'll make a complete recovery. Jefferson is paralyzed on one side, and the doctors aren't sure yet whether or not it's temporary."

"Paralyzed?"

"He was shot and suffered severe trauma to the head and neck which is the source of his paralysis. He has some trauma to some of his internal organs, along with a few cracked ribs."

"My God," Angelica exclaimed again. "Isn't this just coincidental that he and Hamilton would be in the hospital on the same day?" It was a coincidence that would not go unnoticed and Angelica made sure she pointed it out—a way of distancing herself from the situation.

"Very coincidental." Margo's own thoughts had been aroused. She couldn't help but think about her conversation with Malik and what Jefferson had told him. "We're going to get some coffee and some air. Did you say that Hamilton was in ICU?"

"Yeah." Then Angelica reached out to Margo and embraced her with all her might. Tears of sorrow and regret accompanied the hug. Angelica knew she needed to make it right with Margo, and she needed to tell her the truth about whom she was. Although her beginning was what it was, Angelica truly loved Margo. Angelica remained silent, watching Margo and Malik walk out of the hospital.

Angelica was numb. Although her visit to the hospital was to see Hamilton, her greatest concern was for Jefferson. She had been there in the car, lived the ordeal, and survived without a scratch. The police weren't stupid. All too soon, they would realize that another passenger occupied a seat in Jefferson's car. *Such keen minds and modern forensics*, Angelica thought. She hoped she left no tell-tale signs to arouse their curiosity.

CHAPTER 54

Angelica rode the elevator to the third floor. She was apprehensive about taking the few steps to the nurse's station. Her nerves were on edge. She looked about the room that was all but empty, except for the elderly gentleman who seemed to have taken residence there.

Angelica twitched her nose, slumped her shoulders and moved stealthily forward like a secret agent on a mission. She jumped straight in the air when the nurse shouted for an orderly to return to the station to get a lab report that should have been attached to one of the patient's records.

"Are you alright, ma'am?" the nurse asked Angelica.

"She seems awful nervous to me," the nurse whispered to one of the other attendants.

"I'm alright," Angelica said, coming forward. "I'm here to see Hamilton Barnes."

"May I have your name, please?" Angelica hesitated but did not want to seem unreasonable. "Lieutenant Barnes is in a guarded room and only certain people are allowed into the room," the nurse offered.

"I'm Angelica Barnes…his ex-wife."

"Just a moment, I'll escort you."

Angelica followed the nurse down the long, salmon-colored hallway and made a right turn at the end of it. A grumpy-looking police guard sat in front of the door leading to Hamilton's room. He barely looked up when the nurse bounced down the hall. But when he finally noticed that Angelica was in tow, he sat up and asked Angelica for her name—the second time in less than a minute.

The guard's eyes perked up at the mention of her name, and he motioned his permission for them to enter the room. As soon as the door closed, the guard radioed headquarters.

Hamilton was bandaged across his abdomen and lay in a stupor from the effects of the pain medication. He tried to focus but was much too groggy to make out Angelica's face. She stood by his bedside and stroked his arm, wanting him to know that she was there.

The nurse quietly left the two of them. Angelica murmured something to Hamilton. She apologized for not getting to him sooner. If she could have prevented what had happened, she would have. She mumbled something about how she came to be with Santiago and that it was all Hamilton's fault for not making her happy and how her life had turned out. She told him how she had betrayed both him and Jefferson, but in recognizing her mistake tried to warn them.

When she realized it was too late for Hamilton, she warned Jefferson, but it was too late for him also…and the terrible crash…and then her leaving Jefferson in the car to die to save herself…and then walking in the dark for miles once Jefferson had been rescued, and then finally being picked up by the wife of a local minister who was on her way into town to meet her husband for watch night services at their church. Yes, an angel saved her just so she could be with him. Angelica continued to utter inaudible phrases. She abruptly stopped and got up, as if out of a trance and suddenly coming to her senses.

The drugs had worked their magic, and Hamilton snored soundly—probably getting the best sleep of his life. Angelica brushed his hand once more and turned to retreat. She didn't know how long they had been there, but standing by the door was Captain Petrowski and Sergeant Broadnax. By the look on their faces, this was more than a casual visit.

"I'm Mrs. Barnes," Angelica volunteered, extending her arm to Captain Petrowski. She looked at Broadnax. "Hi, Carl."

"I'm Captain Petrowski, Ms. Barnes, with the Fayetteville Police Department. I'm sorry about Hamilton, but I understand he's expected to recover."

"I haven't spoken with the doctor yet about his prognosis, but we're praying that he will fully recover."

"Well, Mrs. Barnes, I'm sure you've noticed the guard

outside. We believe that Hamilton was a target with a contract on his life. The perpetrators might return to finish the job if they find out he's still alive."

Angelica tried to find her breath—shielding her chest as if to brace for an impending heart attack.

"Are you okay?" Captain Petrowski asked.

"Yes, I guess so. Who do you think is after him?" *He seems to be genuinely concerned*, she thought.

"Don't you know?" Sergeant Broadnax cut in. "Seems that you knew who might be after your ex-husband and Jefferson Myles. See, I received a phone call this evening. The caller was Sergeant Walters. Remember her? Sergeant Walters told me that you told her that you needed to warn Lieutenant Barnes and Jefferson Myles about a contract on their life. And even more interesting, they were on a stakeout of Robert Santiago's house. You were tailed leaving his house. What were you doing there? And while you're at it, we'd like for you to tell us all you know."

"Let's take this out into the hallway," Captain Petrowski said, pleased at Sergeant Broadnax's take-charge approach.

"I don't have to answer you, Carl. You don't know what you're talking about."

"I don't? Let me ask you this. Were you in the car with Jefferson Myles this evening?"

"I saw his wife a while ago," Angelica plowed on, ignoring Sergeant Broadnax's question. "She said he was in an accident and in serious condition in this very hospital."

"Maybe you didn't hear the question, Ms. Barnes. I asked, were you with Jefferson Myles this evening?"

"No, the answer is no," Angelica shouted at Sergeant Broadnax. "Hamilton will have your hide for coming at me like that." Angelica pointed her finger shakily in Broadnax's face.

"Lieutenant Barnes won't be having anyone's behind for a long time," Captain Petrowski piped in. "Your ex-husband is in police custody. He's abused the badge and oath he vowed to uphold. But I bet you didn't know that, did you?"

Angelica wrapped her arms around her waist and took a long, hard look at Captain Petrowski. "No, I don't have any idea what you're talking about."

"You will in due time. I suggest you stay close and don't leave the city or the country. Ms. Barnes, you will see us again."

Angelica watched as the two officers plodded down the hallway. She grabbed her coat and purse. She needed to go home and make some decisions. She looked at Hamilton, who was fast asleep, blew him a kiss, and walked out the door.

CHAPTER 55

Malik and Margo headed for the elevator to check on Jefferson's prognosis. Something wasn't quite right, and Margo felt it in every joint of her body.

They slowed their gait to avoid a collision path they found themselves on as Captain Petrowski and Sergeant Broadnax appeared out of nowhere. Petrowski and Broadnax held onto their hot coffees, surprise registering on Petrowski's face, recognizing Margo Myles as soon as she turned the corner.

"Hello, Mrs. Myles," Petrowski said somberly. "This is Sergeant Broadnax from the Richmond Heights police station." Broadnax nodded.

"Hello, Captain Petrowski. This is Malik Mason, a friend of the family." Malik extended his hand to the two officers. "Are you here about my husband's accident?"

Petrowski paused. "May I speak with you in private, Mrs. Myles? There's a lounge around the corner. Sergeant Broadnax and I would like to share a few things we think you should be aware of."

Margo shifted her eyes between Petrowski and Broadnax, then slowly toward Malik.

"Alright, but I'd like for Mr. Mason to accompany me. Whatever you need to say to me, you can say it in front of him."

Petrowski scratched his head and glanced quickly at Broadnax. "Very well, if you like."

"Fine," Margo acknowledged. "Lead the way."

The foursome walked in silence save the sound of their shoes hitting the hard, tiled floor...*click*, *click*, *clickety-click*. They made a quick series of left and right turns until they were in front of a clinic waiting room. Petrowski stood while the others took a seat.

"We are… I…I want you to know that we don't believe that this was an accident but an attempt on your husband's life, Mrs. Myles. I'm not going to beat around the bush. Your husband has been involved with people who are tied to a contra rebel group in Central America.

"They have reportedly stolen guns from Fort Bragg. We believe your husband has embezzled large sums of money from his business accounts to help fund this operation from which he has made huge profits. Then there's the matter of the two homicides—Blake Montgomery and Marsha Wilson. We are almost certain both murders are connected.

Margo looked thoughtfully at Captain Petrowski. Something about him made her skin crawl. It was true

Jefferson had made his bed, but somehow Petrowski seemed to gloat in this minor victory. She could see the adrenaline run through his veins and for a fleeting second saw headlines that could possibly grace the morning paper. *Captain Robert Petrowski, All-American City's Man of the Year Cracks Big Case and Sends Black Businessman Jefferson Myles Straight to Prison.* Margo snapped out of her reverie. "And what's going to happen to Jefferson?"

"He will more than likely be arrested. You may pick up the items we retrieved from your husband's car from the station the day after tomorrow, tomorrow being a holiday."

"Thank you, Captain. I'll be down on Monday. But I do have a question. Will Jefferson be charged with murder?"

"I can't say right now, Mrs. Myles. Oh, and one last question for you. Do you know Angelica Barnes?"

CHAPTER 56

The lobby was still when Petrowski, Broadnax, Margo, and Malik returned. Margo held onto Malik's arm for support, weary from all she had learned. She thanked God over and over for Malik being in the right place at the right time; she could always count on him.

As the foursome prepared to part ways, the lobby door opened and a young woman flew in, running up to the startled group.

"Mother! Malik."

"Ivy? What are you doing here?"

"I'll be talking with you later, Mrs. Myles," Captain Petrowski said. He and Sergeant Broadnax left without another word.

"I didn't feel right being at the party," Ivy began, catching her breath.

"How did you find us?"

"When I got home and didn't find you, I started to panic a little. See…I knew Dad…"

"It's okay, Ivy. I know all about your dad and…and…

Linda. It's a long story, but now my concern is for him. He's battling for his life in more ways than one."

"How is he doing?"

"We haven't been able to see him," Margo continued. "He was in a terrible accident this evening that left his body pretty banged up and his car totaled."

"My God, Mother! How did it happen?"

"Malik will give you the sordid details. Did you say how you found us?"

"The answering machine. Somehow you recorded your conversation with the officer when he called, and as soon as I heard 'hospital,' I got here as fast as I could."

"I'm glad you came, baby," Margo said, pulling Ivy close for one of her motherly hugs. "Your dad is going to need all of our prayers and support. Right, Malik?"

"You know it."

The trio sat in the waiting room hoping to receive a sign that Jefferson would be all right. When they were finally admitted to Jefferson's room in ICU, Margo was the only one who ventured in. The patient encased in mummy's clothing met Margo's staring eyes. Jefferson remained still and lifeless with his eyes closed. The lips Margo had kissed on their first date, the day they were married, their first anniversary together, and the night they celebrated their love, lay swollen and extended beyond the exposed bandages. And she stroked those lips with her own, fell to her knees, and began to pray. If anyone had her back, Margo knew God did. She got up from her knees and continued praying for Jefferson for the next hour until Ivy sent a nurse in to check on her.

Something was amiss. Linda could feel it in her bones which ached from loneliness and betrayal. There was something going on at the Myles' home, and her gut feeling said it had to do with Jefferson.

How could it come to this? Linda asked herself. For six months, she and Jefferson hid a budding romance that started out innocently enough. However, a seed was planted, then a flower bloomed and blossomed. But unlike a flower, she and Jefferson were unwilling to let what happened between them die.

Now, she was just another neighbor—who no longer belonged to the club. Gone were the days when she could run over to Margo's and trade a cup of sugar for a plate of Rice Krispie Treats or accept an invite, "Come on over for dinner if you haven't cooked; we've got plenty." Her access card had been stripped. Linda had ignored the possible consequences until it was too late.

Linda poured herself a cup of coffee and sank down in one of the wooden chairs that flanked her breakfast table. She couldn't understand the scene of Margo and Malik hurrying to his car and driving off like they were responding to a three-alarm fire.

It was a clear, crisp New Year's Day. The sun peered through the kitchen window, adding warmth to what had been forecasted as a dreary day. Linda took another sip of her coffee, then looked about the room that was decorated in country kitchen.

The blue and white wallpaper hosted flock after flock of mother hens and her brood, gingerly walking from one wall to the other. Blue and white gingham curtains hung at the two windows with ruffled tiers strung across the top. Several types of Longaberger Baskets adorned the kitchen counters holding anything from napkins, tea and coffee, to paper and pencils. Country kitchen magnets covered the refrigerator, and hen napkin holders, hen coffee mugs, and hen collector plates normally made Linda want to get up and dance a jig.

But Linda didn't feel like dancing or anything else for that matter. She was very lonely. There was no consoling her, even with all the hens and chickens trying to get her attention. But if Blake had been alive, the day would have been just another day. He hated football. Didn't understand why grown men made a fuss over some jackass kicking a ball and running all over a field with other crazies running after him. Linda lowered her head and sighed at the memory.

She put down her coffee cup, rose from the table, and headed outside to retrieve the morning newspaper. Was Jefferson home? She had not seen him since their meeting the other night. What had Captain Petrowski done with the information she gave him? So much was going through Linda's head. No cops had ventured into their neighborhood; she would have known since she kept a vigil ever since she spilled her guts.

Linda looked out cautiously, not wanting to run into Margo. It seemed awfully quiet next door—nothing seemed to stir. Even the trees stood still without bending—almost as if they stood watch, ready to guard against any outsiders who dared trespass. The blinds and curtains were still drawn which was certainly unusual for Margo. Margo was an early riser and always had the blinds opened by seven. It was now eight a.m.

Linda pulled her paper out of the box and waved back at Vera Watkins across the street. Vera was the neighborhood gossip, and Linda was not up to a session of retold neighbor exploits with Vera this morning. Linda walked briskly ignoring Vera's frantic calls to her, but Vera was moving fast—her legs and arms swinging in perfect formation for the one-hundred-yard dash.

"Linda!" Vera yelled out of breath, hoping to catch her before she closed the door.

"Hey, Vera," Linda said, stepping back out of the house and onto the driveway. "Happy New Year."

"Happy New Year to you, too. Did you hear about…?"

Vera pointed toward the Myles' house with her head.

"Did I hear what, Vera?" Linda asked slowly.

"About Jefferson. He was in a terrible car accident."

Linda gasped, then returned to look at Vera with a blank look on her face. Now it all made sense...Margo and Malik so in a hurry. Linda's heart sank.

"You mean Margo hasn't told you?" Vera plowed on. "She's probably tearing her hair out. I heard it was a bad one."

"What happened? Is Jefferson alright?"

"The news said he was gunned down and run off the road." Linda gasped. "Said that Jefferson was fortunate to be alive, especially finding him when they did. He had lost a lot of blood and may have been in that tangled mess for more than a half-hour. He's at Cape Fear."

"What tangled mess?" Linda inquired as if it wasn't obvious.

"His car. His Mercedes was totaled. Oh, I forgot. A police lieutenant was also gunned down at his precinct less than an hour before Jefferson was hit. Seems there may be a connection."

"Wow," was all Linda could say.

"This is scary, Linda. First Blake, now Jefferson." Vera was talking too much. She wasn't trying to be insensitive, but this was headline news. "Sorry, Linda. I get carried away sometimes. I know all of this has been hard on you."

"Forget it. I'll have to talk about Blake sooner or later."

"Well, let me go. If you should hear anything, let me know."

"Yeah, I'll let you know," Linda said in a half-whisper.

Vera sprinted across the street leaving Linda standing in the driveway.

Linda looked over at the Myles' residence and dropped her head. There had been so much tragedy, and all in a week's time. Linda couldn't take anymore. She tucked her newspaper under her arm and went inside.

Linda picked up the phone to call Margo, hesitated and replaced the receiver in its cradle. Margo didn't want to talk to her. But Margo would have all the answers, and Linda needed some. Regardless of their immediate situation, Linda still cared for Jefferson—they had all been friends for more than ten years.

Linda picked up the newspaper and scoured it for the story. There was only a small blurb. She turned on the television hoping to get some information from the morning news.

She waited ten minutes and finally there was a recap of the morning's top stories. Linda shrank when Jefferson's picture filled the screen. It was the picture on Jefferson's driver's license. She remembered it well, having picked it up from the nightstand and looking at all his vital statistics the first time they made love.

Linda's eyes welled up preparing for tears when she heard the announcer say that Jefferson's accident might have been a contracted hit on his life. *What if I had been in the car with him?*

Now that she had witnessed the news firsthand, Linda wasn't ready to accept what she had heard. She switched to CNN *Headline News,* and again, Jefferson's face exploded onto the screen. *Good Morning America* was at the end of their recap of the story—Diane Sawyer repeating what Linda had already heard on the other channels. Jefferson's story had gone nationwide, and now they were talking about a possible link to an Iran-Contra like operation that may involve stolen weapons from Ft. Bragg, North Carolina. The scandal involved some prominent people and threatened to put Fayetteville, North Carolina back on the national map for months to come.

The remote control shook in her hands. Linda quickly hit the "off" button, silencing the voices that threatened to take control of her senses.

"I've got to know for myself," Linda mused out loud. "I don't need Margo to get answers. I've got my own resources."

CHAPTER 57

New Year's Day had come and gone with little fanfare. Most people enjoyed the day, relaxing, watching the Bowl games and parades that were famous on the first day of the year. Today was January 2nd, and Ebony and Katrina were burying their mother, Marsha.

Margo's timing couldn't have been worse. The last face she wanted to see was Linda's, but there she stood as Margo prepared to leave for Marsha's funeral. Winter and Ivy went ahead, and Margo found herself alone with the wicked witch from the East. How did they end up in their driveways at the same time this morning?

Linda and Margo exchanged glances, and Margo said with her hearty stare—*Don't look at me and forget about trying to have a conversation. Where I'm going and what I do is none of your business. Your friendship card has expired and is non-renewable.* Margo's countenance began to change as she toiled with her inner-self. *Lord, help me to be a good Christian. I can't go there with Linda just yet.*

I get these awful feelings—like I want to slap her like I was her momma. Forgive me, Lord.

Ivy sang "Precious Lord" at the funeral. Her voice made the walls of the tiny chapel shake. Sergeant Broadnax was there to support Ebony, although it appeared that he was playing a lot larger role in her life these days. He was very attentive and sat next to Ebony and Katrina in the long, black stretch limo as it headed to the cemetery. Marsha wasn't much of a mother, but she was their mother.

CHAPTER 58

It was quiet in the house when Margo returned home. Ivy, Winter, Winston, and JR were holed up in their rooms recuperating from the long weekend. Margo had been at the hospital most of the day since the funeral, and all she wanted to do now was take a hot bath and rest. With all that was going on, she hadn't had a moment to herself.

She turned the water on in the tub and plopped a couple of bath beads into the water. She slowly removed her clothes and sat at the vanity while the water was running. She thought about Jefferson lying up in that hospital bed, all bandaged up. So helpless, when only the day before he had walked out on her, had even confessed his love for their next-door neighbor. As it turned out, she was the one praying for him, talking to him, by his side when the others were nowhere around. Then a vision of Angelica flashed before her. She seemed a little distant these past few days. Must be Hamilton. So consumed with Jefferson's well-being, Margo had forgotten about Hamilton. She really needed to go and see him. Margo had been under a lot of stress lately, and she really had no idea what was up with anybody.

The water finally reached the level that Margo wanted and she leaned over the tub to turn it off. *Only seconds away from stress relief*, she thought. And then Ivy's voice shouted throughout the house, calling her name.

"Go away," Margo shouted back, as she continued her descent into the tub.

"Mom, you've got to see this!" Ivy shouted, entering Margo's room. "The late-news headline just announced that they have a late-breaking story. They mentioned that they may have a suspect in Blake Montgomery's and Marsha Wilson's murder."

"What?" Margo retorted, jumping out of the tub. She grabbed a bath towel off the rack and quickly wrapped it around her body to keep from shivering. "Turn my TV on, quick."

Ivy had barely turned on the TV when the newscaster went live to Denver Grey in Fayetteville. "We have a late-breaking story that happened just minutes ago. Robert Santiago, the subject of a six-month FBI investigation into a contra arms deal to Honduras, eluded police this evening after he was sighted at a vacant warehouse with a known arms dealer, also wanted by the FBI. It is believed that Santiago was transferring a cache of stolen arms, those believed to be missing from Fort Bragg.

"Ray Adams, who was arrested last week with another parcel of stolen arms, cooperated with authorities and gave police information to make a possible arrest in this case. Authorities believe Santiago and others not only played major roles in the theft and transport of stolen arms, but may have also been linked to the two murders and two attempted murders that took place in Fayetteville last week. Adams, who plea-bargained for a lighter sentence for his role in this case, still remains behind bars. This is Denver Grey of Station WYZZ, reporting live to you from Fayetteville, North Carolina."

"Did you hear that? They may know who killed Mr. Montgomery and Ebony's mom."

"Don't get overly excited, Ivy. I feel an avalanche getting ready to descend on us."

"Mom, what are you talking about? Is this what Dad was a part of—this Operation Stingray…Dad?"

"What did Malik tell you?"

"Basically, that Dad was in a lot of trouble—mainly for misappropriating funds and that some people were after him because of it, and that the crash might not have been an accident."

"Well, Malik tiptoed around that pretty good. You need to know what's going on, but I'm not up to it at the moment. Our lives are getting ready to change, and things will not be pretty for a while. That's why we need to be of one accord and aware of everything that's going on. Also, remind me to go to the police station tomorrow to pick up your father's things that were taken from his car."

"Mom, you've become a pillar of strength. After all that Dad has put you through, you're still going to stick by his side and take whatever we'll be facing head-on. I feel that somehow I let you down. Winter and I were talking, and you have our support for whatever you need."

"That's right," Winter said, entering her mother's room. "If I need to, I can miss the next semester of school so that I can be here to help in any way I can."

"No, you and Winston are going back to school. There's nothing you can do at this time. I'm not sure what to even expect just yet. I'm leaning on God to help get us through this. Do you girls understand what is going on and what might happen to your dad?"

"Yeah." Winter sighed. "Dad may go to jail. He may lose his business. We might lose the house."

"That's enough, Winter," Ivy piped in. "We get the idea." Both girls sat with Margo on the bed forming a human chain among the three of them. "I feel like singing, 'We Shall Overcome.'"

"Now who's being silly?" Winter pulled up a pillow and hit Ivy in the head.

"Alright, ladies, I've got to take my bath before my water gets cold. But before I do, I want you both to look at me and listen to what I'm going to say. I love your daddy. I'm going to stick by his side to the end. He lost his direction for a minute, but I'm going to be there for him until the end."

Ivy and Winter looked from Margo to each other. There was no mistaking that Margo meant what she said. They saw the pain on her face, but love for their dad was also etched there.

"Now, go on and let me get my bath."

"Okay, Mom. We'll be here when you get out. And I'll go with you to the station tomorrow."

"Me, too," Winter echoed. "And thanks."

Margo looked at her two young ladies and smiled. She was blessed to have four beautiful children, but her girls were her heart.

CHAPTER 59

Margo rose early. She had a full plate on her schedule today. She had several houses to show, but she needed to go to the Fayetteville Police Department to retrieve Jefferson's things before stopping by the hospital. Jefferson was still in a semi-coma. He had some swelling on the brain, but Dr. Graham had reassured Margo that Jefferson would pull through. He was responsive to certain stimuli, and Dr. Graham was hopeful that with vigorous physical therapy treatments, there would be some improvement in his present state.

Jefferson was still paralyzed.

Malik told Margo that Hamilton was doing much better and had been moved to a private room. Margo would have to call Angelica later and get the scoop. Strange that she hadn't heard from her since running into her at the hospital. Malik didn't say much about it either when she mentioned it to him.

"Ivy, Winter, I'm ready to go if you all are going with me!" Margo could still holler like she did when the kids were younger. As long as they were around, she'd have to keep those vocal chords tuned, although she would never use them for singing.

The trio got in the car and backed out of the driveway. Margo gasped. She barely missed hitting Linda, who was obviously waiting for them to pull out. "What does she want now?"

Linda lightly tapped the window, and all three heads turned in her direction looking as if they would devour Linda in one fell swoop.

"You better move before I run over you!" Margo shouted, rolling the window down so that Linda would not miss a word she was saying. "You've got some nerve coming over here. You don't seem to get it, do you?"

Linda sighed. "Margo, please. I know we'll never be friends again, and I don't blame you for the way you feel about me. But I would like for us to talk."

Margo's eyes became sockets of hot coal. She jumped from the car, stood in front of Linda, and jabbed her finger in Linda's chest. "You ought to be glad I'm a Christian woman. Every night since I found out about you and Jefferson, I dream. I dream that I have a gun pointed at your f…n' head, and I pull the trigger. That dream is still crystal clear when I get up each morning, and I beg God with every ounce of my being to erase it from my thoughts. You ought to be grateful, you adulterous hussy…you ought to be grateful."

Not a tear fell from Margo's eyes. She turned away, got back into her car and drove off, leaving Linda standing in the driveway with her mouth wide open—so wide, it looked as if she was preparing for oral surgery.

Linda stood in the driveway another ten minutes. She drew her lips together, nodded her head, and headed into the house to get her purse and keys. Today would be the day. No more putting off what she could not bring herself to do the last few days. She had to see Jefferson, and if her intuition was right, this was the right time to go. She had to make one stop first and then on to the hospital. She'd be in and out. Margo wouldn't be the wiser.

They drove to the police department in silence. Seeing Linda had upset Margo. She wanted to forgive, but it wasn't in her just now. And she wasn't up to bartering with the devil. But if she was going to let God guide and direct her through her trials, she knew her heart had to be open to receive what He had for her. This was probably her test—the test of forgiveness. Naw, she wasn't ready to forgive Linda of her fornicating sins.

This had been a Job experience for Margo. Job had lost everything—his cattle, his wife, and his children. Margo felt all alone—even her best friend, Angelica, seemed to have abandoned her. Maybe God was trying to get her attention.

"God forgive me," Margo cried out. And Ivy and Winter looked at their mother and let her have her moment.

They arrived at the police station without another outburst. The city was getting back to normal. Its maintenance team was already taking down Christmas lights and wreaths that hung from lampposts throughout the city. Margo sat a moment before she attempted to get out of the car. It was less than a week since she had graced this place with her presence, only to find out that her world was in a bigger mess than she knew it to be. She told the girls that she'd be just a minute, but they insisted on going in with her.

The place hadn't changed since she was there last. The same drab walls and uninterested receptionist held up the lobby. The receptionist seemed to recognize Margo, but Margo ignored her and asked for Captain Petrowski.

"Just a moment…and your name?"

"Margo Myles."

They stood in the hallway walking around in an imaginary circle for ten minutes before Captain Petrowski ushered them in. He led them to the property room and told the sergeant behind the counter to retrieve the items taken from Jefferson Myles' car, Item #6248.

Petrowski was rather reserved today, not even the small talk. That was fine with Margo because she didn't feel much like talking either. Another ten minutes had gone by before the sergeant returned with a cardboard box.

"Please sign here," the sergeant said, indicating the location with his index finger. "Thanks."

Captain Petrowski bade farewell and left mother and daughters to their own devices. Ivy pulled Jefferson's wallet from the box, but it was Margo's expression that made Ivy and Winter discontinue their probe.

"Jesus! Oh my God!" Margo wailed. "Jefferson why, why, why, why?"

"Mother, please," Ivy protested. "What's wrong, now?"

Margo couldn't say anything for her out-and-out crying. "May I help?" offered the sergeant.

"Something about the box," Winter said.

The sergeant looked in the box and pulled out the contents. And the girls recognized the culprit as soon as the sergeant said, "This is a phat scarf. One day I'll be able to afford to get my wife one."

Winter and Ivy grabbed Margo. They snatched the box from the sergeant and led their mother to the car. Captain Robert Petrowski stood in the shadows witnessing what he knew was the confirmation to the missing piece in the puzzle. Everybody was going to pay.

"How could she look me in the face and not say a word, and to think I called her my best friend? I cried on her shoulders and bared my soul. No wonder she hasn't been around. She was the *detail at six*, the *breaking headline story*; and all this time I'm thinking that the wench next door was my only enemy. *Yea, though I walk through the valley of the shadow of death, I will fear no evil: for thou art with me; thy rod and thy staff they comfort me.* God was preparing me for this—my Job experience. And Joyce Meyer said it best, 'Double for your trouble.'"

"Calm down, Mom," Ivy admonished. "We'll be home soon. I'm going to call Dr. Graham and tell him you won't be coming today. Maybe he can prescribe something for you."

"No, I've got to go to the hospital. I've got to see Jefferson. This is the only way I'm going to be able to deal with this mess."

"Mom, don't put yourself through this," Winter interjected. "Dad is getting what he deserves, and getting more worked up about it isn't going to do you any good."

"Don't let me hear you say that again!"

"But, Mom."

"Cool it, Winter," Ivy said.

"I want you both to listen to me. This family is going to stay together. Your father and I have a tough road ahead. Sometimes I get so angry that I want to beat him out of his misery. But that's the man I fell in love with over twenty-five years ago…and ladies, I still love him. I don't know why he's done the things he did, but I can't worry about that right now. We haven't come this far to give up everything that ever meant anything to us.

"Look at you two...ready to do battle. The battle is between your father and me. Let us handle it. You stand strong and help keep the family together. Now, I'm going to take you home so I can go to the hospital and be alone with my husband."

"No, we're going with you," Winter said. "We're going to see our father..."

Ivy interrupted. "What about Angelica?"

Margo was silent. Then she turned and looked at Ivy. "Don't ever say her name in my presence again."

No one uttered another word.

CHAPTER 60

Her black wool brim was a perfect fit, falling right at her ears and around the middle of her forehead. The dark sunglasses shaded her eyes, giving her a look of anonymity. She pulled her black wool blazer from a hall closet and grabbed her black leather bag off the wooden chair in the kitchen. She slung the bag across her shoulders and proceeded outside.

The air was brisk with no sign of hurricane Margo. The last thing she wanted to do was run into Margo again. Linda had had about enough of Margo's antics, even if she had brought it on herself. The attempt had been made to bring a peaceful resolve to their decaying friendship, and it was very clear to Linda that there was nothing left to salvage.

The security system on, Linda got in her car and proceeded down Andover Street and out of the Jordan Estates subdivision. Glancing at each house as she drove past—the Davises two houses down, the Barkleys on the left, Vera Watkins across the street, and the Oswalds on the corner—the neighborhood no longer held for

Linda the feeling of home. She seemed estranged from it—more by choice, although she hadn't realized it.

It was amazing what she noticed when she took the time to look. There was a new drugstore being built a half-mile from her subdivision as well as a brand-new Harris Teeter, flanked on either side by several smaller stores yet to be named.

"It would be nice if we could have a real nice restaurant on this end," Linda muttered to herself. The community had grown almost two-fold since she first came to Fayetteville. "One more stoplight to go, and I'll be there."

A lime-green VW Beetle pulled up next to Linda at the light. Heavy metal oozed from the Bose speakers that hung on both sides of the back window. Blond, streaked hair fell over the eyes of the teen in the front passenger seat. He also wore an earring in his right ear and one in his nose.

The teen turned to look at Linda. He stuck out his tongue that had a large steel-colored earring pierced on it. He began to gyrate his tongue and then rapidly stuck it in and out of his mouth, pointing at Linda. Linda gasped, while the other two boys laughed at their friend's antics. The light turned green, and they sped off.

"You prick. You should be in school!" Linda shouted at the wind, repulsed by the young man's innuendo. She had grown kids of her own, and some low-down, sorry-ass punk wasn't going to disrespect her like that. "I wish I knew who your mother was!" Linda continued to yell at no one. "I'd tell her what a terrible job she's done raising you."

Linda's hand shook, and she grabbed the steering wheel tight to avoid veering into the other lane.

"I'm here." She sighed. "I'm here."

Linda turned left into the cemetery and made another right at the end of the first row. Blake was buried at the North end overlooking a small but beautiful man-made lake. Rows upon rows of pretty flowers of all varieties sat in bronze cups just in front of headstones or extended from above-ground vaults. It was a sea of floral splendor—a horizon resting on the ground in beautiful pastel colors of pink, yellow, red, and lavender. Linda drove into the horizon until she located Blake's grave— a mound of fresh flowers waiting to settle.

Linda sat in the car, not quite sure she wanted to get out. She peered out over the calm—the flowers finally becoming a blur as she let her face fall on the steering wheel, a lone tear trickling down her face. She had come to purge her soul and ask Blake for forgiveness. To tell him what she should have told him a long time ago— she was unhappy. Maybe their marriage would have survived if Blake had been given the opportunity to work with her on their problem.

It was too late now. And while Blake would never hear the words she came to utter at the soft mound of dirt, it would certainly make Linda feel better.

She stepped from the car and walked slowly to the

gravesite. She still gave the appearance of a woman in mourning or perhaps a woman who had something to hide.

Words rolled from her tongue as she said her final goodbye. Stooping down, Linda picked up a handful of dirt and let it fall through her fingers like a sifter. Pursing her lips, Linda brought her hands to her mouth and kissed them, finally swinging her arms across the place where Blake lay.

"Goodbye, my love." And she headed back to the car, never once turning around to look back. The tires on her white Honda Accord gave a little screech as she careened from the cemetery. Now she was ready to embark on her most urgent task for today, and that was to see Jefferson. It was ten-thirty a.m.

Linda drove south, then east observing the sights and sounds with renewed interest. All at once the city seemed abuzz. Senior citizens leisurely strolled about, and the working class, the nine-to-fivers, looked forward to a promising economic future now that the new millennium had descended upon them.

"Two blocks to go." Linda sighed out loud. "I've got to get through this. I've got to know that Jefferson will be alright."

The hospital lay ahead. Linda maneuvered her car into the left lane and slowed to a stop when the light changed from yellow to red. She tapped the steering wheel lightly until the taps became loud thuds—a sign that her nervousness was getting the best of her. The light changed, and she turned left into the hospital parking lot and then a right into the visitor's area.

She pulled into the first available parking space, turned off the engine, exhaled, and proceeded to get out of the car. Both of her men were victims of a serious accident. One was dead, the other in serious condition. Blake was her husband, Jefferson her lover. It was reported that her lover's condition had gone from serious to stable and he was in for a long recovery.

A steady stream of people shuffled through the hospital corridors. Linda looked left and right, reading the signs that would lead her to the area where Jefferson lay recuperating. A heavy-set nurse in a crisp, starched white uniform, apparently on her way to obtain blood samples, emerged from an elevator just as Linda contemplated whether to get on or not. Desperate to find Jefferson, Linda solicited the help of the nurse who was able to direct her.

The doors to the elevator closed. Three floors up, and Linda would be closer to the man who for a brief moment gave her hope and promise. Her heart began to flutter. It was much too late now to question whether or not she was doing the right thing. The man she loved lay in a weakened state, unable to lift a finger to touch her. Nor could he move his hands that once held her and tendered her flesh like new money. The elevator door opened causing Linda to lay her thoughts aside. It was the third floor, and Linda walked out, her eyes darting about the room trying to decide what to do next.

Busy with their daily routine, the nurses at their stations barely looked up when Linda entered their ward. Visitors were in and out all day long—many familiar with where they had to go, and Linda was just another face in the crowd. She hesitated, not sure if she should ask about Jefferson's whereabouts. Margo might have a list of preferred visitors and ones not so preferred. Then she spotted it—a board with patient names and their room number listed on it.

Linda moved stealthily past the board. A heavy-set nurse, her braided hair pulled up into a ball, looked up but suddenly looked away when a co-worker asked for a chart. *Jefferson Myles, Room 313.* Linda quickly extracted and continued straight ahead, scanning each door as she passed. Moving as briskly as she could, Linda walked until she came to the end of the corridor.

She turned a corner and stopped abruptly. A uniformed policeman sat slouched in a chair outside of one of the hospital room doors at the far end of the corridor. Linda swallowed, steadied her gait and walked straight ahead.

Upon reaching the officer, Linda stopped and introduced herself as one of Jefferson's neighbors. She was prepared to give Vera's name instead of her own, if she had to. The officer gave her access, and she opened the door to the private room where she found Jefferson bandaged from head to toe, lying quiet and still. She stood at the door for several minutes unable to move forward but not taking her eyes away from the figure that was before her.

The steady beep from the vitals monitor was the only noise in a much-too-quiet room. Glancing around the pale yellow room, Linda saw containers of flowers on the windowsill and throughout the room. Several get-well helium balloons had floated to the ceiling, and a cluster of get-well cards sat together on a tray along with a box of Kleenex and a set of patient instructions.

Linda walked slowly toward Jefferson. She thought she saw him flinch, but as she moved closer, she saw that his eyes were closed. Tubes were running here and there, and an IV drip was attached to his right arm. Jefferson appeared swollen, but Linda was unable to tell a whole lot with so much gauze and tape wrapped around his body.

She reached out and touched him, but he did not move. *He must be drugged.* Linda pulled up a chair and sat down staring upon the battered face.

"I'm so sorry, Jefferson…so sorry. How did you end up like this? Maybe you and I are suffering for our sins. I went by and saw Blake today. He's resting. I told him I loved him and that I had been happy most of our marriage. But I guess it was a little too late.

"I also saw Margo today. She hates my guts. I'm not sure what I'm going to do. I certainly can't continue to live next door with all of this over our heads. I love you, Jefferson, but I do have a confession to make. I went to the police and told them about that night… you know…the night at the house where something strange was going on. I also told the police about a conversation I overheard while you were talking on the phone when we were at the motel. I sold you out, and I'm sorry. I know it was guilt that drove me."

Linda was silent. She continued to gaze upon Jefferson—a faint smile caressing her face. She patted her lover once more, then looked down at her watch.

"I've got to go, sweetie. Maybe I can visit you again. I don't want to be here if Margo should come. That wouldn't be a good thing. I love you." Linda stood and leaned over the bed railing and placed a kiss on Jefferson's bandaged cheek…then his lips. She paused, looking down at him. He seemed so peaceful and without a care in the world. She continued to look as if she'd never see him again.

Then she thought she saw Jefferson's eyelids flutter. Maybe he was dreaming about the first time they made love to each other. "I love you," she said again. And she headed for the door.

"Sit in the car. I need to see your daddy by myself. I have a few things to discuss with him that you don't need to hear."

"Please, Mom," Ivy whined. "Winter and I know what you're going to say to Dad, but I don't understand all the drama since he can't hear you, anyway."

"It's not for you to understand. I've got to get things off my chest. I just can't get over finding An-gel-i-...Angelica's scarf in that box—the scarf that I gave her for Christmas!" Margo sighed. "No wonder she looked at me strangely. If I had known then, I would have killed her right in the hospital. Pathetic bitch. She couldn't keep up with her own husband."

"He's sooooooo fine," Winter reiterated.

"He may have all the tools and a pretty face to go with it, but…," Ivy tried to say.

"Fine," Winter exhorted again.

"Anyway, I was saying that your good-looking Lieutenant Barnes, and I'll agree that he is fine—no *p-h-i-n-e*, is not worth the worry or the time because he's scum."

"How would you know?"

"Because I know, sister dear. Ask Mom. She knows the deal about her sorry-ass friend's sorry-ass husband."

"Ivy, that's enough. Watch your mouth."

"Well, Mom?"

"I don't have time to talk about Hamilton Barnes. Your daddy is my concern. I want him to open up one eye, just one eye, so I can punch him in it." Margo paused. "I'm sorry, ladies. I'm letting this mess get the best of me. It's hard for me to comprehend what has been going on with your daddy, and right up under my nose. All I ever wanted was to be a good wife and mother, be successful and make my family proud. Where did I go wrong?"

"Mom, don't stress yourself," Winter said. "Look at us, you've done a fine job."

"Exactly," Ivy countered. "Look at you."

"Girl, don't play with me. Winston and I are our parents' greatest creation."

"Yeah, right."

"Would you both be quiet? This family is going to make it no matter what. And there's nothing wrong with any of you."

The Myles women rode in silence. The entrance into the hospital parking lot was at the next light. Each entertained her own thoughts, but Ivy and Winter were worried about their mother. She had been hurt by their father's infidelity, and to add insult to injury, finding Angelica's scarf. There was not too much more she could take.

"Visiting hours have started," Margo muttered, looking at the clock on the dash. "Ten fifty-five a.m.; my day has got to be better than it was earlier."

The trio walked silently into the hospital and headed for the elevator. The surroundings were becoming too familiar. Even the medicinal smell that Winter absolutely abhorred was as commonplace as going to the bathroom with a magazine in your hand. But they would tough it out as long as they had to.

Bing. Everyone jumped at the sound of the approaching elevator. Mother and daughters now recovered were reunited with their senses and the purpose of their mission. Margo was on her way to let Jefferson have it, and the girls were there to try and make things as civil as possible. Margo seemed to be much calmer than she was earlier. They stepped in the elevator and the door closed behind them

First floor, second floor, third floor, and the elevator stopped. The door to the elevator opened and out poured mother and daughters. They waved to the nurses at the nurses' station when they passed and continued on to see Jefferson. It was quite busy today, they noted.

At the end of the hall, they turned and saw Sergeant Jeremy Monroe glued to his seat. He was in his late forties and a little on the chubby side—probably used to deskwork.

"Hey, Sergeant Monroe," Margo said softly.

"Good morning to you all."

The girls nodded.

Just as Margo turned the knob, Sergeant Monroe remembered that the neighbor was still in the room.

Before he could get it out of his mouth, the door was open and a startled Linda fell back as Margo pushed the door in.

It was a scene straight from *The Color Purple* where everyone is sitting around the table and Ms. Celie, played by Whoopi Goldberg, grabs the butcher knife and commences to telling Mister, played by Danny Glover, that everything he had done to her had already been done to him. And everything else he'd do would fail. Ms. Celie has everyone's rapt attention—food suspended in mid-air waiting for the bomb to drop, all except Ms. Sophia played by Oprah Winfrey, who is somewhat vindicated for the treatment she received years ago by Mister.

Linda tumbled backward, almost falling onto Jefferson's bed—her eyes bulging from their sockets.

"Jesus, no! Jesus, no!" Margo shouted, waving her hand for emphasis. Her eyes became two huge balls of fire. "Oh my God. I don't believe this! What is this tramp doing in here? Why are you in my husband's room?"

Linda continued to stare.

"Yeah, I'm talking to you, bitch. What the hell are you doing here?"

Linda tried to back up but found she could not move any further. Margo marched up to her and got in her face, ignoring Jefferson's sleeping body. "I came to see how Jefferson was doing," was Linda's weak reply.

Ivy and Winter were close behind Margo, ready to assist in whatever way they saw fit.

Margo grabbed Linda by the collar of her blazer and pulled her within an inch of her nose. "You came to see Jefferson, did you? Well, you came for an ass whooping because I've had it up to here with you. This is the last straw. I thought I made myself perfectly clear this morning that I didn't want to see you ever again, and that also meant sneaking around to see Jefferson."

"I tried to talk to you, Margo."

"You're a stupid bitch if you thought I was going to allow you to come and see *my* husband. I don't know how you got past the guard, but I'm going to have a word with him."

"Let go of me, please."

"When I get good and ready." Hot air rushed to Linda's face as Margo twirled Linda around to face Jefferson. "See what you've done? He wouldn't be lying in here if it wasn't for you."

"That's not true. I had nothing to do with this."

"Look at him. I want you to take a good look," Margo continued, pushing Linda almost on top of Jefferson so that there would be no mistaking what Linda saw.

"I've already seen him, Margo, and…I love him, too. And nothing you do to me will change that."

The room stood still as two pairs of eyes watched their mother's reaction to Linda's very explicit words.

Margo moved in slow motion, her hands absently releasing the collar of Linda's jacket but now set for an all-out assault on the woman who dared to tell her to her face that she was in love with her husband—a dream photo shoot for a still photographer with a wide-open shutter. Margo lunged, catching Linda by the hair while Linda swung her arms widely in a desperate attempt to hit Margo and gain release from her grip. Margo slapped her hands away and let go of her hair causing Linda to trip and land on the floor.

"Mom, stop it!" Winter shouted.

"Get her again!" Ivy yelled.

The door swung open. Sergeant Monroe ran into the room and stopped when he saw Linda lying on the floor.

"What's going on in here? Mrs. Myles? Are you all right, ma'am?" Sergeant Monroe asked Linda, extending a hand to help her off the floor.

"How did she get in here?" Margo screamed, sweat pouring from her brow. "I want her thrown out now, and she is never to enter this room again."

"Calm down, ma'am. Now, tell me what's going on here."

Linda stayed close behind Sergeant Monroe.

"This woman is having an affair with my husband. That's the reason he's all banged up now."

"Miss," Sergeant Monroe said to Linda, "you must leave the room now. I'll walk you to the door."

Margo was ashamed of herself, but Linda and Angelica had driven her to it. She was at her wit's end and was glad that she had the Lord on her side, because if she had a gun today, she'd probably blow somebody's brains out. She hated all these people who were trying to destroy her life—people she had given nothing but her love and heart to. They were making it awfully hard for her to walk in God's footsteps, to be an upstanding Christian when all around her the devil was fighting her tooth and nail.

"Linda, stay away from me and my family," Margo shouted. "I can't ask you to forgive me for my attitude and the way I've acted today, because you know that your very presence has caused this. Whatever your intentions, you should know that you are not welcome here. Security will be advised to be on the lookout for you, and not under any circumstances are they to let you in. You've seen Jefferson; now take a last look. Get your tail out, and don't ever bother coming here again. If you do, the consequences will be hell to pay. Remember that well when you get a wee bitty urge to try and defy me."

Linda hurriedly walked out of the door without glancing back. She had really made a mess of things, and now she was truly alone. She walked from the hospital leaving Jefferson forever behind.

CHAPTER 61

Margo took her remaining Tylenol 3 that was waiting for this rainy day. She crawled in bed, with Ivy and Winter assisting her. One week had taken its toll on Margo, and she was grateful that she wasn't a total basket case. She felt like a Southern buffet—all spread out to be used and abused by this one and that one, shredding her to pieces until nothing was left. But she still loved her husband, despite all that he had put her through. And nothing and no one was going to come between them. If she had to put her dukes up again, she would until everyone got the message…she wasn't going anywhere.

"Mom, we might as well show you now," Ivy said, handing Margo the morning paper she had left in the kitchen.

"Dad's time has run out," Winter interjected.

Margo took the newspaper letting it rest in her lap. "Get my glasses, Winter. They're on the dresser."

Margo picked up the paper having adjusted her glasses on her face and read aloud: "Lieutenant Hamilton Barnes of the Fayetteville Police Department-Richmond Heights station and Mr. Jefferson Myles of Myles and Associates have been indicted on charges of theft, embezzlement, and selling arms as part of a contra rebel activity under the auspices of 'Operation Stingray.' Both Barnes and Myles are currently in intensive care at Cape Fear Valley Hospital after attempts were made on their lives in conjunction with this operation.

"'Operation Stingray' is headed up by wealthy business-man, Robert Santiago. Santiago, a native of Honduras, is still at large. He is believed to have transferred stolen ammunition to an arms dealer. The stolen ammunition is believed to have come from Fort Bragg. Lieutenant Barnes will be held for indictment for murder in the death of Blake Montgomery and involuntary manslaughter in the death of Marsha Wilson. They were both slain last week. Police hope to make several other arrests soon in conjunction with Mr. Montgomery's death and the attempted murders of Lieutenant Hamilton Barnes and Jefferson Myles.

"Lieutenant Barnes was gunned down outside the Richmond Heights Police Station on New Year's Eve while Jefferson Myles was also an apparent shooting victim while he drove on a deserted road. It is theorized that he may have run off the road while an attempt was being made on his life. It also appears that Mr. Myles was not alone in his vehicle. Phone records indicate a

911 call was made from a cellular phone registered to Ms. Angelica Barnes, ex-wife of Lieutenant Hamilton Barnes, alerting authorities to the scene of the accident. Ms. Barnes was reported to also be the girlfriend of Robert Santiago, who allegedly put out a contract on Barnes' and Myles' life. She alerted the police to such. This case will certainly cause lots of speculation and attention in days to come."

Angelica put down her newspaper and prepared herself for the interrogation ahead. She was about to face indictment herself, but she hoped to receive a reduced sentence for her cooperation in helping to apprehend Santiago and his men. There was the matter of the embezzled funds and her leaving Jefferson alone after the accident to avoid detection. Her gut feeling was that her luck had just run out.

Angelica had made a mess of things, and somehow she felt her chance to make it right with Margo had passed. Margo wouldn't believe her, anyway. Angelica had been through a lot, but when Margo needed her the most, Angelica had failed her. For fear of losing Margo as a friend, Angelica hadn't even trusted Margo enough to share the intimate side of her life that was for the most part unpleasant. And Angelica wasn't smart enough to realize that Margo loved her more than she did herself.

Margo meant the world to her. Angelica hoped that one day she would be able to prove to Margo that she loved her—even sharing those parts of her life she felt Margo might not understand. Right now, she needed to deal with the present.

Angelica looked around her condo and then closed the door. Her brother, Edward, would be waiting for her at the police station. Edward had wanted to work this case, but not representing his sister. It was a little nippy outside, but the phat scarf was no more. It was one of the reasons she had to go out in the first place.

Margo ran her hand over the thin, white spread that covered Jefferson. She rubbed the contour of his leg while she prayed silently for his recovery. The continuous beeping of the heart monitor kept perfect rhythm.

She continued to watch Jefferson while her mind played back bits and pieces of the last week and a half. It was hard to look at the images—Linda, then Angelica as they scrolled across her imaginary screen starring in their favorite role as best friend only to turn into deceitful, lying, husband-snatchers. And then there was Jefferson with a smug look on his face denouncing their marriage, their family, and their love for each other.

Margo stopped abruptly and stood up from her chair as Jefferson opened his eyes and attempted to speak. Inaudible sounds came from his mouth, and Margo grabbed Jefferson's hands, squeezed hard and screamed, "Thank you, Jesus!" Margo stopped again as she thought she heard Jefferson say, "Ouch."

Margo cried tears of joy and began to laugh out loud. She was overcome with excitement. She leaned over, kissed Jefferson, and ran out to get a nurse, forgetting in her excitement that all she had to do was ring the bell.

The guard remained planted at the doorway as Margo ran to the nurses' station.

Dr. Graham was on the floor preparing to do his rounds. The excitement was posted on his face as he ran back with Margo and two nurses to witness Jefferson's giant step back to normalcy. Jefferson watched Margo, not taking his eyes from her.

There was something in those eyes that wouldn't let go. They were thankful and grateful eyes—they said Jefferson was sorry for all the trouble he had caused. They were eyes that begged for forgiveness, a second chance at love. He wanted to stare into Margo's eyes for the rest of eternity.

Margo returned Jefferson's gaze and mouthed the words, "I love you." Margo believed that God always has a plan, even though the outcome may not necessarily be what you want. It would have been a slap in

God's face if she rejected His blessing—she and Jefferson getting their second chance, especially after she had begged and begged God for it. She smiled and Jefferson's lips curved upward, and there sat the biggest smile Margo had ever seen.

The room became deathly silent. "M-a-r-g-o." One by one, each person in the room jerked their head toward the sound hoping that another miracle would be wrought. There it was again, although barely audible. "M-a-r-g-o." Margo dropped to her knees and wept openly, thanking God for the sign.

Margo was wracked with pain and jubilation. Her sobbing was out of control, but no one paid her any mind. "I'm going to be right here by your side, Jefferson, no matter what happens. This woman loves you." And she laid her head at Jefferson's side and held him as best she could. There was no doubt this was a moment that Jefferson and Margo were to spend alone. Dr. Graham and the nurses left the room, knowing that Jefferson was indeed in good hands.

CHAPTER 62

There was standing room only. The crowd was noisy and boisterous—mouths open and closed, competing to be heard. Everyone who was somebody in Fayetteville's Black community turned out to see what would become of their Boy Wonder, their Black Businessman of the Year. Frowns, scowls, and arched eyebrows animated, onlookers waited patiently for the show to begin. Then hushed whispers spread across the courtroom like wild fire as Jefferson was wheeled into the courtroom. He sat erect in his wheelchair, dressed in a two-piece, Armani charcoal-gray suit and a starched white, buttoned-to-the-top shirt accentuated with a colorful silk necktie.

News reporters and cameramen vied for the best spot just outside of the courtroom, itching for an exclusive and the opportunity to be first to press. The pens of the few lucky to get inside scrolled feverishly across notepads, recording every detail down to the demeanor of the defendant and his family who sat close behind. The verdict was in and very soon Jefferson would know his fate—handed down by the panel of twelve jurors who took just five hours to deliberate.

Margo twitched in her seat with hands clasped tight, rubbing her thumbs together, trying to control her nerves while the jury reassembled in the jury box. Her chest heaved in and out searching for air in the stifling-hot room. She swatted away a fly that had come to irritate her further.

Margo was flanked on either side by Ivy, JR, Winter, and Winston. Malik sat a few seats down, always the dutiful friend and confidant. The sea of colorful faces that surrounded Margo were a blur—maybe by choice, but she didn't seem to recognize a single person in the room; and she preferred it that way.

Recovery had been an arduous event for Jefferson. The year and four months took its toll on Margo and the rest of the family, too, but Margo remained by his side. Although Jefferson had not regained complete motor function, he was remanded over to the custody of Federal authorities until his trial. Now, Margo glanced in his direction and blew him a kiss. He smiled back and mouthed the words, "I love you."

The bailiff came forward. "The Honorable Judge Mario Rodriguez presiding."

The judge walked from his chambers and took his seat on the bench. He looked into the crowd of hungry faces and in slow motion roamed the room with his eyes.

"Hmph," he said under his breath as he picked up his horn-rimmed glasses and sat them on his face. He glanced in Jefferson's direction, then picked up his gavel and hit the podium once. "Mr. Foreman for the jury. Are you ready with your verdict?"

"Yes, Your Honor. We are ready with our verdict."

"Please pass the verdict to the bailiff."

Margo watched as the bailiff stepped forward and retrieved the verdict from the foreman. The bailiff approached the bench and handed the folded sheet of paper to the judge.

The rustling of the paper unnerved Margo. All eyes were on Judge Rodriguez as he devoured the contents. The large horn-rimmed glasses hung on the bridge of his nose, but his eyes gave no clue.

All of Ivy's and Winter's whispering was getting on Margo's nerves. She had been on her knees until the crack of dawn, praying that the judge would be lenient with Jefferson since he had cooperated with the feds about "Operation Stingray" and the mastermind behind it all, Robert Santiago. Santiago was still at large and had managed to elude all dragnets set out for him. Margo pulled a tissue from her purse and dabbed at a small tear that formed in the corner of her eye, then looked straight ahead and remained that way until the verdict was read.

"Will the defendant, Mr. Jefferson Myles, rise," the

judge ordered. Stacy Greer, a longtime friend of Jefferson's and the best trial lawyer next to Johnnie Cochran, stood for Jefferson. "What is your verdict, Mr. Foreman?"

Each member of the Myles family held and squeezed each others' hands, closing their eyes tight as if it would erase the moment of truth.

"We, the jury, find the defendant, Jefferson Myles, guilty on one count of embezzlement and one count of purchasing and selling stolen arms."

Moans of anguish and unbelief filled the courtroom. "No, no, no," Margo cried aloud as her arms swung violently in the air until they fell silent by her side.

Peering at her over the top of his glasses, the judge dismissed Margo's antics and continued. "Are the members of the jury in agreement with this verdict?" Each head nodded simultaneously. "The sentencing phase will begin tomorrow." He tapped the gavel two times to signal the end.

No one could hear them self think above the clicks and flashes of the news media's cameras and the horde of reporters interviewing prosecution and defense attorneys. Margo lifted her head and reached for the balled-up tissue that lay on her lap. She dabbed at her eyes and barely caught a glimpse of Jefferson as the sheriff prepared to escort him back to the holding cell. Jefferson whispered in the sheriff's ear, and the sheriff turned the wheelchair so Jefferson could get a better view of Margo, who now stood with her mouth pinched. Margo relaxed her face and forced a smile. She waved at Jefferson and quietly mouthed, *I love you.*

Onlookers stood in their places as if in suspended animation afraid to speak—unsure of what to say, numb from the verdict that many already anticipated. The community's heart went out to Margo and Jefferson.

Jefferson lowered his head and his heart as the sheriff grabbed the rear grips of the wheelchair. Jefferson looked up one last time into Margo's wet face, tears streaming down like a waterfall. They held each other's eyes, closing them for a second.

Whoosh!! POP, POP!

"Jesus," Margo yelled as Jefferson's upper body heaved forward, then back.

"Get down," someone yelled above the avalanche of screams. "GET DOWN!"

People dropped to the floor like so many swatted flies. Those who were able scrambled out of the room. Margo, Ivy, JR, Winter, and Winston scooted under the bench they had shared for the past thirty-five minutes, terrified and shaking from the sheer madness that surrounded them.

POP!...POP, POP!...POP!"

Margo, praying mental prayers faster than her lips could carry them, peeked out from the bench just in time to see...*whomp*...the gunman fall onto the defense table and then onto the hardwood floor, but not before he sustained a small gash to his face.

Several deputy sheriffs stormed the room with their guns drawn high, while one officer ran to the middle of the room where the downed sheriff lay motionless—his steel, gray eyes fixed. Jefferson sat slumped over in his wheelchair, his hand hugging his chest. The deputy felt for their pulses, wildly nodded his head and screamed, "Get an ambulance!"

Another deputy walked over to the downed perpetrator who lay on his back in a pool of his own blood. The deputy held a gun to the shooter's face, then checked the shooter's pulse. "He's a goner," he said without sympathy.

Margo had spotted the burly guy—the shooter—earlier. She assumed he was another of Jefferson's clients ready to offer support. Instead, he jumped over the railing that separated the defendant from the rest of the courthouse and overpowered the sheriff. He took the sheriff's gun and then fired it at the sheriff and Jefferson. Malik ran to Jefferson and held his hand. Jefferson managed to lift his head and open his eyes.

"You can't go yet, my friend. We've got a lot of things to do yet, and I know you're going to change your life around."

"I owe you a debt of gratitude, Malik. I can't thank you enough," Jefferson whispered.

The deputies surrounded the entrance to the court-room. Those who remained inside took a seat, now stunned into silence. Activity outside the courtroom was in a chaotic frenzy, with news reporters in search of the hard-nosed truth for the evening news.

Margo inched her way to where Jefferson sat, Malik offering pressure to the wound that nearly pierced Jefferson's heart. Ivy, JR, Winter, and Winston stood back, their mouths gaping while their eyes danced a tune of their own, but in chorus as they watched in horror as Jefferson sat fighting for his life.

On her knees, Margo clutched the side of the wheel-chair and brushed Jefferson's face with the back of her other hand. She kissed him on the cheek and continued to brush the side of his face, rocking back and forth as she did so. She snarled at the deputy who stood close to her with his gun by his side, wary of his prisoner who he was sure had no intention of running away.

"It's going to be alright, baby. You're going to be alright." She dropped her head and continued to brush Jefferson's face.

"Yea, though I walk through the valley of the shadow of death…," Jefferson whispered, his voice deep, ragged.

"I will fear no evil: for thou art with me; thy rod and thy staff they comfort me," Jefferson and Margo repeated simultaneously.

A shadow at Margo's one o'clock made her lift her

head. She saw Malik rise to his feet and raise his hand in a cautionary manner. Margo swung her head to the right and froze at the sight of her—Angelica, a pitiful sight in the midst of so much pain.

Malik stared into Margo's eyes. Margo's stare was cold and icy, a stark contrast to the beautiful autumn day outside. Angelica didn't wait for their blessing. She moved forward, away from Malik's protective shield, fell down beside Margo, and rubbed her shoulder.

"I'm so sorry, Margo." Angelica sniffed, as the tears rolled down her face. "I've made a mess of things, and I don't know how to fix it."

"Not now, Angelica." Malik hissed.

"It's…it's alright, Malik," Margo managed to say, her eyes softening a bit. She threw out her hand to let him know it was okay. Margo turned and looked into Angelica's eyes, and before she could say anything, Angelica plowed on.

"Margo, I don't deserve your love or forgiveness, but I'm asking that if you could find it in your heart to forgive me, I'll spend the rest of my life making it up to you."

"Funny thing is, I've already forgiven you…and Linda. Last night when I was telling God how much I loved and adored Him, how grateful I was to Him for giving Jefferson back to me along with a host of other things, God asked me a very poignant question. He said, *How can you say you love Me whom you haven't seen and hate your sister who you do see…who you haven't forgiven? You've forgiven Jefferson, why not your sister?"*

"Whoa. Wow. What did you tell God?"

"At first I couldn't respond. I guess…I wanted to be angry with you for the rest of my life. Make you pay for what you've done to me, although Jefferson had a big hand in it, too. I felt a little selfish because I was begging God to have mercy on Jefferson in court today, but I couldn't forgive you. Then it came to me. If God forgave Jefferson, why couldn't I forgive you and Linda? Right then, I asked God to forgive me and take the anger and hurt from my heart so that I could feel free to love again. I'll admit that when I saw you standing over there a few moments ago, I forgot what I prayed for. But in the same instant, I remembered how much God loved me and how He wants me to love you the same."

"Thank you, Margo."

"No need to thank me. It's my duty to love you, and I always will. And so that you know, I've forgiven the careless whispers of a good friend."

They rose to their feet. Margo watched as Angelica batted her eyes and blew a thin stream of air from her mouth. Angelica moistened her lips with her tongue, then shut her eyes as she willed the tears not to come. In the steady stream of silence, she wrapped her arms about her body, while her feet remained glued to the floor.

"I go on trial next week," Angelica said. But Margo didn't respond.

They struggled in their silence until Margo inched closer to Angelica and lifted her chin with her finger. Angelica opened her eyes, and the brightest smile met her stained, wet ones. Margo held Angelica's chin a second longer, then embraced her; Angelica did the same.

"The paramedics are here," Malik whispered to Margo. "I'm going to ride in the ambulance with Jefferson."

"I'm going, too," Margo replied. She turned and looked into Angelica's hazel eyes, her reflection staring back at her. "I forgive you."

ABOUT THE AUTHOR

Suzetta Perkins is a native of Oakland, California, but now resides in Fayetteville, North Carolina. Perkins is cofounder and president of the Sistahs Book Club. She is a contributing author to *My Soul to His Spirit*, an anthology of short stories that was featured in the June 2005 issue of *Ebony* magazine. Visit www.suzettaperkins.com

IF YOU ENJOYED "BEHIND THE VEIL," TRY

EX-Terminator:
Life After Marriage
BY SUZETTA PERKINS
AVAILABLE FROM STREBOR BOOKS

Chapter 1: Day of Reckoning

The clock sat quiet on the nightstand, its green fluorescent numbers shouting out three a.m. Heavy breathing was muffled under the layers of bed linen draping the large mass that lay in the middle of the bed. Every now and then the large formation would shift and a new pattern would occur.

In an instant, the still formation erupted—the mass tossing and turning under the bedcovers that rustled as the silk fibers rubbed against each other.

"No, don't go, please don't go," a voice cried out in the darkness. Then quiet.

The dreams were coming again, and Sylvia St. James let them play in her subconscious.

"What did you say, Adonis? I know I didn't hear what I thought I heard."

"I want a divorce, Sylvia. I can't say it any plainer than that."

"But why, Adonis? When did you decide this? I didn't know that our marriage was in trouble."

"That's the problem with you. You're always too busy to notice what's going on right under your nose. Too busy trying to kiss the boss' behind. Too busy trying to be something you're not. Think you're better than everybody else; and—if you remember before we got married, I told you I didn't like fat women."

"I'll get on the treadmill tomorrow, I promise, but can we talk about this…try to work it out? We have invested so much of our lives into this marriage. Our daughter, what is she going to think?"

"Sylvia, I'm unhappy. I've been unhappy a long time, and now it's *my* time. I've got to go."

"But…but what about me?"

"What about you? Look, Sylvia, the love slipped out of our marriage a while ago. Of course, you were too busy to notice. I don't have a lot of time left on this earth, and I'd like to enjoy a little happiness before I go."

"Time left on earth?" Sylvia muttered. "What are you talking about? Where are you going? No one will ever love you like I do, Adonis."

"Sylvia, please don't sound so desperate. You'll do fine. You always do."

"Don't go, Adonis. Don't leave me like this. Nooooooooooooo!" Sylvia screamed.

The cream-colored silk comforter slid to the floor

as Sylvia rolled from side to side, caught up in her dream-memory.

"Nooooooooooo!" she screamed once more into the early morning. "No. No."

Pulling her hand from underneath her, Sylvia began to beat the pillow on which her head rested. She pounded the soft down until her arm tired. She peeled her eyes open, then sat up slowly, sweat pouring from her brow. She scanned the dark room, her eyes out of focus. After a moment, she was able to make out the outline of the "T"-iron that Adonis had left behind: his winning golf club that he had nicknamed "Tiger."

Sylvia slowly brought her hands to her face to catch the stream of water that ran from her eyes and threatened to soak her nightgown. Her breathing was labored as her sobs, soft at first, became loud wails. She sobbed and sobbed, then grabbed her throat to keep from choking. She wrapped her arms around her chest and shook herself from side to side.

"Why, Adonis, why? Why did you leave me? I loved you with all my heart and soul. Why, why?"

Finally, there was quiet…an occasional sniff. Sylvia unfolded her arms, drew her knees up to her chest and wrapped her arms around her legs. She laid her head on the bend of her knees and began to rock back and forth, willing her dream to recede. She sniffed again.

Sylvia lifted her head and turned toward the nightstand that held the clock. It was three fifty-five a.m. She threw her legs over the side of the bed and stood up, almost slipping on the comforter that had fallen to the floor. She moved to the bathroom and relieved herself, washed her hands, then looked into the mirror.

Almond-shaped eyes, which were framed by high-arched brows, stared back at Sylvia. She circled her eyes with her fingers. Even in the dim light, her skin seemed blotchier than it'd been the day before. Her face was discolored something awful, and the older she got the more defined the blotches became.

Sylvia's reflection stared back at her, daring her to speak.

"You don't need him."

Sylvia put her hand to her mouth, not sure whether it was she or the reflection that had spoken.

"Yeah, I don't need him. Get ahold of yourself, girl, and grab the world by its axis. It's time to take my life back and leave this pity party at the doorstep."

Sylvia was sure this time that the reflection in the mirror wasn't talking, but the face that stared back meant serious business.

Chapter 2: D-Day

"Where's my purse?" Sylvia shouted to no one, moving from room to room, looking in corners and closets, pulling on her too-short linen dress every two seconds. "I've got lots to do and I want everything perfect before the ladies come. Ouch, darn! Not my stockings. This is not the time to get a run. Now I've got to stop and change them.

"Here's my purse," Sylvia continued to ramble out loud, her nylon-clad legs making a swishing sound as they rubbed together when she trotted back to her room to put on new hose. "Hiding from me again. I don't have time for this. I've got to get to the beauty shop by ten and I still have to stop and get gas before I go."

Brrng…brrng.

"Damn! Whoever it is, I don't have time to talk." Sylvia let out a sigh when she saw the name on the caller ID.

"Hello, Mother. I'm in a hurry right now. Getting ready to go to the shrink."

"The shrink? I thought you were having a men-hating party today? And hello to you, too."

"I'm sorry. Just got a lot to do and I'm running behind time. Our first meeting is tonight, and I've got to look good for the occasion. Arial, my shrink, is going to give me a touch-up. And I can't wait to get to the shampoo bowl to partake in the divine five-minute head scrub that causes you to have the most wonderful multiple orgasms."

"Sylvia St. James! I know you didn't just say what I thought you said."

"Mom, I'm a forty-five-year-old, good-looking woman—

although lately my attention-grabbing curves have become a series of bumps on a line, hidden under my extra layer of fat."

"Stop beating yourself up. You just need to lay off some of those carbs and get some exercise."

"You're right. And today is the first day of my real healing. I've got a reasonable portion of my health and strength and I know that there is a world of somebodies out there waiting on me."

"Be careful what you ask for."

"A baby and twenty years of my life, Ma, and he had to go and—"

"Let's not talk about it."

"That's the problem. I need to talk about it." Sylvia paused. "I had one of my dreams last night."

"I'm sorry, baby. I wish I could be there for you. He's messin' up your mind and he ain't even thinking about you," her mother said.

"Thanks for the support, Mom. That's why I'm having this meeting. Now, I've gotta go. Love you."

"Love you, too." And the line was dead.

Sylvia stood in the middle of the room with hands on her voluptuous hips—gold bangles dangling from one arm—and surveyed her surroundings. In one corner stood a wooden African fertility statue that looked as lonely as she did. Six months had passed since the judge declared that the marriage of Adonis and Sylvia

St. James was dissolved, but today, Sylvia made her own declaration that she was ready to live again.

Sylvia looked down at her watch. It was almost ten o'clock on a beautiful summer day in June, and she had to get going. Her adrenaline was high, excited about the prospect of sitting with other women who were divorced and sharing ideas about how to move on. She grabbed her belongings and rushed out the door. As she yanked open the door of her silver BMW 530i sedan, her hand slipped. "Aw hell," she muttered, surveying her broken nail, trying to will away the pain. After a couple of seconds she put the key in the ignition and headed for the gas station two blocks down.

✗✗✗

Five minutes away, Sylvia thought. She would still be on time. At the corner, she looked in her purse for her gas card, then remembered she had taken it out and put it on the nightstand. Sylvia shook her head in disbelief. Her road to healing had some major obstacles.

She rummaged through her wallet, which was crammed with receipts. Adonis was always telling her that her purse was going to get stolen one day, and the robber would know her life story. She sifted through the papers until her fingers pulled up a folded twenty-dollar bill. "Thank You, God, You're so good. And I promise to pay careful attention to what I'm doing from now on."

✗✗✗

Arial's mouth was moving a mile a minute when Sylvia walked into the beauty shop. Her petite frame was dressed to the nines: starched white linen slacks and a white short-sleeved blouse with lacy scallops running around the collar; hair piled high into a ponytail revealing the two-carat diamond studs that dotted each earlobe; and her immaculately manicured feet were stuffed in a pair of Dr. Scholl's comfort sandals made for standing long hours— her strappy gold stilettos sitting off to the side. Although Arial was in her late forties, she could easily pass for thirty. But more than that, the girl could hook up some hair. Arial had the gift.

"Be with you in a minute, sweetie…kiss, kiss."

Sylvia blew a kiss back and picked up a hairstyle book to pass the time.

Fifteen minutes later, Arial took the towel from around Ms. Jenkins' neck.

"Looking good, Ms. Jenkins," Sylvia said.

"Thank you, baby. I've got a darned good stylist."

Sylvia gently slid into the chair vacated by Ms. Jenkins.

"How have you been, sweetie? I know you've been through some rough times…"